TV: 2000

Fawcett Crest Books
edited by Isaac Asimov, Charles G. Waugh,
and Martin Harry Greenberg:

☐ CATASTROPHES! 24425 $2.50

☐ THE SEVEN CARDINAL VIRTUES OF
    SCIENCE FICTION 24440 $2.50

☐ THE SEVEN DEADLY SINS OF
    SCIENCE FICTION 24349 $2.50

☐ SPACE MAIL VOLUME II 24481 $2.50

☐ TV: 2000 24493 $2.95

And edited by Isaac Asimov, Martin Harry Greenberg,
and Joseph D. Olander:

☐ THE FUTURE I 24366 $2.50

☐ THE FUTURE IN QUESTION 24266 $2.50

☐ SPACE MAIL 24312 $2.95

Buy them at your local bookstore or use this handy coupon for ordering.

COLUMBIA BOOK SERVICE, CBS Inc.
32275 Mally Road, P.O. Box FB, Madison Heights, MI 48071

Please send me the books I have checked above. Orders for less than 5
books must include 75¢ for the first book and 25¢ for each additional
book to cover postage and handling. Orders for 5 books or more postage
is FREE. Send check or money order only. Allow 3-4 weeks for delivery.

Cost $_____	Name_____
Sales tax*_____	Address_____
Postage_____	City_____
Total $_____	State_____ Zip _____

* The government requires us to collect sales tax in all states except AK,
DE, MT, NH and OR.

Prices and availability subject to change without notice.   8999

TV: 2000

edited by
Isaac Asimov,
Charles G. Waugh, and
Martin Harry Greenberg

Introduction by Isaac Asimov

FAWCETT CREST • NEW YORK

TV: 2000

Published by Fawcett Crest Books, CBS Educational and Professional Publishing, a division of CBS Inc.

ISBN: 0-449-24493-8

Printed in the United States of America

First Fawcett Crest printing: March 1982

10 9 8 7 6 5 4 3 2 1

CONTENTS

PART III: THE CONSEQUENCES OF TV

TV: 2000

Introduction:
It Changed the World!

ISAAC ASIMOV

WE frequently talk about how this or that technological advance changed the world. The use of fire changed the world. So did metallurgy. So did agriculture. So did the mariner's compass. So did printing. So did the steam engine.

Old stuff! Old stuff!

What surprises has technology sprung upon us *lately?*

Quite a few, actually. Since World War II—that is, in a period of less than forty years—we have had to live with the consequences of five major changes that have affected, directly or indirectly, every cranny of our lives. They are:

1. Nuclear bombs and nuclear power stations.
2. Space technology—satellites, probes, and spaceships.
3. Computers and robots.
4. Commercial jet planes.
5. Television.

Of these, television is the most intimate and personal. None of us have satellites, nuclear bombs, or commercial jet planes in the home. To be sure, the computers are now arriving in the home—but television has been our buddy for a whole generation now.

Only those people who are well into middle age can remember a society without television. As for myself, I have very rarely spent a whole day in the second half of my life without a television set in my vicinity being on for at least some part of it. This is so even though I am not much of a television watcher. (I can't be, if I want to keep up the level of my literary output.)

11

There are people who are very proud of not even owning a set, but that scarcely matters. Their entire life is nevertheless affected by television.

Consider some of the ways in which television has affected society.

At the start, it seemed almost certain that television would kill the movie houses. Who on earth would want to get into a movie and sit there in the darkness, surrounded by dubious strangers, so that for a sizable sum of money you could watch very much the same thing you could watch for nothing in the comfort of your home? (Even the TV commercials are an advantage rather than otherwise. They allow the quick stretch, the preparation of a quick snack, even a hurried visit to the bathroom.)

So Hollywood, in desperation, began to make movies of the kind that were not allowed on television. The stag film moved out into the open and, slightly diluted, into the big time, contributing its bit to the sexual revolution.

And now (full circle), cable television is, among other things, moving sexual permissiveness onto the small screen for those who are willing to pay for it.

Again, television is penetrating much of the world; far more than the old motion pictures did, and with a greater immediacy. The picture that television presents the world is, to a great extent, either American or imitation-American; and the life-style is that of a dream couple living on dream street. Even when they experienced trouble, it was not starvation; it was the dishwasher breaking down. And it always got fixed by the end of the program, too.

This didn't make non-Americans (and many Americans, too) living on non-dream streets any poorer, you understand; but it sure made them *feel* poorer, and more resentful. Consequently, societies everywhere grew more unstable. The United States, from being the hope of the impoverished, became their visible and hated oppressor, one which was hogging the resources of the world.

Yet again, television is great on bringing the everyday sight and sound of violence into the home.

Terrorists have never before commanded a world audience; assassins and would-be assassins have never before been assured such instant, widespread fame. How much is this a bribe that encourages such deeds, I wonder? The Iranians who took over the American embassy in late 1978, for instance,

possessed a "bully pulpit," handed them by American television, from which to inflate their importance and express their
angers and hatreds. How much did this encourage their
intransigence?

—But never mind. The point is that television is here now.
It was invented long ago, developed long ago, brought to
maturity long ago—so what has it to do with science fiction?

This goes to the heart of the question as to whether science
is "catching up" with science fiction; whether science is
"killing" science fiction plots; whether science fiction writers
are being left with "nothing to say."

I hear this on all sides from people who know nothing of
science fiction; who think that science fiction consists of a
trip to the moon, and that when a trip to the moon is made in
actual fact, science fiction must sink back, abashed and
mute.

In this book, though, we have a test case. What can be done
with that old science fictional chestnut, television?

Television was predicted by Hugo Gernsback in the 1910s.
It was found in occasional science fiction stories for thirty
years afterward.

And then it came, and one more great science fiction
gimmick was supposed to wither.

But why should it? Television, or *any* technological advance,
is never all of a piece. It doesn't arise, full-blown and thereaf-
ter unchangeable.

Television developed from black-and-white to color; from
small screen to larger screen; from kinescope to tape;
from largely live shows from New York to recorded shows from
Hollywood. We have seen the rise and fall of variety shows,
dramas, Westerns, and so on. The primitive humor and
techniques of Ozzie and Harriet and the slapstick predictabil-
ity of *I Love Lucy* gave way to the more sophisticated comedy
of today.

Right now, we are seeing the rapid development of cable
TV and of TV cassettes and TV recording—which may end up
producing greater changes than television itself did. And
what of the self-righteous censorship efforts of the television
preachers who are enriching themselves on a mixture of
Bible-waving and flag-waving?

Television may be here, but who knows where it is going in
the future and how it will affect society in years to come?

(This is true of any technology, however old and fixed it might seem.)

And it is questions of this sort that are the province of science fiction and that will never fail it. Wherever we go, and in however seemingly science fictional a direction, the legitimate questions will always be: And what next? What does this lead to?

Here, then, we have eighteen stories, all post-television, and all dealing with television, and all nevertheless clearly science fiction that fulfill their important function of exploring technology, people, and the relationship between the two.

Read and enjoy. —And if you want to think a little in response to the reading, go ahead. That, too, is an important part of science fiction.

Part I: The Control of TV

WHO controls television? Part of the answer depends upon which country you are talking about. All nations exercise political control over broadcast frequency assignments and most have copyright laws, but beyond that there are wide variations. In Russia, for example, the Ministry of Culture (shades of 1984) directs TV, while in the USA, stations are federally licensed and subjected to some government regulation, but most are privately owned.

In "Now Inhale," Eric Frank Russell, one of science fiction's premier humorists, has created a government which not only runs TV, but also broadcasts executions in much the same way that England used to conduct public hangings. Psychological impacts of such programming would probably be quite profound, and even though not discussed, they are certainly worth thinking about.

However, national interests are not the only factors influencing television. Usually there are a number of gatekeepers (decision-makers) and forces which interact to produce the final product.

In "Dreaming Is a Private Thing," Isaac Asimov explores the role of network executives by examining the decisions one must make during a typical day. To be successful they must provide products meeting the needs of important interest groups. Otherwise, these men, depending on the country, are likely to be purged by the government or fired by their boards of directors.

Since writers are the source of the initial scripts, and many ideas, they tend to be thought of as exercising more control than they do. Actually, scripts are often altered by producers, directors, actors, network censors, and special-interest groups. And, as James Gunn puts it, writers have little recourse but to "take the money and boogie." Still, there are opportunities to outfox others and slip in wanted messages, as Joseph Patrouch points out in "The Man Who Murdered Television."

Sponsors are another group believed to exercise great control over the content of television. As William Tenn illustrates in "The Jester," one choice they make is whether to buy commercial time during a particular program; programs without sponsors soon fail. Then, too, there is the temptation to fiddle with scripts. For example, Rod Serling once had a coffee company strike out a reference he made to tea. But sponsors, too, are limited in the powers they can exert. Special-interest groups sometimes influence sponsors' choices by threats of boycott, and popular events such as the Superbowl are seller's markets in which one company doesn't have much leverage.

Robert Silverberg presents a good illustration of how special-interest groups can obtain media coverage in "The Man Who Came Back." Indeed, television news' hunger for action footage has caused protests to be labeled the poor man's press conference. To some extent, such sophistication allows important views to be more fully represented than they otherwise might be. But, of course, exploitation by terrorist groups constitutes a negative factor that Dean Ing considers in the Consequences section.

Finally, the viewers exert control collectively by deciding

when and what to watch. Presently, network executives are very nervous about the additional options TV games, video recorders, and cable may offer. But in "I See You," Damon Knight takes this trend even further and considers the control viewers might exert on each other if they were suddenly able to tune in their neighbors.

Now Inhale

ERIC FRANK RUSSELL

HIS leg irons clanked and his wrist chains jingled as they led him into the room. The bonds on his ankles compelled him to move at an awkward shuffle and the guards delighted in urging him onward faster than he could go. Somebody pointed to a chair facing the long table. Somebody else shoved him into it with such force that he lost balance and sat down hard.

The black brush of his hair jerked as his scalp twitched and that was his only visible reaction. Then he gazed across the desk with light gray eyes so pale that the pupils seemed set in ice. The look in them was neither friendly nor hostile, submissive nor angry; it was just impassively and impartially cold, cold.

On the other side of the desk seven Gombarians surveyed him with various expressions: triumph, disdain, satisfaction, boredom, curiosity, glee and arrogance. They were a humanoid bunch in the same sense that gorillas are humanoid. At that point the resemblance ended.

"Now," began the one in the middle, making every third syllable a grunt, "your name is Wayne Taylor?"

No answer.

"You have come from a planet called Terra?"

No response.

"Let us not waste any more time, Palamin," suggested the one on the left. "If he will not talk by invitation, let him talk by compulsion."

"You are right, Eckster." Putting a hand under the desk Palamin came up with a hammer. It had a pear-shaped head with flattened base. "How would you like every bone in your hands cracked finger by finger, joint by joint?"

"I wouldn't," admitted Wayne Taylor.

"A very sensible reply," approved Palamin. He placed the hammer in the middle of the desk, positioning it significantly. "Already many days have been spent teaching you our language. By this time a child could have learned it sufficiently well to understand and answer questions." He favored the prisoner with a hard stare. "You have pretended to be abnormally slow to learn. But you can deceive us no longer. You will now provide all the information for which we ask."

"Willingly or unwillingly," put in Eckster, licking thin lips, "but you'll provide it anyway."

"Correct," agreed Palamin. "Let us start all over again and see if we can avoid painful scenes. Your name is Wayne Taylor and you come from a planet called Terra?"

"I admitted that much when I was captured."

"I know. But you were not fluent at that time and we want no misunderstandings. Why did you land on Gombar?"

"I've told my tutor at least twenty times that I did it involuntarily. It was an emergency landing. My ship was disabled."

"Then why did you blow it up? Why did you not make open contact with us and invite us to repair it for you?"

"No Terran vessel must be allowed to fall intact into hostile hands," said Taylor flatly.

"Hostile?" Palamin tried to assume a look of pained surprise but his face wasn't made for it. "Since you Terrans know nothing whatever about us what right have you to consider us hostile?"

"I wasn't kissed on arrival," Taylor retorted. "I was shot at coming down. I was shot at getting away. I was hunted across twenty miles of land, grabbed and beaten up."

"Our soldiers do their duty," observed Palamin virtuously.

"I'd be dead by now if they were not the lousiest marksmen this side of Cygni."

"And what is Cygni?"

"A star."

"Who are you to criticize our soldiers?" interjected Eckster, glowering.

"A Terran," informed Taylor, as if that were more than enough.

"That means nothing to me," Eckster gave back with open contempt.

"It will."

Palamin took over again. "If friendly contact were wanted the Terran authorities would send a large ship with an official deputation on board, wouldn't they?"

"I don't think so."

"Why not?"

"We don't risk big boats and important people without knowing what sort of a reception they're likely to get."

"And who digs up that information?"

"Space scouts."

"Ah!" Palamin gazed around with the pride of a pygmy who has trapped an elephant. "So at last you admit that you are a spy?"

"I am a spy only in the estimation of the hostile."

"On the contrary," broke in a heavily jowled specimen seated on the right, "you are whatever we say you are—because we say it."

"Have it your own way," conceded Taylor.

"We intend to."

"You can be sure of that, my dear Borkor," soothed Palamin. He returned attention to the prisoner. "How many Terrans are there in existence?"

"About twelve thousand millions."

"He is lying," exclaimed Borkor, hungrily eyeing the hammer.

"One planet could not support such a number," Eckster contributed.

"They are scattered over a hundred planets," said Taylor.

"He is still lying," Borkor maintained.

Waving them down, Palamin asked, "And how many ships have they got?"

"I regret that mere space scouts are not entrusted with fleet statistics," replied Taylor coolly. "I can tell you only that I haven't the slightest idea."

"You must have *some* idea."

"If you want guesses, you can have them for what they are worth,"

"Then make a guess."

"One million."

"Nonsense!" declared Palamin. "Utterly absurd!"

"All right. One thousand. Or any other number you consider reasonable."

"This is getting us nowhere," Borkor complained.

Palamin said to the others, "What do you expect? If we were to send a spy to Terra, would we fill him up with top-secret information to give the enemy when caught? Or would we tell him just enough and only enough to enable him to carry out his task? The ideal spy is a shrewd ignoramus, able to take all, unable to give anything."

"The ideal spy wouldn't be trapped in the first place," commented Eckster maliciously.

"Thank you for those kind words," Taylor chipped in. "If I had come here as a spy, you'd have seen nothing of my ship much less me."

"Well, exactly where were you heading for when forced to land on Gombar?" invited Palamin.

"For the next system beyond."

"Ignoring this one?"

"Yes."

"Why?"

"I go where I'm told."

"Your story is weak and implausible." Palamin lay back and eyed him judicially. "It is not credible that a space explorer should bypass one system in favor of another that is farther away."

"I was aiming for a binary said to have at least forty planets," said Taylor. "This system had only three. Doubtless it was considered relatively unimportant."

"What, with us inhabiting all three worlds?"

"How were we to know that? Nobody has been this way before."

"They know it now," put in Eckster, managing to make it sound sinister.

"This one knows it," Palamin corrected. "The others do not. And the longer they don't, the better for us. When another life form starts poking its snout into our system, we need time to muster our strength."

This brought a murmur of general agreement.

"It's your state of mind," offered Taylor.

"What d'you mean?"

"You're taking it for granted that a meeting must lead to a clash and in turn to a war."

"We'd be prize fools to assume anything else and let ourselves be caught unprepared," Palamin pointed out.

Taylor sighed. "To date we have established ourselves on a hundred planets without a single fight. The reason: we don't go where we're not wanted."

"I can imagine that," Palamin gave back sarcastically. "Someone tells you to beat it and you obligingly beat it. It's contrary to instinct."

"Your instinct," said Taylor. "We see no sense in wasting time and money fighting when we can spend both exploring and exploiting."

"Meaning that your space fleets include no warships?"

"Of course we have warships."

"Many?"

"Enough to cope."

"Pacifists armed to the teeth," said Palamin to the others. He registered a knowing smile.

"Liars are always inconsistent," pronounced Eckster with an air of authority. He fixed a stony gaze upon the prisoner. "If you are so careful to avoid trouble, why do you *need* warships?"

"Because we have no guarantee that the entire cosmos shares our policy of live and let live."

"Be more explicit."

"We chevvy nobody. But someday somebody may take it into their heads to chevvy us."

"Then you will start a fight?"

"No. The other party will have started it. We shall finish it."

"Sheer evasion," scoffed Eckster to Palamin and the rest. "The technique is obvious to anyone but an idiot. They settle themselves upon a hundred planets—if we can believe that number, which I don't! On most there is no opposition because nobody is there to oppose. On the others the natives are weak and backward, know that a struggle is doomed to failure and therefore offer none. But on any planet sufficiently strong and determined to resist—such as Gombar for instance—the Terrans will promptly treat that resistance as unwarranted interference with themselves. They will say they are being chevvied. It will be their moral justification for a war."

Palamin looked at Taylor. "What do you say to that?"

Giving a deep shrug, Taylor said, "That kind of political cynicism has been long out of date where I come from. I can't help it if mentally you're about ten millennia behind us."

"Are we going to sit here and allow ourselves to be insulted by a prisoner in chains?" Eckster angrily demanded of Palamin. "Let us recommend that he be executed. Then we can all go home. I for one have had enough of this futile rigmarole."

Another said, "Me, too." He looked an habitual me-tooer.

"Patience," advised Palamin. He spoke to Taylor. "You claim that you were under orders to examine the twin system of Halor and Ridi?"

"If by that you mean the adjacent binary, the answer is yes. That was my prescribed destination."

"Let us suppose that instead you had been told to take a look over our Gombarian system. Would you have done so?"

"I obey orders."

"You would have come upon us quietly and surreptitiously for a good snoop around?"

"Not necessarily. If my first impression had been one of friendliness, I'd have presented myself openly."

"He is dodging the question," insisted Eckster, still full of ire.

"What would you have done if you had been uncertain of our reaction?" continued Palamin.

"What anyone else would do," Taylor retorted. "I'd hang around until I'd got the measure of it one way or the other."

"Meanwhile taking care to evade capture?"

"Of course."

"And if you had not been satisfied with our attitude, you'd have reported us as hostile?"

"Potentially so."

"That is all we require," decided Palamin. "Your admissions are tantamount to a confession that you are a spy. It does not matter in the least whether you were under orders to poke your inquisitive nose into this system or some other system, you are still a spy." He turned to the others. "Are we all agreed?"

They chorused, "Yes."

"There is only one proper fate for such as you," Palamin

finished. "You will be returned to your cell pending official execution." He made a gesture of dismissal. "Take him away."

The guards took him by simple process of jerking the chair from under him and kicking him erect. They tried to rush him out faster than he could go; he stumbled in his leg irons and almost fell. But he found time to throw one swift glance back from the doorway and his strangely pale eyes looked frozen.

When the elderly warder brought in his evening meal, Taylor asked, "How do they execute people here?"

"How do they do it where you come from?"

"We don't."

"You don't?" The warder blinked in amazement. Putting the tray on the floor, he took a seat on the bench beside Taylor and left the heavily barred grille wide open. The butt of his gun protruded from its holster within easy reach of the prisoner's grasp. "Then how do you handle dangerous criminals?"

"We cure the curable by whatever means are effective no matter how drastic, including brain surgery. The incurable we export to a lonely planet reserved exclusively for them. There they can fight it out between themselves."

"What a waste of a world," opined the warder. In casual manner he drew his gun, pointed it at the wall and pressed the button. Nothing happened. "Empty," he said.

Taylor made no remark.

"No use you snatching it. No use you running for it. The armored doors, multiple locks and loaded guns are all outside."

"I'd have to get rid of these manacles before I could start something with any hope of success," Taylor pointed out. "Are you open to bribery?"

"With what? You have nothing save the clothes you're wearing. And even those will be burned after you're dead."

"All right, forget it." Taylor rattled his irons loudly and looked disgusted. "You haven't yet told me how I'm to die."

"Oh, you'll be strangled in public," informed the warder. He smacked his lips for no apparent reason. "All executions take place in the presence of the populace. It is not enough that justice be done, it must also be seen to be done. So everybody sees it. And it has an excellent disciplinary effect." Again the lip smacking. "It is quite a spectacle."

"I'm sure it must be."

"You will be made to kneel with your back to a post, your arms and ankles tied behind it," explained the warder in tutorial manner. "There is a hole drilled through the post at the level of your neck. A loop of cord goes round your neck, through the hole and around a stick on the other side. The executioner twists the stick, thereby tightening the loop quickly or slowly according to his mood."

"I suppose that when he feels really artistic he prolongs the agony quite a piece by slackening and retightening the loop a few times?" Taylor ventured.

"No, no, he is not permitted to do that," assured the warden, blind to the sarcasm. "Not in a final execution. That method is used only to extract confessions from the stubborn. We are a fair-minded and tenderhearted people, see?"

"You're a great comfort to me," said Taylor.

"So you will be handled swiftly and efficiently. I have witnessed many executions and have yet to see a sloppy, badly performed one. The body heaves and strains against its bonds, the eyes stick out, the tongue protrudes and turns black and complete collapse follows. The effect is invariably the same and is a tribute to the executioner's skill. Really, you have nothing to worry about, nothing at all."

"Looks like I haven't, the way you put it," observed Taylor dryly. "I'm right on top of the world without anything to lose except my breath." He brooded a bit, then asked, "When am I due for the noose?"

"Immediately after you've finished your game," the warder informed.

Taylor eyed him blankly. "Game? What game? What do you mean?"

"It is conventional to allow a condemned man a last game against a skilled player chosen by us. When the game ends he is taken away and strangled."

"Win or lose?"

"The result makes no difference. He is executed regardless of whether he is the winner or the loser."

"Sounds crazy to me," said Taylor frowning.

"It would, being an alien," replied the warder. "But surely you'll agree that a person facing death is entitled to a little bit of consideration if only the privilege of putting up a last-minute fight for his life."

"A pretty useless fight."

"That may be. But every minute of delay is precious to the

one concerned." The warder rubbed hands together appreciatively. "I can tell you that nothing is more exciting, more
thrilling than a person's death-match against a clever player."

"Is that so?"

"Yes. You see, he cannot possibly play in normal manner.
For one thing, his mind is obsessed by his impending fate
while his opponent is bothered by no such burden. For another, he dare not let the other win—and he dare not let him
lose, either. He has to concentrate all his faculties on preventing a decisive result and prolonging the game as much as
possible. And, of course, all the time he is mentally and
morally handicapped by the knowledge that the end is bound
to come."

"Bet it gives you a heck of a kick," said Taylor.

The warder sucked his lips before smacking them. "Many a
felon have I watched playing in a cold sweat with the ingenuity of desperation. Then at last the final move. He has fainted
and rolled off his chair. We've carried him out as limp as an
empty sack. He has come to his senses on his knees facing a
crowd waiting for the first twist."

"It isn't worth the bother," decided Taylor. "No player can
last long."

"Usually they don't but I've known exceptions, tough and
expert gamesters who've managed to postpone death for four
or five days. There was one fellow, a professional *alizik*
player, who naturally chose his own game and contrived to
avoid a decision for sixteen days. He was so good it was a pity
he had to die. A lot of video-watchers were sorry when the
end came."

"Oh, so you put these death-matches on the video?"

"It's the most popular show. Pins them in their chairs, I can
tell you."

"Hm-m-m!" Taylor thought a bit, asked, "Suppose this
video-star had been able to keep the game on the boil for a
year or more, would he have been allowed to do so?"

"Of course. Nobody can be put to death until he has
completed his last game. You could call it a superstition, I
suppose. What's more, the rule is that he gets well fed while
playing. If he wishes he can eat like a king. All the same,
they rarely eat much."

"Don't they?"

"No—they're so nervous that their stomachs refuse to hold
a square meal. Occasionally one of them is actually sick in

the middle of a game. When I see one do that I know he won't last another day."

"You've had plenty of fun in your time," Taylor offered.

"Quite often," the warder admitted. "But not always. Bad players bore me beyond description. They give the video-watchers the gripes. They start a game, fumble it right away, go to the strangling-post and that's the end of them. The greatest pleasure for all is when some character makes a battle of it."

"Fat chance I've got. I know no Gombarian games and you people know no Terran ones."

"Any game can be learned in short time and the choice is yours. Naturally you won't be permitted to pick one that involves letting you loose in a field without your irons. It has to be something that can be played in this cell. Want some good advice?"

"Give."

"This evening an official will arrive to arrange the contest, after which he will find you a suitable partner. Don't ask to be taught one of our games. No matter how clever you may try to be, your opponent will be better because he'll be handling the familiar while you're coping with the strange. Select one of your own planet's games and thus give yourself an advantage."

"Thanks for the suggestion. It might do me some good if defeat meant death—but victory meant life."

"I've told you already that the result makes no difference."

"There you are then. Some choice, huh?"

"You can choose between death in the morning and death the morning after or even the one after that." Getting up from the bench, the warder walked out, closed the grille, said through the bars, "Anyway, I'll bring you a book giving full details of our indoor games. You'll have plenty of time to read it before the official arrives."

"Nice of you," said Taylor. "But I think you're wasting your time."

Left alone, Wayne Taylor let his thoughts mill around. They weren't pleasant ones. Space scouts belonged to a high-risk profession and none knew it better than themselves. Each and every one cheerfully accepted the dangers on the ages-old principle that it always happens to the other fellow, never to oneself. But now it had happened and to him. He ran a forefinger around the inside of his collar, which felt a little tight.

When he'd dived through the clouds with two air-machines blasting fire to port and starboard, he had pressed alarm button D. This caused his transmitter to start flashing a brief but complicated number giving his co-ordinates and defining the planet as enemy territory.

Earlier and many thousands of miles out in space he had reported his intention of making an emergency landing and identified the chosen world with the same coordinates. Button D, therefore, would confirm his first message and add serious doubts about his fate. He estimated that between the time he'd pressed the button and the time he had landed the alarm signal should have been transmitted at least forty times.

Immediately after the landing he'd switched the delayed-action charge and taken to his heels. The planes were still buzzing around. One of them swooped low over the grounded ship just as it blew up. It disintegrated in the blast. The other one gained altitude and circled overhead, directing the search. To judge by the speed with which troops arrived he must have had the misfortune to have dumped himself in a military area full of uniformed goons eager for blood. All the same, he'd kept them on the run for six hours and covered twenty miles before they got him. They'd expressed their disapproval with fists and feet.

Right now, there was no way of telling whether Terran listening-posts had picked up his repeated D-alarm. Odds were vastly in favor of it since it was a top-priority channel on which was kept a round-the-clock watch. He didn't doubt for a moment that, having received the message, they'd do something about it.

The trouble was that whatever they did would come too late. In this very sector patrolled the *Macklin*, Terra's latest, biggest, most powerful battleship. If the *Macklin* happened to be on the prowl, and at her nearest routine point, it would take her ten months to reach Gombar at maximum velocity. If she had returned to port, temporarily replaced by an older and slower vessel, the delay might last two years.

Two years was two years too long. Ten months was too long. He could not wait ten weeks. In fact it was highly probable that he hadn't got ten days. Oh, time, time, how impossible it is to stretch it for a man or compress it for a ship.

The warder reappeared, shoved a book between the bars. "Here you are. You have learned enough to understand it."

"Thanks."

Lying full length on the bench, he read right through it swiftly but comprehensively. Some pages he skipped after brief perusal because they described games too short, simple and childish to be worth considering. He was not surprised to find several games that were alien variations of ones well-known upon Terra. The Gombarians had playing cards, for instance, eighty to a pack with ten suits.

Alizik proved to be a bigger and more complicated version of chess, with four hundred squares and forty pieces per side. This was the one that somebody had dragged out for sixteen days and it was the only one in the book that seemed capable of such extension. For a while he pondered *alizik*, wondering whether the authorities—and the video audience—would tolerate play at the rate of one move in ten hours. He doubted it. Anyway, he could not prevent his skilled opponent from making each answering move in five seconds.

Yes, that was what he really wanted: a game that slowed down the other fellow despite his efforts to speed up. A game that was obviously a game and not a gag because any fool could see with half an eye that it was possible to finish it once and for all. Yet a game that the other fellow could not finish, win or lose, no matter how hard he tried.

There wasn't any such game on the three worlds of Gombar or the hundred worlds of Terra or the multimillion worlds yet unfound. There couldn't be because, if there were, nobody would play it. People like results. Nobody is sufficiently cracked to waste time, thought and patience riding a hobby-horse that got nowhere, indulging a rigmarole that cannot be terminated to the satisfaction of all concerned, including kibitzers.

But nobody!

No?

"When the last move is made God's Plan will be fulfilled; on that day and at that hour and at that moment the universe will vanish in a mighty thunderclap."

He got off the bench, his cold eyes expressionless, and began to pace his cell like a restless tiger.

The official had an enormous potbelly, small, piggy eyes and an unctuous smile that remained permanently fixed. His manner was that of a circus ringmaster about to introduce his best act.

"Ah," he said, noting the book, "so you have been studying our games, eh?"

"Yes."

"I hope you've found none of them suitable."

"Do you?" Taylor surveyed him quizzically. "Why?"

"It would be a welcome change to witness a contest based on something right out of this world. A genuinely new game would give a lot of satisfaction to everybody. Providing, of course," he added hurriedly, "that it was easy to understand and that you didn't win it too quickly."

"Well," said Taylor, "I must admit I'd rather handle something I know than something I don't."

"Good, good!" enthused the other. "You prefer to play a Terran game?"

"That's right."

"There are limitations on your choice."

"What are they?" asked Taylor.

"Once we had a condemned murderer who wanted to oppose his games-partner in seeing who could be the first to catch a sunbeam and put it in a bottle. It was nonsensical. You must choose something that obviously and beyond argument can be accomplished."

"I see."

Secondly, you may not select something involving the use of intricate and expensive apparatus that will take us a long time to manufacture. If apparatus is needed, it must be cheap and easy to construct."

"Is that all?"

"Yes—except that the complete rules of the game must be inscribed by you unambiguously and in clear writing. Once play begins, those rules will be strictly followed and no variation of them will be permitted."

"And who approves my choice after I've described it?"

"I do."

"All right. Here's what I'd like to play." Taylor explained it in detail, borrowed pen and paper and made a rough sketch. When he had finished the other folded the drawing and put it in a pocket.

"A strange game," admitted the official, "but it seems to me disappointingly uncomplicated. Do you really think you can make the contest last a full day?"

"I hope so."

"Even two days perhaps?"

"With luck."

"You'll need it!" He was silent with thought awhile, then shook his head doubtfully. "It's a pity you didn't think up something like a better and trickier version of *alizik*. The audience would have enjoyed it and you might have gained yourself a longer lease of life. Everyone would get a great kick out of it if you beat the record for delay before your execution."

"Would they really?"

"They sort of expect something extra-special from an alien life form."

"They're getting it, aren't they?"

"Yes, I suppose so." He still seemed vaguely dissatisfied. "Oh, well, it's your life and your struggle to keep it a bit longer."

"I'll have only myself to blame when the end comes."

"True. Play will commence promptly at midday tomorrow. After that, it's up to you."

He lumbered away, his heavy footsteps dying along the corridor. A few minutes later the warder appeared.

"What did you pick?"

"Arky-malarkey."

"Huh? What's that?"

"A Terran game."

"That's fine, real fine." He rubbed appreciative hands together. "He approved it, I suppose?"

"Yes, he did."

"So you're all set to justify your continued existence. You'll have to take care to avoid the trap."

"What trap?" Taylor asked.

"Your partner will play to win as quickly and conclusively as possible. That is expected of him. But once he gets it into his head that he can't win, he'll start playing to lose. You've no way of telling exactly when he'll change his tactics. Many a one has been caught out by the sudden switch and found the game finished before he had time to realize it."

"But he must keep to the rules, mustn't he?"

"Certainly. Neither you nor he will be allowed to ignore them. Otherwise the game would become a farce."

"That suits me."

Somewhere outside sounded a high screech like that of a

bobcat backing into a cactus. It was followed by a scuffle of
feet, a dull thud and dragging noises. A distant door creaked
open and banged shut.

"What goes?" said Taylor.

"Lagartine's game must have ended."

"Who's Lagartine?"

"A political assassin." The warder glanced at his watch.
"He chose *ramsid*, a card game. It has lasted a mere four
hours. Serves him right. Good riddance to bad rubbish."

"And now they're giving him the big squeeze?"

"Of course." Eying him, the warder said, "Nervous?"

"Ha-ha," said Taylor without mirth.

The performance did not commence in his cell as he had
expected. A contest involving an alien life form playing an
alien game was too big an event for that. They took him
through the prison corridors to a large room in which stood a
table with three chairs. Six more chairs formed a line against
the wall, each occupied by a uniformed plug-ugly complete
with hand gun. This was the knock-down-and-drag-out squad
ready for action the moment the game terminated.

At one end stood a big, black cabinet with two rectangular
portholes through which gleamed a pair of lenses. From it
came faint ticking sounds and muffled voices. This presumably contained the video camera.

Taking a chair at the table, Taylor sat down and gave the
armed audience a frozen stare. A thin-faced individual with
the beady eyes of a rat took the chair opposite. The potbellied
official dumped himself in the remaining seat. Taylor and
Rat-eyes weighed each other up, the former with cold assurance, the latter with sadistic speculation.

Upon the table stood a board from which arose three long
wooden pegs. The left-hand peg held a column of sixty-four
disks evenly graduated in diameter, the largest at the bottom, smallest at the top. The effect was that of a tapering
tower built from a nursery do-it-yourself kit.

Wasting no time, Potbelly said, "This is the Terran game of
Arky-malarkey. The column of disks must be transferred
from the peg on which it sits to either of the other two pegs.
They must remain graduated in the same order, smallest at
the top, biggest at the bottom. The player whose move com-
pletes the stack is the winner. Do you both understand?"

"Yes," said Taylor.

Rat-eyes assented with a grunt.

"There are three rules," continued Potbelly, "which will be strictly observed. You will make your moves alternately, turn and turn about. You may move only one disk at a time. You may not place a disk upon any other smaller than itself. Do you both understand?"

"Yes," said Taylor.

Rat-eyes gave another grunt.

From his pocket Potbelly took a tiny white ball and carelessly tossed it onto the table. It bounced a couple of times, rolled across and fell off on Rat-eyes' side.

"You start," he said.

Without hesitation Rat-eyes took the smallest disk from the top of the first peg and placed it on the third.

"Bad move," thought Taylor, blank of face. He shifted the second smallest disk from the first peg to the second.

Smirking for no obvious reason, Rat-eyes now removed the smallest disk from the third peg, placed it on top of Taylor's disk on the second. Taylor promptly switched another disk from the pile on the first peg to the empty third peg.

After an hour of this it had become plain to Rat-eyes that the first peg was not there merely to hold the stock. It had to be used. The smirk faded from his face, was replaced by mounting annoyance as hours crawled by and the situation became progressively more complicated.

By bedtime they were still at it, swapping disks around like crazy, and neither had got very far. Rat-eyes now hated the sight of the first peg, especially when he was forced to put a disk back on it instead of taking one off it. Potbelly, still wearing his fixed, meaningless smile, announced that play would cease until sunrise tomorrow.

The next day provided a long, arduous session lasting from dawn to dark and broken only by two meals. Both players worked fast and hard, setting the pace for each other and seeming to vie with one another in an effort to reach a swift conclusion. No onlooker could find cause to complain about the slowness of the game. Four times Rat-eyes mistakenly tried to place a disk on top of a smaller one and was promptly called to order by the referee in the obese shape of Potbelly.

A third, fourth, fifth and sixth day went by. Rat-eyes now played with a mixture of dark suspicion and desperation while the column on the first peg appeared to go up as often as it went down. Though afflicted by his emotions he was no fool. He knew quite well that they were making progress in the task of transferring the column. But it was progress at an appalling rate. What's more, it became worse as time went on. Finally he could see no way of losing the game, much less winning it.

By the fourteenth day Rat-eyes had reduced himself to an automaton wearily moving disks to and fro in the soulless, disinterested manner of one compelled to perform a horrid chore. Taylor remained as impassive as a bronze Buddha and that fact didn't please Rat-eyes either.

Danger neared on the sixteenth day though Taylor did not know it. The moment he entered the room he sensed an atmosphere of heightened interest and excitement. Rat-eyes looked extra glum. Potbelly had taken on added importance. Even the stolid, dull-witted guards displayed faint signs of mental animation. Four off-duty warders joined the audience. There was more activity than usual within the video cabinet.

Ignoring all this, Taylor took his seat and play continued. This endless moving of disks from peg to peg was a lousy way to waste one's life but the strangling-post was lousier. He had every inducement to carry on. Naturally he did so, shifting a disk when his turn came and watching his opponent with his pale gray eyes.

In the midafternoon Rat-eyes suddenly left the table, went to the wall, kicked it good and hard and shouted a remark about the amazing similarity between Terrans and farmyard manure. Then he returned and made his next move. There was some stirring within the video cabinet. Potbelly mildly reproved him for taking time off to advertise his patriotism. Rat-eyes went on playing with the surly air of a delinquent whose mother has forgotten to kiss him.

Late in the evening, Potbelly stopped the game, faced the video lenses and said in portentous manner, "Play will resume tomorrow—the seventeenth day!"

He voiced it as though it meant something or other.

When the warder shoved his breakfast through the grille in the morning, Taylor said, "Late, aren't you? I should be at play by now."

"They say you won't be wanted before this afternoon."

"That so? What's all the fuss about?"

"You broke the record yesterday," informed the other with

reluctant admiration. "Nobody has ever lasted to the seventeenth day."

"So they're giving me a morning off to celebrate, eh? Charitable of them."

"I've no idea why there's a delay," said the warder. "I've never known them to interrupt a game before."

"You think they'll stop it altogether?" Taylor asked, feeling a constriction around his neck. "You think they'll officially declare it finished?"

"Oh, no, they couldn't do that." He looked horrified at the thought of it. "We mustn't bring the curse of the dead upon us. It's absolutely essential that condemned people should be made to choose their own time of execution."

"Why is it?"

"Because it always has been since the start of time."

He wandered off to deliver other breakfasts, leaving Taylor to stew the explanation. "Because it always has been." It wasn't a bad reason. Indeed, some would consider it a good one. He could think of several pointless, illogical things done on Terra solely because they always had been done. In this matter of unchallenged habit the Gombarians were no better or worse than his own kind.

Though a little soothed by the warder's remarks he couldn't help feeling more and more uneasy as the morning wore on without anything happening. After sixteen days of moving disks from peg to peg, it had got so that he was doing it in his sleep. Didn't seem right that he should be enjoying a spell of aimless loafing around his cell. There was something ominous about it.

Again and again he found himself nursing the strong suspicion that officialdom was seeking an effective way of ending the play without appearing to flout convention. When they found it—if they found it—they'd pull a fast one on him, declare the game finished, take him away and fix him up with a very tight necktie.

He was still wallowing in pessimism when the call came in the afternoon. They hustled him along to the same room as before. Play was resumed as if it had never been interrupted. It lasted a mere thirty minutes. Somebody tapped twice on the inside of the video cabinet and Potbelly responded by calling a halt. Taylor went back to his cell and sat there baffled.

*   *   *

Late in the evening he was summoned again. He went with bad grace because these short and sudden performances were more wearing on the nerves than continual day-long ones. Previously he had known for certain that he was being taken to play Arky-malarkey with Rat-eyes. Now he could never be sure that he was not about to become the lead character in a literally breathless scene.

On entering the room he realized at once that things were going to be different this time. The board with its pegs and disks still stood in the center of the table. But Rat-eyes was absent and so was the armed squad. Three people awaited him: Potbelly, Palamin, and a squat, heavily built character who had the peculiar air of being of this world but not with it.

Potbelly was wearing the offended frown of someone burdened with a load of stock in a nonexistent oil well. Palamin looked singularly unpleased and expressed it by snorting like an impatient horse. The third appeared to be contemplating a phenomenon on the other side of the galaxy.

"Sit," ordered Palamin, spitting it out.

Taylor sat.

"Now, Marnikot, you tell him."

The squat one showed belated awareness of being on Gombar, said pedantically to Taylor, "I rarely look at the video. It is suitable only for the masses with nothing better to do."

"Get to the point," urged Palamin.

"But having heard that you were about to break an ages-old record," continued Marnikot, undisturbed, "I watched the video last night." He made a brief gesture to show that he could identify a foul smell at first sniff. "It was immediately obvious to me that to finish your game would require a minimum number of moves of the order of two to the sixty-fourth power minus one." He took flight into momentary dreamland, came back and added mildly, "That is a large number."

"Large!" said Palamin. He let go a snort that rocked the pegs.

"Let us suppose," Marnikot went on, "that you were to transfer these disks one at a time as fast as you could go, morning, noon and night without pause for meals or sleep, do you know how long it would take to complete the game?"

"Nearly six billion Terran centuries," said Taylor as if talking about next Thursday week.

"I have no knowledge of Terran time-terms. But I can tell you that neither you nor a thousand generations of your successors could live long enough to see the end of it. Correct?"

"Correct," Taylor admitted.

"Yet you say that this is a Terran game?"

"I do."

Marnikot spread hands helplessly to show that as far as he was concerned there was nothing more to be said.

Wearing a forbidding scowl, Palamin now took over. "A game cannot be defined as a genuine one unless it is actually played. Do you claim that this so-called game really is played on Terra?"

"Yes."

"By whom?"

"By priests in the Temple of Benares."

"And how long have they been playing it?" he asked.

"About two thousand years."

"Generation after generation?"

"That's right."

"Each player contributing to the end of his days without hope of seeing the result?"

"Yes."

Palamin fumed a bit. "Then *why* do they play it?"

"It's part of their religious faith. They believe that the moment the last disk is placed the entire universe will go bang."

"Are they crazy?"

"No more so than people who have played *alizik* for equally as long and to just as little purpose."

"We have played *alizik* as a series of separate games and not as one never-ending game. A rigmarole without possible end cannot be called a game by any stretch of the imagination."

"Arky-malarkey is not endless. It has a conclusive finish." Taylor appealed to Marnikot as the indisputed authority. "Hasn't it?"

"It is definitely finite," pronounced Marnikot, unable to deny the fact.

"So!" exclaimed Palamin, going a note higher. "You think you are very clever, don't you?"

"I get by," said Taylor, seriously doubting it.

"But we are cleverer," insisted Palamin, using his nastiest manner. "You have tricked us and now we shall trick you. The game is finite. It can be concluded. Therefore it will continue until it reaches its natural end. You will go on playing it days, weeks, months, years until eventually you expire of old age and chronic frustration. There will be times when the very sight of these disks will drive you crazy and you will beg for merciful death. But we shall not grant that favor—and you will continue to play. He waved a hand in triumphant dismissal. "Take him away."

Taylor returned to his cell.

When supper came the warder offered, "I am told that play will go on regularly as from tomorrow morning. I don't understand why they messed it up today."

"They've decided that I'm to suffer fate worse than death," Taylor informed.

The warder stared at him.

"I have been very naughty," said Taylor.

Rat-eyes evidently had been advised of the new setup because he donned the armor of philosophical acceptance and played steadily but without interest. All the same, long sessions of repetitive motions ate corrosively into the armor and gradually found its way through.

In the early afternoon of the fifty-second day, Rat-eyes found himself faced with the prospect of returning most of the disks to the first peg, one by one. He took off the clompers he used for boots. Then he ran barefooted four times around the room, bleating like a sheep. Potbelly got a crick in the neck watching him. Two guards led Rat-eyes away still bleating. They forgot to take his clompers with them.

By the table Taylor sat gazing at the disks while he strove to suppress his inward alarm. What would happen now? If Rat-eyes had given up for keeps it could be argued that he had lost, the game had concluded and the time had come to play okey-chokey with a piece of cord. It could be said with equal truth that an unfinished game remains an unfinished game even though one of the players is in a mental home giving his hair a molasses shampoo.

If the authorities took the former view, his only defense was to assert the latter one. He'd have to maintain with all the energy at his command that, since he had not won or lost, his time could not possibly have come. It wouldn't be easy if he had to make his protest while being dragged by the heels to his doom. His chief hope lay in Gombarian unwillingness to outrage an ancient convention. Millions of video viewers would take a poor look at officialdom mauling a pet superstition. Yes, man, there were times when the Idiot's Lantern had its uses.

He need not have worried. Having decided that to keep the game going would be a highly refined form of hell, the Gombarians had already prepared a roster of relief players drawn from the ranks of minor offenders whose ambitions never rose high enough to earn a strangling. So after a short time another opponent appeared.

The newcomer was a shifty character with a long face and hanging dewlaps. He resembled an especially dopey bloodhound and looked barely capable of articulating three words, to wit, "Ain't talking, copper." It must have taken at least a month to teach him that he must move only one disk at a time and never, never, never place it upon a smaller one. But somehow he had learned. The game went on.

Dopey lasted a week. He played slowly and doggedly as if in fear of punishment for making a mistake. Often he was irritated by the video cabinet, which emitted ticking noises at brief but regular intervals. These sounds indicated the short times they were on the air.

For reasons best known to himself, Dopey detested having his face broadcast all over the planet and, near the end of the seventh day, he'd had enough. Without warning he left his seat, faced the cabinet and made a number of swift and peculiar gestures at the lenses. The signs meant nothing to the onlooking Taylor. But Potbelly almost fell off his chair. The guards sprang forward, grabbed Dopey and frogmarched him through the door.

He was replaced by a huge-jowled, truculent character who dumped himself into the chair, glared at Taylor and wiggled his hairy ears. Taylor, who regarded this feat as one of his own accomplishments, promptly wiggled his own ears back. The other then looked fit to burst a blood vessel.

"This Terran sneak," he roared at Potbelly, "is throwing dirt at me. Do I *have* to put up with that?"

"You will cease to throw dirt," ordered Potbelly.

"I only wiggled my ears," said Taylor.

"That is the same thing as throwing dirt," Potbelly said mysteriously. "You will refrain from doing it and you will concentrate upon the game."

And so it went on, with disks being moved from peg to peg hour after hour, day after day, while a steady parade of opponents arrived and departed. Around the two hundredth day, Potbelly himself started to pull his chair apart with the apparent intention of building a campfire in the middle of the floor. The guards led him out. A new referee appeared. He had an even bigger paunch, and Taylor promptly named him Potbelly Two.

How Taylor himself stood the soul-deadening pace he never knew. But he kept going while the others cracked. He was playing for a big stake while they were not. All the same, there were times when he awoke from horrid dreams in which he was sinking through the black depths of an alien sea with a monster disk like a millstone around his neck. He lost count of the days, and once in a while his hands developed the shakes. The strain was not made any easier by several nighttime uproars that took place during this time. He asked the warder about one of them.

"Yasko refused to go. They had to beat him into submission."

"His game had ended?"

"Yes. The stupid fool matched a five of anchors with a five of stars. Immediately he realized what he'd done, he tried to kill his opponent." He wagged his head in sorrowful reproof. "Such behavior never does them any good. They go to the post cut and bruised. And if the guards are angry with them, they ask the executioner to twist slowly."

"Ugh!" Taylor didn't like to think of it. "Surprises me that none have chosen my game. Everybody must know of it by now."

"They are not permitted to," said the warder. "There is now a law that only a recognized Gombarian game may be selected."

He ambled away. Taylor lay full length on his bench and hoped for a silent, undisturbed night. What was the Earthdate? How long had he been here? How much longer would he remain? How soon would he lose control of himself and go nuts? What would they do with him if and when he became too crazy to play?

Often in the thought-period preceding sleep, he concocted wild plans of escape. None of them were of any use whatever. Conceivably he could break out of this prison despite its grilles, armored doors, locks, bolts, bars and armed guards. It was a matter of waiting for a rare opportunity and seizing it with both hands. But suppose he got out, what then? Any place on the planet he would be as conspicuous as a kangaroo on the sidewalks of New York. If it were possible to look remotely like a Gombarian, he'd have a slight chance. It was not possible. He could do nothing save play for time.

This he continued to do. On and on and on without cease, except for meals and sleep. By the three hundredth day he had to admit to himself that he was feeling somewhat moth-eaten. By the four hundredth he was under the delusion that he had been playing for at least five years and was doomed to play forever, come what may. The four-twentieth day was no different from the rest except in one respect of which he was completely unaware—it was the last.

At down of day four twenty-one, no call came for him to play. Perforce he waited a couple of hours and still no summons. Maybe they'd decided to break him with a cat-and-mouse technique, calling him when he didn't expect it and not calling him when he did. A sort of psychological water torture. When the warder passed along the corridor, Taylor went to the bars and questioned him. The fellow knew nothing and was as puzzled as himself.

The midday meal arrived. Taylor had just finished it when the squad of guards arrived accompanied by an officer. They entered the cell and removed his irons. Ye gods, this was something! He stretched his limbs luxuriously, fired questions at the officer and his plug-uglies. They took no notice, behaved as if he had stolen the green eye of the little yellow god. Then they marched him out of the cell, along the corridors and past the games room.

Finally they passed through a large doorway and into an open yard. In the middle of this area stood six short steel posts each with a hole near its top and a coarse kneeling-mat at its base. Stolidly the squad tramped straight toward the posts. Taylor's stomach turned over. The squad pounded on past the posts and toward a pair of gates. Taylor's stomach turned thankfully back and settled itself.

Outside the gates they climbed aboard a troop-carrier which at once drove off. It took him around the outskirts of the city to a spaceport. They all piled out, marched past the control tower and onto the concrete. There they halted.

Across the spaceport, about half a mile away, Taylor could see a Terran vessel sitting on its fins. It was far too small for a warship, too short and fat for a scoutship. After staring at it with incredulous delight he decided that it was a battleship's lifeboat. He wanted to do a wild dance and yell silly things.

He wanted to run like mad toward it, but the guards stood close around and would not let him move.

They waited there for four long tedious hours, at the end of which another lifeboat screamed down from the sky and landed alongside its fellow. A bunch of figures came out of it, mostly Gombarians. The guards urged him forward.

He was dimly conscious of some sort of exchange ceremony at the halfway mark. A line of surly Gombarians passed him, going the opposite way. Many of them were ornamented with plenty of brass and had the angry faces of colonels come fresh from a general demotion. He recognized one civilian, Borkor, and wiggled his ears at him as he went by.

Then willing hands helped him through an airlock and he found himself sitting in the cabin of a ship going up. A young and eager lieutenant was talking to him but he heard only half of it.

". . . landed, snatched twenty and beat it into space. We cross-examined them by signs . . . bit surprised to learn you were still alive . . . released one with an offer to exchange prisoners. Nineteen Gombarian bums for one Terran is a fair swap, isn't it?"

"Yes," said Taylor, looking around and absorbing every mark upon the walls.

"We'll have you aboard the *Thunderer* pretty soon . . . *Macklin* couldn't make it with that trouble near Cygni . . . got here as soon as we could." The lieutenant eyed him sympathetically. "You'll be heading for home within a few hours. Hungry?"

"No, not at all. The one thing they didn't do was starve me."

"Like a drink?"

"Thanks, I don't drink."

Fidgeting around embarrassedly, the lieutenant asked, "Well, how about a nice, quiet game of draughts?"

Taylor ran a finger around the inside of his collar and said, "Sorry, I don't know how to play and don't want to learn. I am allergic to games."

"You'll change."

"I'll be hanged if I do," said Taylor.

Dreaming Is a Private Thing

ISAAC ASIMOV

JESSE Weill looked up from his desk. His old, spare body, his sharp, high-bridged nose, deep-set, shadowy eyes and amazing shock of white hair had trademarked his appearance during the years that Dreams, Inc., had become world-famous.

He said, "Is the boy here already, Joe?"

Joe Dooley was short and heavy-set. A cigar caressed his moist lower lip. He took it away for a moment and nodded. "His folks are with him. They're all scared."

"You're sure this is not a false alarm, Joe? I haven't got much time." He looked at his watch. "Government business at two."

"This is a sure thing, Mr. Weill." Dooley's face was a study in earnestness. His jowls quivered with persuasive intensity. "Like I told you, I picked him up playing some kind of basketball game in the schoolyard. You should've seen the kid. He stunk. When he had his hands on the ball, his own team had to take it away, and fast, but just the same he had all the stance of a star player. Know what I mean? To me it was a giveaway."

"Did you talk to him?"

"Well, sure. I stopped him at lunch. You know me." Dooley gestured expansively with his cigar and caught the severed ash with his other hand. "Kid, I said—"

"And he's dream material?"

"I said, 'Kid, I just came from Africa and—' "

"All right." Weill held up the palm of his hand. "Your word

41

I'll always take. How you do it I don't know, but when you say a boy is a potential dreamer, I'll gamble. Bring him in."

The youngster came in between his parents. Dooley pushed chairs forward and Weill rose to shake hands. He smiled at the youngster in a way that turned the wrinkles of his face into benevolent creases.

"You're Tommy Slutsky?"

Tommy nodded wordlessly. He was about ten and a little small for that. His dark hair was plastered down unconvincingly and his face was unrealistically clean.

Weill said, "You're a good boy?"

The boy's mother smiled at once and patted Tommy's head maternally (a gesture which did not soften the anxious expression on the youngster's face). She said, "He's always a very good boy."

Weill let this dubious statement pass. "Tell me, Tommy," he said, and held out a lollipop which was first hesitated over, then accepted, "do you ever listen to dreamies?"

"Sometimes," said Tommy trebly.

Mr. Slutsky cleared his throat. He was broad-shouldered and thick-fingered, the type of laboring man who, every once in a while, to the confusion of eugenics, sired a dreamer. "We rented one or two for the boy. Real old ones."

Weill nodded. He said, "Did you like them, Tommy?"

"They were sort of silly."

"You think up better ones for yourself, do you?"

The grin that spread over the ten-year-old face had the effect of taking away some of the unreality of the slicked hair and washed face.

Weill went on gently, "Would you like to make up a dream for me?"

Tommy was instantly embarrassed. "I guess not."

"It won't be hard. It's very easy. . . . Joe."

Dooley moved a screen out of the way and rolled forward a dream recorder.

The youngster looked owlishly at it.

Weill lifted the helmet and brought it close to the boy. "Do you know what this is?"

Tommy shrank away. "No."

"It's a thinker. That's what we call it because people think into it. You put it on your head and think anything you want."

"Then what happens?"

"Nothing at all. It feels nice."

"No," said Tommy, "I guess I'd rather not."

His mother bent hurriedly toward him. "It won't hurt, Tommy. You do what the man says." There was an unmistakable edge to her voice.

Tommy stiffened, and looked as though he might cry but he didn't. Weill put the thinker on him.

He did it gently and slowly and let it remain there for some thirty seconds before speaking again, to let the boy assure himself it would do no harm, to let him get used to the insinuating touch of the fibrils against the sutures of his skull (penetrating the skin so finely as to be insensible almost), and finally to let him get used to the faint hum of the alternating field vortices.

Then he said, "Now would you think for us?"

"About what?" Only the boy's nose and mouth showed.

"About anything you want. What's the best thing you would like to do when school is out?"

The boy thought a moment and said, with rising inflection, "Go on a stratojet?"

"Why not? Sure thing. You go on a jet. It's taking off right now." He gestured lightly to Dooley, who threw the freezer into circuit.

Weill kept the boy only five minutes and then let him and his mother be escorted from the office by Dooley. Tommy looked bewildered by undamaged by the ordeal.

Weill said to the father, "Now, Mr. Slutsky, if your boy does well on this test, we'll be glad to pay you five hundred dollars each year until he finishes high school. In that time, all we'll ask is that he spend an hour a week some afternoon at our special school."

"Do I have to sign a paper?" Slutsky's voice was a bit hoarse.

"Certainly. This is business, Mr. Slutsky."

"Well, I don't know. Dreamers are hard to come by, I hear."

"They are. They are. But your son, Mr. Slutsky, is not a dreamer yet. He might never be. Five hundred dollars a year is a gamble for us. It's not a gamble for you. When he's finished high school, it may turn out he's not a dreamer, yet you've lost nothing. You've gained maybe four thousand dollars altogether. If he *is* a dreamer, he'll make a nice living and you certainly haven't lost then."

"He'll need special training, won't he?"

"Oh, yes, most intensive. But we don't have to worry about that till after he's finished high school. Then, after two years with us, he'll be developed. Rely on me, Mr. Slutsky."

"Will you guarantee that special training?"

Weill, who had been shoving a paper across the desk at Slutsky, and punching a pen wrong-end-to at him, put the pen down and chuckled. "A guarantee? No. How can we when we don't know for sure yet if he's a real talent? Still, the five hundred a year will stay yours."

Slutsky pondered and shook his head. "I tell you straight out, Mr. Weill . . . after your man arranged to have us come here, I called Luster-Think. They said they'll guarantee training."

Weill sighed. "Mr. Slutsky, I don't like to talk against a competitor. If they say they'll guarantee schooling, they'll do as they say, but they can't make a boy a dreamer if he hasn't got it in him, schooling or not. If they take a plain boy without the proper talent and put him through a development course, they'll ruin him. A dreamer he won't be, I guarantee you. And a normal human being he won't be, either. Don't take the chance of doing it to your son.

"Now Dreams, Inc., will be perfectly honest with you. If he can be a dreamer, we'll make him one. If not, we'll give him back to you without having tampered with him and say, 'Let him learn a trade.' He'll be better and healthier that way. I tell you, Mr. Slutsky—I have sons and daughters and grandchildren so I know what I say—I would not allow a child of mine to be pushed into dreaming if he's not ready for it. Not for a million dollars."

Slutsky wiped his mouth with the back of his hand and reached for the pen. "What does this say?"

"This is just an option. We pay you a hundred dollars in cash right now. No strings attached. We'll study the boy's reverie. If we feel it's worth following up, we'll call you in again and make the five-hundred-dollar-a-year deal. Leave yourself in my hands, Mr. Slutsky, and don't worry. You won't be sorry."

Slutsky signed.

Weill passed the document through the file slot and handed an envelope to Slutsky.

Five minutes later, alone in the office, he placed the unfreezer over his own head and absorbed the boy's reverie intently. It was a typically childish daydream. First Person was at the controls of the plane, which looked like a compound of illustrations out of the filmed thrillers that still circulated among those who lacked the time, desire or money for dream cylinders.

When he removed the unfreezer, he found Dooley looking at him.

"Well, Mr. Weill, what do you think?" said Dooley, with an eager and proprietary air.

"Could be, Joe. Could be. He has the overtones and, for a ten-year-old boy without a scrap of training, it's hopeful. When the plane went through a cloud, there was a distinct sensation of pillows. Also the smell of clean sheets, which was an amusing touch. We can go with him a ways, Joe."

"Good."

"But I tell you, Joe, what we really need is to catch them still sooner. And why not? Someday, Joe, every child will be tested at birth. A difference in the brain there positively must be and it should be found. Then we could separate the dreamers at the very beginning."

"Hell, Mr. Weill," said Dooley, looking hurt. "What would happen to my job, then?"

Weill laughed. "No cause to worry yet, Joe. It won't happen in our lifetimes. In mine, certainly not. We'll be depending on good talent scouts like you for many years. You just watch the playgrounds and the streets"—Weill's gnarled hand dropped to Dooley's shoulder with a gentle, approving pressure—"and find us a few more Hillarys and Janows and Luster-Think won't ever catch us.... Now get out. I want lunch and then I'll be ready for my two o'clock appointment. The government, Joe, the government." And he winked portentously.

Jesse Weill's two o'clock appointment was with a young man, apple-cheeked, spectacled, sandy-haired and glowing with the intensity of a man with a mission. He presented his credentials across Weill's desk and revealed himself to be John J. Byrne, an agent of the Department of Art and Sciences.

"Good afternoon, Mr. Byrne," said Weill. "In what way can I be of service?"

"Are we private here?" asked the agent. He had an unexpected baritone.

"Quite private."

"Then, if you don't mind, I'll ask you to absorb this." Byrne produced a small and battered cylinder and held it out between thumb and forefinger.

Weill took it, hefted it, turned it this way and that and said with a denture-revealing smile, "Not the product of Dreams, Inc., Mr. Byrne."

"I didn't think it was," said the agent. "I'd still like you to absorb it. I'd set the automatic cutoff for about a minute, though."

"That's all that can be endured?" Weill pulled the receiver to his desk and placed the cylinder into the unfreeze compartment. He removed it, polished either end of the cylinder with his handkerchief and tried again. "It doesn't make good contact," he said. "An amateurish job."

He placed the cushioned unfreeze helmet over his skull and adjusted the temple contacts, then set the automatic cutoff. He leaned back and clasped his hands over his chest and began absorbing.

His fingers grew rigid and clutched at his jacket. After the cutoff had brought absorption to an end, he removed the unfreezer and looked faintly angry. "A raw piece," he said. "It's lucky I'm an old man so that such things no longer bother me."

Byrne said stiffly, "It's not the worst we've found. And the fad is increasing."

Weill shrugged. "Pornographic dreamies. It's a logical development, I suppose."

The government man said, "Logical or not, it represents a deadly danger for the moral fiber of the nation."

"The moral fiber," said Weill, "can take a lot of beating. Erotica of one form or another have been circulated all through history."

"Not like this, sir. A direct mind-to-mind stimulation is much more effective than smoking room stories or filthy pictures. Those must be filtered through the senses and lose some of their effect in that way."

Weill could scarcely argue that point. He said, "What would you have me do?"

"Can you suggest a possible source for this cylinder?"

"Mr. Byrne, I'm not a policeman."

"No, no, I'm not asking you to do our work for us. The Department is quite capable of conducting its own investigations. Can you help us, I mean, from your own specialized knowledge? You say your company did not put out that filth. Who did?"

"No reputable dream distributor. I'm sure of that. It's too cheaply made."

"That could have been done on purpose."

"And no professional dreamer originated it."

"Are you sure, Mr. Weill? Couldn't dreamers do this sort of thing for some small, illegitimate concern for money—or for fun?"

"They could, but not this particular one. No overtones. It's two-dimensional. Of course, a thing like this doesn't need overtones."

"What do you mean, overtones?"

Weill laughed gently. "You are not a dreamie fan?"

Byrne tried not to look virtuous and did not entirely succeed. "I prefer music."

"Well, that's all right, too," said Weill tolerantly, "but it makes it a little harder to explain overtones. Even people who absorb dreamies would not be able to explain if you asked them. Still they'd know a dreamie was no good if the overtones were missing, even if they couldn't tell you why. Look, when an experienced dreamer goes into reverie, he doesn't think a story like in the old-fashioned television or book films. It's a series of little visions. Each one has several meanings. If you studied them carefully, you'd find maybe five or six. While absorbing in the ordinary way, you would never notice, but careful study shows it. Believe me, my psychological staff puts in long hours on just that point. All the overtones, the different meanings, blend together into a mass of guided emotion. Without them, everything would be flat, tasteless.

"Now, this morning, I tested a young boy. A ten-year-old with possibilities. A cloud to him isn't a cloud, it's a pillow, too. Having the sensations of both, it was more than either. Of course, the boy's very primitive. But when he's through with his schooling, he'll be trained and disciplined. He'll be subjected to all sorts of sensations. He'll store up experience. He'll study and analyze classic dreamies of the past. He'll learn how to control and direct his thoughts, though, mind you, I have always said that when a good dreamer improvises—"

Weill halted abruptly, then proceeded in less impassioned tones, "I shouldn't get excited. All I try to bring out now is

that every professional dreamer has his own type of overtones which he can't mask. To an expert it's like signing his
name on the dreamie. And I, Mr. Byrne, know all the signa-
tures. Now that piece of dirt you brought me has no overtones
at all. It was done by an ordinary person. A little talent,
maybe, but like you and me, he really can't think."

Byrne reddened a trifle. "A lot of people can think, Mr.
Weill, even if they don't make dreamies."

"Oh, tush," and Weill wagged his hand in the air. "Don't be
angry with what an old man says. I don't mean think as in
reason. I mean think as in dream. We all can dream after a
fashion, just like we all can run. But can you and I run a mile
in four minutes? You and I can talk, but are we Daniel
Websters? Now when I think of a steak, I think of the word.
Maybe I have a quick picture of a brown steak on a platter.
Maybe you have a better pictorialization of it and you can see
the crisp fat and the onions and the baked potato. I don't
know. But a *dreamer* . . . he sees it and smells it and tastes it
and everything about it, with the charcoal and the satisfied
feeling in the stomach and the way the knife cuts through it
and a hundred other things all at once. Very sensual. Very
sensual. You and I can't do it."

"Well, then," said Byrne, "no professional dreamer has
done this. That's something anyway." He put the cylinder in
his inner jacket pocket. "I hope we'll have your full co-operation
in squelching this sort of thing."

"Positively, Mr. Byrne. With a whole heart."

"I hope so." Byrne spoke with a consciousness of power.
"It's not up to me, Mr. Weill, to say what will be done and
what won't be done, but this sort of thing"—he tapped the
cylinder he had brought—"will make it awfully tempting to
impose a really strict censorship on dreamies."

He rose. "Good day, Mr. Weill."

"Good day, Mr. Byrne. I'll hope always for the best."

Francis Belanger burst into Jesse Weill's office in his usual
steaming tizzy, his reddish hair disordered and his face aglow
with worry and a mild perspiration. He was brought up
sharply by the sight of Weill's head cradled in the crook of his
elbow and bent on the desk until only the glimmer of white
hair was visible.

Belanger swallowed. "Boss?"

Weill's head lifted. "It's you, Frank?"

"What's the matter, boss? Are you sick?"

"I'm old enough to be sick, but I'm on my feet. Staggering, but on my feet. A government man was here."

"What did he want?"

"He threatens censorship. He brought a sample of what's going round. Cheap dreamies for bottle parties."

"God damn!" said Belanger feelingly.

"The only trouble is that morality makes for good campaign fodder. They'll be hitting out everywhere. And, to tell the truth, we're vulnerable, Frank."

"*We* are? Our stuff is clean. We play up straight adventure and romance."

Weill thrust out his lower lip and wrinkled his forehead. "Between us, Frank, we don't have to make believe. Clean? It depends on how you look at it. It's not for publication, maybe, but you know and I know that every dreamie has its Freudian connotations. You can't deny it."

"Sure, if you *look* for it. If you're a psychiatrist—"

"If you're an ordinary person, too. The ordinary observer doesn't know it's there and maybe he couldn't tell a phallic symbol from a mother image even if you pointed it out. Still, his subconscious knows. And it's the connotations that make many a dreamie click."

"All right, what's the government going to do? Clean up the subconscious?"

"It's a problem. I don't know what they're going to do. What we have on our side, and what I'm mainly depending on, is the fact that the public loves its dreamies and won't give them up. . . . Meanwhile, what did you come in for? You want to see me about something, I suppose?"

Belanger tossed an object onto Weill's desk and shoved his shirttail deeper into his trousers.

Weill broke open the glistening plastic cover and took out the enclosed cylinder. At one end was engraved in a too fancy script in pastel blue "Along the Himalayan Trail." It bore the mark of Luster-Think.

"The Competitor's Product." Weill said it with capitals, and his lips twitched. "It hasn't been published yet. Where did you get it, Frank?"

"Never mind. I just want you to absorb it."

Weill sighed. "Today, everyone wants me to absorb dreams. Frank, it's not dirty?"

Belanger said testily, "It has your Freudian symbols. Narrow crevasses between the mountain peaks. I hope that won't bother you."

"I'm an old man. It stopped bothering me years ago, but that other thing was so poorly done, it hurt. . . . All right, let's see what you've got here."

Again the recorder. Again the unfreezer over his skull and at the temples. This time, Weill rested back in his chair for fifteen minutes or more, while Francis Belanger went hurriedly through two cigarettes.

When Weill removed the headpiece and blinked dream out of his eyes, Belanger said, "Well, what's your reaction, boss?"

Weill corrugated his forehead. "It's not for me. It was repetitious. With competition like this, Dreams, Inc., doesn't have to worry for a while."

"That's your mistake, boss. Luster-Think's going to win with stuff like this. We've got to do something."

"Now, Frank—"

"No, you listen. This is the coming thing."

"This!" Weill stared with half-humorous dubiety at the cylinder. "It's amateurish, it's repetitious. Its overtones are very unsubtle. The snow had a distinct lemon sherbet taste. Who tastes lemon sherbet in snow these days, Frank? In the old days, yes. Twenty years ago, maybe. When Lyman Harrison first made his Snow Symphonies for sale down south, it was a big thing. Sherbet and candy-striped mountaintops and sliding down chocolate-covered cliffs. It's slapstick, Frank. These days it doesn't go."

"Because," said Belanger, "you're not up with the times, boss. I've got to talk to you straight. When you started the dreamie business, when you bought up the basic patents and began putting them out, dreamies were luxury stuff. The market was small and individual. You could afford to turn out specialized dreamies and sell them to people at high prices."

"I know," said Weill, "and we've kept that up. But also we've opened a rental business for the masses."

"Yes, we have and it's not enough. Our dreamies have subtlety, yes. They can be used over and over again. The tenth time you're still finding new things, still getting new enjoyment. But how many people are connoisseurs? And another thing. Our stuff is strongly individualized. They're First Person."

"Well?"

"Well, Luster-Think is opening dream palaces. They've opened one with three hundred booths in Nashville. You walk in, take your seat, put on your unfreezer and get your dream. Everyone in the audience gets the same one."

"I've heard of it, Frank, and it's been done before. It didn't work the first time and it won't work now. You want to know why it won't work? Because, in the first place, dreaming is a private thing. Do you like your neighbor to know what you're dreaming? In the second place, in a dream palace, the dreams have to start on schedule, don't they? So the dreamer has to dream not when he wants to but when some palace manager says he should. Finally, a dream one person likes another person doesn't like. In those three hundred booths, I guarantee you, a hundred fifty people are dissatisfied. And if they're dissatisfied, they won't come back."

Slowly, Belanger rolled up his sleeves and opened his collar. "Boss," he said, "you're talking through your hat. What's the use of proving they won't work? They *are* working. The word came through today that Luster-Think is breaking ground for a thousand-booth palace in St. Louis. People can get used to public dreaming, if everyone else in the same room is having the same dream. And they can adjust themselves to having it at a given time, as long as it's cheap and convenient.

"Damn it, boss, it's a social affair. A boy and a girl go to a dream palace and absorb some cheap romantic thing with stereotyped overtones and commonplace situations, but still they come out with stars sprinkling their hair. They've had the same dream together. They've gone through identical sloppy emotions. Theh're *in tune,* boss. You bet they go back to the dream palace, and all their friends go, too."

"And if they don't like the dream?"

"That's the point. That's the nub of the whole thing. They're bound to like it. If you prepare Hillary specials with wheels within wheels within wheels, with surprise twists on the third-level undertones, with clever shifts of significance and all the other things we're so proud of, why, naturally, it won't appeal to everyone. Specialized dreamies are for specialized tastes. But Luster-Think is turning out simple jobs in Third Person so both sexes can be hit at once. Like what you've just absorbed. Simple, repetitious, commonplace. They're aiming at the lowest common denominator. No one will love it, maybe, but no one will hate it."

Weill sat silent for a long time and Belanger watched him. Then Weill said, "Frank, I started on quality and I'm staying there. Maybe you're right. Maybe dream palaces are the coming thing. If so we'll open them, but we'll use good stuff. Maybe Luster-Think underestimates ordinary people. Let's go slowly and not panic. I have based all my policies on the theory that there's always a market for quality. Sometimes, my boy, it would surprise you how big a market."

"Boss—"

The sounding of the intercom interrupted Belanger.

"What is it, Ruth?" said Weill.

The voice of his secretary said, "It's Mr. Hillary, sir. He wants to see you right away. He says it's important."

"Hillary?" Weill's voice registered shock. Then, "Wait five minutes, Ruth, then send him in."

Weill turned to Belanger. "Today, Frank, is definitely not one of my good days. A dreamer's place is in his home with his thinker. And Hillary's our best dreamer so he especially should be at home. What do you suppose is wrong with him?"

Belanger, still brooding over Luster-Think and dream palaces, said shortly, "Call him in and find out."

"In one minute. Tell me, how was his last dream? I haven't tried the one that came in last week."

Belanger came down to earth. He wrinkled his nose. "Not so good."

"Why not?"

"It was ragged. Too jumpy. I don't mind sharp transitions for the liveliness, you know, but there's got to be some connection, even if only on a deep level."

"Is it a total loss?"

"No Hillary dream is a *total* loss. It took a lot of editing, though. We cut it down quite a bit and spliced in some odd pieces he'd sent us now and then. You know, detached scenes. It's still not Grade A, but it will pass."

"You told him about this, Frank?"

"Think I'm crazy, boss? Think I'm going to say a harsh word to a dreamer?"

And at that point the door opened and Weill's comely young secretary smiled Sherman Hillary into the office.

*   *   *

Sherman Hillary, at the age of thirty-one, could have been recognized as a dreamer by anyone. His eyes, unspectacled, had nevertheless the misty look of one who either needs glasses or who rarely focuses on anything mundane. He was of average height but underweight, with black hair that needed cutting, a narrow chin, a pale skin and a troubled look.

He muttered, "Hello, Mr. Weill," and half-nodded in hang-dog fashion in the direction of Belanger.

Weill said heartily, "Sherman, my boy, you look fine. What's the matter? A dream is cooking only so-so at home? You're worried about it? . . . Sit down, sit down."

The dreamer did, sitting at the edge of the chair and holding his thighs stiffly together as though to be ready for instant obedience to a possible order to stand up once more.

He said, "I've come to tell you, Mr. Weill, I'm quitting."

"Quitting?"

"I don't want to dream any more, Mr. Weill."

Weill's old face looked older now than at any time in the day. "Why, Sherman?"

The dreamer's lips twisted. He blurted out, "Because I'm not *living*, Mr. Weill. Everything passes me by. It wasn't so bad at first. It was even relaxing. I'd dream evenings, week-ends when I felt like, or any other time. And when I felt like I wouldn't. But now, Mr. Weill, I'm an old pro. You tell me I'm one of the best in the business and the industry looks to me to think up new subtleties and new changes on the old reliables like the flying reveries, and the worm-turning skits."

Weill said, "And is anyone better than you, Sherman? Your little sequence on leading an orchestra is selling stead-ily after ten years."

"All right, Mr. Weill. I've done my part. It's gotten so I don't go out any more. I neglect my wife. My little girl doesn't know me. Last week, we went to a dinner party—Sarah made me—and I don't remember a bit of it. Sarah says I was sitting on the couch all evening just staring at nothing and hum-ming. She said everyone kept looking at me. She cried all night. I'm tired of things like that, Mr. Weill. I want to be a normal person and live in this world. I promised her I'd quit and I will, so it's good-by, Mr. Weill." Hillary stood up and held out his hand awkwardly.

Weill waved it gently away. "If you want to quit, Sherman, it's all right. But do an old man a favor and let me explain something to you."

"I'm not going to change my mind," said Hillary.

"I'm not going to try to make you. I just want to explain something. I'm an old man and even before you were born I was in this business so I like to talk about it. Humor me, Sherman? Please?"

Hillary sat down. His teeth clamped down on his lower lip and he stared sullenly at his fingernails.

Weill said, "Do you know what a dreamer is, Sherman? Do you know what he means to ordinary people? Do you know what it is to be like me, like Frank Belanger, like your wife, Sarah? To have crippled minds that can't imagine, that can't build up thoughts? People like myself, ordinary people, would like to escape just once in a while this life of ours. We can't. We need help.

"In olden times it was books, plays, radio, movies, television. They gave us make-believe, but that wasn't important. What was important was that for a little while our own imaginations were stimulated. We could think of handsome lovers and beautiful princesses. We could be beautiful, witty, strong, capable, everything we weren't.

"But, always, the passing of the dream from dreamer to absorber was not perfect. It had to be translated into words in one way or another. The best dreamer in the world might not be able to get any of it into words. And the best writer in the world could put only the smallest part of his dreams into words. You understand?

"But now, with dream recording, any man can dream. You, Sherman, and a handful of men like you, supply those dreams directly and exactly. It's straight from your head into ours, full strength. You dream for a hundred million people every time you dream. You dream a hundred million dreams at once. This is a great thing, my boy. You give all those people a glimpse of something they could not have by themselves."

Hillary mumbled, "I've done my share." He rose desperately to his feet. "I'm through. I don't care what you say. And if you want to sue me for breaking our contract, go ahead and sue. I don't care."

Weill stood up, too. "Would I sue you? . . . Ruth," he spoke into the intercom, "bring in our copy of Mr. Hillary's contract."

He waited. So did Hillary and so did Belanger. Weill smiled faintly and his yellowed fingers drummed softly on his desk.

His secretary brought in the contract. Weill took it, showed its face to Hillary and said, "Sherman, my boy, unless you want to be with me, it's not right you should stay."

Then, before Belanger could make more than the beginning of a horrified gesture to stop him, he tore the contract into four pieces and tossed them down the waste chute. "That's all."

Hillary's hand shot out to seize Weill's. "Thanks, Mr. Weill," he said earnestly, his voice husky. "You've always treated me very well, and I'm grateful. I'm sorry it had to be like this."

"It's all right, my boy. It's all right."

Half in tears, still muttering thanks, Sherman Hillary left.

"For the love of Pete, boss, why did you let him go?" demanded Belanger distractedly. "Don't you see the game? He'll be going straight to Luster-Think. They've bought him off."

Weill raised his hand. "You're wrong. You're quite wrong. I know the boy and this would not be his style. Besides," he added dryly, "Ruth is a good secretary and she knows what to bring me when I ask for a dreamer's contract. What I had was a fake. The real contract is still in the safe, believe me.

"Meanwhile, a fine day I've had. I had to argue with a father to give me a chance at new talent, with a government man to avoid censorship, with you to keep from adopting fatal policies and now with my best dreamer to keep him from leaving. The father I probably won out over. The government man and you, I don't know. Maybe yes, maybe no. But about Sherman Hillary, at least, there is no question. The dreamer will be back."

"How do you know?"

Weill smiled at Belanger and crinkled his cheeks into a network of fine lines. "Frank, my boy, you know how to edit dreamies so you think you know all the tools and machines of the trade. But let me tell you something. The most important tool in the dreamie business is the dreamer himself. He is the one you have to understand most of all, and I understand them.

"Listen. When I was a youngster—there were no dreamies then—I knew a fellow who wrote television scripts. He would complain to me bitterly that when someone met him for the first time and found out who he was, they would say: Where do you get those crazy ideas?

"They honestly didn't know. To them it was an impossibility to even think of one of them. So what could my friend say? He used to talk to me about it and tell me: Could I say, I don't know? When I go to bed, I can't sleep for ideas dancing in my head. When I shave, I cut myself; when I talk, I lose track of what I'm saying; when I drive, I take my life in my hands. And always because ideas, situations, dialogues are spinning and twisting in my mind. I can't tell you where I get my ideas. Can you tell me, maybe, your trick of *not* getting ideas, so I, too, can have a little peace.

"You see, Frank, how it is. *You* can stop work here anytime. So can I. This is our job, not our life. But not Sherman Hillary. Wherever he goes, whatever he does, he'll dream. While he lives, he must think; while he thinks, he must dream. We don't hold him prisoner, our contract isn't an iron wall for him. His own skull is his prisoner, Frank. So he'll be back. What can he do?"

Belanger shrugged. "If what you say is right, I'm sort of sorry for the guy."

Weill nodded sadly. "I'm sorry for all of them. Through the years, I've found out one thing. It's their business; making people happy. *Other* people."

The Man Who Murdered Television

JOSEPH PATROUCH

STRANGE how some people have a social consciousness and others don't. How some look at the way things are and try to figure ways to make things better for everybody, while others figure if they're all right, then everyone's all right. For me, though, the most interesting are those who start out one way and end up the other. My daughter, Carole, for instance.

Carole's twenty-seven now, married, kids of her own. She lives out on Friar Tuck Drive in Sherwood Forest Estates and minds her own business, in a way. For a while, though—when she was in college and just after she graduated—she got kind of radical. One's social consciousness tends to get raised at that age, and it happened to hers too.

Her "thing" was diet. She was anti-starches and anti-cholesterol and anti-additives and anti-I-don't-know-what-all. "You are what you eat," she'd pontificate. "Have you ever seen a cardiovascular system clogged with cholesterol?" This always made me feel nervous and awkward—what do you say to someone who's on a kick and kicking *you?*—so I'd reach in my pocket for a cigarette and light up. That was obviously the wrong thing to do. "Have you ever seen," she'd lecture, "a lung clogged with cigarette tars?"

Sometimes Carole would generalize from all this. "We're a nation, a world, of polluters," she'd proclaim. "Not only do we pollute our own bodies with the wrong foods, with drugs, with cigarettes, but we pollute our air and our water with industrial wastes that . . ." "Not to mention the moral pollution of pornography," I'd add slyly. (She saw nothing wrong with pornography.) "That's an entirely different matter and you know it," she'd snort, "because no one is injured by pornography." "V.D.?" I'd suggest. "From reading a book or looking at pictures? You're talking nonsense. Anyhow, the subject was how we're the only species on this planet that fouls its own nest so badly. . . ." And on and on she'd go.

She carried signs protesting the lack of effective air-pollution control devices at our local gas and electric company, and she carried signs protesting that same company when it raised its rates to pay for the installation of such equipment. She visited welfare mothers to inform them how best to spend their food dollars and wondered why they so often seemed sullen, even smoldering with anger. I'd ask her, "What if someone came to your door and told you what to buy and what not to buy?" "But that's different," she'd protest; "they don't know any better." "Couldn't manage without you, huh?" "They could manage to suffer from heart disease and malnutrition and emphysema and . . . and anyhow, I'm doing it for their own good. It's so frustrating being put down for doing good." "About as frustrating as having good done to you, I expect," I'd remark. She didn't understand that for a long time. But eventually she did, and that's when she started minding her own business.

It happened this way. The husband of one of her welfare mothers had come home and thrown Carole out for putting her nose in where it wasn't wanted. She'd come home all upset. This time she was in to "What can any individual do in a society as corrupt and uncaring as ours? We're killing ourselves with bad diet, drugs, pollution. We're killing our neighbors in unjustified wars. We're the only species that so fouls its own nest. . . ."

I decided the time had come to level with her.

"Carole, sit down," I said. "There are some things I want to explain to you."

Something in my manner combined with her own depression to make her sit down and remain quiet. I was surprised to find myself, not merely reacting to her as usual, but actually in control of the conversation. Where to begin?

"Bear with me for a minute here, Carole. I don't know if I'll make myself clear right away."

"Sure."

"Let's say a neighborhood is infested with rats. What do you think ought to be done?"

"Direct action. Go in there with traps and poison and guns and sticks, whatever it takes, and get rid of them."

"But what about indirect action? What about the man who feels just as strongly as anyone else, but who doesn't go out to set traps?"

"He's a hypocrite, a parlor liberal. Reads his paper and sympathizes at a distance over brandy. No, you've got to go down into the trenches, among the people."

"And how about the fellow who invented the trap in the first place? How about the man who spends years in college and graduate school studying chemistry in order to make a better, safer rat poison? Isn't he at least as important as the ones who set the traps and poison?"

She hesitated. "I never thought of it that way before," she admitted. "I don't know."

"Do you know what I majored in in college?" I asked.

She looked embarrassed. "No," she replied. I could see she was wondering how she could have been so thoughtless as to get to her age without learning such a simple thing about her own father. I had to explain to her that her lack of knowledge wasn't her fault. It was mine. Deliberately.

"When I was a kid, I was interested in radio. Why, when I was eight, I built my own crystal set mostly from pieces of junk I'd found here and there. That set worked, too. I'd sit up at night when my parents thought I was asleep, and I'd listen to music all the way from Chicago."

"So you majored in electrical engineering?"

"No. As it turned out, I was interested in a lot of things. When I had to pick only one, I made it biology. But I liked to combine interests. I couldn't chuck the radio for biology any more than I could chuck biology for radio. Eventually I got a postgraduate fellowship to do research in what today you'd probably call a hybrid between electronics and molecular biology."

"I don't see how those two can be combined," she puzzled.

"I wanted to work on living cells, their health, growth, reproduction. Most people come at that from chemistry. But I thought I was on to something using electromagnetic radiation."

"Radio waves?"

"Of different frequencies."

"And . . .?"

"I didn't have the sophisticated and delicate equipment I'd

have if I were doing the work these days. It was all very crude. I have to admit. But still I believed I had discovered the worst form of environmental pollution that's ever been known to man."

Carole looked skeptical. She couldn't tell whether I was putting her on or not.

"There is always a certain amount of electromagnetic radiation in our natural background. Just as there's always a certain amount of radioactivity around. But too much radioactivity can kill living cells. So can too much electromagnetic radiation."

"How much is too much?"

"Carole, in this country we have so increased the electromagnetic background against which we live that it is now too much. Hundreds of thousands of people are sick and dying from it each year. Only we call it something else because we're looking at the effect not the cause, at what is directly doing the killing and not at what is causing the cause. We call it cancer."

"Wait a minute, Dad. You're moving too fast for me. You mean, you found that radio and television and citizen band radio . . . that all those things cause cancer?"

"The broadcast energy that is received and turned into the sounds and pictures from our sets, yes. That energy causes cancer. The farther into this century we've gotten, the more our bodies have been soaked and saturated by the electromagnetic energy broadcast by our communications systems. And that in turn has caused the incidence of cancer to rise. Oh, the statistics are screened some. We're told that more people live long enough to get cancer now that so many of the other killing diseases are under control, and we're told that we're collecting our statistics more efficiently now, so that on the surface it looks like there are more cases when there aren't. But the correlation is still there: the farther into this electromagnetic century we've come, the more cancer there's been."

Several nights earlier I had been speaking with an astronomer friend about one of the implications of this—though of course I hadn't come right out and explained the whole thing to him. He was talking about how the radio-astronomers were certain that, given powerful and sensitive enough instruments, they could detect the electromagnetic radiation from intelligent civilizations light-years distant. I had been mysteriously skeptical.

"That's why I was insisting to Bill the other night," I went on, referring to the conversation, "that our radio-astronomers aren't likely to detect *intelligent* species by their electromagnetic radiation—the sum total of their daily communications leaking out into interstellar space. Any civilization which knowingly exists bathed constantly in such a field will turn out to be both stupid and short-lived. Too stupid to live long enough to have their civilization overlap ours. You see now why I argued that way."

"Dad, who cares about radio-astronomers and extraterrestrial civilizations? What about our own? You make it sound as if we're committing suicide."

"Not deliberately. Just stupidly. But we are in fact committing racial suicide."

"Can't we do something about it? Tell someone?"

"I tried back then, Carole, during WWII, but no one would take me seriously. Already the money invested in electromagnetic forms of communications was too great. At first they insisted that I needed more proof, not simply the little data I had. Not conclusive, they said. Can't scare the public over nothing. Then they decided I was a crackpot. My postgraduate research money dried up. I was made aware, not very subtly, that if I pushed it—really pushed it—something fatal might happen, an accident."

I paused to get control of myself.

"Carole, I was scared. You're right about one thing. The individual can't do much against powerful, vested interests like those. So I changed my name, dropped completely out of sight, became another person with another career. That's why you didn't know what my major was or anything. It wasn't callousness or lack of interest on your part. It was self-protection on mine. I gave up that research . . . for you and for your mother."

Now I began to feel guilty and ashamed. Carole's mother had died of cancer when Carole was only four. And I was the only one who had known what caused cancer, and I hadn't been able to help her—or any of the others. Not directly. Carole didn't reproach me about my decision to stop research.

I leaned towards her. This next part was important too.

"There is one other thing you absolutely must realize, Carole. It's not a matter of publicizing the relationship between television and cancer. Given the choice, people would rather have the television than live with a drastically reduced incidence of cancer. You see that, don't you?"

"Like with cigarettes," she said quietly. Her example made me cringe. "People would rather smoke than live with the threat of heart disease and lung cancer lowered. It only happens to someone else." She understood.

"Exactly. And fifty thousand a year killed on the highways doesn't lessen the demand for automobiles."

We looked bleakly at one another, trying to feel Channel 7 in the marrow of our bones. Maybe our species wasn't one of the intelligent ones.

"What can we do?" Then suspicion lit in her eyes. "What are you doing? How does a free-lance writer help?"

I smiled thinly. "Well, maybe someday I'll write all this up as a story and plant some seeds of suspicion in some minds where it might do some good. Basically, though, my writing is simply a way of earning money so I can do the really important work."

I probably sounded a little too melodramatic, to judge from the look she gave me. Well, she hadn't heard anything yet.

"I'm part of a group that has decided you can't buck city hall. No way we can exert enough pressure to shut down all the broadcasting stations in the world. Instead, we've decided to do what we can to reduce the demand."

"You mean, get people not to watch television or listen to radio?"

"Exactly. If they don't turn it on, the industry will dry up and blow away."

"How can you stop people from turning on their sets?"

"We decided that programming was the key. We are working to make radio and TV programming so bad that people just won't bother. We've managed to make radio a wasteland of interchangeable DJ's playing interchangeable records. In TV we have members who see to it that really excellent scripts are mangled in production, that good series ideas are run through the grinder until they come out as tasteless paste, that the really excellent series are kept off the air while poorer ones are run, that talent is driven from the industry while only the ordinary and run-of-the-mill remains."

"I don't believe it."

"But it seems to be working." I continued. "More people are

going to the movies than ever before, more books than ever are being sold and read, and neither movies nor books use electromagnetic broadcast energy. But it's slow, very slow. The industry may not topple in my lifetime or yours."

"There's got to be a better way," Carole shook her head slowly. "There's got to be."

I shrugged my shoulders. "We couldn't find it."

"You say it all depends on *broadcast* radiation?"

I nodded. She wandered off mulling the problem over.

Well, that's the story. After that, Carole quit being a social activist. The gas and electric company can put in its pollution control equipment and try to pay for it with rate increases without any protest from her. And the welfare mothers can buy their kids chocolate bars without looking over their shoulders.

This doesn't mean that Carole now thinks my approach will succeed. She doesn't think that I'm about to go down in history as "the man who murdered television and saved the world." She's too cynical to think that people will ever abandon TV no matter how bad the programming gets.

She's taken another approach, and she considers her two children a vote of confidence in the future. She works extremely hard helping her husband.

He's an account executive for a cable television firm.

The Jester

WILLIAM TENN

HISTORY can be as dangerous as a traffic accident: it can happen to people. And cause even more damage. One fine day—about the year 2208, say—a bright, cheerful and maybe too-smart-for-his-own-good young man wakes up to find he's tripped over his cleverest idea and crashed into a brand new age.

Away back when—early in the nineteen hundreds—people began listening to record players instead of trudging off to a vaudeville theater through the cold and wet. Later, in the radio era, most top-level executives were finding dictaphones more efficient than human stenographers and mechanical sorters better than an army of file clerks. And, at the peak of the television boom, every bride dreamed of owning a vocalex kitchen someday that would exactly obey her most casual command to heat a roast for such and such a time and baste it at such and such intervals.

With the deluxe models, of course, came a set of flavor-fix rheostats which, among other talents, could mix salads according to the recipe of a famous chef slightly better than the chef could himself. Then along came All-Purpose Radar Broadcast power; television went three-dimensional and became teledar, inexpensive enough so that every Eskimo could own a set and, incidentally, the only industry where an actor might make a living.

As teledar took over entertainment household devices began to move around in the form of robots powered by APRB, rocket-ships piloted only by automatics made timetable flights to every planet in the system, and everyone agreed that man could hardly ask for more control over his environment.

So one fine day—oh, about the year 2208—

The doorscreen above the valuable antique radiator in Lester's living room fluoresced for a moment, then crackled into a picture of the husky man waiting outside the apartment. He wore the visored helmet of a service mechanic. An enormous yellow box beside him filled most of the doorscreen.

"Lester the Jester? Rholg's Robot Reorganizers. I have your butler-valet combo here all fitted with the special custom-built adjustments you ordered. You have to sign a danger-and-damage release before I can leave him."

"Uhm." The red-haired young man nodded and wiped the sleep from his eyes so that the worry could shine through. He rose from the couch, stretched jerkily. "I'd sign a life-and-liberty waiver to get what I need out of that robot. Hey, door," he called. "Twenty-three, there—twenty-three."

Swiftly the door slid up into its sandwiched recess. The mechanic flipped a switch on his beamlock and the huge crate floated delicately into the apartment, bumped gently to rest against a wall. Lester rubbed his hands nervously. "I hope—"

"You know, Mr. Lester, I never thought a guy like me would ever get to see you in person. In my line I meet all kinds of celebrities—like yesterday, when I returned two receptionist-robots to the police commissioner. We'd equipped them with lie-detectors and flat feet. But wait till I tell my wife I met the biggest comedian in teledar! She always says, Mr. Lester—"

"Not Mr. Lester. Lester—Lester the Jester."

The mechanic grinned widely and appreciatively. "Like on the program, huh?" He pointed his beamlock at the crate, moving the switch from *carry* to *disrupt*. "And when one of the boys at the shop figured you were going to use this robot like a gagwriter I asked him would he like his head broken. I told him your jokes were strictly off the cuff—I heard. Right?"

"Right!" A very loud, vastly amused laugh. "Lester the Jester using a gagwriter! What kind of rumors—imagine that! Me, the glib sahib of ad-lib—as my fans like to call me—working from someone else's boffolas. *Such a thing!* Just because I thought it would be snappy for the hemisphere's top comedian to have a robot valet who can give with gags on demand. *Hah!* Well, let me see him."

A rattling whirr as directive force tore out of the beam-lock, dissolving the yellow crate into quickly scattered dust. When it had settled they were looking at five feet of purple metal man.

"You changed his shape!" Lester yelped accusingly. "I sent you a smooth-lined twenty-two hundred and seven model with the new cylindrical trunk. You bring back a pear-shaped piece of machinery looking squeezed down—as if it had a paunch all the way around. And bowlegged!"

"Look, sir, the techs just had to expand his midsection. Even on microwire that file of jokes took up an awful lot of space. And your order said for him to be able to work out twists on the gags in the file—so they rassled up a new gimmick, what they call a variable modifier. More space, more weight. But let me turn him on."

The man in the visored helmet inserted a convoluted length of iridium—an Official Robot Master Key—into the back of the robot's neck. Two full clicking turns and machinery purred. Metal arms crossed upon a metal chest in the accepted gesture of servility. Eyebrow ridges clinked upward. Multi-linked lips pursed questioningly.

"Migosh!" the mechanic marveled. "I never seen such a snooty expression on any face before."

"My fiancée, Josephine Lissy—she's the singer on my program—designed it," Lester told him proudly. "Her idea of what a butler-valet combo should look like—sort of in the ancient English tradition. She also thought up his name. Hey, Rupert, tell me a joke."

Rupert's mouth opened. His voice clacked out, rising and falling like a sine wave. "On what subject, sir?"

"Oh, anything. A vacation trip. A small belly-laugh joke."

"Ginsberg was making his first voyage to Mars," Rupert began. "He was shown to a small table in the salon and told that his tablemate would be a Frenchman. Since the other had not yet—"

The Rholg's mechanic leaned across his flat purple chest. "That's another gimmick—a meson filter. You said you wanted him able to distinguish between laugh-power in different gags so he could fit them to the audience. And price was no object. That's all you have to tell a tech. They knocked themselves out developing a gadget to do the job just right."

"If it does a couple of writers I know are going to be sorry pigeons. We'll see who's the comedian around here," Lester muttered. "Lester the Jester or Green and Anderson. Greedy little paper-spoilers!"

"—the Frenchman, noticing Ginsberg already at his meal, stopped. He clicked his heels and bowed from the waist. *'Bon appétit,'* he said. Ginsberg, not to be outdone, rose to *his—*"

"A meson filter is what they call it, eh? Well, even that bill in galactic figures your outfit sent me will be worth it if I can get what I want out of Rupert. But I wish you hadn't spoiled his looks!"

"—this succinct dialogue was repeated. Until, the day before the end of the voyage, Ginsberg sought the steward and asked him to explain the meaning of—"

"We'd have found some way of packaging all the stuff or at least distributing it better if you hadn't been in such a hurry. You wanted him back by Wednesday, no matter what."

"Yes, of course. I go on the waves tonight. I needed the—ah, stimulation Rupert would give me." Lester ran nervous fingers through his red hair. "He seems to be okay."

"—approached the Frenchman, who was already at table. He clicked his heels and bowed from the waist. *'Bon appétit,'* Ginsberg told him. Joyfully, the Frenchman leaped to his feet and—"

"Then you won't mind signing this. Regular release form. You take all responsibility for the actions of Rupert. I can't leave him here till I get it."

"Sure." Lester signed. "Anything else?"

"—'Ginsberg,' the Frenchman said!" Rupert had finished.

"Not bad. But I can't use it quite that way. We need a—Holy options, what's that?" Lester teetered backward.

The robot, standing perfectly immobile, was clacking wildly, grinding his gears and *pinging* wires as if he were coming apart.

"Oh, *that.*" The man from Rholg's gestured. "That's another bug the techs didn't have time to clean up. Comes from the meson filter. Near as we can figure out it's what they call an aftereffect of his capacity to distinguish between gags that are partly funny and gags that are very funny. Electronic differentiation of the grotesque, it says in the specifications—in a man, a sense of humor. 'Course, in a robot it only means there's a kink in the exhaust."

"Yeah. I hope he doesn't blow that at me when I have a hangover. A robot that laughs at his own jokes! *Whooee,* what a sound!" Lester shivered. "Rupert, go mix me one of those Three-Ply Lunar Landings."

The mass of purple metal turned and waddled off to the kitchen. Both men chuckled at his bow-legged teetering gait.

"Here's a couple of bucks for your trouble. Sorry I don't have more change on me. Like a carton of Star-Gazers? My sponsor keeps me stocked to the curls on them. Licorice, maple-walnut?"

"I sorta like my cigarettes flavored with crab-apple. The missus too—gee, thanks. Hope everything goes all right."

The service mechanic stuffed his beamlock into his tunic and left. Lester called, "Three-and-twenty," after him. The door slid down into place.

Rupert tottered back with an intricate spiral of transparent tubing filled with a yellow-and-white liquid. The comedian sucked the drink out rapidly, exhaled and combed his hair back into place.

"Right! That was delicious in its own foul way. Whoever built that master bartender unit into you really knew his electronics. Now look, I don't know just how to order you in this deal—though you're able to read now, come to think of it. Here's the script for tonight's teledar show, the straight part.

"Type a companion script for me based on each speech in the original that I've underlined, a gag variation on the statement. That's what I memorize to give the famous ad-lib effect—but you don't have to know that. Start typing."

Without a word, the robot flipped through the sheaf of papers handed to him, instantly "memorizing" on his microwire files every word in them.

Then he dropped the script on the floor again and walked over to the electric typewriter. He pushed the chair in front of it aside. His torso slid down his metallic legs until he was just at the right height for typing. He went to work. Paper boiled up out of the machine.

Lester watched admiringly. "If only his ideas are half as funny as they are fast—hello!" He picked the sheaf of typescript off the floor to which Rupert had returned and set it on a table. "Never did that before. Used to be the neatest piece of machinery on the planet, always picking up after me. But—well, genius has the right to be temperamental!" The phone buzzed almost affirmatively.

He grinned and caught the phone as it bounded into his hands. "Radio Central," said the mouthpiece. "Miss Josephine Lissy calling. Will you take it on your scrambler or on hers?"

"Mine. LY—one hundred thirty-four—YJ. Check."

"Yes sir. Here's your party."

The radio phone sputtered as it adjusted to Lester's personal scrambling system that meant privacy for a conversation on a wavelength shared by millions. A girl with hair as brightly carroty as Lester's appeared in the tiny screen above the mouthpiece.

"Hi, Red." She smiled. "Know something? Jo loves Lester."

"Smart girl—smart. Wait a minute while I get you transferred. Looking at you on this thing strains my eyes—besides, there isn't enough of you."

He twirled a dial, translated the phone's vibrations into the frequency of the doorscreen. Then, while the instrument whizzed back into place on the ceiling, he made a similar adjustment on the doorscreen manual dials, setting it for interior reception.

Josephine Lissy's image was radiant above the imitation radiator as he sighed down into the couch.

"Look, funnyman, this is no love-call. I'll get right down to the most recent mess. Green and Anderson have blabbed to Haskell."

"What!" He leaped to his feet. "I'll sue them! I can, too—the mutual release they signed specified that my use of gag-writers was not to be made public."

She shrugged. "A lot that'll help you. Besides, they didn't publicize it—just told it to Haskell. You couldn't even prove *that*. All I got was grapevine to the effect that Haskell is screaming over to see you.

"Green and Anderson have convinced him that without memorizing their gag copy on the straight part of the show you won't even be able to ad-lib a burp. And Haskell is just scared that the first program under his sponsorship will be a flop."

Lester grinned. "Don't worry, Jo. With any luck—"

"My sacred aunt's favorite space-opera!" she squealed. "What's that?"

That was an ear-splitting series of clanks, bumps, singing metal and siren-like shrieks. Lester whirled.

Rupert had finished typing. He held the long sheet of completed copy between purple fingers and shook over it.

Whirr, he went. *Glongety-glonk. Pingle, pingle, pingle. Ka-zam!* He sounded like a cement mixer inside a cement mixer.

"Oh, that's Rupert. He's got a kink in his exhaust—makes like a mindless sense of humor. Of course he isn't human but does he seem to go for his own stuff! Come here, Rupert!"

The robot stopped clattering and slid up his legs to his full height. He walked to the doorscreen.

"When did they bring him back?" Jo asked. "Did they put all the stuff in him that you—why, they've *ruined* him! He looks like a case of dropsy—as if he has an abdominal ruff! And that beautiful expression on his face I designed—it's all gone! He doesn't look superior any more, just sad—very sad. Poor Rupert!"

"Your imagination," Lester told her. "Rupert can't change his expression even if he wanted to. It's all automatic, built in at the factory. Just because we call him by a name instead of the number cues we use on the rest of the household machinery doesn't mean he has feelings. Outside of his duties as a valet, which he performs as imaginatively as a watch tells time, he's just a glorified filing system with a wadjacallit—a variable modifier to select—"

"Oh, that isn't so. Rupert has feelings, don't you, Rupert?" she cooed at him in a small voice. "You remember me, Rupert? Jo. How are you, Rupert?" The robot stared silently at the screen.

"Of all the unquaint feminine conceits—"

There was a definite *clang* as Rupert's heels smote together. He bowed stiffly from the hips. "Gins—" he began to say. His head went down majestically, kept on going down. It hit the floor with a terrific *zok*.

Jo became almost hysterical. Lester flapped his arms against his sides. Rupert, the back of his paunch peak-high in the air, rested stolidly respectful, his body making a right-angled triangle with the floor.

"—berg," Rupert finished from where his face angled against the floor. He made no move to rise. He *whurgled* softly, reminiscently.

"Well?" Lester glowered at him. "Are you going to lie there and look silly all day? Get up!"

"H-he *c-can't,*" Jo shrieked. "Th-they've shifted h-his center of gra-gravity and he can't get up. If you ever do anything as funny as that bow over the teledar you'll kill two hundred million innocent people!"

Lester the Jester grimaced and bent over his robot. He caught it round the shoulders and tugged. Very slowly, very reluctantly, Rupert straightened. He pointed at Jo's image on the screen.

"That ain't no lady," he enunciated metallically. "That's gonna be your wife. *Or*—it may not be Hades but brother it's gonna be life! *Or*—she's not shady, she's only—"

"Can it!" Lester yelled. "And I do mean *can* it!"

He brooded while the robot went into another gear-clashing paroxysm. "My fine tile floor! The best mid-twentieth-century floor in the whole tower and look at it! A dent the size of—"

Jo clucked at him. "I've told you a dozen times that they only used tiled floors in *bathrooms* in the forties and fifties. Mostly in bathrooms, anyway. And that imitation radiator and roll-top desk are from two widely separated periods—you just don't have a sense of the antique, Lester lad. Wait till we've signed a marriage contract with each other—I'll show you what a Roosevelt-era home really looks like. How are Rupert's gags—on paper, I mean?"

"Don't know yet. He's just finished the script." The screen fluoresced along an edge. "Better get off, Jo. Someone's at the door. Call for me before the 'cast at the usual time. Bye."

At a signal from his master, the robot scuttled to the door and *twenty-three'd* at it. Two things happened simultaneously—the service mechanic from Rholg's Custom-Built Robots walked in and Rupert's head *zokked* against the floor.

Lester sighed and pulled Rupert straight again. "I hope he isn't going to repeat that courtly gesture anytime someone comes here. I'll have shellholes all over the living room."

"Has he done that before? That's not good. Remember, all of his basic control units are in his head and a lot of them have just started meshing the new service patterns. He's liable to fracture a bearing and go choo-choo. Like me to take him back to the plant for recalibration?"

"No, I don't have time. I start 'casting in two hours. That reminds me—did your techs build that word-scanner into his forehead?"

The mechanic nodded. "Sure. See that narrow green plate over his eyes? Just flip that to one side or have him do it whenever you want silent written transmission. The words will flow across like on a regular news sign. I came back for the key. Left it stuck in his neck and I'd be in one sweet fix if I got back to the factory without it."

"Take it. I thought you were somebody else." Lester turned to face the dumpy little man in a striped tunic who had just barged in through the open door. "Hello, Mr. Haskell. Would you have a seat? I'll be with you in a moment."

"Give me the key," the mechanic commanded. Rupert pulled the Official Robot Master Key out of the back of his neck and held it out. The mechanic reached for it. Rupert dropped it.

"Well, I'll be—" the man from Rholg's started. "If I didn't know better, I'd swear he did it on purpose." He bent down to retrieve the key.

As his fingers closed over it, Rupert's right hand flicked forward slightly. The man jumped to his feet and sprang backwards through the doorway.

"No you don't!" he snarled. "Did you see what he was trying to do? Why—"

"Three-and-twenty," said Rupert. The door slid shut, cutting off the service mechanic's last statement. The robot came back into the apartment, clacking ever so slightly. His facial expression seemed even sadder than before—somehow disappointed.

"Two of those Lunar Landing specials," his master told him. He waddled off to prepare them.

"Now look here, Lester," John Haskell boomed in a voice surprising for his size. "I'll come right to the point. I didn't know you were using writers until Green and Anderson told me you'd fired them because they wouldn't take a cut in salary. I go with them when they say they've made you the highest paid comedian in United Americas. Now this show tonight is only an option of a—"

"Wait up, sir. I wrote my own stuff before they came to work for me and they operated entirely from my personal gag files. I fired them because they demanded a higher percentage of my earnings than I got. I can still ad-lib faster than any standup man in the business."

"I don't care whether you ad-lib or whether the stuff comes to you in a dream! I just want laughs on my program to get people in a proper frame of mind to hear my commercials. No, that's not what I mean—oh!" He reached out and grabbed one of the convoluted masses that Rupert had brought in and drained it rapidly. His face didn't even change color. "Not strong enough. Tasteless. Needs stuff."

The robot held the returned and empty receptacle for a

moment and studied it. Then he bow-legged it back to the kitchen.

Lester decided that he didn't agree with the president of Star-Gazers, Inc. This drink had *wowie* in every alcoholic drop. But the drinks at the Planetmasters Club where Haskell lived were reputedly powerful.

"All I care about is this," Haskell was saying. "Can you work up a funny program tonight without Green and Anderson or can't you? You may have a high comic rating but they're spreading the word: people hear what they say in the industry. If Star-Gazers fail to pick up your thirteen-week option tonight after the trial 'cast for our product, you'll have to go back to daytime soap operas."

"Sure, Mr. Haskell, sure. But take a look at this script and *then* make your comments." Lester plucked the long sheet of copy out of the electric typewriter and handed it to the little man.

Dangerous, that. It might stink seven ways from Monday. But he hadn't had time to read it himself. Rupert had better be good!

He was, to judge from Haskell's reaction. The president of Star-Gazers had roared himself into the antique swivel chair and sat there shaking. "Wonderful!" he wiped the tears from his eyes. *"Terrific!* Almost but not quite colossal! I apologize, Lester. You don't need any gag-writers, you really do write comedy. Think you can memorize this before the program?"

"Shouldn't be any trouble. I always have to use a little infra-scopolamine for a rush job anyway. And in case I need an ad-lib suddenly I've got my robot."

"Robot? You mean him?" Mr. Haskell gestured to where Rupert stood *whirring* over his shoulder as he stared at the script. He pulled a dark spiral of tubing out of the purple hand, sucked at it.

"Yes, he has a gag file in his midsection. He'll stand out of camera range and anytime I need a gag I just look at him and the words are spelled out on the forehead scanner. Had it all inserted in my butler-valet combo by the Rholg—Mr. Haskell! What's the matter?"

Haskell had dropped the tube. It lay on the floor, a thin wisp of black smoke steaming out of the open end. "Th-the drink," Haskell said hoarsely. His face, after experimenting with red, green and lavender for a while, compromised and settled on all three in a sort of alternated mottled arrangement. "Where's your—your—"

"In there! Second door to the left!"

The little man scurried off, his body low. He seemed to have lost all of his bones.

"Now what can—" Lester sniffed at the spiral drinking tube. My God! He was abruptly aware that Rupert was going *whirretty-whirretty-klonk.* "Rupert, what did you put in that drink?"

"He asked for something stronger, more tasty—"

"What did you put in that drink?"

The robot considered. "Five parts—(*whizz-clang*)—castor oil to three parts—(*bing-bong*)—Worcestershire sauce to—(*tinkle-tinkle-burr-r-r*)—four parts essence of red pepper—(*g-r-rang*)—to one part Cro—"

Lester whistled and the phone leaped into his hand. "Radio Central? Hospital emergency and I mean emerge! Lester the Jester, Artist's Tower, apartment one thousand and six. Hurry!" He ran down the hall to help his guest sit on his stomach.

When the interne saw the brightly colored mess Haskell was becoming, he shook his head. "Let's get him in the stretcher and out!"

Rupert stood in the corner of the living room as the stretcher, secure in the grip of the interne's beamlock, floated through the door. "Musta been something he et," he clacked.

The interne glared back. "A comedian!"

Lester hurriedly drank three Lunar Landings. He mixed them himself. He had just finished memorizing the robot's ad-lib script with the aid of a heavy dose of infra-scopolamine when Jo breezed in. Rupert opened the door for her. *Clang. Zok.*

"You know, he's been doing this all day," Lester told her as he tugged the robot upright again. "And not only is he adding an original design to my floor but I suspect that he's not helping his bedamned mental processes any. Of course, he's obeyed *me* completely so far and all of his practical jokes have been aimed at others. . . ."

Rupert rolled something around in his mouth. Then he pursed his lips. Multilinked wrinkles appeared in his cheeks. He spat.

A brass hexagonal nut bounced against the floor. The three of them stared at it. Finally, Jo raised her head.

"What practical jokes?"

Lester told her.

"*Whew!* You're lucky your contract has a personal immunity clause. Otherwise Haskell could sue you from Patagonia to Nome. But he still won't feel any affection for you, any *real* affection. He'll probably live, though. Get into your costume."

As Lester hustled into his spangled red suit in the next room, he called at her, "What're you singing tonight?"

"Why don't you come to a rehearsal sometime and find out?"

"Have to keep up my impromptu reputation. What is it?"

"Oh, 'Subjective Me, Objective You' from Googy Garcia's latest hit—*Love Among the Asteroids*. This robot of yours may write good comedy but he sure is a bust as a butler. The junk he leaves scattered around. Paper, cigarettes, drink-tubes! When I enter your life on a permanent basis, young feller . . ." Her voice died as she bent and began picking up the litter from the floor of the living room. Behind her Rupert meditated at her back. *"Whirr?"* he went.

His right hand flashed up. He came at her fast. He reached her.

"Yeeee-eeee!" Jo screamed as she climbed halfway up the opposite wall. She turned as she came down. Her eyes literally crackled.

"Who—what—" she began menacingly. Then she noticed Rupert standing, his hand still out, all of his machinery going *whistle-clong-ka-bankle* all at once.

"Why, he's laughing at me! Think it funny do you, you mechanical pervert?" She sped at him in fury, her right hand going far back for a terrific slap.

Lester had torn out of the kitchen when she screamed. Now he saw her hand whistling around in a great arc, almost at Rupert's face.

"Jo!" he yelled. "Not in the head!"

Moing-g-g-g-g-g!

"Think you'll be all right, Miss Lissy," the doctor said. "Just keep your hand in this cast for two weeks. Then we'll X-ray again."

"Let's get started for the studio, Jo," Lester said nervously. "We'll be late. Shame this had to happen."

"Isn't it though? But before I let you accompany me anywhere I want to get one thing straight. You get rid of Rupert."

"But, Jo darling, honey, sweet, do you know what a writer he is?"

"I don't care. I wouldn't think of bringing children up in a home that he infested. According to the Robot Laws you have to keep him at home. I frankly think he's gone dotty in a humorous way. But I don't like it. So—you'll have to choose between me and that gear-happy gagman." She smoothed the cast on her arm as she waited for his reply.

Now Rupert, in his present condition—for all of his eccentricities—meant that Lester's career as a comedian was assured, that never again would he have to worry about material, that he was set for life. On the other hand, he doubted he'd ever meet a woman who was as close to what he wanted in a wife as Jo. She was—well, Lester's ideal—she alone among the girls he knew met his requirements for a successful marriage.

It was a clear choice between money and the woman he loved.

"Well," Lester told Jo at last. "We can still be good friends?"

Jo was finishing her song by the time he arrived at the studio. She didn't even glower at him as she walked away from the camera-mikes. The commercial began.

Lester stationed Rupert against the wall of the control booth where no camera could pick up a view of his purple body. Then he joined the other actors under the dead camera who were waiting for the end of the commercial before starting their combination drama and comedy.

The announcer came to the end of the last rolling syllable of admiration. The five Gloppus sisters came up for the finale:

S—G—F, F, C!
Star-Gazer's Fifteen Flavored Cigarettes!
Stay away from tastes like hay!
Days are gay with nasal play,
Star-Gazer's Fifteen Flavored Way!
S—G—F, F, C! From Choc-o-late—to chereèee!

The camera above Lester sparked colors as he and the actors took over. A simple playlet—romance in a fueling station on Phobos. Lester was extraneous to the plot—he merely came in with gags from time to time, gags based on some action or line in the straight story.

Good gags tonight—even the program manager was laughing. Well, not laughing—but he *smiled* now and then. And, buddy, if a program manager smiles, then people all over the western hemisphere have collapsed into a cataleptic hysteria. This is a fact as demonstrably certain and changeless as that the third vice-president of a teledar corporation shall always be the butt of the very worst jokes or, as it is known sociologically, the Throttlebottom Effect.

From time to time Lester glanced at his robot. The creature was not staring at him always—that was annoying. He had turned to examine the interior of the control booth through the transparent door which shut it off from the rest of the studio. Lester had removed the narrow green plate from above Rupert's eyes in case an ad-lib were necessary.

One was suddenly necessary. The second ingenue worked her way into a line beginning, "So when Harold said he had come to Mars to get away from militarism and regimentation" —and expired into a frantic "I told him—I told him—um, I had to tell him that—that—" She gaped, snapped her fingers spasmodically as she tried to remember.

Out of camera range, the prompter's fingers flew over the keys of the silent typewriter which projected the entire line on a screen above their heads. Meanwhile there was dead air. Everyone waited for Lester to make a crack that would fill the horrible space.

He spun to his robot. Thankfully he noticed that Rupert was staring at him. Good! Now if he could only meson-filter an ad-lib!

Words flowed across the screen on Rupert's forehead. Lester read them off as fast as they appeared.

"Say, Barbara, why don't you tell the station manager to switch from atomics to petroleum?"

"I don't know," she said, feeding the line back like a good straight-man while she memorized the passage she had forgotten. "Why should I tell him to switch from atomics to petroleum?"

From the corner, Rupert roared, "Because there's no fuel like an oil fuel!"

The studio guffawed. Rupert guffawed. Only he sounded as if he were coming apart. All over United Americas, people grabbed at their teledar sets and tried to hold them together as the electronic apparatus *klunked, pingled* and *whirrety-whirred.*

Even Lester laughed. Beautiful! A lot more sophisticated than the crud he'd been getting from Green and Anderson, yet mixed with the pure old Iowa corn on which all belly-laughter is based. The robot was—

Hey! Rupert hadn't fed him that line—he'd used it himself. People weren't laughing at Lester the Jester—they were laughing at Rupert, even if they couldn't see him. *Hey-y-y!*

When the playlet ended the camera-mikes shifted to Josephine Lissy and the orchestra.

Lester took advantage of the break to charge up to Rupert. He pointed imperiously at the control booth.

"Get inside, you topper-copper, and don't come out until I'm ready to leave. Save the punch-line for yourself, will you? Bite the hand that oils you? Git, damn you, git!"

Rupert moved back a pace, almost crushing a property man. *"Bing-bing?"* he chuckled inquiringly. *""Honk-beeper-bloogle?"*

"No, I'm not kidding," Lester told him. "Get inside that control booth and stay there!"

With a dragging step that cut a thin groove in the plastic floor, Rupert went off to St. Helena.

Going on with the show, Lester watched him take his place behind the technicians, his shoulders slumped in a dejection the smoothlined 2207 model was never designed to register. From time to time he noticed the robot stride jerkily about the tiny booth, the word-scanner in his forehead making such abortive efforts as "Why is hyperspace like a paperweight?" and "When is a mutant not a mutant?" Lester indignantly ignored these attempts to make amends.

The mid-program commercial—"Have you ever asked yourself," the announcer put it to them, "why among the star-blazers it's Star-Gazers one thousand to one? Impartial tests show that these adventurous seekers in empty space always prefer—*what in*—"

Rupert slammed the door shut behind the last of three angry control technicians. Then he began pulling switches. He turned dials.

"He just up and threw us out!"

"That robot's gone psycho! Listen, he can shift the control to the inside of the booth. It's very simple. Is he a talking robot—no, please God!"

"Yeah! He can broadcast himself! Can he talk?"

"*Can* he!" Lester groaned. "Better blast him out fast!"

"Blast him?" An engineer laughed painfully. "He's locked the door. And do you know what the doors and walls of that booth are made of? He can stay in there until we get clearance from the IPCC. Which—"

"You know why they call them Star-Gazers, don't you?" Rupert's voice boomed over the teledar speaker which carried through the studio and incidentally all through the western hemisphere. "One puff and you're flat on your back! *Wongle-wangle-ding-ding!* Yes sir, you see stars all right—all colors. You smoke 'em and novas go off in your head. *Gr-r-rung! Ka-bam-ka-blooie!* Fifteen flavors and all of them worth a raspberry! *Zingambong*—"

The walls of the control booth shivered with huge scraping laughter. And not only the walls were shivering.

Jo soothed Lester as best she could.

"He can't go on forever, darling. He's got to stop!"

"Not with that file he has—and that variable modifier—and that meson-filter. I'm through. I'll never 'cast again—they'll never let me in anywhere. And I don't know how to do anything else. No other skills, no other experience. I'm through for life, Jo!"

The engineers finally had to shut off all power in Teledar City. That meant all 'casting stopped, including messages to spaceships and emergency calls to craft on the ground. It meant that elevators in the building stopped between floors, that lights went out in government offices all over the tower. Then they were able to open the doors with an auxiliary remote control unit and drag the inert robot out.

When the radiant power was shut off, so was he.

So Lester married Jo. But he didn't live happily ever after. He was barred from teledar for life.

He didn't starve, though. He wished he had from time to time. Because the 'cast that ruined him made Rupert. People wrote in demanding to hear more of this terrific robot who kidded the crass off sponsors. And Star-Gazers tripled their sales. Which, after all, is the ultimate test. . . .

Lester manages Rupert the Rollicking Robot ("The screwiest piece of machinery since the invention of the nut"). He lives with him too, has to by Robot Law. He can't sell him—who'd want to get rid of his only source of bread and marmalade? And he can't hire anyone to take care of Rupert—anyone in his right mind, that is. But worst of all Lester has to *live* with Rupert. He finds it difficult.

Once a week he visits Jo and his children. He looks very haggard then. Rupert's practical jokes get more complicated all the time.

The Man Who Came Back

ROBERT SILVERBERG

NATURALLY, there was a tremendous fuss made over him, since he was the first man actually to buy up his indenture and return from a colony-world. He had been away eighteen years, farming on bleak Novotny IX, and who knew how many of those years he had been slaving and saving to win his passage home?

Besides, rumor had it that a girl was involved. It could be the big romance of the century, maybe. Even before the ship carrying him had docked at Long Island Spaceport, John Burkhardt was a system-famed celebrity. Word of his return had preceded him—word, and all manner of rumor, legend and myth.

The starship *Lincoln,* returning from a colony-seeding trip in the outer reaches of the galaxy, for the first time in its history, was carrying an Earthward-bound passenger. A small army of newsmen impatiently awaited the ship's landing, and the nine worlds waited with them.

When he stepped into the unloading elevator and made his descent, a hum of comment rippled through the gathered crowd. Burkhardt looked his part perfectly. He was a tall man, spare and lean. His face was solemn, his lips thin and pale, his hair going gray though he was only in his forties.

And his eyes—deepset, glowering, commanding. Everything fit the myth: the physique, the face, the eyes. They were those of a man who could renounce Earth for unrequited love, then toil eighteen years out of the sheer strength of that love.

Cameras ground. Bulbs flashed. Five hundred reporters felt their tongues going dry with anticipation of the big story.

Burkhardt smiled coldly and waved at the horde of newsmen. He did not blink, shield his eyes, or turn away. He seemed almost unnaturally in control of himself. They had expected him to weep, maybe kneel and kiss the soil of Mother Earth. He did none of those things. He merely smiled and waved.

The Global Wire man stepped forward. He had won the lottery. It was his privilege to conduct the first interview.

"Welcome to Earth, Mr. Burkhardt. How does it feel to be back?"

"I'm glad to be here." Burkhardt's voice was slow, deep, measured, controlled like every other aspect of him.

"This army of pressmen doesn't upset you, does it?"

"I haven't seen this many people all at once in eighteen years. But no—they don't upset me."

"You know, Mr. Burkhardt, you've done something special. You're the only man ever to return to Earth after signing out on an indenture."

"Am I the only one?" Burkhardt responded easily. "I wasn't aware of that."

"You are indeed, sir. And I'd like to know, if I may—for the benefit of billions of viewers—if you care to tell us a little of the story behind your story? Why did you leave Earth in the first place, Mr. Burkhardt? And why did you decide to return?"

Burkhardt smiled gravely. "There was a woman." he said. "A lovely woman, a famous woman now. We loved each other, once, and when she stopped loving me I left Earth. I have reason to believe I can regain her love now, so I have returned. And now, if you'll pardon me—"

"Couldn't you give us any details?"

"I've had a long trip, and I prefer to rest now. I'll be glad to answer your questions at a formal press conference tomorrow afternoon."

And he cut through the crowd toward a waiting cab supplied by the Colonization Bureau.

Nearly everyone in the system had seen the brief interview or had heard reports of it. It had certainly been a masterly job. If people had been curious about Burkhardt before, they were obsessed with him now. To give up Earth out of unrequited love, to labor eighteen years for a second chance—why, he was like some figure out of Dumas, brought to life in the middle of the 24th Century.

It was no mean feat to buy oneself back out of a colonization indenture, either. The Colonization Bureau of the Solar Federation undertook to transport potential colonists to distant worlds and set them up as homesteaders. In return for one-way transportation, tools and land, the colonists merely had to promise to remain settled, to marry, and to raise the maximum practical number of children. This program, a hundred years old now, had resulted in the seeding of Terran colonies over a galactic radius of better than five hundred light-years.

It was theoretically possible for a colonist to return to Earth, of course. But few of them seemed to want to, and none before Burkhardt ever had. To return, you had first to pay off your debt to the government—figured theoretically at $20,000 for round-trip passage, $5000 for land, $5000 for tools—plus 6% interest per year. Since nobody with any assets would ever become a colonist, and since it was next to impossible for a colonist, farming an unworked world, to accumulate any capital, no case of an attempted buy-out had ever arisen.

Until Burkhardt. He had done it, working round the clock, outproducing his neighbors on Novotny IX and selling his surplus, cabling his extra pennies back to Earth to be invested in blue-chip securities, and finally—after eighteen years—amassing the $30,000 plus accrued interest that would spring him from indenture.

Twenty billion people on nine worlds wanted to know why.

The day after his return, he held a press conference in the hotel suite provided for him by the Colonization Bureau. Admission was strictly limited—one man from each of the twenty leading news services, no more.

Wearing a faded purplish tunic and battered sandals, Burkhardt came out to greet the reporters. He looked tremendously dignified—an overbearing figure of a man, thin but solid, with enormous gnarled hands and powerful forearms. The gray in his hair gave him a patriarchal look on a world dedicated to cosmetic rejuvenation. And his eyes, shining like twin beacons, roved around the room, transfixing everyone once, causing discomfort and uneasiness. No one had seen eyes like that on a human being before. But no one had ever seen a returned colonist before, either.

He smiled without warmth. "Very well, gentlemen. I'm at your disposal."

They started with the peripheral questions first.

"What sort of planet is Novotny IX, Mr. Burkhardt?"

"Cold. The temperature never gets above sixty. The soil is marginally fertile. A man has to work ceaselessly if he wants to stay alive there."

"Did you know that when you signed up to go there?"

Burkhardt nodded. "I asked for the least desirable of the available colony worlds."

"Are there many colonists there?"

"About twenty thousand, I think. It isn't a popular planet, you understand."

"Mr. Burkhardt, part of the terms of the colonist's indenture specify that he must marry. Did you fulfill this part of the contract?"

Burkhardt smiled sadly. "I married less than a week after my arrival there in 2319. My wife died the first winter of our marriage. There were no children. I didn't remarry."

"And when did you get the idea of buying up your indenture and returning to Earth?"

"In my third year on Novotny IX."

"In other words, you devoted fifteen years to getting back to Earth?"

"That's correct."

It was a young reporter from Transuniverse News who took the plunge toward the real meat of the universe. "Could you tell us why you changed your mind about remaining a colonist? At the spaceport you said something about there being a woman—"

"Yes." Burkhardt chuckled mirthlessly. "I was pretty young when I threw myself into the colonization plan—twenty-five, in point of fact. There was a woman; I loved her; she married someone else. I did the romantic thing and signed up for Novotny IX. Three years later, the newstape from Earth told me that she had been divorced. This was in 2322. I resolved to return to Earth and try to persuade her to marry me."

"So for fifteen years you struggled to get back so you could patch up your old romance," another newsman said. "But how did you know she hadn't remarried in all that time?"

"She did remarry," Burkhardt said stunningly.

"But—"

"I received word of her remarriage in 2324, and of her subsequent divorce in 2325. Of her remarriage in 2327, and of her subsequent divorce in 2329. Of her remarriage in the same year, and her subsequent divorce in 2334. Of her remarriage in 2335, and of her divorce four months ago. Unless I have missed the announcement, she has not remarried this last time."

"Did you abandon your project every time you heard of one of these marriages?"

Burkhardt shook his head. "I kept on saving. I was confident that none of her marriages would last. All these years, you see, she's been trying to find a substitute for me. But human beings are unique. There are no substitutes. I weathered five of her marriages. Her sixth husband will be myself."

"Could you tell us—could you tell us the name of this woman, Mr. Burkhardt?"

The returned colonist's smile was frigid. "I'm not ready to reveal her name just yet," he said. "Are there any further questions?"

Along toward midafternoon, Burkhardt ended the conference. He had told them in detail of his efforts to pile up the money; he had talked about life as a colonist; he had done everything but tell them the name of the woman for whose sake he had done all this.

Alone in the suite after they had gone, Burkhardt stared out at the other glittering towers of New York. Jet liners droned overhead; a billion lights shattered the darkness. New York, he thought, was as chaotic and as repugnant to him as ever. He missed Novotny IX.

But he had had to come back. Smiling gently, he opaqued the windows of his suite. It was winter, now, on Novotny IX's colonized continent. A time for burrowing away, for digging in against the mountain-high drifts of blue-white snow. Winter was eight standard months long, on Novotny IX; only four out of the sixteen standard months of the planet's year were really livable. Yet a man could see the results of his own labor, out there. He could use his hands and measure his gains.

And there were friends there. Not the other settlers, though they were good people and hard workers. But the natives, the Euranoi.

The survey charts said nothing about them. There were only about five hundred of them left, anyway, or so Donnoi had claimed. Burkhardt had never seen more than a dozen of the Euranoi at any one time, and he had never been able to tell one from another. They looked like slim elves, half the height of a man, gray-skinned, chinless, sad-eyed. They went naked against their planet's bitter cold. They lived in caves, somewhere below the surface. And Donnoi had become Burkhardt's friend.

Burkhardt smiled, remembering. He had found the little alien in a snowdrift, so close to dead it was hard to be certain one way or the other. Donnoi had lived, and had recovered, and had spent the winter in Burkhardt's cabin, talking a little, but mostly listening.

Burkhardt had done the talking. He had talked it all out, telling the little being of his foolishness, of his delusion that Lily loved him, of his wild maniac desire to get back to Earth.

And Donnoi had said, when he understood the situation. *"You will get back to Earth. And she will be yours."*

That had been between the first divorce and the second marriage. The day the newstapes had brought word of Lily's remarriage had nearly finished Burkhardt, but Donnoi was there, comforting, consoling, and from that day on Burkhardt never worried again. Lily's marriages were made, weakened, broke up, and Burkhardt worked unfalteringly, knowing that when he returned to Earth he could have Lily at last.

Donnoi had told him solemnly, *"It is all a matter of channeling your desires. Look: I lay dying in a snowdrift, and I willed you to find me. You came; I lived."*

"But I'm not Euranoi," Burkhardt had protested. "My will isn't strong enough to influence another person."

"Any creature that thinks can assert its will. Give me your hand, and I will show you."

Burkhardt smiled back across fifteen years, remembering the feel of Donnoi's limp, almost boneless hand in his own, remembering the stiff jolt of power that had flowed from the alien. His hand had tingled for days afterward. But he knew, from that moment, that he would succeed.

Burkhardt had a visitor the next morning. A press conference was scheduled again for the afternoon, and Burkhardt had said he would grant no interviews before then, but the visitor had been insistent. Finally, the desk had phoned up to tell Burkhardt that a Mr. Richardson Elliott was here, and demanded to see him.

The name rang a bell. "Send him up," Burkhardt said.

A few minutes later, the elevator disgorged Mr. Richardson Elliott. He was shorter than Burkhardt, plump, pink-skinned, clean-shaven. A ring glistened on his finger, and there was a gem of some alien origin mounted on a stickpin near his throat.

He extended his hand. Burkhardt took it. The hand was carefully manicured, pudgy, somehow oily.

"You're not at all as I pictured you," Burkhardt said.

"You are. Exactly."

"Why did you come here?"

Elliott tapped the newsfax crumpled under his arm. He unfolded it, showing Burkhardt that front-page spread. "I read the story, Burkhardt. I knew at once who the girl—the woman—was. I came to warn you not to get involved with her."

Burkhardt's eyes twinkled. "And why not?"

"She's a witch," Elliott muttered. "She'll drain a man dry and throw the husk away. Believe me, I know. You only loved her. I married her."

"Yes," Burkhardt said. "You took her away from me eighteen years ago."

"You know that isn't true. She walked out on you because she thought I could further her career, which was so. I didn't even know another man had been in the picture until she got that letter from you, postmarked the day your ship took off. She showed it to me—laughing. I can't repeat the things she said about you, Burkhardt. But I was shocked. My marriage to her started to come apart right then and there, even though it was another three years before we called it quits. She threw herself at me. I didn't steal her from anybody. Believe me, Burkhardt."

"I believe you."

Elliott mopped his pink forehead. "It was the same way with all the other husbands. I've followed her career all along. She exists only for Lily Leigh, and nobody else. When she left me, it was to marry Alderson. Well, she killed him as good as if she'd shot him, when she told him she was pulling out. Man his age had no business marrying her. And then it was Michaels, and after him Dan Cartwright, and then Jim

Thorne. Right up the ladder to fame and fortune, leaving a trail of used-up husbands behind her."

Burkhardt shrugged. "The past is of no concern to me."

"You actually think Lily will marry you?"

"I do," Burkhardt said. "She'll jump at it. The publicity values will be irresistible. The sollie star with five broken marriages to millionaires now stooping to wed her youthful love, who is now a penniless ex-colonist."

Elliott moistened his lips unhappily. "Perhaps you've got something there," he admitted. "Lily might just do a thing like that. But how long would it last? Six months, a year—until the publicity dies down. And then she'll dump you. She doesn't want a penniless husband."

"She won't dump me."

"You sound pretty confident, Burkhardt."

"I am."

For a moment there was silence. Then Elliott said, "You seem determined to stick your head in the lion's mouth. What is it—an obsession to marry her?"

"Call it that."

"It's crazy. I tell you, she's a witch. You're in love with an imaginary goddess. The real Lily Leigh is the most loathsome female ever spawned. As the first of her five husbands, I can take oath to that."

"Did you come here just to tell me that?"

"Not exactly," Elliott said. "I've got a proposition for you. I want you to come into my firm as a Vice President. You're system-famous, and we can use the publicity. I'll start you at sixty thousand. You'll be the most eligible bachelor in the universe. We'll get you a rejuvenation and you'll look twenty-five again. Only none of this Lily Leigh nonsense. I'll set you up, you'll marry some good-looking kid, and all your years on Whatsis Nine will be just so much nightmare."

"The answer is no."

"I'm not doing this out of charity, you understand. I think you'll be an asset to me. But I also think you ought to be protected against Lily. I feel I owe you something, for what I did to you unknowingly eighteen years ago."

"You don't owe me a thing. Thanks for the warning, Mr. Elliott, but I don't need it. And the answer to the proposition is No. I'm not for sale."

"I beg you—"

"No."

Color flared in Elliott's cheeks for a moment. He rose, started to say something, stopped. "All right," he said heavily. "Go to Lily. Like a moth drawn to a flame. The offer remains, Mr. Burkhardt. And you have my deepest sympathy."

At his press conference that afternoon, Burkhardt revealed her name. The system's interest was at peak, now; another day without the revelation and the peak would pass, frustration would cause interest to subside. Burkhardt told them. Within an hour it was all over the system.

Glamorous Lily Leigh, for a decade and a half queen of the solido-films, was named today as the woman for whom John Burkhardt bought himself out of indenture. Burkhardt explained that Miss Leigh, then an unknown starlet, terminated their engagement in 2319 to marry California industrialist Richardson Elliott. The marriage, like Miss Leigh's four later ones, ended in divorce.

"I hope now to make her my wife," the mystery man from Novotny IX declared. "After eighteen years I still love her as strongly as ever."

Miss Leigh, in seclusion at her Scottsdale, Arizona home following her recent divorce from sollie-distributing magnate James Thorne, refused to comment on the statement.

For three days, Lily Leigh remained in seclusion, seeing no one, issuing no statements to the press. Burkhardt was patient. Eighteen years of waiting teaches patience. And Donnoi had told him, as they trudged through the gray slush of rising spring, *"The man who rushes ahead foolishly forfeits all advantages in a contest of wills."*

Donnoi carried the wisdom of a race at the end of its span. Burkhardt remained in his hotel suite, mulling over the advice of the little alien. Donnoi had never passed judgment on the merits and drawbacks of Burkhardt's goal; he had simply advised, and suggested, and taught.

The press had run out of things to say about Burkhardt, and he declined to supply them with anything new to print. So, inevitably, they lost interest in him. By the third day, it was no longer necessary to hold a press conference. He had come back; he had revealed his love for the sollie queen, Lily Leigh; now he was sitting tight. There was nothing to do but wait for further developments, if any. And neither Burkhardt nor Lily Leigh seemed to be creating further developments.

It was hard to remain calm, Burkhardt thought. It was

queer to be here on Earth, in the quiet autumn, while winter fury raged on Novotny IX. Fury of a different kind raged here, the fury of a world of five billion eager, active human beings, but Burkhardt kept himself aloof from all that. Eighteen years of near-solitude had left him unfit for that sort of world.

It was hard to sit quietly, though, with Lily just a visicall away. Burkhardt compelled himself to be patient. She would call, sooner or later.

She called on the fourth day. Burkhardt's skin crawled as he heard the hotel operator say—in tones regulated only with enormous effort—"Miss Leigh is calling from Arizona, Mr. Burkhardt."

"Put the call on."

She had not used the visi-circuit. Burkhardt kept his screen blank too.

She said, without preliminaries, "Why have you come back after all these years, John?"

"Because I love you."

"Still?"

"Yes."

She laughed—the famous LL laugh, for his benefit alone. "You're a bigger fool now than you were then, John."

"Perhaps," he admitted.

"I suppose I ought to thank you, though. This is the best publicity I've had all year. And at my age I need all the publicity I can get."

"I'm glad for you," he said.

"You aren't serious, though, about wanting to marry me, are you? Not after all these years. Nobody stays in love that long."

"I did."

"Damn you, what do you want from me?" The voice, suddenly shrill, betrayed a whisper of age.

"Yourself," Burkhardt said calmly.

"What makes you think I'll marry you? Sure, you're a hero today. The Man Who Came Back from the Stars. But you're nothing, John. All you have to show for eighteen years is calluses. At least back then you had your youth. You don't even have that any more."

"Let me come to see you, Lily."

"I don't want to see you."

"Please. It's a small thing—let me have half an hour alone with you."

She was silent.

"I've given you half a lifetime of love, Lily. Let me have half an hour."

After a long moment she said, simply, hoarsely. "All right. You can come. But I won't marry you."

He left New York shortly before midnight. The Colonization Bureau had hired a private plane for him, and he slipped out unnoticed, in the dark. Publicity now would be fatal. The plane was a chemically powered jet, somewhat out of date; they were using photon-rockets for the really fast travel. But, obsolete or no, it crossed the continent in three hours. It was just midnight, local time, when the plane landed in Phoenix. As they had arranged it, Lily had her chauffeur waiting, with a long, sleek limousine. Burkhardt climbed in. Turbines throbbed; the car glided out toward Lily's desert home.

It was a mansion, a sprawled-out villa moated off—a *moat*, in water-hungry Arizona!—and topped with a spiring pink stucco tower. Burkhardt was ushered through open fern-lined courtyards to an inner maze of hallways, and through them into a small room where Lily Leigh sat waiting.

He repressed a gasp. She wore a gown worth a planet's ransom, but the girl within the gown had not changed in eighteen years. Her face was the same, impish, the eyes dancing and gay. Her hair had lost none of its glossy sheen. Her skin was the skin of a girl of nineteen.

"It's like stepping back in time," he murmured.

"I have good doctors. You wouldn't believe I'm forty, would you? But everyone knows it, of course." She laughed. "You look like an old man, John."

"Forty-three isn't old."

"It is when you let your age show. I'll give you some money, John, and you can get fixed up. Better still, I'll send my doctors to you."

Burkhardt shook his head. "I'm honest about the passing of time. I look this way because of what I've done these past eighteen years. I wouldn't want a doctor's skill to wipe out the traces of those years."

She shrugged lightly. "It was only an offer, not a slur. What do you want with me, John?"

"I want you to marry me."

Her laughter was a silvery tinkle, ultimately striking a false note. "That made sense in 2319. It doesn't now. People would say you married me for my money. I've got lots of money, John, you know."

"I'm not interested in your money. I want *you.*"

"You think you love me, but how can you? I'm not the sweet little girl you once loved. I never was that sweet little girl. I was a grasping, greedy little girl—and now I'm a grasping, greedy old woman who still looks like a little girl. Go away, John. I'm not for you."

"Marry me, Lily. We'll be happy. I know we will."

"You're a stupid monomaniac."

Burkhardt only smiled. "It'll be good publicity. After five marriages for profit, you're marrying for love. All the worlds love a lover, Lily. You'll be everyone's sweetheart again. Give me your hand, Lily."

Like a sleepwalker, she extended it. Burkhardt took the hand, frowning at its coldness, its limpness.

"But I don't love you, John."

"Let the world think you do. That's all that matters."

"I don't understand you. You—"

She stopped. Burkhardt's grip tightened on her thin hand. He thought of Donnoi, a gray shadow against the snow, holding his hand, letting the power flow from body to body, from slim alien to tall Earthman. *It is all a matter of channeling your desires,* he had said. *Any creature that thinks can learn how to assert its will. The technique is simple.*

Lily lowered her head. After a moment, she raised it. She was smiling.

"It won't last a month," Richardson Elliott grunted, at the sight of the announcement in the paper.

"The poor dumb bastard," Jim Thorne said, reading the news at his Martian ranch. "Falling in love with a dream-Lily that never existed, and actually marrying her. She'll suck him dry."

On nine worlds, people read the story and talked about it. Many of them were pleased; it was the proper finish for the storybook courtship. But those who knew Lily Leigh were less happy about it. "She's got some angle." they said. "It's all a publicity stunt. She'll drop him as soon as the fanfare dies down. And she'll drop him so hard he won't ever get up."

Burkhardt and Lily were married on the tenth day after

his return from space. It was a civil ceremony, held secretly.
Their honeymoon trip was shrouded in mystery. While they
were gone, gossip columnists speculated. How could the brit-
tle, sophisticated, much-married Lily be happy with a simple
farmer from a colony-world?

Two days after their return to Earth from the honeymoon,
Burkhardt and his wife held a joint press conference. It lasted
only five minutes. Burkhardt, holding his wife's hand tightly, said, "I'm happy to announce that Miss Leigh is distributing all of her possessions to charity. We've both signed up as
indentured colonists and we're leaving for Novotny IX
tomorrow."

"Really, Miss Leigh?"

"Yes," Lily said. "I belong at John's side. We'll work his old
farm together. It'll be the first useful thing I've ever done in
my life."

The newsmen, thunderstruck, scattered to shout their story
to the waiting worlds. Mr. and Mrs. John Burkhardt closed
the door behind them.

"Happy?" Burkhardt asked.

Lily nodded. She was still smiling. Burkhardt, watching
her closely, saw the momentary flicker of her eyes, the brief
clearing-away of the cloud that shrouded them—as though
someone were trapped behind those lovely eyes, struggling to
get out. But Burkhardt's control never lapsed. Bending, he
kissed her soft lips lightly.

"Bedtime," he said.

"Yes. Bedtime."

Burkhardt kissed her again. Donnoi had been right, he
thought. Control was possible. He had channeled desire eighteen years, and now Lily was his. Perhaps she was no longer
Lily as men had known her, but what did that matter? She
was the Lily of his lonely dreams. He had created her in the
tingling moment of a handshake, from the raw material of
her old self.

He turned off the light and began to undress. He thought
with cozy pleasure that in only a few weeks he would be
setting foot once again on the bleak tundra of Novotny
IX—this time, with his loving bride.

I See You

DAMON KNIGHT

YOU are five, hiding in a place only you know. You are covered with bark dust, scratched by twigs, sweaty and hot. A wind sighs in the aspen leaves. A faint steady hiss comes from the viewer you hold in your hands; then a voice: "Lorie, I see you—under the barn, eating an apple!" A silence. "Lorie, come on out, I see you." Another voice. "That's right, she's in there." After a moment, sulkily: "Oh, okay."

You squirm around, raising the viewer to aim it down the hill. As you turn the knob with your thumb, the bright image races toward you, trees hurling themselves into red darkness and vanishing, then the houses in the compound; and now you see Bruce standing beside the corral, looking into his viewer, slowly turning. His back is to you; you know you are safe, and you sit up. A jay passes with a whir of wings, settles on a branch. With your own eyes now you can see Bruce, only a dot of blue beyond the gray shake walls of the houses. In the viewer, he is turning toward you, and you duck again. Another voice: "Children, come in and get washed for dinner now." "Aw, Aunt Ellie!" "Mom, we're playing hide and seek. Can't we just stay fifteen minutes more?" "Please, Aunt Ellie!" "No, come on in now—you'll have plenty of time after dinner." And Bruce: "Aw, okay. All out's in free." And once more they have not found you; your secret place is yours alone.

Call him Smith. He was the president of a company that bore his name and which held more than a hundred patents in the scientific instrument field. He was sixty, a widower.

His only daughter and her husband had been killed in a plane crash in 1978. He had a partner who handled the business operations now; Smith spent most of his time in his own lab. In the spring of 1990 he was working on an image intensification device that was puzzling because it was too good. He had it on his bench now, aimed at a deep shadow box across the room; at the back of the box was a card ruled with black, green, red and blue lines. The only source of illumination was a single ten-watt bulb hung behind the shadow box; the light reflected from the card did not even register on his meter, and yet the image in the screen of his device was sharp and bright. When he varied the inputs to the components in a certain way, the bright image vanished and was replaced by shadows, like the ghost of another image. He had monitored every television channel, had shielded the device against radio frequencies, and the ghosts remained. Increasing the illumination did not make them clearer. They were vaguely rectilinear shapes without any coherent pattern. Occasionally a moving blur traveled slowly across them.

Smith made a disgusted sound. He opened the clamps that held the device and picked it up, reaching for the power switch with his other hand. He never touched it. As he moved the device, the ghost images had shifted; they were dancing now with the faint movements of his hand. Smith stared at them without breathing for a moment. Holding the cord, he turned slowly. The ghost images whirled, vanished, reappeared. He turned the other way; they whirled back.

Smith set the device down on the bench with care. His hands were shaking. He had the thing clamped down on the bench all the time until now. "Christ almighty, how dumb can one man get?" he asked the empty room.

You are six, almost seven, and you are being allowed to use the big viewer for the first time. You are perched on a cushion in the leather chair at the console; your brother, who has been showing you the controls with a bored and superior air, has just left the room, saying, "All right, if you know so much, do it yourself."

In fact, the controls on this machine are unfamiliar; the little viewers you have used all your life have only one knob, for nearer or farther—to move up/down, or left/right, you just point the viewer where you want to see. This machine has dials and little windows with numbers in them, and switches and pushbuttons, most of which you don't understand, but you know they are for special purposes and don't matter. The main control is a metal rod, right in front of you, with a gray plastic knob on the top. The knob is dull from years of handling; it feels warm and a little greasy in your hand. The console has a funny electric smell, but the big screen, taller than you are, is silent and dark. You can feel your heart beating against your breastbone. You grip the knob harder, push it forward just a little. The screen lights, and you are drifting across the next room as if on huge silent wheels, chairs and end tables turning into reddish silhouettes that shrink, twist and disappear as you pass through them, and for a moment you feel dizzy because when you notice the red numbers jumping in the console to your left, it is as if the whole house were passing massively and vertiginously through itself; then you are floating out the window with the same slow and steady motion, on across the sunlit pasture where two saddle horses stand with their heads up, sniffing the wind; then a stubbled field, dropping away; and now, below you, the co-op road shines like a silver-gray stream. You press the knob down to get closer, and drop with a giddy swoop; now you are rushing along the road, overtaking and passing a yellow truck, turning the knob to steer. At first you blunder into the dark trees on either side, and once the earth surges up over you in a chaos of writing red shapes, but now you are learning, and you soar down past the crossroads, up the farther hill, and now, now you are on the big road, flying eastward, passing all the cars, rushing toward the great world where you long to be.

It took Smith six weeks to increase the efficiency of the image intensifier enough to bring up the ghost pictures clearly. When he succeeded, the image on the screen was instantly recognizable. It was a view of Jack McCranie's office; the picture was still dim, but sharp enough that Smith could see the expression on Jack's face. He was leaning back in his chair, hands behind his head. Beside him stood Peg Spatola in a purple dress, with her hand on an open folder. She was talking, and McCranie was listening. That was wrong, because Peg was not supposed to be back from Cleveland until next week.

Smith reached for the phone and punched McCranie's number.

"Yes, Tom?"

"Jack, is Peg in there?"

"Why, no—she's in Cleveland, Tom."

"Oh, yes."

McCranie sounded puzzled. "Is anything the matter?" In the screen, he had swiveled his chair and was talking to Peg, gesturing with short, choppy motions of his arm.

"No, nothing," said Smith. "That's all right, Jack, thank you." He broke the connection. After a moment he turned to the breadboard controls of the device and changed one setting slightly. In the screen, Peg turned and walked backward out of the office. When he turned the knob the other way, she repeated these actions in reverse. Smith tinkered with the other controls until he got a view of the calendar on Jack's desk. It was Friday, June 15th—last week.

Smith locked up the device and all his notes, went home and spent the rest of the day thinking.

By the end of July he had refined and miniaturized the device and had extended its sensitivity range into the infrared. He spent most of August, when he should have been on vacation, trying various methods of detecting sound through the device. By focusing on the interior of a speaker's larynx and using infrared, he was able to convert the visible vibrations of the vocal cords into sound of fair quality, but that did not satisfy him. He worked for a while on vibrations picked up from panes of glass in windows and on framed pictures, and he experimented briefly with the diaphragms in speaker systems, intercoms and telephones. He kept on into October without stopping and finally achieved a system that would give tinny but recognizable sound from any vibrating surface—a wall, a floor, even the speaker's own cheek or forehead.

He redesigned the whole device, built a prototype and tested it, tore it down, redesigned, built another. It was Christmas before he was done. Once more he locked up the device and all his plans, drawings and notes.

At home he spent the holidays experimenting with commercial adhesives in various strengths. He applied these to coated paper, let them dry, and cut the paper into rectangles. He numbered these rectangles, pasted them onto letter envelopes, some of which he stacked loose; others he bundled together and secured with rubber bands. He opened the stacks and bundles and examined them at regular intervals. Some of the labels curled up and detached themselves after twenty-six hours without leaving any conspicuous trace. He made up another batch of these, typed his home address on six of them. On each of six envelopes he typed his office address, then covered it with one of the labels. He stamped the envelopes and dropped them into a mailbox. All six, minus their labels, were delivered to the office three days later.

Just after New Year's, he told his partner that he wanted to sell out and retire. They discussed it in general terms.

Using an assumed name and a post office box number which was not his, Smith wrote to a commission agent in Boston with whom he had never had any previous dealings. He mailed the letter, with the agent's address covered by one of his labels on which he had typed a fictitious address. The label detached itself in transit; the letter was delivered. When the agent replied, Smith was watching and read the letter as a secretary typed it. The agent followed his instruction to mail his reply in an envelope without return address. The owner of the post office box turned it in marked "not here"; it went to the dead-letter office and was returned in due time, but meanwhile Smith had acknowledged the letter and had mailed, in the same way, a large amount of cash. In subsequent letters he instructed the agent to take bids for components, plans for which he enclosed, from electronics manufacturers, for plastic casings from another, and for assembly and shipping from still another company. Through a second commission agent in New York, to whom he wrote in the same way, he contracted for ten thousand copies of an instruction booklet in four colors.

Late in February he bought a house and an electronics dealership in a small town in the Adirondacks. In March he signed over his interest in the company to his partner, cleaned out his lab and left. He sold his co-op apartment in Manhattan and his summer house in Connecticut, moved to his new home and became anonymous.

You are thirteen, chasing a fox with the big kids for the first time. They have put you in the north field, the worst place, but you know better than to leave it.

"He's in the glen."

"I see him, he's in the brook, going upstream."

You turn the viewer, racing forward through dappled shade, a brilliance of leaves: there is the glen, and now you see the fox, trotting through the shallows, blossoms of bright water at its feet.

"Ken and Nell, you come down ahead of him by the spring-house. Wanda, you and Tim and Jean stay where you are. Everybody else come upstream, but stay back till I tell you."

That's Leigh, the oldest. You turn the viewer, catch a glimpse of Bobby running downhill through the woods, his long hair flying. Then back to the glen: the fox is gone.

"He's heading up past the corncrib!"

"Okay, keep spread out on both sides everybody. Jim, can you and Edie head him off before he gets to the woods?"

"We'll try. There he is!"

And the chase is going away from you, as you knew it would, but soon you will be older, as old as Nell and Jim; then you will be in the middle of things, and your life will begin.

By trial and error, Smith has found the settings for Dallas, November 22, 1963: Dealey Plaza, 12:25 p.m. He sees the Presidential motorcade making the turn onto Elm Street. Kennedy slumps forward, raising his hands to his throat. Smith presses a button to hold the moment in time. He scans behind the motorcade, finds the sixth floor of the Book Depository Building, finds the window. There is no one behind the barricade of cartons; the room is empty. He scans the nearby rooms, finds nothing. He tries the floor below. At an open window a man kneels, holding a high-powered rifle. Smith photographs him. He returns to the motorcade, watches as the second shot strikes the President. He freezes time again, scans the surrounding buildings, finds a second marks-man on a roof, photographs him. Back to the motorcade. A third and fourth shot, the last blowing off the side of the President's head. Smith freezes the action again, finds two gunmen on the grassy knoll, one aiming across the top of a station wagon, one kneeling in the shrubbery. He photo-graphs them. He turns off the power, sits for a moment, then goes to the washroom, kneels beside the toilet and vomits.

The viewer is your babysitter, your television, your tele-phone (the telephone lines are still up, but they are used only as signaling devices; when you know that somebody wants to talk to you, you focus your viewer on him), your library, your school. Before puberty you watch other people having sex, but even then your curiosity is easily satisfied; after an older cousin initiates you at fourteen, you are much more interested in doing it yourself. The co-op teacher monitors your studies, sometimes makes suggestions, but more and more, as you grow older, leaves you to your own devices. You are intensely interested in African prehistory, in the European theater, and in the anti-civilization of Epsilon Eridani IV. Soon you will have to choose.

New York Harbor, November 4, 1872—a cold, blustery day. A two-masted ship rides at anchor; on her stern is lettered: *Mary Celeste*. Smith advances the time control. A flicker of darkness, light again, and the ship is gone. He turns back again until he finds it standing out under light canvas past Sandy Hook. Manipulating time and space controls at once, he follows it eastward through a flickering of storm and sun—loses it, finds it again, counting days as he goes. The farther eastward, the more he has to tilt the device downward, while the image of the ship tilts correspondingly away from him. Because of the angle, he can no longer keep the ship in view from a distance but must track it closely. November 21 and 22, violent storms: the ship is dashed upward by waves, falls again, visible only intermittently; it takes him five hours to pass through two days of real time. The 23rd is calmer, but on the 24th another storm blows up. Smith rubs his eyes, loses the ship, finds it again after a ten-minute search.

The gale blows itself out on the morning of the 26th. The sun is bright, the sea almost dead calm. Smith is able to catch glimpses of figures on deck, tilted above dark cross-sections of the hull. A sailor is splicing a rope in the stern, two others lowering a triangular sail between the foremast and the bowsprit, and a fourth is at the helm. A little group stands leaning on the starboard rail; one of them is a woman. The next glimpse is that of a running figure who advances into the screen and disappears. Now the men are lowering a boat over the side; the rail has been removed and lies on the deck. The men drop into the boat and row away. He hears them shouting to each other but cannot make out the words.

Smith turns to the ship again: the deck is empty. He dips below to look at the hold, filled with casks, then the cabin, then the forecastle. There is no sign of anything wrong—no explosion, no fire, no trace of violence. When he looks up again, he sees the sails flapping, then bellying out full. The

sea is rising. He looks for the boat, but now too much time
has passed and he cannot find it. He returns to the ship and
now reverses the time control, tracks it backward until the
men are again in their places on deck. He looks again at the
group standing at the rail; now he sees that the woman has a
child in her arms. The child struggles, drops over the rail.
Smith hears the woman shriek. In a moment she too is over
the rail and falling into the sea.

He watches the men running, sees them launch the boat.
As they pull away, he is able to keep the focus near enough to
see and hear them. One calls, "My God, who's at the helm?"
Another, a bearded man with a face gone tallow-pale, replies,
"Never mind—row!" They are staring down into the sea.
After a moment one looks up, then another. The *Mary Celeste*,
with three of the four sails on her foremast set, is gliding
away, slowly, now faster; now she is gone.

Smith does not run through the scene again to watch the
child and her mother drown, but others do.

The production model was ready for shipping in September. It was a simplified version of the prototype, with only
two controls, one for space, one for time. The range of the
device was limited to one thousand miles. Nowhere on the
casing of the device or in the instruction booklet was a patent
number or a pending patent mentioned. Smith had called the
device Ozo, perhaps because he thought it sounded vaguely
Japanese. The booklet described the device as a distant
viewer and gave clear, simple instructions for its use. One
sentence read cryptically: "Keep Time Control set at zero." It
was like "Wet Paint—Do Not Touch."

During the week of September 23, seven thousand Ozos
were shipped to domestic and Canadian addresses supplied
by Smith: five hundred to electronics manufacturers and
suppliers, six thousand, thirty to a carton, marked "On
Consignment," to TV outlets in major cities, and the rest to
private citizens chosen at random. The instruction booklets
were in sealed envelopes packed with each device. Three
thousand more went to Europe, South and Central America,
and the Middle East.

A few of the outlets which received the cartons opened
them the same day, tried the devices out, and put them on
sale at prices ranging from $49.95 to $125. By the following

day the word was beginning to spread, and by the close of business on the third day every store was sold out. Most people who got them, either through the mail or by purchase, used them to spy on their neighbors and on people in hotels.

In a house in Cleveland, a man watches his brother-in-law in the next room, who is watching his wife getting out of a taxi. She goes into the lobby of an apartment building. The husband watches as she gets into the elevator, rides to the fourth floor. She rings the bell beside the door marked 410. The door opens; a dark-haired man takes her in his arms; they kiss.

The brother-in-law meets him in the hall. "Don't do it, Charlie."

"Get out of my way."

"I'm not going to get out of your way, and I tell you, don't do it. Not now and not later."

"Why the hell shouldn't I?"

"Because if you do I'll kill you. If you want a divorce, OK, get a divorce. But don't lay a hand on her or I'll find you the farthest place you can go."

Smith got his consignment of Ozos early in the week, took one home and left it to his store manager to put a price on the rest. He did not bother to use the production model but began at once to build another prototype. It had controls calibrated to one-hundredth of a second and one millimeter, and a timer that would allow him to stop a scene, or advance or regress it at any desired rate. He ordered some clockwork from an astronomical supply house.

A high-ranking officer in Army Intelligence, watching the first demonstration of the Ozo in the Pentagon, exclaimed, "My God, with this we could dismantle half the establishment—all we've got to do is launch interceptors when we see them push the button."

"It's a good thing Senator Burkhart can't hear you say that," said another officer. But by the next afternoon everybody had heard it.

A Baptist minister in Louisville led the first mob against an Ozo assembly plant. A month later, while civil and criminal suits against all the rioters were still pending, tapes showing each one of them in compromising or ludicrous activities were widely distributed in the area.

The commission agents who had handled the orders for the first Ozos were found out and had to leave town. Factories were firebombed, but others took their place.

The first Ozo was smuggled into the Soviet Union from West Germany by Katerina Belov, a member of a dissident group in Moscow, who used it to document illegal government actions. The device was seized on December 13 by the KGB; Belov and two other members of the group were arrested, imprisoned and tortured. By that time over forty other Ozos were in the hands of dissidents.

You are watching an old movie, *Bob and Ted and Carol and Alice.* The humor seems infantile and unimaginative to you; you are not interested in the actresses' occasional seminudity. What strikes you as hilarious is the coyness, the sidelong glances, smiles, grimaces hinting at things that will never be shown on the screen. You realize that these people have never seen anyone but their most intimate friends without clothing, have never seen any adult shit or piss, and would be embarrassed or disgusted if they did. Why did children say "pee-pee" and "poo-poo," and then giggle? You have read scholarly books about taboos on "bodily functions," but why was shitting worse than sneezing?

Cora Zickwolfe, who lived in a remote rural area of Arizona and whose husband commuted to Tucson, arranged with her nearest neighbor, Phyllis Mell, for each of them to keep an Ozo focused on the bulletin board in the other's kitchen. On the bulletin board was a note that said "OK." If there was any trouble and she couldn't get to the phone, she would take down the note, or if she had time, write another.

In April, 1992, about the time her husband usually got home, an intruder broke into the house and seized Mrs. Zickwolfe before she had time to get to the bulletin board. He dragged her into the bedroom and forced her to disrobe. The state troopers got there in fifteen minutes, and Cora never spoke to her friend Phyllis again.

Between 1992 and 2002 more than six hundred improvements and supplements to the Ozo were recorded. The most important of these was the power system created by focusing the Ozo at a narrow aperture on the interior of the Sun. Others included the system of satellite slave units in stationary orbits and a computerized tracer device which would keep the Ozo focused on any subject.

Using the tracer, an entomologist in Mexico City is following the ancestral line of a honey bee. The images bloom and expire, ten every second: the tracer is following each queen back to the egg, then the egg to the queen that laid it, then that queen to the egg. Tens of thousands of generations have passed; in two thousand hours, beginning with a Paleocene bee, he has traveled back into the Cretaceous. He stops at intervals to follow the bee in real time, then accelerates again. The hive is growing smaller, more primitive. Now it is only a cluster of round cells, and the bee is different, more like a wasp. His year's labor is coming to fruition. He watches, forgetting to eat, almost to breathe.

In your mother's study after she dies you find an elaborate chart of her ancestors and your father's. You retrieve the program for it, punch it in, and idly watch a random sampling, back into time, first the female line, then the male . . . a teacher of biology in Boston, a suffragette, a corn merchant, a singer, a Dutch farmer in New York, a British sailor, a German musician. Their faces glow in the screen, bright-eyes, cheeks flushed with life. Someday you too will be only a series of images in a screen.

Smith is watching the planet Mars. The clockwork which turns the Ozo to follow the planet, even when it is below the horizon, makes it possible for him to focus instantly on the surface, but he never does this. He takes up his position hundreds of thousands of miles away, then slowly approaches, in order to see the red spark grow to a disk, then to a yellow sunlit ball hanging in darkness. Now he can make out the surface features: Syrtis Major and Thoth-Nepenthes leading in a long gooseneck to Utopia and the frostcap.

The image as it swells hypnotically toward him is clear and sharp, without tremor or atmospheric distortion. It is summer in the northern hemisphere: Utopia is wide and dark. The planet fills the screen, and now he turns northward, over the cratered desert still hundreds of miles distant. A dust

storm, like a yellow veil, obscures the curved neck of Thoth-
Nepenthes; then he is beyond it, drifting down to the edge of
the frostcap. The limb of the planet reappears; he floats like a
glider over the dark surface tinted with rose and violet-gray;
now he can see its nubbly texture; now he can make out
individual plants. He is drifting among their gnarled gray
stems, their leaves of violet horn; he sees the curious mis-
shapen growths that may be air bladders or some grotesque
analogue of blossoms. Now, at the edge of the screen, something black and spindling leaps. He follows it instantly, finds
it, brings it hugely magnified into the center of the screen: a
thing like a hairy beetle, its body covered with thick black
hairs or spines; it stands on six jointed legs, waving its
antennae, its mouth parts busy. And its four bright eyes
stare into his, across forty million miles.

Smith's hair got whiter and thinner. Before the 1992
Crash, he made heavy contributions to the International Red
Cross and to volunteer organizations in Europe, Asia and
Africa. He got drunk periodically, but always alone. From
1993 to 1996 he stopped reading the newspapers.

He wrote down the coordinates for the plane crash in which
his daughter and her husband had died, but never used them.

At intervals while dressing or looking into the bathroom
mirror, he stared as if into an invisible camera and raised one
finger. In his last years he wrote some poems.

We know his name. Patient researchers, using advanced
scanning techniques, followed his letters back through the
postal system and found him, but by that time he was safely
dead.

The whole world has been at peace for more than a generation. Crime is almost unheard of. Free energy has made the
world rich, but the population is stable, even though early
detection has wiped out most diseases. Everyone can do
whatever he likes, providing his neighbors would not disap-
prove, and after all, their views are the same as his own.

You are forty, a respected scholar, taking a few days out to
review your life, as many people do at your age. You have
watched your mother and father coupling on the night they
conceived you, watched yourself growing in her womb, first a
red tadpole, then a thing like an embryo chicken, then a
big-headed baby kicking and squirming. You have seen your-

self delivered, seen the first moment when your bloody head
broke into the light. You have seen yourself staggering about
the nursery in rompers, clutching a yellow plastic duck. Now
you are watching yourself hiding behind the fallen tree on
the hill, and you realize that there are no secret places. And
beyond you in the ghostly future you know that someone is
watching you as you watch; and beyond that watcher another,
and beyond that another . . . forever.

Part II: The Content of TV

THE '30s and '40s were the golden years of radio, and those
of us old enough to remember them know only too well how
the content of a medium can change over time.

One major reason for change is that new media, or
technical advances in old, change audience options, hence
changing the size and nature of all media audiences. Today,
with cables, satellite transmission, pay TV, and video
recorders, TV stands on the same threshold radio did in
the '50s. Of course, nobody knows exactly what will happen, but several stories in this section suggest tantalizing
possibilities.

Game shows have traditionally been popular television
fare. They offer drama, viewer participation, and low production costs. Prime-time game shows (from eight to eleven P.M.,
when the audience is largest) have never recovered from the
cheating scandals of the '50s. But just recently people have
been seriously injured trying to perform crazy stunts on the
so called "real life" shows, and it doesn't take too much
imagination to see that one day we may very well end up

with the combat-type game show Robert Sheckley depicts in "The Prize of Peril."

With the exception of football and certain special contests such as the world series, sports events have never done well in prime time. But with cable TV's potential for shattering audiences into small pieces, sporting fans may emerge as one of the largest lumps, and some stations may run nothing but sports. In any case, no matter what happens, you can bet that an interworld series between earthmen and Arcturians would draw viewers. Particularly if, as in Jack C. Haldeman's "Home Team Advantage," the winner got to eat the loser, and the play-by-play was performed by a certain loud-mouthed sports announcer.

To the networks, news programs have always been more a matter of status and public service than big ratings successes. However, there have been exceptions such as *60 Minutes*, and local news shows are good money makers. With the blossoming of cable, though, some stations, just like radio, may decide to specialize in news. And since wars provide good action, they might, as Mack Reynolds suggests in "Mercenary," be covered live—with soldiers getting fan letters.

Advertising has always been the backbone of network television, but what will be its future on pay TV? Some of these embryonic networks don't carry it, others do. And as the demand for new programming expands to fill the channels available, advertisers may very well begin producing their own programs (with appropriate plugs) for free distribution. Indeed, as James Gunn points out in "Without Portfolio," it is even possible that our government will become a major advertiser.

Series seem to be cyclical. Westerns appeared, became popular, were cloned, lost appeal, and vanished. Ditto for cop shows and so on. While series do fail because they are bad or have bad time slots, they can also flop because they are too familiar, too far behind the times, or even too far ahead. In "The Idea," presumably this latter problem plagues Barry Malzberg's protagonist.

To satisfy the policies of the Federal Communications Commission, networks carry some educational programs, but rarely in prime time, since the ratings are usually low. Public television presents many educational programs with fine production values (*Sesame Street, Nova*, etc.). And universities often offer "talking heads" guaranteed to cure the worst cases of insomnia. However, as sophistication increases, school systems may come to depend more on video instructors and less on classroom instruction, as in Lloyd Biggle's "And Madly Teach."

The Prize of Peril

ROBERT SHECKLEY

RAEDER lifted his head cautiously above the window sill. He saw the fire escape, and below it a narrow alley. There was a weatherbeaten baby carriage in the alley, and three garbage cans. As he watched, a black-sleeved arm moved from behind the farthest can, with something shiny in its fist. Raeder ducked down. A bullet smashed through the window above his head and punctured the ceiling, showering him with plaster.

Now he knew about the alley. It was guarded, just like the door.

He lay at full length on the cracked linoleum, staring at the bullet hole in the ceiling, listening to the sounds outside the door. He was a tall man with bloodshot eyes and a two-day stubble. Grime and fatigue had etched lines into his face. Fear had touched his features, tightening a muscle here and twitching a nerve there. The results were startling. His face had character now, for it was reshaped by the expectation of death.

There was a gunman in the alley and two on the stairs. He was trapped. He was dead.

Sure, Raeder thought, he still moved and breathed; but that was only because of death's inefficiency. Death would take care of him in a few minutes. Death would poke holes in his face and body, artistically dab his clothes with blood, arrange his limbs in some grotesque position of the grave-yard ballet . . . Raeder bit his lip sharply. He wanted to live. There had to be a way.

He rolled onto his stomach and surveyed the dingy cold-water apartment into which the killers had driven him. It was a perfect little one-room coffin. It had a door, which was watched, and a fire escape, which was watched. And it had a tiny windowless bathroom.

He crawled to the bathroom and stood up. There was a ragged hole in the ceiling, almost four inches wide. If he could enlarge it, crawl through into the apartment above . . .

He heard a muffled thud. The killers were impatient. They were beginning to break down the door.

He studied the hole in the ceiling. No use even considering it. He could never enlarge it in time.

They were smashing against the door, grunting each time they struck. Soon the lock would tear out, or the hinges would pull out of the rotting wood. The door would go down, and the two blank-faced men would enter, dusting off their jackets. . . .

But surely someone would help him! He took the tiny television set from his pocket. The picture was blurred, and he didn't bother to adjust it. The audio was clear and precise.

He listened to the well-modulated voice of Mike Terry addressing his vast audience.

". . . *terrible spot,*" Terry was saying. "*Yes, folks, Jim Raeder is in a truly terrible predicament. He had been hiding, you'll remember, in a third-rate Broadway hotel under an assumed name. It seemed safe enough. But the bellhop recognized him, and gave that information to the Thompson gang.*"

The door creaked under repeated blows. Raeder clutched the little television set and listened.

"*Jim Raeder just managed to escape from the hotel! Closely pursued, he entered a brownstone at one fifty-six West End Avenue. His intention was to go over the roofs. And it might have worked, folks, it just might have worked. But the roof door was locked. It looked like the end. . . . But Raeder found that apartment seven was unoccupied and unlocked. He entered . . .*"

Terry paused for emphasis, then cried: "*—and now he's*

trapped there, trapped like a rat in a cage! The Thompson gang is breaking down the door! The fire escape is guarded! Our camera crew, situated in a nearby building, is giving you a closeup now. Look, folks, just look! Is there no hope for Jim Raeder?"

Is there no hope? Raeder silently echoed, perspiration pouring from him as he stood in the dark, stifling little bathroom, listening to the steady thud against the door.

"Wait a minute!" Mike Terry cried. *"Hang on, Jim Raeder, hang on a little longer. Perhaps there is hope! I have an urgent call from one of our viewers, a call on the Good Samaritan Line! Here's someone who thinks he can help you, Jim. Are you listening, Jim Raeder?"*

Raeder waited, and heard the hinges tearing out of rotten wood.

"Go right ahead, sir," said Mike Terry. *"What is your name, sir?"*

"Er—Felix Bartholemow."

"Don't be nervous, Mr. Bartholemow. Go right ahead."

"Well, OK. Mr. Raeder," said an old man's shaking voice, *"I used to live at one five six West End Avenue. Same apartment you're trapped in, Mr. Raeder—fact! Look, that bathroom has got a window, Mr. Raeder. It's been painted over, but it has got a—"*

Raeder pushed the television set into his pocket. He located the outlines of the window and kicked. Glass shattered, and daylight poured startlingly in. He cleared the jagged sill and quickly peered down.

Below was a long drop to a concrete courtyard.

The hinges tore free. He heard the door opening. Quickly Raeder climbed through the window, hung by his fingertips for a moment, and dropped.

The shock was stunning. Groggily he stood up. A face appeared at the bathroom window.

"Tough luck," said the man, leaning out and taking careful aim with a snub-nosed .38.

At that moment a smoke bomb exploded inside the bathroom.

The killer's shot went wide. He turned, cursing. More smoke bombs burst in the courtyard, obscuring Raeder's figure.

He could hear Mike Terry's frenzied voice over the TV set in his pocket. *"Now run for it!"* Terry was screaming. *"Run,*

Jim Raeder, run for your life. Run now, *while the killers' eyes are filled with smoke. And thank Good Samaritan Sarah Winters, of three four one two Edgar Street, Brockton, Mass., for donating five-smoke bombs and employing the services of a man to throw them!"*

In a quieter voice, Terry continued: *"You've saved a man's life today,*Mrs. Winters. *Would you tell our audience how it—"*

Raeder wasn't able to hear any more. He was running through the smoke-filled courtyard, past clotheslines, into the open street.

He walked down 63d Street, slouching to minimize his height, staggering slightly from exertion, dizzy from lack of food and sleep.

"Hey you!"

Raeder turned. A middle-aged woman was sitting on the steps of a brownstone, frowning at him.

"You're Raeder, aren't you? The one they're trying to kill?"

Raeder started to walk away.

"Come inside here, Raeder," the woman said.

Perhaps it was a trap. But Raeder knew that he had to depend upon the generosity and goodheartedness of the people. He was their representative, a projection of themselves, an average guy in trouble. Without them, he was lost. With them, nothing could harm him.

Trust in the people, Mike Terry had told him. They'll never let you down.

He followed the woman into her parlor. She told him to sit down and left the room, returning almost immediately with a plate of stew. She stood watching him while he ate, as one would watch an ape in the zoo eat peanuts.

Two children came out of the kitchen and stared at him. Three overalled men came out of the bedroom and focused a television camera on him. There was a big television set in the parlor. As he gulped his food, Raeder watched the image of Mike Terry, and listened to the man's strong, sincere, worried voice.

"There he is, folks," Terry was saying. *"There's Jim Raeder now, eating his first square meal in two days. Our camera crews have really been working to cover this for you! Thanks, boys. . . . Folks, Jim Raeder has been given a brief sanctuary by Mrs. Velma O'Dell, of three forty-three Sixty-Third Street.*

Thank you, Good Samaritan O'Dell! It's really wonderful how people from all walks of life have taken Jim Raeder to their hearts!"

"You better hurry," Mrs. O'Dell said.

"Yes, ma'am," Raeder said.

"I don't want no gunplay in my apartment."

"I'm almost finished, ma'am."

One of the children asked, "Aren't they going to kill him?"

"Shut up," said Mrs. O'Dell.

"Yes, Jim," chanted Mike Terry, *"you'd better hurry. Your killers aren't far behind. They aren't stupid men, Jim. Vicious, warped, insane—yes! But not stupid. They're following a trail of blood—blood from your torn hand, Jim!"*

Raeder hadn't realized until now that he'd cut his hand on the window sill.

"Here, I'll bandage that," Mrs. O'Dell said. Raeder stood up and let her bandage his hand. Then she gave him a brown jacket and a gray slouch hat.

"My husband's stuff," she said.

"He has a disguise, folks!" Mike Terry cried delightedly. *"This is something new! A* disguise! *With seven hours to go until he's safe!"*

"Now get out of here," Mrs. O'Dell said.

"I'm going, ma'am," Raeder said. "Thanks."

"I think you're stupid," she said. "I think you're stupid to be involved in this."

"Yes, ma'am."

"It just isn't worth it."

Raeder thanked her and left. He walked to Broadway, caught a subway to 59th Street, then an uptown local to 86th. There he bought a newspaper and changed for the Manhasset through-express.

He glanced at his watch. He had six and a half hours to go.

The subway roared under Manhattan. Raeder dozed, his bandaged hand concealed under the newspaper, the hat pulled over his face. Had he been recognized yet? Had he shaken the Thompson gang? Or was someone telephoning them now?

Dreamily he wondered if he had escaped death. Or was he still a cleverly animated corpse, moving around because of death's inefficiency? (My dear, death is so *laggard* these days! Jim Raeder walked about for hours after he died, and actually answered people's *questions* before he could be decently buried!)

Raeder's eyes snapped open. He had dreamed something . . . unpleasant. He couldn't remember what.

He closed his eyes again and remembered, with mild astonishment, a time when he had been in no trouble.

That was two years ago. He had been a big, pleasant young man working as a truck driver's helper. He had no talents. He was too modest to have dreams.

The tight-faced little truck driver had the dreams for him. "Why not try for a television show, Jim? I would if I had your looks. They like nice average guys with nothing much on the ball. As contestants. Everybody likes guys like that. Why not look into it?"

So he had looked into it. The owner of the local television store had explained it further.

"You see, Jim, the public is sick of highly trained athletes with their trick reflexes and their professional courage. Who can feel for guys like that? Who can identify? People want to watch exciting things, sure. But not when some joker is making it his business for fifty thousand a year. That's why organized sports are in a slump. That's why the thrill shows are booming."

"I see," said Raeder.

"Six years ago, Jim, Congress passed the Voluntary Suicide Act. Those old senators talked a lot about free will and self-determinism at the time. But that's all crap. You know what the Act really means? It means that amateurs can risk their lives for the big loot, not just professionals. In the old days you had to be a professional boxer or footballer or hockey player if you wanted your brains beaten out legally for money. But now that opportunity is open to ordinary people like you, Jim."

"I see," Raeder said again.

"It's a marvelous opportunity. Take you. You're no better than anyone, Jim. Anything you can do, anyone can do. You're *average*. I think the thrill shows would go for you."

Raeder permitted himself to dream. Television shows looked like a sure road to riches for a pleasant young fellow with no particular talent or training. He wrote a letter to a show called *Hazard* and enclosed a photograph of himself.

Hazard was interested in him. The JBC network investigated, and found that he was average enough to satisfy the wariest viewer. His parentage and affiliations were checked. At last he was summoned to New York, and interviewed by Mr. Moulian.

Moulian was dark and intense, and chewed gum as he talked. "You'll do," he snapped. "But not for *Hazard*. You'll appear on *Spills*. It's a half-hour daytime show on Channel Three."

"Gee," said Raeder.

"Don't thank me. There's a thousand dollars if you win or place second, and a consolation prize of a hundred dollars if you lose. But that's not important."

"No, sir."

"*Spills* is a *little* show. The JBC network uses it as a testing ground. First- and second-place winners on *Spills* move on to *Emergency*. The prizes are much bigger on *Emergency*."

"I know they are, sir."

"And if you do well on *Emergency* there are the first-class thrill shows, like *Hazard* and *Underwater Perils*, with their nationwide coverage and enormous prizes. And then comes the really big time. How far you go is up to you."

"I'll do my best, sir," Raeder said.

Moulian stopped chewing gum for a moment and said, almost reverently, "You can do it, Jim. Just remember. You're *the people*, and *the people* can do anything."

The way he said it made Raeder feel momentarily sorry for Mr. Moulian, who was dark and frizzy-haired and pop-eyed, and was obviously not *the people*.

They shook hands. Then Raeder signed a paper absolving the JBC of all responsibility should he lose his life, limbs or reason during the contest. And he signed another paper exercising his rights under the Voluntary Suicide Act. The law required this, and it was a mere formality.

In three weeks, he appeared on *Spills*.

The program followed the classic form of the automobile race. Untrained drivers climbed into powerful American and European competition cars and raced over a murderous twenty-mile course. Raeder was shaking with fear as he slid his big Maserati into the wrong gear and took off.

The race was a screaming, tire-burning nightmare. Raeder stayed back, letting the early leaders smash themselves up on the counter-banked hairpin turns. He crept into third place when a Jaguar in front of him swerved against an Alfa-Romeo, and the two cars roared into a plowed field. Raeder gunned for second place on the last three miles, but couldn't find passing room. An S-curve almost took him, but he fought the car back on the road, still holding third. Then the lead driver broke a crankshaft in the final fifty yards, and Jim ended in second place.

He was now a thousand dollars ahead. He received four fan letters, and a lady in Oshkosh sent him a pair of argyles. He was invited to appear on *Emergency*.

Unlike the others, *Emergency* was not a competition-type program. It stressed individual initiative. For the show, Raeder was knocked out with a non-habit-forming narcotic. He awoke in the cockpit of a small airplane, cruising on auto-pilot at ten thousand feet. His fuel gauge showed nearly empty. He had no parachute. He was supposed to land the plane.

Of course, he had never flown before.

He experimented gingerly with the controls, remembering that last week's participant had recovered consciousness in a submarine, had opened the wrong valve, and had drowned.

Thousands of viewers watched spellbound as this average man, a man just like themselves, struggled with the situation just as they would do. Jim Raeder was *them*. Anything he could do, they could do. He was representative of *the people*.

Raeder managed to bring the ship down in some semblance of a landing. He flipped over a few times, but his seat belt held. And the engine, contrary to expectation, did not burst into flames.

He staggered out with two broken ribs, three thousand dollars, and a chance, when he healed, to appear on *Torero*.

At last, a first-class thrill show! *Torero* paid ten thousand dollars. All you had to do was kill a black Miura bull with a sword, just like a real trained matador.

The fight was held in Madrid, since bullfighting was still illegal in the United States. It was nationally televised.

Raeder had a good cuadrilla. They liked the big, slow-moving American. The picadors really leaned into their lances, trying to slow the bull for him. The banderilleros tried to run the beast off his feet before driving in their banderillas. And the second matador, a mournful man from Algeciras, almost broke the bull's neck with fancy cape work.

But when all was said and done it was Jim Raeder on the sand, a red muleta clumsily gripped in his left hand, a sword in his right, facing a ton of black, blood-streaked, wide-horned bull.

Someone was shouting, "Try for the lung, *hombre*. Don't be a hero, stick him in the lung." But Jim only knew what the technical adviser in New York had told him: Aim with the sword and go in over the horns.

Over he went. The sword bounced off bone, and the bull tossed him over its back. He stood up, miraculously ungouged, took another sword and went over the horns again with his eyes closed. The god who protects children and fools must have been watching, for the sword slid in like a needle through butter, and the bull looked startled, stared at him unbelievingly, and dropped like a deflated balloon.

They paid him ten thousand dollars, and his broken collar bone healed in practically no time. He received twenty-three fan letters, including a passionate invitation from a girl in Atlantic City, which he ignored. And they asked him if he wanted to appear on another show.

He had lost some of his innocence. He was now fully aware that he had been almost killed for pocket money. The big loot lay ahead. Now he wanted to be almost killed for something worthwhile.

So he appeared on *Underwater Perils,* sponsored by Fairlady's Soap. In face mask, respirator, weighted belt, flippers and knife, he slipped into the warm waters of the Caribbean with four other contestants, followed by a cage-protected camera crew. The idea was to locate and bring up a treasure which the sponsor had hidden there.

Mask diving isn't especially hazardous. But the sponsor had added some frills for public interest. The area was sown with giant clams, moray eels, sharks of several species, giant octopuses, poison coral, and other dangers of the deep.

It was a stirring contest. A man from Florida found the treasure in a deep crevice, but a moray eel found him. Another diver took the treasure, and a shark took him. The brilliant blue-green water became cloudy with blood, which photographed well on color TV. The treasure slipped to the bottom and Raeder plunged after it, popping an eardrum in the process. He plucked it from the coral, jettisoned his weighted belt and made for the surface. Thirty feet from the top he had to fight another diver for the treasure.

They feinted back and forth with their knives. The man struck, slashing Raeder across the chest. But Raeder, with the self-possession of an old contestant, dropped his knife and tore the man's respirator out of his mouth.

That did it. Raeder surfaced, and presented the treasure at the stand-by boat. It turned out to be a package of Fairlady's Soap—"The Greatest Treasure of All."

That netted him twenty-two thousand dollars in cash and prizes, and three hundred and eight fan letters, and an interesting proposition from a girl in Macon, which he seriously considered. He received free hospitalization for his knife slash and burst eardrum, and injections for coral infection.

But best of all, he was invited to appear on the biggest of the thrill shows, *The Prize of Peril*.

And that was when the real trouble began. . . .

The subway came to a stop, jolting him out of his reverie. Raeder pushed back his hat and observed, across the aisle, a man staring at him and whispering to a stout woman. Had they recognized him?

He stood up as soon as the doors opened, and glanced at his watch. He had five hours to go.

At the Manhasset station he stepped into a taxi and told the driver to take him to New Salem.

"New Salem?" the driver asked, looking at him in the rear-vision mirror.

"That's right."

The driver snapped on his radio. "Fare to New Salem. Yep, that's right. *New Salem*."

They drove off. Raeder frowned, wondering if it had been a signal. It was perfectly usual for taxi drivers to report to their dispatchers, of course. But something about the man's voice . . .

"Let me off here," Raeder said.

He paid the driver and began walking down a narrow country road that curved through sparse woods. The trees were too small and too widely separated for shelter. Raeder walked on, looking for a place to hide.

There was a heavy truck approaching. He kept on walking, pulling his hat low on his forehead. But as the truck drew near, he heard a voice from the television set in his pocket. It cried, *"Watch out!"*

He flung himself into the ditch. The truck careened past, narrowly missing him, and screeched to a stop. The driver was shouting, "There he goes! Shoot, Harry, shoot!"

Bullets clipped leaves from the trees as Raeder sprinted into the woods.

"It's happened again!" Mike Terry was saying, his voice high-pitched with excitement. *"I'm afraid Jim Raeder let himself be lulled into a false sense of security. You can't do that, Jim! Not with your life at stake! Not with killers pursuing you! Be careful, Jim, you still have four and a half hours to go!"*

The driver was saying, "Claude, Harry, go around with the truck. We got him boxed."

"They've got you boxed, Jim Raeder!" Mike Terry cried. *"But they haven't got you yet! And you can thank Good Samaritan Susy Peters of twelve Elm Street, South Orange, New Jersey, for that warning shout just when the truck was bearing down on you. We'll have little Susy on stage in just a moment. . . . Look, folks, our studio helicopter has arrived on the scene. Now you can see Jim Raeder running, and the killers pursuing, surrounding him . . ."*

Raeder ran through a hundred yards of woods and found himself on a concrete highway, with open woods beyond. One of the killers was trotting through the woods behind him. The truck had driven to a connecting road, and was now a mile away, coming toward him.

A car was approaching from the other direction. Raeder ran into the highway, waving frantically. The car came to a stop.

"Hurry!" cried the blond young woman driving it.

Raeder dived in. The woman made a U-turn on the highway. A bullet smashed through the windshield. She stamped on the accelerator, almost running down the lone killer who stood in the way.

The car surged away before the truck was within firing range.

Raeder leaned back and shut his eyes tightly. The woman concentrated on her driving, watching for the truck in her rear-vision mirror.

"It's happened again!" cried Mike Terry, his voice ecstatic. *"Jim Raeder has been plucked again from the jaws of death, thanks to Good Samaritan Janice Morrow of four three three Lexington Avenue, New York City. Did you ever see anything like it, folks? The way Miss Morrow drove through a fusillade of bullets and plucked Jim Raeder from the mouth of doom! Later we'll interview Miss Morrow and get her reactions. Now, while Jim Raeder speeds away—perhaps to safety, perhaps to further peril—we'll have a short announcement from our sponsor. Don't go away! Jim's got four hours and ten minutes until he's safe. Anything* can *happen!"*

"OK," the girl said. "We're off the air now. Raeder, what in the hell is the matter with you?"

"Eh?" Raeder asked. The girl was in her early twenties. She looked efficient, attractive, untouchable. Raeder noticed that she had good features, a trim fiure. And he noticed that she seemed angry.

"Miss," he said, "I don't know how to thank you for—"

"Talk straight," Janice Morrow said. "I'm no Good Samaritan. I'm employed by the JBC network."

"So the program had me rescued!"

"Cleverly reasoned," she said.

"But why?"

"Look, this is an expensive show, Raeder. We have to turn in a good performance. If our rating slips, we'll all be in the street selling candy apples. And you aren't co-operating."

"What? Why?"

"Because you're terrible," the girl said bitterly. "You're a flop, a fiasco. Are you trying to commit suicide? Haven't you learned *anything* about survival?"

"I'm doing the best I can."

"The Thompsons could have had you a dozen times by now. We told them to take it easy, stretch it out. But it's like shooting a clay pigeon six feet tall. The Thompsons are co-operating, but they can only fake so far. If I hadn't come along, they'd have had to kill you—air-time or not."

Raeder stared at her, wondering how such a pretty girl could talk that way. She glanced at him, then quickly looked back to the road.

"Don't give me that look!" she said. *"You* chose to risk your life for money, buster. And plenty of money! You knew the score. Don't act like some innocent little grocer who finds the nasty hoods are after him. That's a different plot."

"I know," Raeder said.

"If you can't live well, at least try to die well."

"You don't mean that," Raeder said.

"Don't be too sure. . . . You've got three hours and forty minutes until the end of the show. If you can stay alive, fine. The boodle's yours. But if you can't, at least try to give them a run for the money."

Raeder nodded, staring intently at her.

"In a few moments we're back on the air. I develop engine trouble, let you off. The Thompsons go all out now. They kill you when and if they can, as soon as they can. Understand?"

"Yes," Raeder said. "If I make it, can I see you some time?"

She bit her lip angrily. "Are you trying to kid me?"

"No. I'd like to see you again. May I?"

She looked at him curiously. "I don't know. Forget it. We're almost on. I think your best bet is the woods to the right. Ready?"

"Yes. Where can I get in touch with you? Afterward, I mean."

"Oh, Raeder, you aren't paying attention. Go through the woods until you find a washed-out ravine. It isn't much, but it'll give you some cover."

"Where can I get in touch with you?" Raeder asked again.

"I'm in the Manhattan telephone book." She stopped the car. "OK, Raeder, start running."

He opened the door.

"Wait." She leaned over and kissed him on the lips. "Good luck, you idiot. Call me if you make it."

And then he was on foot, running into the woods.

He ran through birch and pine, past an occasional split-level house with staring faces at the big picture window. Some occupant of those houses must have called the gang, for they were close behind him when he reached the washed-out little ravine. Those quiet, mannerly, law-abiding people didn't want him to escape, Raeder thought sadly. They wanted to see a killing. Or perhaps they wanted to see him *narrowly escape* a killing.

It came to the same thing, really.

He entered the ravine, burrowed into the thick underbrush

and lay still. The Thompsons appeared on both ridges, moving slowly, watching for any movement. Raeder held his breath as they came parallel to him.

He heard the quick explosion of a revolver. But the killer had only shot a squirrel. It squirmed for a moment, then lay still.

Lying in the underbrush, Raeder heard the studio helicopter overhead. He wondered if any cameras were focused on him. It was possible. And if someone was watching, perhaps some Good Samaritan would help.

So looking upward, toward the helicopter, Raeder arranged his face in a reverent expression, clasped his hands and prayed. He prayed silently, for the audience didn't like religious ostentation. But his lips moved. That was every man's privilege.

And a real prayer was on his lips. Once, a lip-reader in the audience had detected a fugitive *pretending* to pray, but actually just reciting multiplication tables. No help for that man!

Raeder finished his prayer. Glancing at his watch, he saw that he had nearly two hours to go.

And he din't want to die! It wasn't worth it, no matter how much they paid! He must have been crazy, absolutely insane to agree to such a thing. . . .

But he knew that wasn't true. And he remembered just how sane he had been.

One week ago he had been on the *Prize of Peril* stage, blinking in the spotlight, and Mike Terry had shaken his hand.

"Now, Mr. Raeder," Terry had said solemnly, "do you understand the rules of the game you are about to play?"

Raeder nodded.

"If you accept, Jim Raeder, you will be a *hunted man* for a week. *Killers* will follow you, Jim. *Trained* killers, men wanted by the law for other crimes, granted immunity for this single killing under the Voluntary Suicide Act. They will be trying to kill *you*, Jim. Do you understand?"

"I understand," Raeder said. He also understood the two hundred thousand dollars he would receive if he could live out the week.

"I ask you again, Jim Raeder. We force no man to play for stakes of death."

"I want to play," Raeder said.

Mike Terry turned to the audience. "Ladies and gentlemen, I have here a copy of an exhaustive psychological test which an impartial psychological testing firm made on Jim Raeder at our request. Copies will be sent to anyone who desires them for twenty-five cents to cover the cost of mailing. The test shows that Jim Raeder is sane, well-balanced, and fully responsible in every way." He turned to Raeder. "Do you still want to enter the contest, Jim?"

"Yes, I do."

"Very well!" cried Mike Terry. "Jim Raeder, meet your would-be killers!"

The Thompson gang moved on stage, booed by the audience.

"Look at them, folks," said Mike Terry, with undisguised contempt. "Just look at them! Antisocial, thoroughly vicious, completely amoral. These men have no code but the criminal's warped code, no honor but the honor of the cowardly hired killer. They are doomed men, doomed by our society, which will not sanction their activities for long, fated to an early and unglamorous death."

The audience shouted enthusiastically.

"What have you to say, Claude Thompson?" Terry asked.

Claude, the spokesman of the Thompsons, stepped up to the microphone. He was a thin, clean-shaven man, conservatively dressed.

"I figure," Claude Thompson said hoarsely, "I figure we're no worse than anybody. I mean, like soldiers in a war, *they* kill. And look at the graft in government, and the unions. Everybody's got their graft."

That was Thompson's tenuous code. But how quickly, with what precision, Mike Terry destroyed the killer's rationalizations! Terry's questions pierced straight to the filthy soul of the man.

At the end of the interview Claude Thompson was perspiring, mopping his face with a silk handkerchief and casting quick glances at his men.

Mike Terry put a hand on Raeder's shoulder. "Here is the man who has agreed to become your victim—if you can catch him."

"We'll catch him," Thompson said, his confidence returning.

"Don't be too sure," said Terry. "Jim Raeder has fought wild bulls—now he battles jackals. He's an average man.

He's *the people*—who mean ultimate doom to you and your kind."

"We'll get him," Thompson said.

"And one thing more," Terry said, very softly. "Jim Raeder does not stand alone. The folks of America are for him. Good Samaritans from all corners of our great nation stand ready to assist him. Unarmed, defenseless, Jim Raeder can count on the aid and goodheartedness of *the people,* whose representative he is. So don't be too sure, Claude Thompson! The average men are for Jim Raeder—and there are a lot of average men!"

Raeder thought about it, lying motionless in the underbrush. Yes, *the people* had helped him. But they had helped the killers, too.

A tremor ran through him. He had chosen, he reminded himself. He alone was responsible. The psychological test had proved that.

And yet, how responsible were the psychologists who had given him the test? How responsible was Mike Terry for offering a poor man so much money? Society had woven the noose and put it around his neck, and he was hanging himself with it, and calling it free will.

Whose fault?

"Aha!" someone cried.

Raeder looked up and saw a portly man standing near him. The man wore a loud tweed jacket. He had binoculars around his neck, and a cane in his hand.

"Mister," Raeder whispered, "please don't tell—"

"Hi!" shouted the portly man, pointing at Raeder with his cane. "Here he is!"

A madman, thought Raeder. The damned fool must think he's playing Hare and Hounds.

"Right over here!" the man screamed.

Cursing, Raeder sprang to his feet and began running. He came out of the ravine and saw a white building in the distance. He turned toward it. Behind him he could still hear the man.

"That way, over there. Look, you fools, can't you see him yet?"

The killers were shooting again. Raeder ran, stumbling over uneven ground, past three children playing in a tree house.

"Here he is!" the children screamed. "Here he is!"

Raeder groaned and ran on. He reached the steps of the building, and saw that it was a church.

As he opened the door, a bullet struck him behind the right kneecap.

He fell, and crawled inside the church.

The television set in his pocket was saying, *"What a finish, folks, what a finish! Raeder's been hit! He's been hit, folks, he's crawling now, he's in pain, but he hasn't given up! Not Jim Raeder!"*

Raeder lay in the aisle near the altar. He could hear a child's eager voice saying, "He went in there, Mr. Thompson. Hurry, you can still catch him!"

Wasn't a church considered a sanctuary? Raeder wondered.

Then the door was flung open, and Raeder realized that the custom was no longer observed. He gathered himself together and crawled past the altar, out the back door of the church.

He was in an old graveyard. He crawled past crosses and stars, past slabs of marble and granite, past stone tombs and rude wooden markers. A bullet exploded on a tombstone near his head, showering him with fragments. He crawled to the edge of an open grave.

They had deceived him, he thought. All of those nice average normal people. Hadn't they said he was their representative? Hadn't they sworn to protect their own? But no, they loathed him. Why hadn't he seen it? Their hero was the cold, blank-eyed gunman, Thompson, Capone, Billy the Kid, Young Lochinvar, El Cid, Cuchulain, the man without human hopes or fears. They worshiped him, that dead, implacable, robot gunman, and lusted to feel his foot in their face.

Raeder tried to move, and slid helplessly into the open grave.

He lay on his back, looking at the blue sky. Presently a black silhouette loomed above him, blotting out the sky. Metal twinkled. The silhouette slowly took aim.

And Raeder gave up all hope forever. *"WAIT, THOMPSON!"* roared the amplified voice of Mike Terry.

The revolver wavered.

"It is one second past five o'clock! The week is up! JIM RAEDER HAS WON!"

There was a pandemonium of cheering from the studio audience.

The Thompson gang, gathered around the grave, looked sullen.

"He's won, friends, he's won!" Mike Terry cried. "Look, look on your screen! The police have arrived, they're taking the Thompsons away from their victim—the victim they could not kill. And all this is thanks to you, Good Samaritans of America. Look, folks, tender hands are lifting Jim Raeder from the open grave that was his final refuge. Good Samaritan Janice Morrow is there. Could this be the beginning of a romance? Jim seems to have fainted, friends, they're giving him a stimulant. He's won two hundred thousand dollars! Now we'll have a few words from Jim Raeder!"

There was a short silence.

"That's odd," said Mike Terry. "Folks, I'm afraid we can't hear from Jim just now. The doctors are examining him. Just one moment . . ."

There was a silence. Mike Terry wiped his forehead and smiled.

"It's the strain, folks, the terrible strain. The doctor tells me . . . Well, folks, Jim Raeder is temporarily not himself. But it's only temporary! JBC is hiring the best psychiatrists and psychoanalysts in the country. We're going to do everything humanly possible for this gallant boy. And entirely at our own expense."

Mike Terry glanced at the studio clock. "Well, it's about time to sign off, folks. Watch for the announcement of our next great thrill show. And don't worry, I'm sure that very soon we'll have Jim Raeder back with us."

Mike Terry smiled, and winked at the audience. "He's bound to get well, friends. After all, we're all pulling for him!"

Home Team Advantage

JACK C. HALDEMAN II

SLUGGER walked down the deserted hallway, his foot-steps making a hollow ringing sound under the empty stadi-um. Turning a corner, he headed for the dugout. He was early. He was always early. Sportscasters said he'd probably be early for his own funeral.

He was.

Slugger sat on the wooden bench. It was too quiet. He picked up a practice bat and tapped it against the concrete floor. Normally he and Lefty would be razzing Pedro. Coach Weinraub would be pacing up and down, cursing the players, the umpire. There would be a lot of noise, gum popping, tobacco spitting, and good-natured practical jokes. The Kid would be sitting at the far end of the bench, worrying about his batting average and keeping his place in the starting lineup. The Kid always did that, even though he had a .359 average. The Kid was a worrier, but he wouldn't worry any more. Not after yesterday. Not after the Arcturians won the series and ended the season. Not after they won the right to eat all the humans.

Tough luck about being eaten, but Slugger couldn't let himself feel too bad about that; he had led the league in homers and the team had finished the regular season 15 games out in front. Except for the series with the Arcturians, it had been a good year. Slugger hefted the practice bat over his shoulder and climbed the dugout steps, as he had done so many times before, up to the field. This time there were no cheers.

The early morning wind blew yesterday's hot dog wrappers and beer cups across the infield. It was cool; dew covered the artificial grass, fog drifted in the bleachers. Slugger strode firmly up to the plate, took his stance, and swung hard at an imaginary ball. In his mind there was a solid crack, a roar from the crowd, and the phantom ball sailed over the center field fence. He dropped the bat and started to run the bases. By the time he rounded third, he had slowed to a walk. The empty stadium closed in on him, and when he reached home plate he sat down in the batter's box to wait for the Arcturians.

He wasn't alone very long. A television crew drove up in a large van and started setting up their cameras. Some carpenters quickly erected a temporary stage on the pitcher's mound. The ground crew halfheartedly picked up the hot dog wrappers and paper cups. Slugger started back to the dugout but he didn't make it. He ran into the Hawk.

Julius Hawkline was a character, an institution of sorts in the sports world. In his early days as a manager, the Hawk had been crankier and more controversial than the legendary Stengel. In his present role as television announcer and retired S.O.B., the Hawk was more irritating and opinionated than the legendary Cosell. True to his name, the Hawk was descending on Slugger for an interview.

"Hey Slugger!"

"Gotta go."

"Just take a minute." A man was running around with a camera, getting it all on tape. "You owe it to the fans."

The fans. That got to Slugger. It always did.

"Okay, Hawk. Just a minute. Gotta get back to the locker room. The guys'll be there soon."

"How's it feel to have blown the game, the series—to be responsible for the Arcturians earning the right to eat all the humans?"

"We played good," said Slugger, backing away. "They just played better. That's all."

"That's *all*? They're going to *eat* us and you blew it four to three. Not to mention Lefty—"

"Don't blame Lefty. He couldn't help it. Got a trick ankle, that's all."

"*All*? They're going to gobble us up—you know, knives, forks, pepper, Worcestershire sauce, all that stuff; every man, woman, and child. Imagine all those poor children out there covered with catsup. All because of a trick ankle and a couple of bonehead plays. Sure we can blame Lefty. The whole world will blame Lefty, blame you, blame the entire team. You let us down. It's all over, buddy, and your team couldn't win the big one. What do you have to say to that?"

"We played good. They played better."

The Hawk turned from Slugger and faced the camera. "And now you have it, ladies and gentlemen, the latest word from down here on the field while we wait the arrival of the Arcturians for their post-game picnic. Slugger says we played good, but let me tell you that this time 'good' just wasn't good enough. We had to be *great* and we just couldn't get it up for the final game. The world will little note nor long remember that Slugger went ten for seventeen in the series, or that we lost the big one by only one run. What they *will* remember is Lefty falling down rounding first, *tripping* over his own shoelaces, causing us to lose the whole ball of wax."

Slugger walked over to the Hawk, teeth clenched. He reached out and crumpled the microphone with one hand.

"Lefty's my friend. We played good." He turned and walked back to the dugout.

The Hawk was delighted. They'd gotten it all on tape.

When Slugger got back to the dressing room, most of the team was there, suiting up. Everything was pretty quiet, there was none of the horseplay that usually preceded a game. Slugger went to his locker and started to dress. Someone had tied his shoelaces together. He grinned. It was a tough knot.

Usually coach Weinraub would analyze the previous day's game—giving pointers, advice, encouragement, and cussing a few of the players out. Today he just sat on the bench, eyes downcast. Slugger had to keep reminding himself that there wouldn't be any more games; not today, not tomorrow. Never again. It just didn't seem possible. He slipped his glove on, the worn leather fitting his hand perfectly. It felt good to be in uniform, even if it was just for a picnic.

The noise of the crowd filtered through to the dressing room; the stadium was filling up. The Arcturians would be here soon. Reporters were crowding at the door, slipping inside. Flashbulbs were popping.

Lefty snuck in the back way and slipped over to his locker. It was next to Slugger's. They had been friends a long time, played in the minors together.

"Mornin', Lefty," said Slugger. "How's the wife and kids?"

"Fine," mumbled Lefty, pulling off the false mustache he'd worn to get through the crowd.

"Ankle still bothering you?"

"Naw. It's fine now."

"Can't keep a good man down," said Slugger, patting Lefty on the back.

A microphone appeared between them, followed by the all too familiar face of the Hawk.

"Hey Lefty, how about a few words for the viewing public? How does it feel to be the meathead that blew the whole thing?"

"Aw, come on, Hawk, gimme a break."

"It was a team effort all the way," said Slugger, reaching for the microphone.

"These things cost money," said the Hawk, stepping back. The coach blew his whistle.

"Come on team, this is it. Everybody topside." The dressing room emptied quickly. Nobody wanted to be around the Hawk. Even being the main course at the picnic was better than that.

On the field the Arcturians had already been introduced, and they stood at attention along the third base line. One by one the humans' names were called, and they took their places along the first base line. The crowd cheered Slugger and booed Lefty. Slugger felt bad about that. The stage on the pitcher's mound had a picnic table on it and the Arcturian managers and coaches were sitting around it, wearing bibs.

After they played both planets' anthems, George Alex, the league president, went to the podium set up on the stage.

"Ladies and gentlemen, I won't keep you in suspense much longer. The name of the first human to be eaten will be announced shortly. But first I would like to thank you, the fans, for casting so many ballots to choose the person we will honor today. As with the All-Star game, the more votes that are cast make for a more representative selection. All over the country—the world for that matter—fans like you, just plain people, have been writing names on the backs of hot dog wrappers and stuffing them in the special boxes placed in all major league stadiums. I'm proud to say that over ten million votes were cast and we have a winner. The envelope, please."

A man in a tuxedo, flanked by two armed guards, presented the envelope.

"The results are clear. The first human to be eaten will be
. . . the Hawk! Let's hear it for *Julius W. Hawkline!*"

The stadium rocked with cheers. The Hawk was obviously
the crowd's favorite. He was, however, reluctant to come
forward and had to be dragged to the stage. The other
reporters stuck microphones in his face, asking him how it
felt to be the chosen one.

For the first time in his life the Hawk was at a loss for
words.

The coach of the Arcturians held the Hawk with four of his
six arms and ceremoniously bit off his nose. Everyone cheered
and the Arcturian chewed. And chewed. The crowd went
wild. He chewed some more. Finally, he spat the Hawk's nose
out and went into a huddle with the other coaches.

Undigestible, was the conclusion, unchewable; humans
were definitely inedible. Something else would have to be
arranged.

Slugger smiled to himself, thinking ahead to next season.
You had to hand it to the Hawk; he was one tough old bird.

Mercenary

MACK REYNOLDS

I

JOSEPH Mauser spotted the recruiting line-up from two or
three blocks down the street, shortly after driving into Kingston. The local offices of Vacuum Tube Transport, undoubtedly. Baron Haer would be doing his recruiting for the fracas
with Continental Hovercraft there if for no other reason than
to save on rents. The Baron was watching pennies on this one
and that was bad.

In fact, it was so bad that even as Joe Mauser let his sport hovercar sink to a parking level and vaulted over its side he was still questioning his decision to sign up with the Vacuum Tube outfit rather than with their opponents. Joe was an old pro and old pros do not get to be old pros in the Category Military without developing an instinct to stay away from losing sides.

Fine enough for Low-Lowers and Mid-Lowers to sign up with this outfit as opposed to that, motivated by no other reasoning than the snappiness of the uniform and the stock shares offered, but an old pro considered carefully such matters as budget. Baron Haer was watching every expense, was, it was rumored, figuring on commanding himself and calling upon relatives and friends for his staff. Continental Hovercraft, on the other hand, was heavy with variable capital and was in a position to hire Stonewall Cogswell himself for their tactician.

However, the die was cast. You didn't run up a caste level, not to speak of two at once, by playing it careful. Joe had planned this out; for once, old pro or not, he was taking risks.

Recruiting line-ups were not for such as he. Not for many a year, many a fracas. He strode rapidly along this one, heading for the offices ahead, noting only in passing the quality of the men who were taking service with Vacuum Tube Transport. These were the soldiers he'd be commanding in the immediate future, and the prospects looked grim. There were few veterans among them. Their stance, their demeanor, their . . . well, you could tell a veteran even though he be Rank Private. You could tell a veteran of even one fracas. It showed.

He knew the situation. The word had gone out. Baron Malcolm Haer was due for a defeat. You weren't going to pick up any lush bonuses signing up with him, and you definitely weren't going to jump a caste. In short, no matter what Haer's past record, choose what was going to be the winning side—Continental Hovercraft. Continental Hovercraft and old Stonewall Cogswell who had lost so few fracases that many a Telly buff couldn't remember a single one.

Individuals among these men showed promise, Joe Mauser estimated even as he walked, but promise means little if you don't live long enough to cash in on it.

Take that small man up ahead. He'd obviously got himself into a hassle maintaining his place in line against two or three heftier would-be soldiers. The little fellow wasn't back-

ing down a step in spite of the attempts of the other Lowers to
usurp his place. Joe Mauser liked to see such spirit. You
could use it when you were in the dill.

As he drew abreast of the altercation, he snapped from the
side of his mouth, "Easy, lads. You'll get all the scrapping
you want with Hovercraft. Wait until then."

He'd expected his tone of authority to be enough, even
though he was in mufti. He wasn't particularly interested in
the situation, beyond giving the little man a hand. A veteran
would have recognized him as an old timer and probable
officer, and heeded, automatically.

These evidently weren't veterans.

"Says who?" one of the Lowers growled back at him. "You
one of Baron Haer's kids, or something?"

Joe Mauser came to a halt and faced the other. He was
irritated, largely with himself. He didn't want to be bothered.
Nevertheless, there was no alternative now.

The line of men, all Lowers so far as Joe could see, had
fallen silent in an expectant hush. They were bored with
their long wait. Now something would break the monotony.

By tomorrow, Joe Mauser would be in command of some of
these men. In as little as a week he would go into a full
fledged fracas with them. He couldn't afford to lose face. Not
even at this point when all, including himself, were still
civilian garbed. When matters pickled, in a fracas, you wanted
men with complete confidence in you.

The man who had grumbled the surly response was a near
physical twin of Joe Mauser, which put him in his early
thirties, gave him five foot eleven of altitude and about one
hundred and eighty pounds. His clothes casted him Low-
Lower—nothing to lose. As with many who have nothing to
lose, he was willing to risk all for principle. His face now
registered that ideal. Joe Mauser had no authority over him,
nor his friends.

Joe's eyes flicked to the other two who had been pestering
the little fellow. They weren't quite so aggressive and as yet
had come to no conclusion about their stand. Probably the
three had been unacquainted before their bullying alliance to
deprive the smaller man of his place. However, a moment of
hesitation and Joe would have a trio on his hands.

He went through no further verbal preliminaries. Joe
Mauser stepped closer. His right hand lanced forward, not
doubled in a fist but fingers close together and pointed,

spearlike. He sank it into the other's abdomen, immediately below the rib cage—the solar plexus.

He had misestimated the other two. Even as his opponent crumpled, they were upon him, coming in from each side. And at least one of them, he could see now, had been in hand-to-hand combat before. In short, another pro, like Joe himself.

He took one blow, rolling with it, and his feet automatically went into the shuffle of the trained fighter. He retreated slightly to erect defenses, plan attack. They pressed him strongly, sensing victory in his retreat.

The one mattered little to him. Joe Mauser could have polished off the oaf in a matter of seconds, had he been allotted seconds to devote. But the second, the experienced one, was the problem. He and Joe were well matched, and with the oaf as an ally really he had all the best of it.

Support came from a forgotten source, the little chap who had been the reason for the whole hassle. He waded in now as big as the next man so far as spirit was concerned, but a sorry fate gave him to attack the wrong man, the veteran rather than the tyro. He took a crashing blow to the side of his head which sent him sailing back into the recruiting line, now composed of excited, shouting verbal participants of the fray.

However, the extinction of Joe Mauser's small ally had taken a moment or two, and time was what Joe needed most. For a double second he had the oaf alone on his hands, and that was sufficient. He caught a flailing arm, turned his back and automatically went into the movements which result in that spectacular hold of the wrestler, the Flying Mare. Just in time he recalled that his opponent was a future comrade-in-arms and twisted the arm so that it bent at the elbow, rather than breaking. He hurled the other over his shoulder and as far as possible, to take the scrap out of him, and twirled quickly to meet the further attack of his sole remaining foe.

That phase of the combat failed to materialize.

A voice of command bit out, "Hold it, you lads!"

The original situation which had precipitated the fight was being duplicated. But while the three Lowers had failed to respond to Joe Mauser's tone of authority, there was no similar failure now.

The owner of the voice, beautifully done up in the uniform of Vacuum Tube Transport, complete to kilts and the swagger stick of the officer of Rank Colonel or above, stood glaring at them. Age, Joe estimated even as he came to attention, somewhere in the late twenties—an Upper in caste. Born to command. His face holding that arrogant, contemptuous expression once common to the patricians of Rome, the Prussian Junkers, the British ruling class of the Nineteenth Century. Joe knew the expression well. How well he knew it. On more than one occasion, he had dreamt of it.

Joe said, "Yes, sir."

"What in Zen goes on here? Are you lads overtranked?"

"No, sir," Joe's veteran opponent grumbled, his eyes on the ground, a schoolboy before the principal.

Joe said, evenly, "A private disagreement, sir."

"Disagreement!" the Upper snorted. His eyes went to the three fallen combatants, who were in various stages of reviving. "I'd hate to see you lads in a real scrap."

That brought a response from the noncombatants in the recruiting line. The *bon mot* wasn't that good but caste has its privileges and the laughter was just short of uproarious.

Which seemed to placate the kilted officer. He tapped his swagger stick against the side of his leg while he ran his eyes up and down Joe Mauser and the others, as though memorizing them for future reference.

"All right," he said. "Get back into the line, and you troublemakers quiet down. We're processing as quickly as we can." And at that point he added insult to injury with an almost word-for-word repetition of what Joe had said a few moments earlier. "You'll get all the fighting you want from Hovercraft, if you can wait until then."

The four original participants of the rumpus resumed their places in various stages of sheepishness. The little fellow, nursing an obviously aching jaw, made a point of taking up his original position even while darting a look of thanks to Joe Mauser, who still stood where he had when the fight was interrupted.

The Upper looked at Joe. "Well, lad, are you interested in signing up with Vacuum Tube Transport or not?"

"Yes, sir," Joe said evenly. Then, "Joseph Mauser, sir. Category Military, Rank Captain."

"Indeed." The officer looked him up and down all over again, his nostrils high. "A Middle, I assume. And brawling with recruits." He held a long silence. "Very well, come with me." He turned and marched off.

Joe inwardly shrugged. This was a fine start for his pitch—a
fine start. He had half a mind to give it all up, here and now,
and head on up to Catskill to enlist with Continental Hovercraft. His big scheme would wait for another day. Nevertheless, he fell in behind the aristocrat and followed him to the
offices which had been his original destination.

Two Rank Privates with 45-70 Springfields and wearing
the Haer kilts in such wise as to indicate permanent status in
Vacuum Tube Transport came to the salute as they approached.
The Upper preceding Joe Mauser flicked his swagger stick in
an easy nonchalance. Joe felt envious amusement. How long
did it take to learn how to answer a salute with that degree of
arrogant ease?

There were desks in here, and typers humming, as Vacuum Tube Transport office workers, mobilized for this special
service, processed volunteers for the company forces. Harried
noncoms and junior-grade officers buzzed everywhere, failing
miserably to bring order to the chaos. To the right was a door
with a medical cross newly painted on it. When it occasionally popped open to admit or emit a recruit, white-robed
doctors, male nurses and half-nude men could be glimpsed
beyond.

Joe followed the other through the press and to an inner
office at which door he didn't bother to knock. He pushed his
way through, waved in greeting with his swagger stick to the
single occupant who looked up from the paper- and tape-
strewn desk at which he sat.

Joe Mauser had seen the face before on Telly, though never
so tired as this and never with the element of defeat to be
read in the expression. Bullet-headed, barrel-figured Baron
Malcolm Haer of Vacuum Tube Transport. Category Transportation, Mid-Upper, and strong candidate for Upper-Upper
upon retirement. However, there would be few who expected
retirement in the immediate future. Hardly. Malcolm Haer
found too obvious a lusty enjoyment in the competition between
Vacuum Tube Transport and its stronger rivals.

Joe came to attention, bore the sharp scrutiny of his chosen
commander-to-be. The older man's eyes went to the kilted
Upper officer who had brought Joe along. "What is it, Balt?"

The other gestured with his stick at Joe. "Claims to be
Rank Captain. Looking for a commission with us, Dad. I
wouldn't know why." The last sentence was added lazily.

The older Haer shot an irritated glance at his son. "Possibly for the same reason mercenaries usually enlist for a fracas, Balt." His eyes came back to Joe.

Joe Mauser, still at attention even though in mufti, opened his mouth to give his name, category and rank, but the older man waved a hand negatively. "Captain Mauser, isn't it? I caught the fracas between Carbonaceous Fuel and United Miners, down on the Panhandle Reservation. Seems to me I've spotted you once or twice before, too."

"Yes, sir," Joe said. This was some improvement in the way things were going.

The older Haer was scowling at him. "Confound it, what are you doing with no more rank than captain? On the face of it, you're an old hand, a highly experienced veteran."

An old pro, we call ourselves, Joe said to himself. *Old pros, we call ourselves, among ourselves.*

Aloud, he said, "I was born a Mid-Lower, sir."

There was understanding in the old man's face, but Balt Haer said loftily, "What's that got to do with it? Promotion is quick and based on merit in Category Military."

At a certain point, if you are good combat officer material, you speak your mind no matter the rank of the man you are addressing. On this occasion, Joe Mauser needed few words. He let his eyes go up and down Balt Haer's immaculate uniform, taking in the swagger stick of the Rank Colonel or above. Joe said evenly, "Yes, sir."

Balt Haer flushed quick temper. "What do you mean by—"

But his father was chuckling. "You have spirit, captain. I need spirit now. You are quite correct. My son, though a capable officer, I assure you, has probably not participated in a fraction of the fracases you have to your credit. However, there is something to be said for the training available to we Uppers in the academies. For instance, captain, have you ever commanded a body of lads larger than, well, a *company?*"

Joe said flatly, "In the Douglas-Boeing versus Lockheed-Cessna fracas we took a high loss of officers when the Douglas-Boeing outfit rang in some fast-firing French *mitrailleuse* we didn't know they had. As my superiors took casualties I was field promoted to acting battalion commander, to acting regimental commander, to acting brigadier. For three days I held the rank of acting commander of brigade. We won."

Balt Haer snapped his fingers. "I remember that. Read quite a paper on it." He eyed Joe Mauser, almost respectfully.

"Stonewall Cogswell got the credit for the victory and received his marshal's baton as a result."

"He was one of the few other officers that survived," Joe said dryly.

"But, Zen! You mean you got no promotion at all?"

Joe said, "I was upped to Low-Middle from High-Lower, sir. At my age, at the time, quite a promotion."

Baron Haer was remembering, too. "That was the fracas that brought on the howl from the Sovs. They claimed those *mitrailleuse* were post-1900 and violated the Universal Disarmament Pact. Yes, I recall that. Douglas-Boeing was able to prove that the weapon was used by the French as far back as the Franco-Prussian War." He eyed Joe with new interest now. "Sit down, captain. You too, Balt. Do you realize that Captain Mauser is the only recruit of officer rank we've had today?"

"Yes," the younger Haer said dryly. "However, it's too late to call the fracas off now. Hovercraft wouldn't stand for it, and the Category Military Department would back them. Our only alternative is unconditional surrender, and you know what that means."

"It means our family would probably be forced from control of the firm," the older man growled. "But nobody has suggested surrender on any terms. Nobody, thus far." He glared at his officer son, who took it with an easy shrug and swung a leg over the edge of his father's desk in the way of a seat.

Joe Mauser found a chair and lowered himself into it. Evidently, the foppish Balt Haer had no illusions about the spot his father had got the family corporation into. And the younger man was right, of course.

But the Baron wasn't blind to reality any more than he was a coward. He dismissed Balt Haer's defeatism from his mind and came back to Joe Mauser. "As I say, you're the only officer recruit today. Why?"

Joe said evenly, "I wouldn't know, sir. Perhaps free lance Category Military men are occupied elsewhere. There's always a shortage of trained officers."

Baron Haer was waggling a finger negatively. "That's not what I mean, captain. You are an old hand. This is your category and you must know it well. Then why are *you* signing up with Vacuum Tube Transport rather than Hovercraft?"

Joe Mauser looked at him for a moment without speaking.

"Come, come, captain. I am an old hand too, in my category, and not a fool. I realize there is scarcely a soul in the West-world that expects anything but disaster for my colors. Pay rates have been widely posted. I can offer only five common shares of Vacuum Tube for a Rank Captain, win or lose. Hovercraft is doubling that, and can pick and choose among the best officers in the hemisphere."

Joe said softly, "I have all the shares I need."

Balt Haer had been looking back and forth between his father and the newcomer and becoming obviously more puzzled. He put in, "Well, what in Zen motivates you if it isn't the stock we offer?"

Joe glanced at the younger Haer to acknowledge the question but he spoke to the Baron. "Sir, as you said, you're no fool. However, you've been sucked in, this time. When you took on Hovercraft, you were thinking in terms of a regional dispute. You wanted to run one of your vacuum tube deals up to Fairbanks from Edmonton. You were expecting a minor fracas, involving possibly five thousand men. You never expected Hovercraft to parlay it up, through their connections in the Category Military Department, to a divisional magnitude fracas which you simply aren't large enough to afford. But Hovercraft was getting sick of your corporation. You've been nicking away at them too long. So they decided to do you in. They've hired Marshal Cogswell and the best combat officers in North America, and they're hiring the most competent veterans they can find. Every fracas buff who watches Telly figures you've had it. They've been watching you come up the aggressive way, the hard way, for a long time, but now they're all going to be sitting on the edges of their sofas waiting for you to get it."

Baron Haer's heavy face had hardened as Joe Mauser went on relentlessly. He growled, "Is this what everyone thinks?"

"Yes. Everyone intelligent enough to have an opinion." Joe made a motion of his head to the outer offices where the recruiting was proceeding. "Those men out there are rejects from Catskill, where old Baron Zwerdling is recruiting. Either that or they're inexperienced Low-Lowers, too stupid to realize they're sticking their necks out. Not one man in ten is a veteran. And when things begin to pickle, you want veterans."

Baron Malcolm Haer sat back in his chair and stared coldly at Captain Joe Mauser. He said, "At first I was moderately surprised that an old-time mercenary like yourself should

chose my uniform, rather than Zwerdling's. Now I am increasingly mystified about motivation. So all over again I ask you,
captain: Why are you requesting a commission in my forces
which you seem convinced will meet disaster?"

Joe wet his lips carefully. "I think I know a way you can
win."

II

His permanent military rank the Haers had no way to
alter, but they were short enough of competent officers that
they gave him an acting rating and pay scale of major and
command of a squadron of cavalry. Joe Mauser wasn't interested in a cavalry command this fracas, but he said nothing.
Immediately, he had to size up the situation; it wasn't time as
yet to reveal the big scheme. And, meanwhile, they could use
him to whip the Rank Privates into shape.

He had left the offices of Baron Haer to go through the red
tape involved in being signed up on a temporary basis in the
Vacuum Tube Transport forces and reentered the confusion of
the outer offices where the Lowers were being processed and
given medicals. He reentered in time to run into a Telly team
which was doing a live broadcast.

Joe Mauser remembered the news reporter who headed the
team. He'd run into him two or three times in fracases. As a
matter of fact, although Joe held the standard Military
Category prejudices against Telly, he had a basic respect for
this particular newsman. On the occasions he'd seen him
before, the fellow was hot in the midst of the action even
when things were in the dill. He took as many chances as did
the average combatant, and you can't ask for more than that.

The other knew him, too, of course. It was part of his job to
be able to spot the celebrities and near celebrities. He zeroed
in on Joe now, making flicks of his hand to direct the
cameras. Joe, of course, was fully aware of the value of Telly
and was glad to co-operate.

"Captain! Captain Mauser, isn't it? Joe Mauser who held
out for four days in the swamps of Louisiana with a single
company while his ranking officers reformed behind him."

That was one way of putting it, but both Joe and the
newscaster who had covered the debacle knew the reality of
the situation. When the front had collapsed, his commanders—
of Upper caste, of course—had hauled out, leaving him to

fight a delaying action while they mended their fences with the enemy, coming to the best terms possible. Yes, that had been the United Oil versus Allied Petroleum fracas, and Joe had emerged with little either in glory or pelf.

The average fracas fan wasn't on an intellectual level to appreciate anything other than victory. The good guys win, the bad guys lose—that's obvious, isn't it? Not one out of ten Telly followers of the fracases was interested in a well-conducted retreat or holding action. They wanted blood, lots of it, and they identified with the winning side.

Joe Mauser wasn't particularly bitter about this aspect. It was part of his way of life. In fact, his pet peeve was the *real* buff. The type, man or woman, who could remember every fracas you'd ever been in, every time you'd copped one, and how long you'd been in the hospital. Fans who could remember, even better than you could, every time the situation had pickled on you and you'd had to fight your way out as best you could. They'd tell you about it, their eyes gleaming, sometimes a slightest trickle of spittle at the sides of their mouths. They usually wanted an autograph, or a souvenir such as a uniform button.

Now Joe said to the Telly reporter, "That's right, Captain Mauser. Acting major, in this fracas, ah—"

"Freddy. Freddy Soligen. You remember me, captain—"

"Of course I do, Freddy. We've been in the dill, side by side, more than once, and even when I was too scared to use my side arm, you'd be scanning away with your camera."

"Ha ha, listen to the captain, folks. I hope my boss is tuned in. But seriously, Captain Mauser, what do you think the chances of Vacuum Tube Transport are in this fracas?"

Joe looked into the camera lens, earnestly. "The best, of course, or I wouldn't have signed up with Baron Haer, Freddy. Justice triumphs, and anybody who is familiar with the issues in this fracas knows that Baron Haer is on the side of true right."

Freddy said, holding any sarcasm he must have felt, "What would you say the issues were, captain?"

"The basic North American free enterprise right to compete. Hovercraft has held a near monopoly in transport to Fairbanks. Vacuum Tube Transport wishes to lower costs and bring the consumers of Fairbanks better service through running a vacuum tube to that area. What could be more in the traditions of the West-world? Continental Hovercraft stands in the way and it is they who have demanded of the Category Military Department a trial by arms. On the face of it, justice is on the side of Baron Haer."

Freddy Soligen said into the camera, "Well, all you good people of the Telly world, that's an able summation the captain has made, but it certainly doesn't jibe with the words of Baron Zwerdling we heard this morning, does it? However, justice triumphs and we'll see what the field of combat will have to offer. Thank you, thank you very much, Captain Mauser. All of us, all of us tuned in today, hope that you personally will run into no dill in this fracas."

"Thanks, Freddy. Thanks all," Joe said into the camera, before turning away. He wasn't particularly keen about this part of the job, but you couldn't underrate the importance of pleasing the buffs. In the long run it was your career, your chances for promotion both in military rank and ultimately in caste. It was the way the fans took you up, boosted you, idolized you, worshipped you if you really made it. He, Joe Mauser, was only a minor celebrity; he appreciated every chance he had to be interviewed by such a popular reporter as Freddy Soligen.

Even as he turned, he spotted the four men with whom he'd had his spat earlier. The little fellow was still to the fore. Evidently, the others had decided the one place extra that he represented wasn't worth the trouble he'd put in their way defending it.

On an impulse he stepped up to the small man, who began a grin of recognition, a grin that transformed his feisty face. A revelation of an inner warmth beyond average in a world which had lost much of its human warmth.

Joe said, "Like a job, soldier?"

"Name's Max. Max Mainz. Sure I want a job. That's why I'm in this everlasting line."

Joe said, "First fracas for you, isn't it?"

"Yeah, but I had basic training in school."

"What do you weigh, Max?"

Max's face soured. "About one twenty."

"Did you check out on semaphore in school?"

"Well, sure. I'm Category Food, Sub-division Cooking, Branch Chef, but, like I say, I took basic military training, like most everybody else."

"I'm Captain Joe Mauser. How'd you like to be my batman?"

Max screwed up his already not overly handsome face. "Gee, I don't know. I kinda joined up to see some action. Get into the dill. You know what I mean."

Joe said dryly, "See here, Mainz, you'll probably find more pickled situations next to me than you'll want—and you'll come out alive."

The recruiting sergeant looked up from the desk. It was Max Mainz's turn to be processed. The sergeant said, "Lad, take a good opportunity when it drops in your lap. The captain is one of the best in the field. You'll learn more, get better chances for promotion, if you stick with him."

Joe couldn't remember ever having run into the sergeant before, but he said, "Thanks, sergeant."

The other said, evidently realizing Joe didn't recognize him, "We were together on the Chihuahua Reservation, on the jurisdictional fracas between the United Miners and the Teamsters, sir."

It had been almost fifteen years ago. About all that Joe Mauser remembered of that fracas was the abnormal number of casualties they'd taken. His side had lost, but from this distance in time Joe couldn't even remember what force he'd been with. But now he said, "That's right. I thought I recognized you, sergeant."

"It was my first fracas, sir." The sergeant went business-like. "If you want I should hustle this lad though, captain—"

"Please do, sergeant." Joe added to Max, "I'm not sure where my billet will be. When you're through all this, locate the officer's mess and wait there for me."

"Well, O.K.," Max said doubtfully, still scowling but evidently a servant of an officer, if he wanted to be or not.

"Sir," the sergeant added ominously. "If you've had basic, you know enough how to address an officer."

"Well, yes sir," Max said hurriedly.

Joe began to turn away, but then spotted the man immediately behind Max Mainz. He was one of the three with whom Joe had tangled earlier, the one who'd obviously had previous combat experience. He pointed the man out to the sergeant. "You'd better give this lad at least temporary rank of corporal. He's a veteran and we're short of veterans."

The sergeant said, "Yes, sir. We sure are." Joe's former foe looked properly thankful.

* * *

Joe Mauser finished off his own red tape and headed for the street to locate a military tailor who could do him up a set of the Haer kilts and fill his other dress requirements. As he went, he wondered vaguely just how many different uniforms he had worn in his time.

In a career as long as his own from time to time you took semi-permanent positions in bodyguards, company police, or possibly the permanent combat troops of this corporation or that. But largely, if you were ambitious, you signed up for the fracases, and that meant into a uniform and out of it again in as short a period as a couple of weeks.

At the door he tried to move aside but was too slow for the quick-moving young woman who caromed off him. He caught her arm to prevent her from stumbling. She looked at him with less than thanks.

Joe took the blame for the collision. "Sorry," he said. "I'm afraid I didn't see you, Miss."

"Obviously," she said coldly. Her eyes went up and down him, and for a moment he wondered where he had seen her before. Somewhere, he was sure.

She was dressed as they dress who have never considered cost and she had an elusive beauty which would have been even the more hadn't her face projected quite such a serious outlook. Her features were more delicate than those to which he was usually attracted. Her lips were less full, but still—he was reminded of the classic ideal of the British Romantic Period, the women sung of by Byron and Keats, Shelley and Moore.

She said, "Is there any particualr reason why you should be staring at me, Mr.—"

"Captain Mauser," Joe said hurriedly. "I'm afraid I've been rude, Miss—well, I thought I recognized you."

She took in his civilian dress, typed it automatically, and came to an erroneous conclusion. She said, "Captain? You mean that with everyone else I know drawing down ranks from Lieutenant Colonel to Brigadier General, you can't make anything better than Captain?"

Joe winced. He said carefully, "I came up from the ranks, Miss. Captain is quite an achievement, believe me."

"Up from the ranks!" She took in his clothes again. "You mean you're a Middle? You neither talk nor look like a Middle, captain." She used the caste rating as though it was not *quite* a derogatory term.

Not that she meant to be deliberately insulting, Joe knew, wearily. How well he knew. It was simply born in her. As once a well-educated aristocracy had, not necessarily unkindly, named their status inferiors *niggers;* or other aristocrats, in another area of the country, had named theirs *greasers.* Yes, how well he knew.

He said very evenly, "Mid-Middle now, Miss. However, I was born in the Lower castes."

An eyebrow went up. "Zen! You must have put in many an hour studying. You talk like an Upper, captain." She dropped all interest in him and turned to resume her journey.

"Just a moment," Joe said. "You can't go in there, Miss—"

Her eyebrows went up again. "The name is Haer," she said. "Why can't I go in here, captain?"

Now it came to him why he had thought he recognized her. She had basic features similar to those of that overbred poppycock Balt Haer.

"Sorry," Joe said. "I suppose under the circumstances, you can. I was about to tell you that they're recruiting with lads running around half clothed. Medical inspections, that sort of thing."

She made a noise through her nose and said over her shoulder, even as she sailed on. "Besides being a Haer, I'm an M.D., captain. At the ludicrous sight of a man shuffling about in his shorts, I seldom blush."

She was gone.

Joe Mauser looked after her. "I'll bet you don't," he muttered.

Had she waited a few minutes he could have explained his Upper accent and his unlikely education. When you'd copped one you had plenty of opportunity in hospital beds to read, to study, to contemplate—and to fester away in your own schemes of rebellion against fate. And Joe had copped many in his time.

III

By the time Joe Mauser called it a day and retired to his quarters he was exhausted to the point where his basic dissatisfaction with the trade he followed was heavily upon him.

He had met his immediate senior officers, largely dilettante Uppers with precious little field experience, and was unimpressed. And he'd met his own junior officers and was

shocked. By the looks of things at this stage, Captain Mauser's squadron would be going into this fracas both under-
manned with Rank Privates and with junior officers composed
largely of temporarily promoted noncoms. If this was typical
of Baron Haer's total force, then Balt Haer had been correct;
unconditional surrender was to be considered, no matter how
disastrous to Haer family fortunes.

Joe had been able to take immediate delivery of one kilted
uniform. Now, inside his quarters, he began stripping out of
his jacket. Somewhat to his surprise, the small man he had
selected earlier in the day to be his batman entered from an
inner room, also resplendent in the Haer uniform and obviously happily so.

He helped his superior out of the jacket with an ease that
held no subservience but at the same time was correctly
respectful. You'd have thought him a batman specially trained.

Joe grunted, "Max, isn't it? I'd forgotten about you. Glad
you found our billet all right."

Max said, "Yes, sir. Would the captain like a drink? I
picked up a bottle of applejack. Applejack's the drink around
here, sir. Makes a topnotch highball with gingerale and a
twist of lemon."

Joe Mauser looked at him. Evidently his tapping this man
for orderly had been sheer fortune. Well, Joe Mauser could
use some good luck on this job. He hoped it didn't end with
selecting a batman.

Joe said, "An applejack highball sounds wonderful, Max.
Got ice?"

"Of course, sir." Max left the small room.

Joe Mauser and his officers were billeted in what had once
been a motel on the old road between Kingston and Wood-
stock. There was a shower and a tiny kitchenette in each
cottage. That was one advantage in a fracas held in an area
where there were plenty of facilities. Such military reservations as that of the Little Big Horn in Montana and particularly some of those in the Southwest and Mexico were another
thing.

Joe lowered himself into the room's easy chair and bent
down to untie his laces. He kicked his shoes off. He could use
that drink. He began wondering all over again if his scheme
for winning this Vacuum Tube Transport versus Continental
Hovercraft fracas would come off. The more he saw of Baron
Haer's inadequate forces, the more he wondered. He hadn't

expected Vacuum Tube to be in *this* bad a shape. Baron Haer
had been riding high for so long that one would have thought
his reputation for victory would have lured many a veteran
to his colors. Evidently they hadn't bitten. The word was out
all right.

Max Mainz returned with the drink.

Joe said, "You had one yourself?"

"No, sir."

Joe said, "Well, Zen, go get yourself one and come on back
and sit down. Let's get acquainted."

"Well, yessir." Max disappeared back into the kitchenette
to return almost immediately. The little man slid into a
chair, drink awkwardly in hand.

His superior sized him up, all over again. Not much more
than a kid, really. Surprisingly aggressive for a Lower who
must have been raised from childhood in a trank-bemused,
Telly-entertained household. The fact that he'd broken away
from that environment at all was to his credit; it was considerably easier to conform. But then it is always easier to
conform, to run with the herd, as Joe well knew. His own
break hadn't been an easy one. "Relax," he said now.

Max said, "Well, this is my first day."

"I know. And you've been seeing Telly shows all your life
showing how an orderly conducts himself in the presence of
his superior." Joe took another pull and yawned. "Well,
forget about it. With any man who goes into a fracas with me,
I like to be on close terms. When things pickle, I want him to
be on my side, not nursing some peeve brought on by his
officer trying to give him an inferiority complex."

The little man was eying him in surprise.

Joe finished his highball and came to his feet to get
another one. He said, "On two occasions I've had an orderly
save my life. I'm not taking any chances but that there might
be a third opportunity."

"Well, yessir. Does the captain want me to get him—"

"I'll get it," Joe said.

When he'd returned to his chair, he said, "Why did you join
up with Baron Haer, Max?"

The other shrugged it off. "The usual. The excitement. The
idea of all those fans watching me on Telly. The share of
common stock I'll get. And, you never know, maybe a promotion in caste. I wouldn't mind making Upper-Lower."

Joe said sourly, "One fracas and you'll be over that desire

to have the buffs watching you on Telly while they sit around in their front rooms sucking on tranks. And you'll probably be over the desire for the excitement, too. Of course, the share of stock is another thing."

"You aren't just countin' down, captain," Max said, an almost surly overtone in his voice. "You don't know what it's like being born with no more common stock shares than a Mid-Lower."

Joe held his peace, sipping at his drink, taking this one more slowly. He let his eyebrows rise to encourage the other to go on.

Max said doggedly, "Sure, they call it People's Capitalism and everybody gets issued enough shares to insure him a basic living all the way from the cradle to the grave, like they say. But let me tell you, you're a Middle and you don't realize how basic the basic living of a Lower can be."

Joe yawned. If he hadn't been so tired, there would have been more amusement in the situation.

Max was still dogged. "Unless you can add to those shares of stock, it's pretty drab, captain. You wouldn't know."

Joe said, "Why don't you work? A Lower can always add to his stock by working."

Max stirred in indignity. "Work? Listen, sir, that's just one more field that's been automated right out of existence. Category Food Preparation, Sub-division Cooking, Branch Chef. Cooking isn't left in the hands of slobs who might drop a cake of soap into the soup. It's done automatic. The only new changes made in cooking are by real top experts, almost scientists like. And most of them are Uppers, mind you."

Joe Mauser sighed inwardly. So his find in batmen wasn't going to be as wonderful as all that, after all. The man might have been born into the food preparation category from a long line of chefs, but evidently he knew precious little about his field. Joe might have suspected. He himself had been born into Clothing Category, Sub-division Shoes, Branch Repair— Cobbler—a meaningless trade since shoes were no longer repaired but discarded upon showing signs of wear. In an economy of complete abundance, there is little reason for repair of basic commodities. It was high time the government investigated category assignment and reshuffled and reassigned half the nation's population. But then, of course, was the question of what to do with the technologically unemployed.

Max was saying, "The only way I could figure on a promotion to a higher caste, or the only way to earn stock shares, was by crossing categories. And you know what that means. Either Category Military or Category Religion, and I sure as Zen don't know nothing about religion."

Joe said mildly, "Theoretically, you can cross categories into any field you want, Max."

Max snorted. "Theoretically is right ... sir. You ever heard about anybody born a Lower, or even a Middle like yourself, cross categories to, say, some Upper category like banking?"

Joe chuckled. He liked this peppery little fellow. If Max worked out as well as Joe thought he might, there was a possibility of taking him along to the next fracas.

Max was saying, "I'm not saying anything against the old-time way of doing things or talking against the government, but I'll tell you, captain, every year goes by it gets harder and harder for a man to raise his caste or to earn some additional stock shares."

The applejack had worked enough on Joe for him to rise against one of his pet peeves. He said, "That term, the old-time way, is strictly Telly talk, Max. We don't do things *the old-time way*. No nation in history ever has—with the possible exception of Egypt. Socioeconomics are in a continual flux, and here in this country we no more do things in the way they did fifty years ago than fifty years ago they did them the way the American Revolutionists outlined back in the Eighteenth Century."

Max was staring at him. "I don't get that, sir."

Joe said impatiently, "Max, the politico-economic system we have today is an outgrowth of what went earlier. The welfare state, the freezing of the status quo, the Frigid Fracas between the West-world and the Sov-world, industrial automation until useful employment is all but needless—all these things were to be found in embryo more than fifty years ago."

"Well, maybe the captain's right, but you gotta admit, sir, that mostly we do things the old way. We still got the Constitution and the two-party system and—"

Joe was wearying of the conversation now. You seldom ran into anyone, even in Middle caste, the traditionally professional class, interested enough in such subjects to be worth arguing with. He said, "The Constitution, Max, has got to the point of the Bible. Interpret it the way you wish, and you can find anything. If not, you can always make a new amendment. So far as the two-party system is concerned, what effect does it have when there are no differences between the two parties? That phase of pseudo-democracy was beginning as far back as the 1930s when they began passing State laws hindering the emerging of new political parties. By the time they were insured against a third party working its way through the maze of election laws, the two parties had become so similar that elections became almost as big a farce as over in the Sov-world."

"A farce?" Max ejaculated indignantly, forgetting his servant status. "That means not so good, doesn't it? Far as I'm concerned, election day is tops. The one day a Lower is just as good as an Upper. The one day how many shares you got makes no difference. Everybody has everything."

"Sure, sure, sure," Joe sighed. "The modern equivalent of the Roman Bacchanalia. Election day in the West-world when no one, for just that one day, is freer than anyone else."

"Well, what's wrong with that?" The other was all but belligerent. "That's the trouble with you Middles and Uppers, you don't know how it is to be a Lower and—"

Joe snapped suddenly, "I was born a Mid-Lower myself, Max. Don't give me that nonsense."

Max gaped at him, utterly unbelieving.

Joe's irritation fell away. He held out his glass. "Get us a couple of more drinks, Max, and I'll tell you a story."

By the time the fresh drink came, Joe Mauser was sorry he'd made the offer. He thought back. He hadn't told anyone the Joe Mauser story in many a year. And, as he recalled, the last time had been when he was well into his cups, on an election day at that, and his listener had been a Low-Upper, a hereditary aristocrat, one of the one per cent of the upper strata of the nation. Zen! How the man had laughed. He'd roared his amusement till the tears ran.

However, Joe said, "Max, I was born in the same caste you were—average father, mother, sisters and brothers. They subsisted on the basic income guaranteed from birth, sat and watched Telly for an unbelievable number of hours each day, took trank to keep themselves happy. And thought I was crazy because I didn't. Dad was the sort of man who'd take his belt off to a child of his who questioned such school-taught slogans as *What was good enough for Daddy is good enough for me.*

"They were all fracas fans, of course. As far back as I can remember the picture is there of them gathered around the Telly, screaming excitement." Joe Mauser sneered, uncharacteristically.

"You don't sound much like you're in favor of your trade, captain," Max said.

Joe came to his feet, putting down his still half-full glass. "I'll make this epic story short, Max. As you said, the two actually valid methods of rising above the level in which you were born are in the Military and Religious Categories. Like you, even I couldn't stomach the latter."

Joe Mauser hesitated, then finished it off. "Max, there have been few societies that man has evolved that didn't allow in some manner for the competent or sly, the intelligent or the opportunist, the brave or the strong, to work his way to the top. I don't know which of these I personally fit into, but I rebel against remaining in the lower categories of a stratified society. Do I make myself clear?"

"Well, no sir, not exactly."

Joe said flatly, "I'm going to fight my way to the top and nothing is going to stand in the way. Is that clearer?"

"Yessir," Max said, taken aback.

IV

After routine morning duties, Joe Mauser returned to his billet and mystified Max Mainz by not only changing into mufti himself but having Max do the same.

In fact, the new batman protested faintly. He hadn't nearly, as yet, got over the glory of wearing his kilts and was looking forward to parading around town in them. He had a point, of course. The appointed time for the fracas was getting closer and buffs were beginning to stream into town to bask in the atmosphere of threatened death. Everybody knew what a military center, on the outskirts of a fracas reservation such as the Catskills, was like immediately preceding a clash between rival corporations. The high-strung gaiety, the drinking, the overtranking, the relaxation of mores. Even a Rank Private had it made. Admiring civilians to buy drinks and hang on your every word, and more important still, sensuous-eyed women, their faces slack in thinly suppressed passion. It was a recognized phenomenon, even Max Mainz knew—this desire on the part of women Telly fans to date a man, and then watch him later, killing or being killed.

"Time enough to wear your fancy uniform," Joe Mauser growled at him. "In fact, tomorrow's a local election day. Parlay that up on top of all the fracas fans gravitating into town and you'll have a wingding the likes of nothing you've seen before."

"Well, yessir," Max begrudged. "Where're we going now, captain?"

"To the airport. Come along."

Joe Mauser led the way to his sports hovercar and as soon as the two were settled into the bucket seats, hit the lift lever with the butt of his left hand. Aircushion-borne, he tread down on the accelerator.

Max Mainz was impressed. "You know," he said. "I never been in one of these swanky sports jobs before. The kinda car you can afford on the income of a Mid-Lower's stock aren't—"

"Knock it off," Joe said wearily. "Carping we'll always have with us evidently, but in spite of all the beefing in every strata from Low-Lower to Upper-Middle, I've yet to see any signs of organized protest against our present politico-economic system."

"Hey," Max said. "Don't get me wrong. What was good enough for Dad is good enough for me. You won't catch me talking against the government."

"Hm-m-m," Joe murmured. "And all the other cliches taught to us to preserve the status quo, our People's Capitalism." They were reaching the outskirts of town, crossing the Esopus. The airport lay only a mile or so beyond.

It was obviously too deep for Max, and since he didn't understand, he assumed his superior didn't know what he was talking about. He said, tolerantly, "Well, what's wrong with People's Capitalism? Everybody owns the corporations. Damnsight better than the Sovs have."

Joe said sourly. "We've got one optical illusion, they've got another, Max. Over there they claim the proletariat owns the means of production. Great. But the Party members are the ones who control it, and, as a result they manage to do all right for themselves. The Party hierarchy over there are like our Uppers over here."

"Yeah." Max was being particularly dense. "I've seen a lot about it on Telly. You know, when there isn't a good fracas on, you tune to one of them educational shows, like—"

Joe winced at the term *educational,* but held his peace.

"It's pretty rugged over there. But in the West-world, the people own a corporation's stock and they run it and get the benefit."

"At least it makes a beautiful story," Joe said dryly. "Look, Max. Suppose you have a corporation that has two hundred thousand shares out and they're distributed among one hundred thousand and one persons. One hundred thousand of these own one share apiece, but the remaining stockholder owns the other hundred thousand."

"I don't know what you're getting at," Max said.

Joe Mauser was tired of the discussion. "Briefly," he said, "we have the illusion that this is a People's Capitalism, with all stock in the hands of the People. Actually, as ever before, the stock is in the hands of the Uppers, all except a mere dribble. They own the country and they run it for their own benefit."

Max shot a less than military glance at him. "Hey, you're not one of these Sovs yourself, are you?"

They were coming into the parking area near the Administration Building of the airport. "No," Joe said so softly that Max could hardly hear his words. "Only a Mid-Middle on the make."

Followed by Max, he strode quickly to the Administration Building, presented his credit identification at the desk and requested a light aircraft for a period of three hours. The clerk, hardly looking up, began going through motions, speaking into telescreens.

The clerk said finally, "You might have a small wait, sir. Quite a few of the officers involved in this fracas have been renting out taxi-planes almost as fast as they're available."

That didn't surprise Joe Mauser. Any competent officer made a point of an aerial survey of the battle reservation before going into a fracas. Aircraft, of course, couldn't be used *during* the fray, since they postdated the turn of the century, and hence were relegated to the cemetery of military devices along with such items as nuclear weapons, tanks, and even gasoline-propelled vehicles of size to be useful.

Use an aircraft in a fracas, or even *build* an aircraft for military usage, and you'd have a howl go up from the military attachés from the Sov-world that would be heard all the way to Budapest. Not a fracas went by but there were scores, if not hundreds, of military observers, keen-eyed to check whether or not any really modern tools of war were being illegally utilized. Joe Mauser sometimes wondered if the West-world observers, over in the Sov-world, were as hair-fine in their living up to the rules of the Universal Disarmament Pact. Probably. But, for that matter, they didn't have the same system of fighting fracases over there as in the West.

Max took a chair while he waited and thumbed through a fan magazine. From time to time he found his own face in such publications. He was a third-rate celebrity, really. Luck hadn't been with him so far as the buffs were concerned. They wanted spectacular victories, murderous situations in which they could lose themselves in vicarious sadistic thrills. Joe had reached most of his peaks while in retreat, or commanding a holding action. His officers appreciated him and so did the ultra-knowledgable fracas buffs—but he was all but an unknown to the average dimwit who spent most of his life glued to the Telly set, watching men butcher each other.

On the various occasions when matters had pickled and Joe had to fight his way out against difficult odds, using spectacular tactics in desperation, he was almost always off camera. Purely luck. On top of skill, determination, experience and courage, you had to have luck in the Military Category to get anywhere.

This time Joe was going to manufacture his own.

A voice said, "Ah, Captain Mauser."

Joe looked up, then came to his feet quickly. In automatic reflex, he began to come to the salute but then caught himself. He said stiffly, "My compliments, Marshal Cogswell."

The other was a smallish man, but strikingly strong of face and strongly built. His voice was clipped, clear and had the air of command as though born with it. He, like Joe, wore mufti and now extended his hand to be shaken.

"I hear you've signed up with Baron Haer, captain. I was rather expecting you to come in with me. Had a place for a good aide de camp. Liked your work in that last fracas we went through together."

"Thank you, sir," Joe said. Stonewall Cogswell was as good a tactician as freelanced, and he was more than that. He was a judge of men and a stickler for detail. And right now, if Joe Mauser knew Marshal Stonewall Cogswell as well as he thought, Cogswell was smelling a rat. There was no reason why old pro Joe Mauser should sign up with a sure loser like Vacuum Tube when he could have earned more shares taking a commission with Hovercraft.

He was looking at Joe brightly, the question in his eyes. Three or four of his staff were behind a few paces, looking polite, but Cogswell didn't bring them into the conversation. Joe knew most by sight. Good men all. Old pros all. He felt another twinge of doubt.

Joe had to cover. He said, "I was offered a particularly good contract, sir. Too good to resist."

The other nodded, as though inwardly coming to a satisfactory conclusion. "Baron Haer's connections, eh? He's probably offered to back you for a bounce in caste. Is that it, Joe?"

Joe Mauser flushed. Stonewall Cogswell knew what he was talking about. He'd been born into Middle status himself and had become an Upper the hard way. His path wasn't as long as Joe's was going to be, but long enough, and he knew how rocky the climb was. How very rocky.

Joe said stiffly, "I'm afraid I'm in no position to discuss my commander's military contracts, marshal. We're in mufti, but after all—"

Cogswell's lean face registered one of his infrequent grimaces of humor. "I understand, Joe. Well, good luck and I hope things don't pickle for you in the coming fracas. Possibly we'll find ourselves aligned together again at some future time."

"Thank you, sir," Joe said, once more having to catch himself to prevent an automatic salute.

Cogswell and his staff went off, leaving Joe looking after them. Even the marshal's staff members were top men any of whom could have conducted a divisional magnitude fracas. Joe felt the coldness in his stomach again. Although it must have looked like a cinch, the enemy wasn't taking any chances whatsoever. Cogswell and his officers were undoubtedly here at the airport for the same reason as Joe. They wanted a thorough aerial reconnaissance of the battlefield-to-be, before the issue was joined.

Max was standing at his elbow. "Who was that, sir? Looks like a real tough one."

"He is a real tough one," Joe said sourly. "That's Stonewall Cogswell, the best field commander in North America."

Max pursed his lips. "I never seen him out of uniform before. Lots of times on Telly, but never out of uniform. I thought he was taller than that."

"He fights with his brains," Joe said, still looking after the craggy field marshal. "He doesn't have to be any taller."

Max scowled. "Where'd he ever get that nickname, sir?"

"Stonewall?" Joe was turning to resume his chair and magazine. "He's supposed to be a student of a top general back in the American Civil War. Uses some of the original Stonewall's tactics."

Max was out of his depth. "American Civil War? Was that much of a fracas, captain? It musta been before my time."

"It was quite a fracas," Joe said dryly. "Lot of good lads died. A hundred years after it was fought, the *reasons* it was fought seemed about as valid as those we fight fracases for today. Personally I—"

He had to cut it short. They were calling him on the address system. His aircraft was ready. Joe made his way to the hangars, followed by Max Mainz. He was going to pilot the airplane himself and old Stonewall Cogswell would have been surprised at what Joe Mauser was looking for.

V

By the time they had returned to quarters, there was a message waiting for Captain Mauser. He was to report to the officer commanding reconnaissance.

Joe redressed in the Haer kilts and proceeded to headquarters.

The officer commanding reconnaissance turned out to be none other than Balt Haer, natty as ever, and, as ever, arrogantly tapping his swagger stick against his leg.

"Zen! Captain," he complained. "Where have you been? Off on a trank kick? We've got to get organized."

Joe Mauser snapped him a salute. "No, sir. I rented an aircraft to scout out the terrain over which we'll be fighting."

"Indeed. And what were your impressions, captain?" There was an overtone which suggested that it made little difference what impressions a captain of cavalry might have gained.

Joe shrugged. "Largely mountains, hills, woods. Good reconnaissance is going to make the difference in this one. And in the fracas itself cavalry is going to be more important

than either artillery or infantry. A Nathan Forrest fracas,
sir. A matter of getting there fustest with the mostest."

Balt Haer said amusedly, "Thanks for your opinion, captain. Fortunately, our staff has already come largely to the
same conclusions. Undoubtedly, they'll be glad to hear your
wide experience bears them out."

Joe said evenly, "It's a rather obvious conclusion, of course."
He took this as it came, having been through it before. The
dilettante amateur's dislike of the old pro. The amateur in
command who knew full well he was less capable than many
of those below him in rank.

"Of course, captain," Balt Haer flicked his swagger stick
against his leg. "But to the point. Your squadron is to be
deployed as scouts under my overall command. You've had
cavalry experience, I assume."

"Yes, sir. In various fracases over the past fifteen years."

"Very well. Now then, to get to the reason I have summoned you. Yesterday in my father's office you intimated
that you had some grandiose scheme which would bring
victory to the Haer colors. But then, on some thin excuse,
refused to divulge just what the scheme might be."

Joe Mauser looked at him unblinkingly.

Balt Haer said: "Now I'd like to have your opinion on just
how Vacuum Tube Transport can extract itself from what
would seem a poor position at best."

In all there were four others in the office, two women clerks
fluttering away at typers, and two of Balt Haer's junior
officers. They seemed only mildly interested in the conversation between Balt and Joe.

Joe wet his lips carefully. The Haer scion was his commanding officer. He said, "Sir, what I had in mind is a new
gimmick. At this stage, if I told anybody and it leaked, it'd
never be effective, not even this first time."

Haer observed him coldly. "And you think me incapable of
keeping your secret, ah, *gimmick,* I believe is the idiomatic
term you used."

Joe Mauser's eyes shifted around the room, taking in the
other four, who were now looking at him.

Balt Haer rapped, "These members of my staff are all
trusted Haer employees, Captain Mauser. They are not fly-
by-night freelancers hired for a week or two."

Joe said, "Yes, sir. But it's been my experience that one

person can hold a secret. It's twice as hard for two, and from there on it's a decreasing probability in a geometric ratio."

The younger Haer's stick rapped the side of his leg, impatiently. "Suppose I inform you that this is a command, captain? I have little confidence in a supposed gimmick that will rescue our forces from disaster and I rather dislike the idea of a captain of one of my squadrons dashing about with such a bee in his bonnet when he should be obeying my commands."

Joe kept his voice respectful. "Then, sir, I'd request that we take the matter to the Commander in Chief, your father."

"Indeed!"

Joe said, "Sir, I've been working on this a long time. I can't afford to risk throwing the idea away."

Balt Haer glared at him. "Very well, captain. I'll call your bluff. Come along." He turned on his heel and headed from the room.

Joe Mauser shrugged in resignation and followed him.

The old Baron wasn't much happier about Joe Mauser's secrets than was his son. It had only been the day before that he had taken Joe on, but already he had seemed to have aged in appearance. Evidently, each hour that went by made it increasingly clear just how perilous a position he had assumed. Vacuum Tube Transport had elbowed, buffaloed, bluffed and edged itself up to the outskirts of the really big time. The Baron's ability, his aggressiveness, his flair, his political pull, had all helped, but now the chips were down. He was up against one of the biggies, and this particular biggy was tired of ambitious little Vacuum Tube Transport.

He listened to his son's words, listened to Joe's defense.

He said, looking at Joe, "If I understand this, you have some scheme which you think will bring victory in spite of what seems a disastrous situation."

"Yes, sir."

The two Haers looked at him, one impatiently, the other in weariness.

Joe said, "I'm gambling everything on this, sir. I'm no Rank Private in his first fracas. I deserve to be given some leeway."

Balt Haer snorted. "Gambling everything! What in Zen would *you* have to gamble, captain? The whole Haer family fortunes are tied up. Hovercraft is out for blood. They won't be satisfied with a token victory and a negotiated compromise. They'll devastate us. Thousands of mercenaries killed, with all that means in indemnities; millions upon millions in expensive military equipment, most of which we've had to hire and will have to recompensate for. Can you imagine the value of our stock after Stonewall Cogswell has finished with us? Why, every two-by-four trucking outfit in North America will be challenging us, and we won't have the forces to meet a minor skirmish."

Joe reached into an inner pocket and laid a sheaf of documents on the desk of Baron Malcolm Haer. The Baron scowled down at them.

Joe said simply, "I've been accumulating stock since before I was eighteen and I've taken good care of my portfolio in spite of taxes and the various other pitfalls which make the accumulation of capital practically impossible. Yesterday, I sold all of my portfolio I was legally allowed to sell and converted to Vacuum Tube Transport." He added, dryly, "Getting it at an excellent rate, by the way."

Balt Haer mulled through the papers, unbelievingly. "Zen!" he ejaculated. "The fool really did it. He's sunk a small fortune into our stock."

Baron Haer growled at his son, "You seem considerably more convinced of our defeat than the captain, here. Perhaps I should reverse your positions of command."

His son grunted, but said nothing.

Old Malcolm Haer's eyes came back to Joe. "Admittedly, I thought you on the romantic side yesterday, with your hints of some scheme which would lead us out of the wilderness, so to speak. Now I wonder if you might not really have something. Very well, I respect your claimed need for secrecy. Espionage is not exactly an antiquated military field."

"Thank you, sir."

But the Baron was still staring at him. "However, there's more to it than that. Why not take this great scheme to Marshal Cogswell? And yesterday you mentioned that the Telly sets of the nation would be tuned in on this fracas, and obviously you are correct. The question becomes, what of it?"

The fat was in the fire now. Joe Mauser avoided the haughty stare of young Balt Haer and addressed himself to the older man. "You have political pull, sir. Oh, I know you don't make and break presidents. You couldn't even pull enough wires to keep Hovercraft from making this a divisional magnitude fracas—but you have pull enough for my needs."

Baron Haer leaned back in his chair, his barrellike body causing that article of furniture to creak. He crossed his hands over his stomach. "And what are your needs, Captain Mauser?"

Joe said evenly, "If I can bring this off, I'll be a fracas buff celebrity. I don't have any illusions about the fickleness of the Telly fans, but for a day or two I'll be on top. If at the same time I had your all-out support, pulling what strings you could reach—"

"Why then, you'd be promoted to Upper, wouldn't you, captain?" Balt Haer finished for him, amusement in his voice.

"That's what I'm gambling on," Joe said evenly.

The younger Haer grinned at his father superciliously. "So our captain says he will defeat Stonewall Cogswell in return for your sponsoring his becoming a member of the nation's elite."

"Good Heavens, is the supposed cream of the nation now selected on no higher a level than this?" There was sarcasm in the words.

The three men turned. It was the girl Joe had bumped into the day before. The Haers didn't seem surprised at her entrance.

"Nadine," the older man growled. "Captain Joseph Mauser, who has been given a commission in our forces."

Joe went through the routine of a Middle of officer's rank being introduced to a lady of Upper caste. She smiled at him, somewhat mockingly, and failed to make standard response.

Nadine Haer said, "I repeat, what is this service the captain can render the house of Haer so important that pressure should be brought to raise him to Upper caste? It would seem unlikely that he is a noted scientist, an outstanding artist, a great teacher—"

Joe said, uncomfortably, "They say the military is a science, too."

Her expression was almost as haughty as that of her brother. "Do they? I have never thought so."

"Really, Nadine," her father grumbled. "This is hardly your affair."

"No? In a few days I shall be repairing the damage you

have allowed, indeed sponsored, to be committed upon the bodies of possibly thousands of now healthy human beings."

Balt said nastily, "Nobody asked you to join the medical staff, Nadine. You could have stayed in your laboratory, figuring out new methods of preventing the human race from replenishing itself."

The girl was obviously not the type to redden, but her anger was manifest. She spun on her brother. "If the race continues its present maniac course, possibly more effective methods of birth control *are* the most important development we could make. Even to the ultimate discovery of preventing all future conception."

Joe caught himself in mid-chuckle.

But not in time. She spun on him in his turn. "Look at yourself in that silly skirt. A professional soldier! A killer! In my opinion the most useless occupation ever devised by man. Parasite on the best and useful members of society. Destroyer by trade!"

Joe began to open his mouth, but she overrode him. "Yes, yes. I know. I've read all the nonsense that has accumulated down through the ages about the need for, the glory of, the sacrifice of the professional soldier. How they defend their country. How they give all for the common good. Zen! What nonsense."

Balt Haer was smirking sourly at her. "The theory today is, Nadine, old thing, that professionals such as the captain are gathering experience in case a serious fracas with the Sovs ever develops. Meanwhile his training is kept at a fine edge fighting in our inter-corporation, inter-union, or union-corporation fracases that develop in our private enterprise society."

She laughed her scorn. "And what a theory! Limited to the weapons which prevailed before 1900. If there was ever real conflict between the Sov-world and our own, does anyone really believe either would stick to such arms? Why, aircraft, armored vehicles, yes, and nuclear weapons and rockets, would be in overnight use."

Joe was fascinated by her furious attack. He said, "Then, what would you say was the purpose of the fracases, Miss—"

"Circuses," she snorted. "The old Roman games, all over again, and a hundred times worse. Blood-and-guts sadism. The quest of a frustrated person for satisfaction in another's pain. Our Lowers of today are as useless and frustrated as the Roman proletariat, and potentially they're just as dangerous as the mob that once dominated Rome. Automation, the second industrial revolution, has eliminated for all practical purposes the need for their labor. So we give them bread and circuses. And every year that goes by the circuses must be increasingly sadistic, death on an increasing scale, or they aren't satisfied. Once it was enough to have fictional mayhem, cowboys and Indians, gangsters, or G.I.s versus the Nazis, Japs or Commies, but that's passed. Now we need *real* blood and guts."

Baron Haer snapped finally, "All right, Nadine. We've heard this lecture before. I doubt if the captain is interested, particularly since you don't seem to be able to get beyond the protesting stage and have yet to come up with an answer."

"I have an answer!"

"Ah?" Balt Haer raised his eyebrows, mockingly.

"Yes! Overthrow this silly status society. Resume the road to progress. Put our people to useful endeavor, instead of sitting in front of their Telly sets, taking trank pills to put them in a happy daze and watching sadistic fracases to keep them in thrills, and their minds from their condition."

Joe had figured on keeping out of the controversy with this firebrand, but now, really interested, he said, "Progress to where?"

She must have caught in his tone that he wasn't needling. She frowned at him. "I don't know man's goal, if there is one. I'm not even sure it's important. It's the road that counts. The endeavor. The dream. The effort expended to make a world a better place than it was at the time of your birth."

Balt Haer said mockingly, "That's the trouble with you, Sis. Here we've reached Utopia and you don't admit it."

"Utopia!"

"Certainly. Take a poll. You'll find nineteen people out of twenty happy with things just the way they are. They have full tummies and security, lots of leisure and trank pills to make matters seem even rosier than they are—and they're rather rosy already."

"Then what's the necessity of this endless succession of bloody fracases, covered to the most minute bloody detail on the Telly?"

Baron Haer cut things short. "We've hashed and rehashed

this before, Nadine, and now we're too busy to debate further." He turned to Joe Mauser. "Very well, captain, you have my pledge. I wish I felt as optimistic as you seem to be about your prospects. That will be all for now, captain."

Joe saluted and executed an about-face.

In the outer offices, when he had closed the door behind him, he rolled his eyes upward in mute thanks to whatever powers might be. He had somehow gained the enmity of Balt, his immediate superior, but he'd also gained the support of Baron Haer himself, which counted considerably more.

He considered, for a moment, Nadine Haer's words. She was obviously a malcontent, but, on the other hand, her opinions of his chosen profession weren't too different than his own. However, given this victory, this upgrading in caste, and Joe Mauser would be in a position to retire.

The door opened and shut behind him, and he half turned.

Nadine Haer, evidently still caught up in the hot words between herself and her relatives, glared at him. All of which stressed the beauty he had noticed the day before. She was an almost unbelievably pretty girl, particularly when flushed with anger.

It occurred to him with a blowlike suddenness that, if his caste was raised to Upper, he would be in a position to woo such as Nadine Haer.

He looked into her furious face and said, "I was intrigued, Miss Haer, with what you had to say, and I'd like to discuss some of your points. I wonder if I could have the pleasure of your company at some nearby refreshment—"

"My, how formal an invitation, captain. I suppose you had in mind sitting and flipping back a few trank pills."

Joe looked at her. "I don't believe I've had a trank in the past twenty years, Miss Haer. Even as a boy, I didn't particularly take to having my senses dulled with drug-induced pleasure."

Some of her fury was abating, but she was still critical of the professional mercenary. Her eyes went up and down his uniform in scorn. "You seem to make pretenses of being cultivated, captain. Then why your chosen profession?"

He'd had the answer to that for long years. He said now, simply, "I told you I was born a Lower. Given that, little counts until I fight my way out of it. Had I been born in a feudal society, I would have attempted to batter myself into the nobility. Under classical capitalism, I would have done my utmost to accumulate a fortune, enough to reach an effective position in society. Now, under People's Capitalism . . ."

She snorted. "Industrial Feudalism would be the better term."

". . . I realize I can't even start to fulfill myself until I am a member of the Upper caste."

Her eyes had narrowed, and the anger was largely gone. "But you chose the military field in which to better yourself?"

"Government propaganda to the contrary, it is practically impossible to raise yourself in other fields. I didn't build this world, possibly I don't even approve of it, but since I'm in it I have no recourse but to follow its rules."

Her eyebrows arched. "Why not try to change the rules?"

Joe blinked at her.

Nadine Haer said, "Let's look up that refreshment you were talking about. In fact, there's a small coffee bar around the corner where it'd be possible for one of Baron Haer's brood to have a cup with one of her father's officers of Middle caste."

VI

The following morning, hands on the pillow beneath his head, Joe Mauser stared up at the ceiling of his room and rehashed his session with Nadine Haer. It hadn't taken him five minutes to come to the conclusion that he was in love with the girl, but it had taken him the rest of the evening to keep himself under rein and not let the fact get through to her.

He wanted to talk about the way her mouth tucked in at the corners, but she was hot on the evolution of society. He would have liked to have kissed that impossibly perfectly shaped ear of hers, but she was all for exploring the reasons why man had reached his present impasse. Joe was for holding hands, and staring into each other's eyes, she was for delving into the differences between the West-world and the Sov-world and the possibility of resolving them.

Of course, to keep her company at all it had been necessary to suppress his own desires and to go along. It obviously had never occurred to her that a Middle might have romantic ideas involving Nadine Haer. It had simply not occurred to her, no matter the radical teachings she advocated.

Most of their world was predictable from what had gone before. In spite of popular fable to the contrary, the division between classes had become increasingly clear. Among other things, tax systems were such that it became all but impossible for a citizen born poor to accumulate a fortune. Through ability he might rise to the point of earning fabulous sums—and wind up in debt to the tax collector. A great inventor, a great artist, had little chance of breaking into the domain of what finally became the small percentage of the population now known as Uppers. Then, too, the rising cost of a really good education became such that few other than those born into the Middle or Upper castes could afford the best of schools. Castes tended to perpetuate themselves.

Politically, the nation had fallen increasingly deeper into the two-party system, both parties of which were tightly controlled by the same group of Uppers. Elections had become a farce, a great national holiday in which stereotyped patriotic speeches, pretenses of unity between all castes, picnics, beer busts and trank binges predominated for one day.

Economically, too, the augurs had been there. Production of the basics had become so profuse that poverty in the old sense of the word had become nonsensical. There was an abundance of the necessities of life for all. Social security, socialized medicine, unending unemployment insurance, old age pensions, pensions for veterans, for widows and children, for the unfit, pensions and doles for this, that and the other, had doubled, and doubled again, until everyone had security for life. The Uppers, true enough, had opulence far beyond that known by the Middles and lived like gods compared to the Lowers. But all had security.

They had agreed, thus far, Joe and Nadine. But then had come debate.

"Then why," Joe had asked her, "haven't we achieved what your brother called it? Why isn't this Utopia? Isn't it what man has been yearning for, down through the ages? Where did the wheel come off? What happened to the dream?"

Nadine had frowned at him—beautifully, he thought. "It's not the first time man has found abundance in a society, though never to this degree. The Incas had it, for instance."

"I don't know much about them," Joe admitted. "An early form of communism with a sort of military-priesthood at the top."

She had nodded, her face serious, as always. "And for themselves, the Romans more or less had it—at the expense of the nations they conquered, of course."

"And—" Joe prodded.

"And in these examples the same thing developed. Society ossified. Joe," she said, using his first name for the first time, and in a manner that set off a new count down in his blood, "a ruling caste and a socioeconomic system perpetuates itself, just so long as it ever can. No matter what damage it may do to society as a whole, it perpetuates itself even to the point of complete destruction of everything.

"Remember Hitler? Adolf the Aryan and his Thousand Year Reich? When it became obvious he had failed, and the only thing that could result from continued resistance would be destruction of Germany's cities and millions of her people, did he and his clique resign or surrender? Certainly not. They attempted to bring down the whole German structure in a Götterdämmerung."

Nadine Haer was deep into her theme, her eyes flashing her conviction. "A socioeconomic system reacts like a living organism. It attempts to live on, indefinitely, agonizingly, no matter how antiquated it might have become. The Roman politico-economic system continued for centuries after it should have been replaced. Such reformers as the Gracchus brothers were assassinated or thrust aside so that the entrenched elements could perpetuate themselves, and when Rome finally fell, darkness descended for a thousand years on Western progress."

Joe had never gone this far in his thoughts. He said now, somewhat uncomfortably, "Well, what would replace what we have now? If you took power from you Uppers, who could direct the country? The Lowers? That's not even funny. Take away their fracases and their trank pills and they'd go berserk. They don't *want* anything else."

Her mouth worked. "Admittedly, we've already allowed things to deteriorate much too far. We should have done something long ago. I'm not sure I know the answer. All I know is that in order to maintain the status quo, we're not utilizing the efforts of more than a fraction of our people. Nine out of ten of us spend our lives sitting before the Telly, sucking tranks. Meanwhile, the motivation for continued progress seems to have withered away. Our Upper political

circles are afraid some seemingly minor change might ava-
lanche, so more and more we lean upon the old way of doing
things."

Joe had put up mild argument. "I've heard the case made
that the Lowers are fools and the reason our present socioeconomic system makes it so difficult to rise from Lower to
Upper is that you cannot make a fool understand he is one.
You can only make him angry. If some, who are not fools, are
allowed to advance from Lower to Upper, the vast mass who
are fools will be angry because they are not allowed to. That's
why the Military Category is made a channel of advance. To
take that road, a man gives up his security, and he'll die if
he's a fool."

Nadine had been scornful. "That reminds me of the old
contention by racial segregationalists that the Negroes *smelled*
bad. First they put them in a position where they had
insufficient bathing facilities, their diet inadequate, and their
teeth uncared for, and then protested that they couldn't be
associated with because of their odor. Today, we are born
within our castes. If an Upper is inadequate, he nevertheless
remains an Upper. An accident of birth makes him an aristocrat; environment, family, training, education, friends, traditions and laws maintain him in that position. But a Lower
who potentially has the greatest of value to society, is born
handicapped and he's hard put not to wind up before a Telly,
in a mental daze from trank. Sure he's a fool, he's never been
allowed to develop himself."

Yes, Joe reflected now, it had been quite an evening. In a
life of more than thirty years devoted to rebellion, he had
never met anyone so outspoken as Nadine Haer, nor one who
had thought it through as far as she had.

He grunted. His own revolt was against the level at which
he had found himself in society, not the structure of society
itself. His whole *raison d'être* was to lift himself to Upper
status. It came as a shock to him to find a person he admired
who had been born into Upper caste, desirous of tearing the
whole system down.

His thoughts were interrupted by the door opening and the
face of Max Mainz grinning in at him. Joe was mildly
surprised at his orderly's not knocking before opening the
door. Max evidently had a lot to learn.

The little man blurted, "Come on, Joe. Let's go out on the town!"

"*Joe?*" Joe Mauser raised himself to one elbow and stared at the other. "Leaving aside the merits of your suggestion for the moment, do you think you should address an officer by his first name?"

Max Mainz came fully into the bedroom, his grin still wider. "You forgot! It's election day!"

"Oh." Joe Mauser relaxed into his pillow. "So it is. No duty for today, eh?"

"No duty for anybody," Max crowed. "What'd you say we go into town and have a few drinks in one of the Upper bars?"

Joe grunted, but began to arise. "What'll that accomplish? On election day, most of the Uppers get done up in their oldest clothes and go slumming down in the Lower quarters."

Max wasn't to be put off so easily. "Well, wherever we go, let's get going. Zen! I'll bet this town is full of fracas buffs from as far as Philly. And on election day, to boot. Wouldn't it be something if I found me a real fracas fan, some Upper-Upper dame?"

Joe laughed at him, even as he headed for the bathroom. As a matter of fact, he rather liked the idea of going into town for the show. "Max," he said over his shoulder, "you're in for a big disappointment. They're all the same. Upper, Lower, or Middle."

"Yeah?" Max grinned back at him. "Well, I'd like the pleasure of finding out if that's true by personal experience."

VII

In a faraway past, Kingston had once been the capital of the United States. For a short time, when Washington's men were in flight after the debacle of their defeat in New York City, the government of the United Colonies had held session in this Hudson River town. It had been its one moment of historic glory, and afterward Kingston had slipped back into being a minor city on the edge of the Catskills, approximately halfway between New York and Albany.

Of most recent years, it had become one of the two recruiting centers which bordered the Catskill Military Reservation, which in turn was one of the score or so population-cleared areas throughout the continent where rival corporations or unions could meet and settle their differences in combat—

given permission of the Military Category Department of the government. And permission was becoming ever easier to acquire.

It had slowly evolved, the resorting to trial by combat to settle disputes between competing corporations, disputes between corporations and unions, disputes between unions over jurisdiction. Slowly, but predictably. Since the earliest days of the first industrial revolution, conflict between these elements had often broken into violence, sometimes on a scale comparable to minor warfare. An early example was the union organizing in Colorado when armed elements of the Western Federation of Miners shot it out with similarly armed "detectives" hired by the mine owners, and later with the troops of an unsympathetic State government.

By the middle of the Twentieth Century, unions had become one of the biggest businesses in the country, and by this time a considerable amount of the industrial conflict had shifted to fights between them for jurisdiction over dues-paying members. Battles on the waterfront, assassination and counter-assassination by gun-toting goon squads dominated by gangsters, industrial sabotage, frays between pickets and scabs—all were common occurrences.

But it was the coming of Telly which increasingly brought such conflicts literally before the public eye. Zealous reporters made ever greater effort to bring the actual mayhem before the eyes of their viewers, and never were their efforts more highly rewarded.

A society based upon private endeavor is as jealous of a vacuum as is mother nature. Give a desire that can be filled profitably, and the means can somehow be found to realize it.

At one point in the nation's history, the railroad lords had dominated the economy, later it became the petroleum princes of Texas and elsewhere, but toward the end of the Twentieth Century the communications industries slowly gained prominence. Nothing was more greatly in demand than feeding the insatiable maw of the Telly fan; nothing, ultimately, became more profitable.

And increasingly, the Telly buff endorsed the more sadistic of the fictional and nonfictional programs presented him. Even in the earliest years of the industry, producers had found that murder and mayhem, war and frontier gunfights, took precedence over less gruesome subjects. Music was drowned out by gunfire, the dance replaced by the shuffle of cowboy and rustler advancing down a dusty street toward each other, their fingertips brushing the grips of their six-shooters, the comedian's banter fell away before the chatter of the gangster's tommy gun.

And increasing realism was demanded. The Telly reporter on the scene of a police arrest, preferably a murder, a rumble between rival gangs of juvenile delinquents, a longshoreman's fray in which scores of workers were hospitalized. When attempts were made to suppress such broadcasts, the howl of freedom of speech and the press went up, financed by tycoons clever enough to realize the value of the subjects they covered so adequately.

The vacuum was there, the desire, the *need*. Bread the populace had. Trank was available to all. But the need was for the circus, the vicious, sadistic circus, and bit by bit, over the years and decades, the way was found to circumvent the country's laws and traditions to supply the need.

Aye, a way is always found. The final Universal Disarmament Pact which had totally banned all weapons invented since the year 1900 and provided for complete inspection, had not ended the fear of war. And thus there was excuse to give the would-be soldier, the potential defender of the country in some future internation conflict, practical experience.

Slowly tolerance grew to allow union and corporation to fight it out, hiring the services of mercenaries. Slowly rules grew up to govern such fracases. Slowly a department of government evolved. The Military Category became as acceptable as the next, and the mercenary a valued, even idolized, member of society. And the field became practically the only one in which a status-quo-orientated socioeconomic system allowed for advancement in caste.

Joe Mauser and Max Mainz strolled the streets of Kingston in an extreme of atmosphere seldom to be enjoyed. Not only was the advent of a divisional magnitude fracas only a short period away, but the freedom of an election day as well. The carnival, the Mardi Gras, the fete, the fiesta, of an election. Election day, when each aristocrat became only a man, and each man an aristocrat, free of all society's artificially conceived, caste perpetuating rituals and taboos.

Carnival! The day was young, but already the streets were thick with revelers, with dancers, with drunks. A score of bands played, youngsters in particular ran about attired in costume, there were barbecues and flowing beer kegs. On the outskirts of town were roller coasters and ferris wheels, fun houses and drive-it-yourself miniature cars. Carnival!

Max said happily, "You drink, Joe? Or maybe you like trank, better." Obviously, he loved to roll the other's first name over his tongue.

Joe wondered in amusement how often the little man had found occasion to call a Mid-Middle by his first name. "No trank," he said. "Alcohol for me. Mankind's old faithful."

"Well," Max debated, "get high on alcohol and bingo, a hangover in the morning. But trank? You wake up with a smile."

"And a desire for more trank to keep the mood going," Joe said wryly. "Get smashed on alcohol and you suffer for it eventually."

"Well, that's one way of looking at it," Max argued happily. "So let's start off with a couple of quick ones in this here Upper joint."

Joe looked the place over. He didn't know Kingston overly well, but by the appearance of the building and by the entry, it was probably the swankiest hotel in town. He shrugged. So far as he was concerned, he appreciated the greater comfort and the better service of his Middle caste bars, restaurants and hotels over the ones he had patronized when a Lower. However, his wasn't an immediate desire to push into the preserves of the Uppers; not until he had won rightfully to their status.

But on this occasion the little fellow wanted to drink at an Upper bar. Very well, it was election day. "Let's go," he said to Max.

In the uniform of a Rank Captain of the Military Category, there was little to indicate caste level, and ordinarily given the correct air of nonchalance, Joe Mauser, in uniform, would have been able to go anywhere, without so much as a raised eyebrow—until he had presented his credit card, which indicated his caste. But Max was another thing. He was obviously a Lower, and probably a Low-Lower at that.

But space was made for them at a bar packed with election day celebrants, politicians involved in the day's speeches and voting, higher ranking officers of the Haer forces, having a day off, and various Uppers of both sexes in town for the excitement of the fracas to come.

"Beer," Joe said to the bartender.

"Not me," Max crowed. "Champagne. Only the best for Max Mainz. Give me some of that champagne liquor I always been hearing about."

Joe had the bill credited to his card, and they took their bottles and glasses to a newly abandoned table. The place was too packed to have awaited the services of a waiter, although poor Max probably would have loved such attention. Lower and even Middle bars and restaurants were universally automated, and the waiter or waitress a thing of yesteryear.

Max looked about the room in awe. "This is living," he announced. "I wonder what they'd say if I went to the desk and ordered a room."

Joe Mauser wasn't as highly impressed as his batman. In fact, he'd often stayed in the larger cities in hostelries as sumptuous as this, though only of Middle status. Kingston's best was on the mediocre side. He said, "They'd probably tell you they were filled up."

Max was indignant. "Because I'm a Lower? It's *election* day."

Joe said mildly, "Because they probably are filled up. But for that matter, they might brush you off. It's not as though an Upper went to a Middle or Lower hotel and asked for accommodations. But what do you want, justice?"

Max dropped it. He looked down into his glass. "Hey," he complained, "what'd they give me? This stuff tastes like weak hard cider."

Joe laughed. "What did you think it was going to taste like?"

Max took another unhappy sip. "I thought it was supposed to be the best drink you could buy. You know, really strong. It's just bubbly wine."

A voice said, dryly, "Your companion doesn't seem to be a connoisseur of the French vintages, captain."

Joe turned. Balt Haer and two others occupied the table next to them.

Joe chuckled amiably and said, "Truthfully, it was my own reaction, the first time I drank sparkling wine, sir."

"Indeed," Haer said. "I can imagine." He fluttered a hand. "Lieutenant Colonel Paul Warren of Marshal Cogswell's staff, and Colonel Lajos Arpàd, of Budapest—Captain Joseph Mauser."

Joe Mauser came to his feet and clicked his heels, bowing

from the waist in approved military protocol. The other two didn't bother to come to their feet, but did condescend to shake hands.

The Sov officer said, disinterestedly, "Ah yes, this is one of your fabulous customs, isn't it? On an election day, everyone is quite entitled to go anywhere. Anywhere at all. And, ah"—he made a sound somewhat like a giggle—"associate with anyone at all."

Joe Mauser resumed his seat, then looked at him. "That is correct. A custom going back to the early history of the country when all men were considered equal in such matters as law and civil rights. Gentlemen, may I present Rank Private Max Mainz, my orderly."

Balt Haer, who had obviously already had a few, looked at him dourly. "You can carry these things to the point of the ludicrous, captain. For a man with your ambitions, I'm surprised."

The infantry officer the younger Haer had introduced as Lieutenant Colonel Warren, of Stonewall Cogswell's staff, said idly, "Ambitions? Does the captain have ambitions? How in Zen can a Middle have ambitions, Balt?" He stared at Joe Mauser superciliously, but then scowled. "Haven't I seen you somewhere before?"

Joe said evenly, "Yes, sir. Five years ago we were both with the marshal in a fracas on the Little Big Horn reservation. Your company was pinned down on a knoll by a battery of field artillery. The marshal sent me to your relief. We sneaked in, up an arroyo, and were able to get most of you out."

"I was wounded," the colonel said, the superciliousness gone and a strange element in his voice above the alcohol there earlier.

Joe Mauser said nothing to that. Max Mainz was stirring unhappily now. These officers were talking above his head, even as they ignored him. He had a vague feeling that he was being defended by Captain Mauser, but he didn't know how, or why.

Balt Haer had been occupied in shouting fresh drinks. Now he turned back to the table. "Well, colonel, it's all very secret, these ambitions of Captain Mauser. I understand he's been an aide de camp to Marshal Cogswell in the past, but the marshal will be distressed to learn that on this occasion Captain Mauser has a secret by which he expects to rout your forces. Indeed, yes, the captain is quite the strategist." Balt

Haer laughed abruptly. "And what good will this do the captain? Why on my father's word, if he succeeds, all efforts will be made to make the captain a caste equal of ours. Not just on election day, mind you, but all three hundred sixty-five days of the year."

Joe Mauser was on his feet, his face expressionless. He said, "Shall we go, Max? Gentlemen, it's been a pleasure. Colonel Arpàd, a privilege to meet you. Colonel Warren, a pleasure to renew acquaintance." Joe Mauser turned and, trailed by his orderly, left.

Lieutenant Colonel Warren, pale, was on his feet too.

Balt Haer was chuckling. "Sit down, Paul. Sit down. Not important enough to be angry about. The man's a clod."

Warren looked at him bleakly. "I wasn't angry, Balt. The last time I saw Captain Mauser I was slung over his shoulder. He carried, tugged and dragged me some two miles through enemy fire."

Balt Haer carried it off with a shrug. "Well, that's his profession. Category Military. A mercenary for hire. I assume he received his pay."

"He could have left me. Common sense dictated that he leave me."

Balt Haer was annoyed. "Well, then we see what I've contended all along. The ambitious captain doesn't have common sense."

Colonel Paul Warren shook his head. "You're wrong there. Common sense Joseph Mauser has. Considerable ability, he has. He's one of the best combat men in the field. But I'd hate to serve under him."

The Hungarian was interested. "But why?"

"Because he doesn't have luck, and in the dill you need luck." Warren grunted in sour memory. "Had the Telly cameras been focused on Joe Mauser, there at the Little Big Horn, he would have been a month-long sensation to the Telly buffs, with all that means." He grunted again. "There wasn't a Telly team within a mile."

"The captain probably didn't realize that," Balt Haer snorted. "Otherwise his heroics would have been modified."

Warren flushed his displeasure and sat down . He said, "Possibly we should discuss the business before us. If your father is in agreement, the fracas can begin in three days." He turned to the representative of the Sov-world. "You have satisfied yourselves that neither force is violating the Disarmament Pact?"

Lajos Arpàd nodded. "We will wish to have observers on the field, itself, of course. But preliminary observation has been satisfactory." He had been interested in the play between these two and the lower caste officer. He said now, "Pardon me. As you know, this is my first visit to the, uh, *West*. I am fascinated. If I understand what just transpired, our Captain Mauser is a capable junior officer ambitious to rise in rank and status in your society." He looked at Balt Haer. "Why are you opposed to his so rising?"

Young Haer was testy about the whole matter. "Of what purpose is an Upper caste if every Tom, Dick and Harry enters it at will?"

Warren looked at the door through which Joe and Max had exited from the cocktail lounge. He opened his mouth to say something, closed it again, and held his peace.

The Hungarian said, looking from one of them to the other, "In the Sov-world we seek out such ambitious persons and utilize their abilities."

Lieutenant Colonel Warren laughed abruptly. "So do we here, *theoretically*. We are *free*, whatever that means. However," he added sarcastically, "it does help to have good schooling, good connections, relatives in positions of prominence, abundant shares of good stocks, that sort of thing. And these one is born with, in this free world of ours, Colonel Arpàd."

The Sov military observer clucked his tongue. "An indication of a declining society."

Balt Haer turned on him. "And is it any different in your world?" he said sneeringly. "Is it merely coincidence that the best positions in the Sov-world are held by Party members, and that it is all but impossible for anyone not born of Party member parents to become one? Are not the best schools filled with the children of Party members? Are not only Party members allowed to keep servants? And isn't it so that—"

Lieutenant Colonel Warren said, "Gentlemen, let us not start World War Three at this spot, at this late occasion."

VIII

Baron Malcolm Haer's field headquarters were in the ruins of a farmhouse in a town once known as Bearsville. His forces, and those of Marshal Stonewall Cogswell, were on the march but as yet their main bodies had not come in contact. Save for skirmishes between cavalry units, there had been no action. The ruined farmhouse had been a victim of an earlier fracas in this reservation, which had seen in its comparatively brief time more combat than Belgium, that cockpit of Europe.

There was a sheen of oily moisture on the Baron's bulletlike head, and his officers weren't particularly happy about it. Malcolm Haer characteristically went into a fracas with confidence, an aggressive confidence so strong that it often carried the day. In battles past, it had become a tradition that Haer's morale was worth a thousand men; the energy he expended was the despair of his doctors, who had been warning him for a decade. But now, something was missing.

A forefinger traced over the military chart before them. "So far as we know, Marshal Cogswell has established his command here in Saugerties. Anybody have any suggestions as to why?"

A major grumbled, "It doesn't make much sense, sir. You know the marshal. It's probably a fake. If we have any superiority at all, it's our artillery."

"And the old fox wouldn't want to join the issue on the plains, down near the river," a colonel added. "It's his game to keep up into the mountains with his cavalry and light infantry. He's got Jack Alshuler's cavalry. Most experienced veterans in the field."

"I know who he's got," Haer growled in irritation. "Stop reminding me. Where in the devil is Balt?"

"Coming up, sir," Balt Haer said. He had entered only moments ago, a sheaf of signals in his hand. "Why didn't they make that date 1910, instead of 1900? With radio, we could speed up communications—"

His father interrupted testily. "Better still, why not make it 1945? Then we could speed up to the point where we could polish ourselves off. What have you got?"

Balt Haer said, his face in sulk, "Some of my lads based in West Hurley report concentrations of Cogswell's infantry and artillery near Ashokan reservoir."

"Nonsense," somebody snapped. "We'd have him."

The younger Haer slapped his swagger stick against his bare leg and kilt. "Possibly it's a feint," he admitted.

"How much were they able to observe?" his father demanded.

"Not much. They were driven off by a superior squadron. The Hovercraft forces are screening everything they do with heavy cavalry units. I told you we needed more—"

"I don't need your advice at this point," his father snapped. The older Haer went back to the map, scowling still. "I don't see what he expects to do, working out of Saugerties."

A voice behind them said, "Sir, may I have your permission—"

Half of the assembled officers turned to look at the newcomer.

Balt Haer snapped, "Captain Mauser. Why aren't you with your lads?"

"Turned them over to my second in command, sir," Joe Mauser said. He was standing to attention, looking at Baron Haer.

The Baron glowered at him. "What is the meaning of this cavalier intrusion, captain? Certainly you must have your orders. Are you under the illusion that you are part of my staff?"

"No, sir," Joe Mauser clipped. "I came to report that I am ready to put into execution—"

"The great plan!" Balt Haer ejaculated. He laughed brittlely. "The second day of the fracas, and nobody really knows where old Cogswell is, or what he plans to do. And here comes the captain with his secret plan."

Joe looked at him. He said evenly, "Yes, sir."

The Baron's face had gone dark, as much in anger at his son as with the upstart cavalry captain. He began to growl ominously, "Captain Mauser, rejoin your command and obey your orders."

Joe Mauser's facial expression indicated that he had expected this. He kept his voice level, however, even under the chuckling scorn of his immediate superior, Balt Haer.

He said, "Sir, I will be able to tell you where Marshal Cogswell is, and every troop at his command."

For a moment there was silence, all but a stunned silence. Then the major who had suggested the Saugerties field command headquarters were a fake blurted a curt laugh.

"This is no time for levity, captain," Balt Haer clipped. "Get to your command."

A colonel said, "Just a moment, sir. I've fought with Joe Mauser before. He's a good man."

"Not that good," someone else huffed. "Does he claim to be clairvoyant?"

Joe Mauser said flatly, "Have a semaphore man posted here this afternoon. I'll be back at that time." He spun on his heel and left them.

Balt Haer rushed to the door after him, shouting, "Captain! That's an order! Return—"

But the other was obviously gone. Enraged, the younger Haer began to shrill commands to a noncom in the way of organizing a pursuit.

His father called wearily, "That's enough, Balt. Mauser has evidently taken leave of his senses. We made the initial mistake of encouraging this idea he had, or thought he had."

"We?" his son snapped in return. "I had nothing to do with it."

"All right, all right. Let's tighten up, here. Now, what other information have your scouts come up with?"

IX

At the Kingston airport, Joe Mauser rejoined Max Mainz, his face drawn now.

"Everything go all right?" the little man said anxiously.

"I don't know," Joe said. "I still couldn't tell them the story. Old Cogswell is as quick as a coyote. We pull this little caper today, and he'll be ready to meet it tomorrow."

He looked at the two-place sailplane which sat on the tarmac. "Everything all set?"

"Far as I know," Max said. He looked at the motorless aircraft. "You sure you been checked out on these things, captain?"

"Yes," Joe said. "I bought this particular soaring glider more than a year ago, and I've put almost a thousand hours in it. Now, where's the pilot of that light plane?"

A single-engined sports plane was attached to the glider by a fifty-foot nylon rope. Even as Joe spoke, a youngster poked his head from the plane's window and grinned back at them. "Ready?" he yelled.

"Come on, Max," Joe said. "Let's pull the canopy off this thing. We don't want it in the way while you're semaphoring."

A figure was approaching them from the Administration Building. A uniformed man, and somehow familiar.

"A moment, Captain Mauser!"

Joe placed him now. The Sov-world representative he'd met at Balt Haer's table in the Upper bar a couple of days ago. What was his name? Colonel Arpàd. Lajos Arpàd.

The Hungarian approached and looked at the sailplane in interest. "As a representative of my government, a military attaché checking upon possible violations of the Universal Disarmament Pact, may I request what you are about to do, captain?"

Joe Mauser looked at him emptily. "How did you know I was here and what I was doing?"

The Sov colonel smiled gently. "It was by suggestion of Marshal Cogswell. He is a great man for detail. It disturbed him that an ... what did he call it? ... an *old pro* like yourself should join with Vacuum Tube Transport, rather than Continental Hovercraft. He didn't think it made sense and suggested that possibly you had in mind some scheme that would utilize weapons of a post-1900 period in your efforts to bring success to Baron Haer's forces. So I have investigated, Captain Mauser."

"And the marshal knows about this sailplane?" Joe Mauser's face was blank.

"I didn't say that. So far as I know, he doesn't."

"Then, Colonel Arpàd, with your permission, I'll be taking off."

The Hungarian said, "With what end in mind, captain?"

"Using this glider as a reconnaissance aircraft."

"Captain, I warn you! Aircraft were not in use in warfare until—"

But Joe Mauser cut him off, equally briskly. "Aircraft were first used in combat by Pancho Villa's forces a few years previous to World War I. They were also used in the Balkan Wars of about the same period. But those were powered craft. This is a glider, invented and in use before the year 1900 and hence open to utilization."

The Hungarian clipped, "But the Wright brothers didn't fly even gliders until—"

Joe looked him full in the face. "But you of the Sov-world do not admit that the Wrights were the first to fly, do you?"

The Hungarian closed his mouth, abruptly.

Joe said evenly, "But even if Ivan Ivanovitch, or whatever you claim his name was, didn't invent flight of heavier-than-air craft, the glider was flown variously before 1900, including by Otto Lilienthal in the 1890s, and was designed as far back as Leonardo da Vinci."

The Sov-world colonel stared at him for a long moment, then gave an inane giggle. He stepped back and flicked Joe

Mauser a salute. "Very well, captain. As a matter of routine, I shall report this use of an aircraft for reconnaissance purposes, and undoubtedly a commission will meet to investigate the propriety of the departure. Meanwhile, good luck!"

Joe returned the salute and swung a leg over the cockpit's side. Max was already in the front seat, his semaphore flags, maps and binoculars on his lap. He had been staring in dismay at the Sov officer, now was relieved that Joe had evidently pulled it off.

Joe waved to the plane ahead. Two mechanics had come up to steady the wings for the initial ten or fifteen feet of the motorless craft's passage over the ground behind the towing craft.

Joe said to Max, "did you explain to the pilot that under no circumstances was he to pass over the line of the military reservation, that we'd cut before we reached that point?"

"Yes, sir," Max said nervously. He'd flown before, on the commercial lines, but he'd never been in a glider.

They began lurching across the field, slowly, then gathering speed. And as the sailplane took speed, it took grace. After it had been pulled a hundred feet or so, Joe eased back the stick and it slipped gently into the air, four or five feet off the ground. The towing airplane was still taxiing, but with its tow airborne it picked up speed quickly. Another two hundred feet and it, too, was in the air and beginning to climb. The glider behind held it to a speed of sixty miles or so.

At ten thousand feet, the plane leveled off and the pilot's head swiveled to look back at them. Joe Mauser waved to him and dropped the release lever which ejected the nylon rope from the glider's nose. The plane dove away, trailing the rope behind it. Joe knew that the plane pilot would later drop it over the airport where it could easily be retrieved.

In the direction of Mount Overlook he could see cumulus clouds and the dark turbulence which meant strong updraft. He headed in that direction.

Except for the whistling of wind, there is complete silence in a soaring glider. Max Mainz began to call back to his superior, was taken back by the volume, and dropped his voice. He said, "Look, captain. What keeps it up?"

Joe grinned. He liked the buoyance of glider flying, the nearest approach of man to the bird, and thus far everything was going well. He told Mac, "An airplane plows through the air currents, a glider rides on top of them."

"Yeah, but suppose the current is going down?"

"Then we avoid it. This sailplane only has a gliding angle ratio of one to twenty-five, but it's a workhorse with a payload of some four hundred pounds. A really high-performance glider can have a ratio of as much as one to forty."

Joe had found a strong updraft where a wind ran up the side of a mountain. He banked, went into a circling turn. The gauge indicated they were climbing at the rate of eight meters per second, nearly fifteen hundred feet a minute.

Max hadn't got the rundown on the theory of the glider. That was obvious in his expression.

Joe Mauser, even while searching the ground below keenly, went into it further. "A wind up against a mountain will give an updraft, or storm clouds will, even a newly plowed field in a bright sun. So you go from one of these to the next."

"Yeah, great, but when you're between," Max protested.

"Then, when you have a one to twenty-five ratio, you go twenty-five feet forward for each one you drop. If you started a mile high, you could go twenty-five miles before you touched ground." He cut himself off quickly. "Look, what's that, down there? Get your glasses on it."

Max caught his excitement. His binoculars were tight to his eyes. "Sojers. Cavalry. They sure ain't ours. They must be Hovercraft lads. And look, field artillery."

Joe Mauser was piloting with his left hand, his right smoothing out a chart on his lap. He growled, "What are they doing there? That's at least a full brigade of cavalry. Here, let me have those glasses.

With his knees gripping the stick, he went into a slow circle, as he stared down at the column of men. "Jack Alshuler," he whistled in surprise. "The marshal's crack heavy cavalry. And several batteries of artillery." He swung the glasses in a wider scope and the whistle turned into a hiss of comprehension. "They're doing a complete circle of the reservation. They're going to hit the Baron from the direction of Phoenecia."

X

Marshal Stonewall Cogswell directed his old-fashioned telescope in the direction his chief of staff indicated.

"What is it?" he grunted.

"It's an airplane, sir."

"Over a military reservation with a fracas in progress?"

"Yes, sir." The other put his glasses back on the circling
object. "Then what is it, sir? Certainly not a free balloon."

"Balloons," the marshal snorted, as though to himself.
"Legal to use. The Union forces had them toward the end of
the Civil War. But practically useless in a fracas of movement."

They were standing before the former resort hotel which
housed the marshal's headquarters. Other staff members
were streaming from the building, and one of the ever-present
Telly reporting crews were hurriedly setting up cameras.

The marshal turned and barked, "Does anybody know
what in Zen that confounded thing, circling up there, is?"

Baron Zwerdling, the aging Category Transport magnate,
head of Continental Hovercraft, hobbled onto the wooden
veranda and stared with the others. "An airplane," he croaked.
"Haer's gone too far this time. Too far, too far. This will strip
him. Strip him, understand." Then he added, "Why doesn't it
make any noise?"

Lieutenant Colonel Paul Warren stood next to his commanding officer. "It looks like a glider, sir."

Cogswell glowered at him. "A what?"

"A glider, sir. It's a sport not particularly popular these
days."

"What keeps it up, confound it?"

Paul Warren looked at him. "The same thing that keeps a
hawk up, an albatross, a gull—"

"A vulture, you mean," Cogswell snarled. He watched it for
another long moment, his face working. He whirled on his
chief of artillery. "Jed, can you bring that thing down?"

The other had been viewing the craft through field binoculars, his face as shocked as the rest of them. Now he faced his
chief, and lowered the glasses, shaking his head. "Not with
the artillery of pre-1900. No, sir."

"What can you do?" Cogswell barked.

The artillery man was shaking his head. "We could mount
some Maxim guns on wagon wheels, or something. Keep him
from coming low."

"He doesn't have to come low," Cogswell growled unhappily. He spun on Lieutenant Colonel Warren again. "When
were they invented?" He jerked his thumb upward. "Those
things."

Warren was twisting his face in memory. "Some time
about the turn of the century."

"How long can the things stay up?"

Warren took in the surrounding mountainous countryside. "Indefinitely, sir. A single pilot, as long as he is physically able to operate. If there are two pilots up there to relieve each other, they could stay until food and water ran out."

"How much weight do they carry?"

"I'm not sure. One that size, certainly enough for two men and any equipment they'd need. Say, five hundred pounds."

Cogswell had his telescope glued to his eyes again; he muttered under his breath, "Five hundred pounds! They could even unload dynamite over our horses. Stampede them all over the reservation."

"What's going on?" Baron Zwerdling shrilled. "What's going on, Marshal Cogswell?"

Cogswell ignored him. He watched the circling, circling craft for a full five minutes, breathing deeply. Then he lowered his glass and swept the assembled officers of his staff with an indignant glare. "Ten Eyck!" he grunted.

An infantry colonel came to attention. "Yes, sir."

Cogswell said heavily, deliberately. "Under a white flag. A dispatch to Baron Haer. My compliments and request for his terms. While you're at it, my compliments also to Captain Joseph Mauser."

Zwerdling was bug-eyeing him. "Terms!" he rasped.

The marshal turned to him. "Yes, sir. Face reality. We're in the dill. I suggest you sue for terms as short of complete capitulation as you can make them."

"You call yourself a soldier—!" the transport tycoon began to shrill.

"Yes, sir," Cogswell snapped. "A soldier, not a butcher of the lads under me." He called to the Telly reporter who was getting as much of this as he could. "Mr. Soligen, isn't it?"

The reporter scurried forward, flicking signals to his cameramen for proper coverage. "Yes, sir. Freddy Soligen, marshal. Could you tell the Telly fans what this is all about, Marshal Cogswell? Folks, you all know the famous marshal. Marshal Stonewall Cogswell, who hasn't lost a fracas in nearly ten years, now commanding the forces of Continental Hovercraft."

"I'm losing one now," Cogswell said grimly. "Vacuum Tube Transport has pulled a gimmick out of the hat and things have pickled for us. It will be debated before the Military Category Department, of course, and undoubtedly the Sov-world military attachés will have things to say. But as it appears now, the fracas, as we have known it, has been revolutionized."

"Revolutionized?" Even the Telly reporter was flabbergasted. "You mean by that thing?" He pointed upward, and the lenses of the cameras followed his finger.

"Yes," Cogswell growled unhappily. "Do all of you need a blueprint? Do you think I can fight a fracas with that thing dangling above me, throughout the day hours? Do you understand the importance of reconnaissance in warfare?" His eyes glowered. "Do you think Napoleon would have lost Waterloo if he'd had the advantage of perfect reconnaissance such as that thing can deliver? Do you think Lee would have lost Gettysburg? Don't be ridiculous." He spun on Baron Zwerdling, who was stuttering his complete confusion.

"As it stands, Baron Haer knows every troop dispensation I make. All I know of his movements are from my cavalry scouts. I repeat, I am no butcher, sir. I will gladly cross swords with Baron Haer another day, when I, too, have . . . what did you call the confounded things, Paul?"

"Gliders," Lieutenant Colonel Warren said.

XI

Major Joseph Mauser, now attired in his best off-duty Category Military uniform, spoke his credentials to the receptionist. "I have no definite appointment, but I am sure the Baron will see me," he said.

"Yes, sir." The receptionist did the things that receptionists do, then looked up at him again. "Right through that door, major."

Joe Mauser gave the door a quick double rap and then entered before waiting an answer.

Balt Haer, in mufti, was standing at a far window, a drink in his hand, rather than his customary swagger stick. Nadine Haer sat in an easychair. The girl Joe Mauser loved had been crying.

Joe Mauser, suppressing his frown, made with the usual amenities.

Balt Haer, without answering them, finished his drink in a gulp and stared at the newcomer. The old stare, the aloof stare, an aristocrat looking at an underling as though wondering what made the fellow tick. He said, finally, "I see you have been raised to Rank Major."

"Yes, sir," Joe said.

"We are obviously occupied, major. What can either my sister or I possibly do for you?"

Joe kept his voice even. He said, "I wanted to see the Baron."

Nadine Haer looked up, a twinge of pain crossing her face.

"Indeed," Balt Haer said flatly. "You are talking to the Baron, Major Mauser."

Joe Mauser looked at him, then at his sister, who had taken to her handkerchief again. Consternation ebbed up and over him in a flood. He wanted to say something such as, "Oh *no*," but not even that could he utter.

Haer was bitter. "I assume I know why you are here, major. You have come for your pound of flesh, undoubtedly. Even in these hours of our grief—"

"I . . . I didn't know. Please believe . . ."

". . . You are so constituted that your ambition has no decency. Well, Major Mauser, I can only say that your arrangement was with my father. Even if I thought it a reasonable one, I doubt if I would sponsor your ambitions myself."

Nadine Haer looked up wearily. "Oh, Balt, come off it," she said. "The fact is, the Haer fortunes contracted a debt to you, major. Unfortunately, it is a debt we cannot pay." She looked into his face. "First, my father's governmental connections do not apply to us. Second, six months ago, my father, worried about his health and attempting to avoid certain death taxes, transferred the family stocks into Balt's name. And Balt saw fit, immediately before the fracas, to sell all Vacuum Tube Transport stocks, and invest in Hovercraft."

"That's enough, Nadine," her brother snapped nastily.

"I see," Joe said. He came to attention. "Dr. Haer, my apologies for intruding upon you in your time of bereavement." He turned to the new Baron. "Baron Haer, my apologies for *your* bereavement."

Balt Haer glowered at him.

Joe Mauser turned and marched for the door, which he opened then closed behind him.

On the street, before the New York offices of Vacuum Tube Transport, he turned and for a moment looked up at the splendor of the building.

Well, at least the common shares of the concern had skyrocketed following the victory. His rank had been upped to Major, and old Stonewall Cogswell had offered him a permanent position on his staff in command of aerial operations, no small matter of prestige. The difficulty was, he wasn't interested in the added money that would accrue to him, nor the higher rank—nor the prestige, for that matter.

He turned to go to his hotel.

An unbelievably beautiful girl came down the steps of the building. She said, "Joe."

He looked at her. "Yes?"

She put a hand on his sleeve. "Let's go somewhere and talk, Joe."

"About what?" He was infinitely weary now.

"About goals," she said. "As long as they exist, whether for individuals, or nations, or a whole species, life is still worth the living. Things are a bit bogged down right now, but at the risk of sounding very trite, there's tomorrow."

Without Portfolio

JAMES E. GUNN

"**R**EADY?" the Secretary asked. He pushed his chair back from the wide, polished darkness of the desk and stood up.

In his sixties, he was still tall and broad-shouldered and straight, and he carried his beautifully modeled head proudly. To *Time*, he was good and gray, as Cordell Hull had once been. But it wasn't dignity or honor or the pride of integrity that peeked out of the dark, deep-set eyes under the thick, white eyebrows. It was fear.

"Ready," Stephen Judy said calmly and picked up his brief case and followed the Secretary's gray back through the doorway and down the long hall and out into the green and the blue and the brightness.

As they came out of the side door, grim-faced men formed a protective circle around them. The helicopter, that had been hanging above, dropped lower. They started along the broad, white walk that bisected the cropped lawn and walked quickly toward the domed Capitol. Around it, the antimissile radar installations searched restlessly for targets, and the obedient guns raked stiff, taloned fingers across the sky, as if the tender Earth, in final rebellion, had grown hands to tear its tormentors from above.

Judy was undistinguished. Everything about him was medium, from his height and weight to his brown hair and eyes. Even his age fell somewhere between the young and the old. His face was firm but not hard. He had thickened noticeably around the middle. He seemed successful in an unspectacular way, a small businessman say, an executive in a larger business, a lawyer—civil, not criminal—a lobbyist.

There is a quality of ruthlessness that clings to ambitious men long after they have reached their goals; that Judy seemed to lack.

In a sense he was what he seemed to be, and the brief case was his professional badge.

As they approached the long, high steps, the Secretary slowed and turned toward Judy. "Have you got the . . . the documents?" he asked. His voice trembled just a little.

"Right here," Judy said, patting the brief case.

Just before the Secretary stepped into the shadow of the Capitol, he glanced once toward the unspecked blueness above. There the artificial satellites raced unseen, but they were neutral like the stars, and death might lurk there. But no one would know until knowledge was futile. And so the glance was folly, and he knew it.

Death is invisible.

Judy smiled as if he could read the Secretary's thoughts. He pointed up where the Secretary had been looking. "The fate of the world isn't up there—but there!" And he pointed toward the great doors that waited for them in front.

Excerpts from a recorded session of the United States Senate standing committee on Foreign Relations, August 20, 1975, Senator Mullins presiding:

Chairman: Mr. Judy . . .

Judy: Call me Stephen—or Steve, if you like . . .

Chairman: Before we start, Mr. Judy, I'd like to ask whether you have any objections to this meeting of the committee in secret session.

Judy: No, sir. But then I wouldn't object to a public meeting, either. . . .

Senator Peterson: With this country expecting attack at any moment, and you think the meetings of the Foreign Relations committee should be open to the public—which includes foreign agents?

Judy: You might as well. It will leak out anyhow. But I suppose it depends on your philosophy. . . .

Chairman: The session will proceed much faster if the witness confines himself to simply answering the questions.

Secretary: I'd like to remind this committee that Mr. Judy is appearing here of his own free will. He has not been subpoenaed, and he is not required by law to appear before you, as I am.

Chairman: That, Mr. Secretary, is the crux of the matter, and I suggest we get down to it as soon as possible so that we can get to the bomb shelters.

You are, Mr. Judy, an employee of the government?

Judy: No, sir. My firm has been hired by the government to perform certain duties. . . .

Chairman: And how would you describe those duties?

Judy: Well, I suppose it could be called the handling of foreign relations. . . .

(Uproar. After several minutes, the chairman succeeded in quieting the committee, and the session continued.)

Chairman: The present crisis—it would be due to your performance of those duties. Is that correct?

Judy: I suppose. . . .

Chairman: Because the government abdicated its diplomatic function. . . ?

Judy: That's hard to . . .

Chairman: Suppose you start at the beginning, Mr. Judy, and tell us—explain to us so that we can understand—how the United States, without committing a single official act, can find itself facing all-out war—can wonder whether missiles with hydrogen-bomb warheads are plunging down toward it.

Judy: (removing several sheafs of paper from his brief case) Here are files—one for each member of the committee—of documents excerpted and duplicated. The first one, you will notice, is a copy of a letter to the Eurasian Ambassador:

COOK & JUDY
DIPLOMATIC SERVICES
"Extraterritorial claims a specialty"
March 26, 1975

Mr. Josef Petrovsky, Ambassador
Eurasian Union
Eurasian Embassy
179. . . .

Dear Sir:
   This will inform you and your government that we are, as of this date, the appointed diplomatic representative of the United States of America. All further correspondence should be directed to us.
   We are in the process of reviewing the State Department files in preparation for putting these affairs on a businesslike basis, converting treaties into contracts, and so forth. If you have anything to discuss with us in pursuance of this matter, we will be glad to have our representative call on you or arrange a meeting at your convenience.
   We are especially anxious to clean up the German situation so that we can get on to more important matters. Perhaps we can get together soon for lunch?

Sincerely yours,
Stephen Judy

Chairman: Don't you consider this unusual, Mr. Judy—I might even say unprecedented—for a business firm to assume responsibility for a nation's foreign relations?

Judy: For a nation this size? Unusual? Yes. Unprecedented? No. There are precedents aplenty, ever since the formation, in the early Fifties, of the partnership between Ernest Gross and Louis Hyde, Jr. I might even say that this development was inevitable. It has been obvious for many years that the conduct of foreign relations has outgrown the capabilities of amateurs—even such gifted amateurs as our present

Secretary of State. It is long past time for the professional to take over, as he has done in many countries, including the Eurasian Union. The difference here—and the blessing, too, as I hope to prove—was that the American institution best suited to accept and carry out this function was the business firm.

(Mr. Judy slipped a small object out of his brief case. This caused considerable consternation before it was recognized as a miniature projector. When he focused the picture on the wall, it revealed two men. They were in an office. One of the men was immediately identified as Josef Petrovsky, the Eurasian Ambassador.)

Petrovsky stared down at the sheet of paper in his hand, frowning so darkly that his heavy black eyebrows met in a single line. He sneered, started to crumple the sheet, changed his mind, smoothed it out, and tossed it aside. It fluttered to the wide expanse of polished desk top.

"So," he rumbled heavily. "What does it mean, Ivor?"

"I suggest, ambassador," Ivor submitted cautiously, "that it is a trick."

Petrovsky tugged at his chin, sneering. "A trick? Perhaps. But I do not think so. I think it is a sign of weakness. We will ignore it. They will get weaker and more desperate."

Chairman: Do you expect us to believe that this was an actual recording of a conversation in the office of the Eurasian ambassador? Even a child would be aware of the impossibility of that, not to mention the fact that they are speaking English. . . .

Judy: Impossible as you consider it, that was the Eurasian ambassador and his personal secretary, Ivor Rilikov, not actors. English translations were dubbed in as a matter of standard operating procedure. The originals are, of course, on file. S.O.P., too, was to plant numerous small devices in the offices and homes of the men we expected to deal with. You wouldn't expect a business firm to work properly without a knowledge of its competitors' intentions. . . .

Chairman: All right. Go on.

Judy: The next few items in the file are diplomatic notes from the Eurasian Embassy to the State Department. We acknowledged these in a general letter with the observation that they had been turned over to us for action, and we would be glad to discuss them at the ambassador's convenience, preferably over lunch or dinner, there being a new and rather delightful floor show in town. . . .

Senator Peterson: Do you consider this in keeping with the dignity of the United States. . .?

Judy: One of the advantages of the conduct of foreign relations by independent contractors is the decline in importance of dignity, formality, honor. . . . The vital thing is results. Fortunately, though, Petrovsky felt the same way about it as you. He was goaded into answering us. His reply was short, brusque, and protocolic. . . .

Chairman: Protocolic?

Judy: Sorry. An office term. We gave him a pain in his protocol.

Chairman: And while you were playing these little games, the German situation was drawing us closer to war. . . .

Judy: True. But that's the privilege of the professional. Things assume their proper proportion, including games, as you say. It was vital not to appear eager, you see. I think you will get a better picture of what we were trying to do if you imagine us as two business firms interested in coming to agreement over a potential market, neither one knowing the exact extent of the other's resources, how much it is willing to gamble on this venture, or how much it knows of the other's intentions. It is, if you like, a game situation. As such, it is covered by the Theory of Games, and our computer section gave us all the information on odds and probabilities we could use. And we were aware, too, that Eurasia, in spite of Petrovsky's attitude, wasn't ready to act until our position and capabilities had been explored.

Senator Peterson: You were just trying to keep Eurasia guessing.

Judy: Of course. Always. But that wasn't our primary goal. We had to get Eurasia in a mood to bargain, to meet us at least halfway. That, as a matter of fact, turned out to be the Rocket Club.

Senator Peterson: As a place for conducting State business, that has, at least, the virtue of novelty.

Judy: For State business, perhaps. But not for business. More deals have been consummated over night club tables than over office desks. The atmosphere urges agreement, and alcohol and the female body divine speak all languages.

Petrovsky had condescended to exchange a few letters with us muddying Eurasia's position on the German situation and ignoring our requests that Eurasia live up to its contractual obligations. He agreed to the meeting place, because he had just discovered one of our recorders in his office. I give you—Petrovsky in the Rocket Club. We were speaking French, incidentally, and the recorder was in the table decoration. . . .

Against a mottled background of spotlights and darkness, white flesh and whiter shirt fronts, loud music and louder voices, Petrovsky, clothed in a conservative, diplomatic pinstripe, cautiously approached the table.

Judy jumped up to grab the Eurasian ambassador's hand and pump it enthusiastically. "It's a pleasure to meet you at last, sir, and I'm sure we can reach a quick settlement of our mutual problems. But first, shall we eat?"

"Never mind," Petrovsky grumbled. "I've already eaten. Let's get on with the business. . . ."

"You won't mind then," Judy broke in blandly, "if I order?"

The film flickered as it changed to a scene of Judy lifting a dripping bite of steak toward his mouth and saying, "How about another drink? Don't hesitate. All this goes on the expense account."

Petrovsky glanced once more out of the corner of his eye at the stripper carved in half by the lights and said heavily, "I find these proceedings exceedingly undignified, and I would appreciate your saying what you have to say so that I may leave. This whole matter has been handled with absurd informality, and I shall so report it to my government."

"Dignity?" Judy said. "Formality? What are they worth on the free market? Come now, we're reasonable men. We can sit down and work these matters out together. Take the German situation, for instance. . . ."

Petrovsky straightened up; his eyes sharpened like little black pins. "Yes. Go on."

"It's a simple matter of contract which any court could dispose of within minutes—"

"Simple matter?" Petrovsky exclaimed. He was frowning as his hand came down heavily on the table. "This question of freedom and democracy? And what is this about court and contract? We have neither of these things."

"Treaty, then, if you prefer the word. We hope, though, to regularize them into contract form as soon as possible. As for

the court, of course we don't have any. But we must act as if
we had, eh?"

"Absurd!" Petrovsky drew back as if he were across the
table from a madman. "Act as if we had a court! The foreign
relations of the Eurasian Union have always been conducted
realistically."

"But how else can we discover the right thing to do?" Judy
asked in bewilderment. "Self-interest is anarchy; don't you
agree?"

"Of course not," Petrovsky growled, his head turning to
watch the gleam of white flesh. "There is no law where there
is no method of enforcing it. There is merely agreement, and
agreement is dependent on the continuation of the original
state of affairs."

Judy shook his head gently, as if he were tutoring a pupil.
"That is obviously, demonstrably unworkable. It leads to war
as the only punishment. That's like a man taking the law
into his own hands, and it punishes him, even if he wins, as
much as the criminal. Society could never survive that, and
the society of nations has crumbled before it time after time."

"So?" Petrovsky asked, shrugging massive shoulders.

"So, until the establishment, through the United Nations,
or some such agency, of international law and effective
international sanctions by which international criminals can
be punished, we must act as if that law and those sanctions
exist."

"Fantasy!" Petrovsky sneered. "That situation will never
arrive. It would mean a surrender of national sovereignty—"

"Just as the establishment of society and laws and police-
men was a surrender of individual sovereignty," Judy agreed.
"But it made it possible for men to live together. It is the
price we pay for peace. I am a man, Mr. Petrovsky, not a wild
animal; I restrict myself and I allow myself to be restricted. I
am also a businessman, and I conduct my business within the
boundaries laid down by law."

"But there is no law," Petrovsky insisted, and this time
there was a puzzled frown on his face. "We must be realistic."

Judy shrugged helplessly. "That's just the point I'm trying
to make. You speak of 'realism,' 'freedom,' and 'democracy.'
To you they mean one thing; to me they mean another. A
contract would define the terms; a court would enforce them.
You are realistic, you say? Nonsense. You live by a set of
ancient fictions."

"I?" Petrovsky's face flushed.

"You subscribe—like all other diplomats—to the three basic principles of international law: the recognition of the existence and integrity of other states, of their independence, and of their equality. The last two are obvious fictions. Nations are no more independent than people are. And they aren't equal, except perhaps before the law that you refuse to recognize."

Petrovsky sneered. "When I speak of reality, I mean the reality of divisions."

"There, you see?" Judy sighed. "We disagree already. But this isn't solving the German situation. You have your 'real' divisions massed on the border in breach of the contract—I beg your pardon—treaty."

"When freedom and democratic government are endangered," Petrovsky said piously, "the Eurasian government is always ready to defend them."

"In other words, if the East Germans choose to join the West Germans in the coming plebescite, the Eurasian armies will roll in—"

"Such a choice," Petrovsky said blandly, "would be proof, *per se*, of fascist intervention, falsification of ballots, miscount, fraud—"

"Your government, then," Judy said calmly, "won't recognize any result except in your favor?"

"Exactly."

"In spite of the treaty?"

"We must agree with Bismarck—treaties are only valid so long as they are reinforced by the interests of the parties to them."

"You're going to risk war on this issue?" Judy asked.

Petrovsky shrugged. "What risk is there? You won't go to war over such a minor matter."

"That," Judy said grimly, "is where you are wrong. . . ."

Chairman: So. We can discard the night club approach.

Judy: Well, it made Petrovsky say more than he intended. He outlined his government's position very well. Unfortunately, my implied threat wasn't effective. As soon as this became obvious, we started Plan No. 5.

Senator Peterson: What was that?

Judy: We declared war—

(Mr. Judy was interrupted by an uproar which took several minutes to quiet.)

Chairman: On the basis of what we have already heard, it is my opinion that no time should be lost in setting impeachment proceedings underway against the Secretary of State and whoever else is responsible for placing the conduct of foreign relations in the hands of this . . . this traitor! And there must be some charges we can press against the witness himself. . . .

Judy: This is another proof of the superiority of business methods over political methods. The Secretary must act as if one hundred election-conscious senators were peering over his shoulder, knives in hand. Naturally, he sticks to precedent. My firm, on the other hand, can concentrate on the most effective measures and the desired results. . . .

Senator Peterson: There has been no constitutional amendment, I believe, eliminating the right of the Senate to approve treaties and the right of Congress to declare war. . . .

(Applause.)

Judy: There have been no treaties signed, and when I speak of war, I mean, of course, a businessman's war—a commercial war. . . .

Chairman: It's unfortunate that Eurasia doesn't mean the same thing.

(Laughter.)

Judy: That's true. It is unfortunate. Our job is to make Eurasia realize that. We must act, you see, as if there were laws and other nations abided by them. When they do not, we must protect ourselves; we must make other nations lawabiding. . . .

Chairman: You did not quail before the task. . . ?

Judy: No, sir. How vital it was has been demonstrated in the last few hours and the last few minutes. Upon it depended the future of our firm, of the administration that had faith in us, of the continued existence of the United States of America, and of the world's chances for real international law.

Senator Peterson: You realized, of course, that we were not prepared to go to war over the German question?

Judy: Certainly. But in the face of inevitable war, it is better to stand firm rather than let the borders and determination of the free world be nibbled away. . . .

Secretary: Yesterday the German plebiscite was held under U.N. auspices. . . .

Chairman: The Secretary will please refrain from comment. If he will be patient, he will get his turn upon the stand. . . .

Judy: The results, which will be announced shortly but are already generally known, are an overwhelming victory for the free world.

Secretary: The vote was, to a large measure, the direct result of the efforts and methods of Steve's firm in presenting the question to the voters. . . .

Senator Peterson: If it is the occasion for the marching of the Eurasian divisions and the outbreak of atomic war, I should think Mr. Judy's efforts might better have been spent in persuading the East Germans to vote the other way.

Judy: We can't surrender to blackmail. That would make us criminals. Besides, we were prepared. . . .

Chairman: Prepared? How? Have you taken over the command of the Armed Forces, too?

Judy: Oh, no. Nothing like that. We had been preparing for some time. Plan No. 5.

Chairman: War?

Judy: Right. In preparation, we had sold several million cheap, sturdy TV sets to the Eurasian government. As we expected, they were distributed immediately. The hunger of the Eurasian masses for consumer goods perpetually unsatisfied. After that our methods were the tested methods of persuasion, proven in the fire of more than a century of commercial competition.

Senator Peterson: It seems to me that this hearing might well adjourn to the bomb shelter. . . .

Judy: That won't be necessary. I'm almost finished. In the month before the plebiscite, our campaign went into full swing. Under the guise of vast distress sales, we undersold Eurasia on the world market, as you'll notice in the file. . . .

GIANT PRE-WAR SALE!
Soft Goods   Hard Goods
Grain—Butter—Cheese—Dried Milk
Metals

WE NEED THE MONEY
10% off for Cash and Carry
YOU NAME THE TERMS
WE'LL TRADE YOUR WAY

Chairman: You were selling these things when they would be the very things we would need in the event of war! . . .

Judy: In the event of the kind of war the sales were designed to prevent, the things we sold would have been worthless. Actually, we made some very profitable sales and got rid of some embarrassing surpluses. . . .

Senator Peterson: Now we have the real reason for your interest in foreign relations: profit!

Judy: Of course. That's business. Call us profiteers, if you like, but add "of peace." If more people could profit by peace, there'd be no war. But let me go on—time is growing short. We spread rumors about our competitor—I mean Eurasia, of course. Their goods were shoddy, we said; their methods were disreputable—all perfectly true. Eurasia's trade with the world was cut off cleanly. She had come to depend on it more than she realized.

Chairman: And that was another incentive to war.

Judy: Oh, no. Eurasia couldn't hope to re-establish trade by war. That would only result in conquest and destruction. Finally we bought time on the Worldwide TV Network.

Senator Peterson: You mean the artificial satellites thing that the U.N. neutralized?

Judy: Precisely. We bought advertising time, and the TV sets sold to Eurasia came into use. A hidden relay turned them on, and they picked up the program from the satellite racing overhead. Advertising is, of course, only a method of shaping convictions. We bought listeners with irresistible entertainment and advertised—consumer goods. Within a few days, the sets had all been smashed by government agents, but their work was done. Seven hundred million Eurasians were convinced that our products were the best available, that they could get them only from us, and they wanted them with a great and overwhelming hunger.

Chairman: And that, I suppose, wasn't a reason for war?

Judy: Only a madman would think that. We broadcast no propaganda. We did nothing that Eurasia could not do, freely and legally. We did what any salesman would do: we advertised what we had for sale. Of course, we were prepared for the fact that we might be dealing with madmen.

Senator Peterson: How do you mean?

Judy: On the eve of the plebiscite, by stratospheric rocket, we showered leaflets throughout Eurasia but especially over the border areas and troop concentrations.

Chairman: Leaflets have never won a war.

Judy: Until now. You'll find a translation in the file in front of you . . .

$50 $50

This coupon is good for
$50   FIFTY DOLLARS $50
in trade
at the nearest port of entry
on any REFRIGERATOR,
RANGE, TV SET,
AUTOMOBILE or HELI
(Void if not redeemed
within one month)

$50 $50

Chairman: This is unprecedented folly!

Judy: Folly? That depends on results, and the results are not yet in. But not unprecedented. Let me cite Radio Free Europe and other civilian activities. . . .

(The senators stared at Mr. Judy as he cocked his head and stared at the ceiling as if he were listening to voices.)

Judy: It's a great pleasure to inform you that Petrovsky is frantic for a meeting. . . .

Senator Peterson: What does that mean?

Judy: It means that Eurasia has surrendered. Good thing, too. A few hours more and the government would have toppled.

Chairman: Would you tell us how you learned this?

Judy: A receiver, Mr. Chairman, imbedded in my mastoid.

Senator Peterson: What do you intend to do?

Judy: Why we'll sign a contract with Eurasia, of course. It should be very profitable, even after redeeming the coupons. I think that law and the conduct of foreign relations in a businesslike way have won striking victories. The technique was simple: arouse desires which only peace can satisfy.

Chairman: Wait a minute! Why not let the Eurasian government fall?

Judy: But that would be instigating revolution! Very illegal. Besides, I doubt if this country wants the responsibility of caring for seven hundred million Eurasians.

(The committee members whispered for a moment or two among themselves.)

Chairman: It is the decision of this committee not to press charges against the witness or the Secretary of State.

Judy: Very wise, too, since a recording of this session is now in my office, transmitted there by a little device in my brief case. . . .

Outside the Capitol a few minutes later, in the green and the blue and the brightness, the restless radar saucers slowly came to a stop. The antimissile guns froze. They no longer looked alive; they were like something stiff and old and useless.

But the sun beamed down very warmly.

The Idea

BARRY N. MALZBERG

IT came to me out of the blue that Thursday morning. The conception, I mean. Its coming had absolutely nothing to do with the top level meeting that was scheduled upstairs later in the day. If I had remembered the meeting, I'm sure the idea would never have come in the first place. I function poorly under pressure, an old predicament.

"Educational," I told Miller after I had sketched in the outlines to him. Miller is my immediate superior so he deserves the courtesy, up to a point. "That's the hook. It's educational."

"Not enough," said Miller. He is one of those bleak, desperate men in their upper forties who remind me now and then that even I am mortal. Sometimes I consider his history, which so approximates my own progress through network to date as to be distressing.

"It's more than enough. Would I lead you wrong? The atmosphere, the times. The social tension. Everything's ready for it. Would I lead you wrong? Trust your instincts. Think of your children. Wouldn't they understand?"

"I won't propose it, Howard. I won't get before that meeting and present this. We'll be slaughtered. I'm thinking of you more than of myself."

"Did I ask *you* to propose it? I will. All I wanted was to clear with you." This was after Miller had reminded me of the meeting which he had done as soon as he had told me that he had no time for ideas, but too late for me to give him mine.

"I refuse to clear it."

"We've never had a serious disagreement. Must I go over your head?"

That made him think, as it was meant to. I could see him playing off the one thing against the other thing: an official complaint from a subordinate against the question of approval. It was a difficult decision. Part of the immediate beauty of the idea was that it made decisions difficult for everyone. Right away, it vaulted us into a new world of possibilities. Everything had implications beyond the simple dilemma of *need money; hate job,* which was the ordinary key to existence. "I can't put up with it, Howard," he said finally.

"Then I should go higher?"

"Not exactly. No. Just bring it up. At the meeting. As something you were discussing. Not as a recommendation or anything, though. Just as an idea. That's as far as I can authorize you to move on it."

"No good. A full presentation or nothing."

"You haven't got the material for a full presentation." Then he said it. "I think you're crazy, Howard."

"No, I'm not. Besides, we're all crazy. What I do is think; think all the time. It beats response, beats precision, it even beats competence. No substitute for original human thought."

"You can pose it but just as a curiosity. Say that you had this silly way-out idea and here it goes up the chute for laughs. No more. I'm a desperate man, Howard, you can see that, but I won't go beyond that."

"Fine," I said, having satisfied himself. "That's fair enough. I wasn't even thinking of the meeting to tell you the truth. If I had remembered the meeting before I came in here I wouldn't have thought it out. Pressure, you know?"

"No," said Miller.

So I pitched it to them and it went over fantastic. I had figured it would. Bald men, wigged men, old men, young men . . . all of these responded as one by the time I finally got out of the full sense of the idea. I had help, of course. Several of them were bright enough to catch the implications right off and Miller himself, once he saw the drift, had a few angles himself. The meeting broke up at about five after five—which meant that half of these guys had missed connections of one sort or another and would have to rearrange the whole evening if not most of the next day—and a whole group of them wanted to go out to a restaurant and finish the discussion. They couldn't get off it, were on the point of arranging for a private room in Sardi's until I said that I had an important previous engagement and would have to personally bow out.

Well, for some reason, that killed it. None of them wanted to go out or stay with it without me. They said that I was the guiding star or motivating force or things like that but it took me until a long time later that I finally figured out the real reason. Not that it matters any more, of course.

The pilot went up for production four weeks after that, and it was terrific. They had hired the two best bodies available, big show business names as well, to do it, and it quickly became something of a classic. The price was right for those kids and they were glad to have the work. I was there at the filming and they got everything, didn't miss a nuance. About that time or shortly after, Miller had a mild heart attack and was put on leave for three months and it was just natural to move me into his spot. Just temporarily, of course. So I was able to add a few little personal touches to the pilot.

It glided right through network approval, of course, because this was one of the few pilots in history which had network money in it from the start, which kind of gave us a break on coverage, not to say the decision-making process. The go-ahead orders came right through, but it was decided to hold up production for the fall until the pilot itself was slotted as a one-shot midsummer special and we could get some reactions. If they went as we hoped they would, it could then be full-speed ahead. It was about that time that the first glimmers of trepidation seemed to come around. Until then it had been a real spin, a voyage toward destiny conducted in as full, frank and comradely a way as I had ever seen in television—because all of us, at last, felt we were beating the biggest rap of all—but now, with the pilot in the can and actually scheduled, things began to break the other way. Rumors: too many party girls hanging around outside board meetings, stuff like that. Nothing definite.

About that time, too, was when it became "Howard's idea." Not the "fall spot" or the "turn-around gig" but "Howard's conception." I began to be asked about a lot of things which really weren't my responsibility, placement angles and sustaining spots and stuff like that. And which we wanted to tie into primarily: Nielsen or Arbitron. These were all landing at my desk and it was at about that time that I realized the fix was being put in. I remembered what Miller had said to me the only time he called from the hospital. "It's going to work, Howard," he said, "and they'll eat all of us alive for having shown them how badly they wanted it."

Prophecy from an oxygen tent. I began to find my evenings booked solid with receptions, interview shows, guest shots. Of course I couldn't come out and really say what was going to happen—we had decided to keep as tight an official lid on as possible—but the point was to hint a lot. The more I did, the more the applause meters went up.

August 3rd was pilot day. I watched it in my own home surrounded by my own family from 8:30 to 9:00 and it was like nothing that had ever happened before in the history of the world. The thing took to the tube even better than it had to the screen. The closeness, the *compression* fitted it. It was impossible not to be moved by it.

When it was over, my wife cursed me and took the children upstairs and left me to have a drink all alone and when I came out of the kitchen they were gone. I haven't seen them since, but I get messages.

About five minutes after the third drink, the phone started ringing and it hasn't stopped since. Not for a moment. Outside, inside, all I am is a message center, all clogged by grief. Right? Right.

The final trial will begin this week and I wish that Miller

were here to see it, only Miller is still in this spa in Arizona. Anyone else you can think of will be there, though. As they say, they want to see Howard get what's coming to him. Howard being the man who almost destroyed America.

"Educational," I try to tell my lawyer. The first thing was, it was educational. How can you knock the accretion of knowledge in this highly technologized age, I ask you.

And my lawyer, an old friend, very short, smart guy who used to bail T&T out of all kinds of trouble before they dropped below 50 and the trouble stopped, says, "What you got to understand, Howard, is that the world is full of guys all as unique as you and when it thinks that the time for something has come it is going to make one of them do it but then the world, not liking the great man theory of history, is going to lay it on the one who did it. So it can say it never happened. So it can go on its way and blame the Communists or the drinking water for the kick. But if it's any comfort, Howard, the next time it's done—and thanks to you, it will be very soon—it will be a lot easier and in the meantime I promise you that I will charge you a very small fee, nothing that the company policy won't be able to pay in full if the ultimate happens which, of course, we don't want it to."

And Madly Teach

LLOYD BIGGLE, JR.

MISS Mildred Boltz clasped her hands and exclaimed, "What a lovely school!"

It shimmered delightfully in the bright morning sunlight, a pale, delicate blue-white oasis of color that lay gemlike amidst the nondescript towers and domes and spires of the sprawling metropolitan complex.

But even as she spoke she qualified her opinion. The building's form was boxlike, utilitarian, ugly. Only its color made it beautiful.

The aircab driver had been muttering to himself because he'd gotten into the wrong lane and missed his turn. He turned quickly, and said, "I beg your pardon?"

"The school," Miss Boltz said. "It has a lovely color."

They threaded their way through an interchange, circled, and maneuvered into the proper lane. Then the driver turned to her again. "I've heard of schools. They used to have some out west. But that isn't a school."

Miss Boltz met his serious gaze confusedly, and hoped she wasn't blushing. It just wasn't proper for a woman of her age to blush. She said, "I must have misunderstood you. I thought that was—"

"Yes, Ma'am. That's the address you gave me."

"Then—of course it's a school! I'm a teacher. I'm going to teach there."

He shook his head. "No, Ma'am. We don't have any schools."

The descent was so unsettlingly abrupt that Miss Boltz had to swallow her protests and clutch at her safety belt. Then they were in the ground level parking area, and he had the door open. She paid him, and stepped out with the dignity demanded of a middle-aged school teacher. She would have liked to investigate this queer notion of his about schools, but she didn't want to be late for her appointment. And anyway— the idea! If it wasn't a school, what was it?

In the maze of lettered and double-lettered corridors, each turning she took seemed to be the wrong one, and she was breathing heavily and fighting off a mild seizure of panic when she reached her destination. A receptionist took her name and said severely, "Mr. Wilbings is expecting you. Go right in."

The office door bore a bristling label. ROGER A. WILBINGS. DEPUTY SUPERINTENDENT OF EDUCATION (SECONDARY). NORTHEASTERN UNITED STATES SCHOOL DISTRICT. PRIVATE. Miss Boltz hesitated, and the receptionist said again, "Go right in."

"Thank you," Miss Boltz said and opened the door.

The gentleman behind the desk at the distant center of the

room was awaiting her with a fiercely blank expression which resolved into the hair-framed oval of a bald head as she moved forward. She blinked her eyes nervously and wished she'd worn her contact lenses. Mr. Wilbings's attention was fixed upon the papers that littered the top of his desk, and he indicated a chair for her without bothering to look up. She walked tightrope-fashion across the room and seated herself.

"One moment, please," he said.

She ordered herself to relax. She was not a young lass just out of college, hoping desperately for a first job. She had a contract and twenty-five years of tenure, and she was merely reporting for reassignment.

Her nerves disregarded the order.

Mr. Wilbings gathered up his papers, tapped them together, and returned them to a folder. "Miss—ah—Boltz," he said. His curiously affected appearance fascinated her. He was wearing spectacles, a contrivance which she hadn't seen for years; and he had a trim little patch of hair on his upper lip, the like of which she had never seen outside of films and theatricals. He held his head thrust forward and tilted back, and he sighted at her distastefully along the high arc of his nose.

He nodded suddenly, and turned back to his desk. "I've gone through your file, Miss—ah—Boltz." He pushed the folder aside impatiently. "My recommendation is that you retire. My secretary will give you the necessary papers to fill out. Good morning."

The suddenness of the attack startled her out of her nervousness. She said calmly, "I appreciate your interest, Mr. Wilbings, but I have no intention of retiring. Now—about my new assignment."

"My dear Miss Boltz!" He had decided to be nice to her. His expression altered perceptibly, and hovered midway between a smile and a sneer. "It is your own welfare that concerns me. I understand that your retirement might occasion some financial sacrifice, and under the circumstances I feel that we could obtain an appropriate adjustment in your pension. It would leave you secure and free to do what you like, and I can assure you that you are *not*"—he paused, and tapped his desk with one finger —"*not* suited for teaching. Painful as the idea may be for you, it is the blunt truth, and the sooner you realize it—"

For one helpless moment she could not control her laughter. He broke off angrily and stared at her.

"I'm sorry," she said, dabbing at her eyes. "I've been a teacher for twenty-five years—a good teacher, as you know if you've checked over my efficiency reports. Teaching is my whole life, and I love it, and it's a little late to be telling me that I'm not suited for it."

"Teaching is a young people's profession, and you are nearly fifty. And then—we must consider your health."

"Which is perfectly good," she said. "Of course I had cancer of the lung. It isn't uncommon on Mars. It's caused by the dust, you know, and it's easily cured."

"You had it four times, according to your records."

"I had it four times and I was cured four times. I returned to Earth only because the doctors felt that I was unusually susceptible to Martian cancer."

"Teaching on Mars—" He gestured disdainfully. "You've never taught anywhere else, and at the time you were in training your college was specializing in training teachers for Mars. There's been a revolution in education, Miss Boltz, and it has completely passed you by." He tapped his desk again, sternly. "You are not suited for teaching. Certainly not in this district."

She said stubbornly, "Will you honor my contract, or do I have to resort to legal action?"

He shrugged, and picked up her file. "Written and spoken English. Tenth grade. I assume you think you can handle that."

"I can handle it."

"Your class meets from ten-fifteen to eleven-fifteen, Monday through Friday."

"I am not interested in part-time teaching."

"This is a full-time assignment."

"Five hours a week?"

"The position assumes forty hours of class preparation. You'll probably need much more than that."

"I see," she said. She had never felt more bewildered.

"Classes begin next Monday. I'll assign you to a studio and arrange an engineering conference for you immediately."

"A—*studio?*"

"Studio." There was a note of malicious satisfaction in his voice. "You will have approximately forty thousand students."

From a drawer he took two books, one a ponderous volume

entitled *Techniques and Procedures in TV Teaching,* and the other, mecha-typed and bound with a plastic spiral, a course outline of tenth-grade English, Northeastern United States School District. "These should contain all the information you'll need," he said.

Miss Boltz said falteringly, "TV teaching? Then—my students will attend class by television?"

"Certainly."

"Then I'll never see them."

"They will see you, Miss Boltz. That is quite sufficient."

"I suppose the examinations will be machine-graded, but what about papers? I couldn't get through one assignment in an entire semester."

He scowled at her. "There are no assignments. There are no examinations, either. I suppose the educational system on Mars still uses examinations and assignments to coerce its students into learning, but we have progressed beyond those dark ages of education. If you have some idea of bludgeoning your material into your students with examinations and papers and the like, just forget it. Those things are symptomatic of bad teaching, and we would not permit it if it were possible, which it isn't."

"If there are no examinations or papers, and if I never see my students, how can I evaluate the results of my teaching?"

"We have our own method for that. You receive a Trendex rating every two weeks. Is there anything else?"

"Just one thing." She smiled faintly. "Would you mind telling me why you so obviously resent my presence here?"

"I wouldn't mind," he answered indifferently. "You have an obsolete contract that we have to honor, but we know that you will not last the term out. When you do leave we will have the problem of finding a midyear replacement for you, and forty thousand students will have been subjected to several weeks of bad instruction. You can hardly blame us for taking the position that it would be better for you to retire now. If you change your mind before Monday I will guarantee full retirement benefits for you. If not, remember this: the courts have upheld our right to retire a teacher for incompetence, regardless of tenure."

Mr. Wilbings's secretary gave her a room number. "This will be your office," she said. "Wait there, and I'll send someone."

It was a small room with a desk, bookshelves, a filing cabinet, a book-film cabinet, and a film reader. A narrow window looked out onto long rows of narrow windows. On the wall opposite the desk was a four-foot TV screen. It was the first office Miss Boltz had ever had, and she sat at her desk with the drab brown walls frowning down at her and felt lonely, and humble, and not a little frightened.

The telephone rang. After a frantic search she located it under a panel in the desk top, but by then it had stopped ringing. She examined the desk further, and found another panel that concealed the TV controls. There were four dials, each with numbers zero through nine. With almost no calculation she deduced the possible number of channels as 9,999. She tried various numbers and got a blank screen except for channel 0001, which carried an announcement: CLASSES BEGIN MONDAY, SEPTEMBER 9. REGISTRATION IS NOW IN PROGRESS. YOU MUST BE REGISTERED TO RECEIVE GRADUATION CREDITS.

A knock sounded on her door. It was a kindly-looking, graying man of fifty plus, who introduced himself as Jim Pargrin, chief engineer. He seated himself on the edge of her desk and grinned at her. "I was afraid you'd gotten lost. I telephoned, and no one answered."

"By the time I found the telephone, you'd hung up," Miss Boltz said.

He chuckled and then said seriously, "So you're the Martian. Do you know what you're getting into?"

"Did they send you up here to frighten me?"

"I don't frighten anyone but the new engineers. I just wondered—but never mind. Come over to your studio, and I'll explain the setup."

They quickly left the rows of offices behind them, and each room that they passed featured an enormous glass window facing on the corridor. Miss Boltz was reminded of the aquarium on Mars, where she sometimes took her students to show them the strange marine life on Earth.

Pargrin unlocked a door, and handed her the key. "Six-four-three-nine. A long way from your office, but at least it's on the same floor."

A hideous black desk with stubby metal legs squatted in front of a narrow blackboard. The camera stared down from the opposite wall, and beside it was a pilot screen. Pargrin unlocked a control box, and suddenly lights blinded her.

"Because you're an English teacher, they figure you don't need any special equipment," he said. "See these buttons? Number one gives you a shot of the desk and the blackboard and just about the space enclosed by that floor line. Number two is a closeup of the desk. Number three is a closeup of the blackboard. Ready to try it out?"

"I don't understand."

He touched another switch. "There."

The pilot screen flickered to life. Miss Boltz faced it—faced the dumpy-looking, middle-aged woman who stared back at her—and thought she looked cruelly old. The dress she had purchased with such care and for too much money the day before was a blur of repulsive colors. Her face was shockingly pale. She told herself sadly that she really should have spent more time on the sun deck, coming back from Mars.

"Try number two," Pargrin suggested.

She seated herself at the desk and pressed button number two. The camera twitched, and she contemplated the closeup of herself and shuddered. Number three, with herself at the blackboard, was equally bad.

Pargrin switched off the camera and closed the control box. "Here by the door is where you check in," he said. "If you haven't pressed this button by ten-fifteen, your class is automatically canceled. And then—you must leave immediately when your class is over at eleven-fifteen, so the next teacher can get ready for the eleven-thirty class. Except that it's considered good manners to clean the blackboard and tidy things up. The stuff is in the desk. Everything clear?"

"I suppose," she said. "Unless you can tell me how I'm to teach written and spoken English without ever hearing my students speak or reading anything that they write."

He was silent as they left the studio. "I know what you mean," he said, when they reached her office. "Things were different when I was a kid. TV was something you watched when your folks let you, and you went to school with all the other kids. But it's changed, now, and it seems to work out this way. At least, the big shots say it does. Anyway—the best of luck to you."

She returned to her desk, and thoughtfully opened *Techniques and Procedures in TV Teaching.*

At five minutes after ten o'clock on the following Monday morning, Miss Boltz checked in at her studio. She was rewarded with a white light over the pilot screen. She seated herself at the desk, and after pressing button number two she folded her hands and waited.

At precisely ten-fifteen the white light changed to red, and from the pilot screen her own image looked down disapprovingly. "Good morning," she said. "This is tenth-grade English. I am Miss Boltz."

She had decided to devote that first class period to introducing herself. Although she could never become acquainted with her thousands of students, she felt that they should know something about her. She owed them that much.

She talked about her years of teaching on Mars—how the students attended school together, how there were only twenty or twenty-five students in one room, instead of forty thousand attending class by way of as many TV sets. She described the recess period, when the students who went outside the dome to play had to wear air masks in order to breathe. She told about the field trips, when the class, or perhaps the entire school, would go out to study Martian plant life, or rocks and soil formations. She told them some of the questions her Martian students liked to ask about Earth.

The minutes dragged tediously. She felt imprisoned under the unblinking eye of the camera, and her image on the pilot screen began to look haggard and frightened. She had not realized that teaching could be such a strain.

The end of the hour came as a death throe. She smiled weakly, and from the pilot screen a hideous caricature of a smile grimaced back at her. "I'll be seeing you tomorrow," she said. "Good morning."

The red light faded to white. Miss Boltz took a last, shuddering look at the camera and fled.

She was seated at her desk, forlornly fighting to hold back her tears, when Jim Pargrin looked in on her.

"What's the matter?" he asked.

"Just wishing I'd stayed on Mars."

"Why would you be wishing that? You got off to a very good start."

"I didn't think so."

"I did." He smiled at her. "We took a sample Trendex on you this morning, during the last ten minutes. We sometimes do that with a new teacher. Most students will start off with their assigned classes, but if the teacher isn't good they switch to something else in a hurry. So we check at the end of the first hour to see how a new teacher is doing. Wilbings asked for a Trendex on you, and he came down to watch us take it. I think he was disappointed." He chuckled slyly. "It was just a fraction under one hundred, which is practically perfect."

He departed before she could thank him, and when she turned to her desk again her gloom had been dispelled as if by magic. Cheerfully she plunged into the task of rewriting the outline of tenth grade English.

She had no objection to the basic plan, which was comprehensive and well-constructed and at times almost logical. But the examples, the meager list of stories and novels and dramas supplied for study and supplemental reading—these were unbelievable. Just unbelievable.

"Recommended drama," the outline said. *"You Can't Marry an Elephant,* by H. N. Varga. This delightful farce—"

She crossed it out with firm strokes of her pen and wrote in the margin, "W. Shakespeare: *The Merchant of Venice.*" She substituted Dickens's *A Tale of Two Cities* for *Saddle Blankets and Six Guns,* a thrilling novel of the Old West, by Percivale Oliver. She found no unit at all which concerned itself with poetry, so she created one. Her pen slashed its way relentlessly through the outline, and her conscience troubled her not at all. Didn't the manual say that originality was encouraged in teachers?

The next morning, when she started down the corridor toward her studio, she was no longer nervous.

The vast unfriendliness of the building and the drab solitude of her office so depressed her that she decided to prepare her classes in her apartment. It was the middle of the third week before she found her way to the tenth floor, where, according to her manual, there was a cafeteria. As she awaited her turn at the vending machines the young teachers who silently surrounded her made her feel positively prehistoric.

A hand waved at her when she turned toward the tables. Jim Pargrin bounded to his feet and took her tray. A younger man helped her with her chair. After so many hours of solitude, the sudden attention left her breathless.

"My nephew," Pargrin said. "Lyle Stewart. He teaches physics. Miss Boltz is the teacher from Mars."

He was a dark-complexioned, good-looking young man

with a ready smile. She said she was pleased to meet him and meant it. "Why, you're the first teacher I've spoken to!" she exclaimed.

"Mostly we ignore each other," Stewart agreed. "It's strictly a survival-of-the-fittest occupation."

"But I'd think that some kind of co-operation—"

He shook his head. "Supposing you come up with something that clicks. You have a high Trendex, and the other teachers notice. So they watch your class, and if they can steal your stuff they will. Then you watch them, to see if they have something you can steal, and you see them using your technique. Naturally you don't like it. We've had teachers involved in assault cases, and lawsuits, and varying degrees of malicious mischief. At best, we just don't speak to each other."

"How do you like it here?" Pargrin asked her.

"I miss the students," Miss Boltz said. "It worries me, not being able to know them, or check on their progress."

"Don't you go trying to drag in an abstraction like *progress*," Stewart said bitterly. "The New Education looks at it this way: we expose the child to the proper subject matter. The exposure takes place in his home, which is the most natural environment for him. He will absorb whatever his individual capacity permits, and more than that we have no right to expect."

"The child has no sense of accomplishment—no incentive to learn," she protested.

"Under the New Education, both are irrelevant. What we are striving for is the technique that has made advertising such an important factor in our economy. Hold the people's attention, and make them buy in spite of themselves. Or hold the student's attention, and make him learn whether he wants to or not."

"But the student learns no social values."

Stewart shrugged. "On the other hand, the school has no discipline problems. No extracurricular activities to supervise. No problem of transporting the children to school and home again. You aren't convinced?"

"Certainly not!"

"Keep it to yourself. And just between us, I'll tell you the most potent factor in the philosophy of the New Education. It's money. Instead of a fortune invested in buildings and real estate, with thousands of schools to maintain, we have one

TV studio. We save another fortune in teachers' salaries by having one teacher for a good many thousands of students instead of one for maybe twenty or thirty. The bright kids will learn no matter how badly they are taught, and that's all our civilization needs—a few bright people to build a lot of bright machines. And the school tax rate is the lowest it's been in the last century and a half." He pushed back his chair. "Nice to meet you, Miss Boltz. Maybe we can be friends. Since you're an English teacher, and I'm a physics teacher, we aren't likely to steal from each other. Now I have to go think up some new tricks. My Trendex is way down."

She watched thoughtfully as he walked away. "He looks as if he's been working too hard," she announced.

"Most teachers don't have contracts like yours," Pargrin said. "They can be dismissed at any time. Lyle wants to go into industry after this year, and he may have a tough time finding a job if he's fired."

"He's leaving teaching? That's a shame!"

"There's no future in it."

"There's always a future for a good teacher."

Pargrin shook his head. "Look around you. The teachers are all young. They hang on as long as they can, because the pay is very good, but there comes a time when security means more than money. Anyway, in the not too distant future there won't be any teachers. Central District is experimenting now with filmed classes. Take a good teacher, film a year of his work, and you don't need the teacher any longer. You just run the films. No, there's very little future in teaching. Did you get your copy of the Trendex ratings?"

"Why, no. Should I have gotten one?"

"They come out every two weeks. They were distributed yesterday."

"I didn't get one."

He swore under his breath, and then looked at her apologetically. "Wilbings can be downright deceitful when he wants to. He probably thinks he'll take you by surprise."

"I'm afraid I don't understand these ratings."

"There's nothing complicated about them. Over a two-week period we'll take a thousand samples of a teacher's students. If all of them are watching their assigned class, as they should be, the teacher's Trendex is 100. If only half are watching, then the Trendex is 50. A good teacher will have about a 50 Trendex. If a teacher's Trendex falls below 20, he's dismissed. Incompetence."

"Then the children don't have to watch their classes unless they want to?"

"The parents have to provide the TV sets," Pargrin said. "They have to see that their children are present during their assigned class hours—'in attendance,' it's called—but they aren't responsible for making them watch any particular class. They'd have to supervise them every minute if that were so, and the courts have held that this would be unreasonable. It would also be unreasonable to require sets that worked only on assigned channels, and even if that were done the students could still watch classes on channels they're supposed to use at another time. So the students are there, and their sets are on, but if they don't like your class they can watch something else. You can see how important it is for the teacher to make the classes interesting."

"I understand. What was my Trendex?"

He looked away. "Zero."

"You mean—*no one* is watching me? I thought I was doing things correctly."

"You must have done something that interested them that first day. Perhaps they just got tired of it. That happens. Have you watched any of the other teachers?"

"Goodness, no! I've been so busy I just never thought of it."

"Lyle may have some ideas for you. I'll ask him to meet us at your office for the two o'clock class. And then—well, we'll see."

Lyle Stewart spread some papers on the desk in front of her, and bent over them. "These are the Trendex ratings," he said. "You were supposed to get a copy."

She glanced down the list of names, and picked out hers. Boltz, Mildred. English, tenth grade. Time, 10:15. Channel 6439. Zero. Year's average, zero.

"The subject has something to do with the tricks you can use," Stewart said. "Here's a Marjorie McMillan at two o'clock. She teaches eleventh-grade English, and her Trendex is 64. That's very high. Let's see how she does it." He set the dials.

At precisely two o'clock Marjorie McMillan appeared, and Miss Boltz's first horrified impression was that she was disrobing. Her shoes and stockings were piled neatly on the floor. She was in the act of unzipping her blouse. She glanced up at the camera.

"What are you cats and toms doing in here?" she cooed. "I thought I was alone."

She was a trim blonde, with a flashy, brazen kind of prettiness. Her profile displayed sensational curves. She smiled, tossed her head, and started to tiptoe away.

"Oh, well, as long as I'm among friends—"

The blouse came off. So did the skirt. She stood before them in an alluringly brief costume, consisting exclusively of shorts and halter. The camera recorded its scarlet and gold colors brilliantly. She pranced about in a shuffling dance step, flicking the switch for a closeup of the blackboard as she danced past her desk.

"Time to go to work, all you cats and toms," she said. "This is called a sentence." She read aloud as she wrote on the blackboard. "The—man—ran—down—the—street. 'Ran down the street' is what the man did. We call that the predicate. Funny word, isn't it? Are you with me?"

Miss Boltz uttered a bewildered protest. "*Eleventh*-grade English?"

"Yesterday we talked about verbs," Marjorie McMillan said. "Do you remember? I'll bet you weren't paying attention. I'll bet you aren't even paying attention now."

Miss Boltz gasped. The halter suddenly came unfastened. Its ends flapped loosely, and Miss McMillan snatched at it just as it started to fall. "Nearly lost it that time," she said. "Maybe I will lose it, one of these days. And you wouldn't want to miss that, would you? Better pay attention. Now let's take another look at that nasty old predicate."

Miss Boltz said quietly, "A little out of the question for me, isn't it?"

Stewart darkened the screen. "Her high rating won't last," he said. "As soon as her students decide she's really not going to lose that thing—but let's look at this one. Tenth-grade English. A male teacher. Trendex 45."

He was young, reasonably good-looking, and clever. He balanced chalk on his nose. He juggled erasers. He did imitations. He took up the reading of that modern classic, *Saddle Blankets and Six Guns,* and he read very well, acting out parts of it, creeping behind his desk to point an imaginary six-gun at the camera. It was quite realistic.

"The kids will like him," Stewart said. "He'll probably last pretty well. Now let's see if there's anyone else."

There was a history teacher, a sedate-looking young woman with a brilliant artistic talent. She drew sketches and caricatures with amazing ease and pieced them together with sprightly conversation. There was an economics teacher who performed startling magic tricks with cards and money. There were two young women whose routines approximated that of Marjorie McMillan, though in a more subdued manner. Their ratings were also much lower.

"That's enough to give you an idea of what you're up against," Stewart said.

"A teacher who can't do anything but teach is frightfully handicapped," Miss Boltz said thoughtfully. "These teachers are just performers. They aren't teaching their students—they're entertaining them."

"They have to cover the subject matter of their courses. If the students watch, they can't help learning *something*."

Jim Pargrin had remained silent while they switched from channel to channel. Now he stood up and shook his graying head solemnly. "I'll check engineering. Perhaps we could show some films for you. Normally that's frowned upon, because we haven't the staff or the facilities to do it for everyone, but I think I could manage it."

"Thank you," she said. "That's very kind of you. And thank you, Lyle, for helping out with a lost cause."

"The cause is never lost while you're still working," he said.

They left together, and long after the door closed after them Miss Boltz sat looking at the blank TV screen and wondering how long she would be working.

For twenty-five years on barren, inhospitable Mars she had dreamed of Earth. She had dreamed of walking barefoot on the green grass, with green trees and shrubs around her; and over her head, instead of the blurring transparency of an atmosphere dome, the endless expanse of blue sky. She had stood in the bleak Martian desert and dreamed of high-tossing ocean waves racing toward a watery horizon.

Now she was back on Earth, living in the unending city complex of Eastern United States. Streets and buildings impinged upon its tiny parks. The blue sky was almost obscured by air traffic. She had glimpsed the ocean once or twice, from an aircab.

But they were there for the taking, the green fields and the lakes and rivers and ocean. She had only to go to them. Instead she had worked. She had slaved over her class materials. She had spent hours writing and revising and gathering her examples, and more hours rehearsing herself meticulously, practicing over and over her single hour of teaching before she exposed it to the devouring eye of the camera.

And no one had been watching. During those first two weeks her students had turned away from her by the tens and hundreds and thousands, until she had lost them all.

She shrugged off her humiliation and took up the teaching of *The Merchant of Venice*. Jim Pargrin helped out personally, and she was able to run excellent films of background material and scenes from the play.

She said sadly, "Isn't it a shame to show these wonderful things when no one is watching?"

"*I'm* watching," Pargrin said. "I enjoy them."

His kindly eyes made her wistful for something she remembered from long ago—the handsome young man who had seen her off for Mars and looked at her in very much the same way as he promised to join her when he completed his engineering studies. He'd kissed her goodbye, and the next thing she heard he'd been killed in a freak accident. There were long years between affectionate glances for Miss Mildred Boltz, but she'd never thought of them as empty years. She had never thought of teaching as an unrewarding occupation until she found herself in a small room with only a camera looking on.

Pargrin called her when the next Trendex ratings came out. "Did you get a copy?"

"No," she said.

"I'll find an extra one, and send it up."

He did, but she knew without looking that the rating of Boltz, Mildred, English, tenth grade, and so on, was still zero.

She searched the libraries for books on the technique of TV teaching. They were replete with examples concerning those subjects that lent themselves naturally to visual presentation, but they offered very little assistance in the teaching of tenth-grade English.

She turned to the education journals and probed the mysteries of the New Education. She read about the sanctity of the individual and the right of the student to an education in his own home, undisturbed by social distractions. She read about the psychological dangers of competition in learning and the evils of artificial standards; about the dangers of old-fashioned group teaching and its sinister contribution to delinquency.

Pargrin brought in another Trendex rating. She forced herself to smile. "Zero again?"

"Well—not exactly."

She stared at the paper, blinked, and stared again. Her rating was .1—one tenth of one per cent. Breathlessly she did some mental arithmetic. She had one student! At that moment she would have waived all of her retirement benefits for the privilege of meeting that one loyal youngster.

"What do you suppose they'll do?" she asked.

"That contract of yours isn't anything to trifle with. Wilbings won't take any action until he's certain he has a good case."

"Anyway, it's nice to know that I have a student. Do you suppose there are any more?"

"Why don't you ask them to write to you? If you got a lot of letters, you could use them for evidence."

"I'm not concerned about the evidence," she said, "but I will ask them to write. Thank you."

"Miss—ah—Mildred—"

"Yes?"

"Nothing. I mean, would you like to have dinner with me tonight?"

"I'd love to."

A week went by before she finally asked her students to write. She knew only too well why she hesitated. She was afraid there would be no response.

But the morning came when she finished her class material with a minute to spare, and she folded her hands and forced a smile at the camera. "I'd like to ask you a favor. I want each of you to write me a letter. Tell me about yourself. Tell me how you like the things we've been studying. You know all about me, and I don't know anything about you. Please write to me."

She received eleven letters. She handled them reverently, and read them lovingly, and she began her teaching of *A Tale of Two Cities* with renewed confidence.

She took the letters to Jim Pargrin, and when he'd finished reading them she said, "There must be thousands like them—

bright, eager children who would love to learn if they weren't drugged into a kind of passive indifference by all this entertainment."

"Have you heard anything from Wilbings?"

"Not a thing."

"He asked me to base your next Trendex on two thousand samples. I told him I'd need a special order from the board. I doubt if he'll bother."

"He must be getting ready to do something about me."

"I'm afraid so," Pargrin said. "We really should start thinking of some line of defense for you. You'll need a lawyer."

"I don't know if I'll offer any defense. I've been wondering if I shouldn't try to set myself up as a private teacher."

"There are private schools, you know. Those that could afford it would send their children there. Those that couldn't wouldn't be able to pay you, either."

"Just the same, when I have some time I'm going to call on the children who wrote to me."

"The next Trendex is due Monday," Pargrin said. "You'll probably hear from Wilbings then."

Wilbings sent for her on Monday morning. She had not seen him since that first day, but his absurd appearance and his testy mannerisms had impressed themselves firmly upon her memory. "Are you familiar with the Trendex ratings?" he asked her.

Because she knew that he had deliberately attempted to keep her in ignorance, she shook her head innocently. Her conscience did not protest.

He patiently explained the technique and its purpose.

"If the Trendex is as valuable as you say it is," she said, "why don't you let the teachers know what their ratings are?"

"But they do know. They receive a copy of every rating."

"I received none."

"Probably an oversight, since this is your first term. However, I have all of them except today's, and that one will be sent down as soon as it's ready. You're welcome to see them."

He went over each report in turn, ceremoniously pointing out her zeros. When he reached the rating of .1, he paused. "You see, Miss Boltz, out of the thousands of samples taken, we have found only one student who was watching you. This is by far the worst record we have ever had. I must ask you to retire voluntarily, and if you refuse, then I have no alternative—"

He broke off as his secretary tiptoed in with the new
Trendex. "Yes. Thank you. Here we are. Boltz, Mildred—"

His finger wavered comically. Paralysis seemed to have
clogged his power of speech. Miss Boltz found her name, and
followed the line across the page to her rating.

It was 27.

"Evidently I've improved," she heard herself say. "Is there
anything else?"

It took him a moment to find his voice, and when he did its
pitch had risen perceptibly. "No. Nothing else."

As she went through the outer office she heard his voice
again, still high-pitched, squawking angrily in his secretary's communicator. "Pargrin. I want Pargrin down here
immediately."

He was waiting for her in the cafeteria. "It went all right, I
suppose," he said, with studied casualness.

"It went too well."

He took a large bite of sandwich, and chewed solemnly.

"Jim, why did you do it?" she demanded.

He blushed. "Do what?"

"Arrange my Trendex that way."

"Nobody *arranges* a Trendex. It isn't possible. Even Wilbings
will tell you that." He added softly, "How did you know?"

"It's the only possible explanation, and you shouldn't have
done it. You might get into trouble, and you're only postpon-
ing the inevitable. I'll be at zero again on the next rating."

"That doesn't matter. Wilbings will take action eventually,
but now he won't be impulsive about it."

They ate in silence until the cafeteria manager came in
with an urgent message for Mr. Pargrin from Mr. Wilbings.
Pargrin winked at her. "I think I'm going to enjoy this. Will
you be in your office this afternoon?"

She shook her head. "I'm going to visit my students."

"I'll see you tomorrow, then."

She looked after him thoughtfully. She sincerely hoped
that he hadn't gotten himself in trouble.

On the rooftop landing area she asked the manager to call
an aircab for her. While she waited she took a letter from her
purse and reread it.

*My name is Darrel Wilson. I'm sixteen years old, and I have
to stay in my room most of the time because I had Redger
disease and part of me is paralyzed. I like your class, and
please, could we have some more Shakespeare?*

"Here's your cab, ma'am."

"Thank you," Miss Boltz said. She returned the letter to her purse and stepped briskly up the cab ramp.

Jim Pargrin ruffled his hair and stared at her. "Whoa, now. What was that again? *Class*room?"

"I have nine students who are coming here every day to go to school. I'll need some place to teach them."

Pargrin clucked his tongue softly. "Wilbings would have a hemorrhage!"

"My TV class takes only five hours a week, and I have the entire year's work planned. Why should anyone object to my holding classes for a selected group of students on my own time?" She added softly, "These students *need* it."

They were wonderful children, brilliant children, but they needed to be able to ask questions, to articulate their thoughts and feelings, to have their individual problems dealt with sympathetically. They desperately needed each other. Tens of thousands, hundreds of thousands of gifted children were being intellectually and emotionally stifled in the barren solitude of their TV classes.

"What Wilbings doesn't know won't hurt him," Pargrin said. "At least, I hope it won't. But—a classroom? There isn't a thing like that in the building. Could you use a large studio? We could hang a curtain over the glass so you wouldn't be disturbed. What hours would your class meet?"

"All day. Nine to three. They'll bring their lunches."

"Whoa, now. Don't forget your TV class. Even if no one is watching—"

"I'm not forgetting it. My students will use that hour for a study period. Unless you could arrange for me to hold my TV class in this larger studio."

"Yes. I can do that."

"Wonderful! I can't thank you enough."

He shrugged his shoulders, and shyly looked away.

"Did you have any trouble with Mr. Wilbings?" she asked.

"Not much. He thought your Trendex was a mistake. Since I don't take the ratings personally, the best I could do was refer him to the Trendex engineer."

"Then I'm safe for a little while. I'll start my class tomorrow."

Three of the students arrived in power chairs. Ella was a lovely, sensitive girl who had been born without legs, and though science had provided her with a pair, she did not like to use them. Darrel and Charles were victims of Redger disease. Sharon was blind. The TV entertainers failed to reach her with their tricks, but she listened to Miss Boltz's every word with a rapt expression on her face.

Their intelligence level exceeded by far that of any other class in Miss Boltz's experience. She felt humble, and not a little apprehensive; but her apprehension vanished as she looked at their shining faces that first morning and welcomed them to her venture into the Old Education.

She had two fellow conspirators. Jim Pargrin personally took charge of the technical aspects of her hour on TV and gleefully put the whole class on camera. Lyle Stewart, who found the opportunity to work with real students too appealing to resist, came in the afternoon to teach two hours of science and mathematics. Miss Boltz laid out her own study units firmly. History, English, literature, and social studies. Later, if the class continued, she would try to work in a unit on foreign language. That Wednesday was her happiest day since she returned to Earth.

On Thursday morning a special messenger brought in an official-looking envelope. It contained her dismissal notice.

"I already heard about it," Jim Pargrin said, when she telephoned him. "When is the hearing?"

"Next Tuesday."

"It figures. Wilbings got board permission for a special Trendex. He even brought in an outside engineer to look after it, and just to be doubly sure they used two thousand samples. You'll need an attorney. Know any?"

"No. I know hardly anyone on Earth." She sighed. She'd been so uplifted by her first day of actual teaching that this abrupt encounter with reality stunned her. "I'm afraid an attorney would cost a lot of money, and I'm going to need what money I have."

"A little thing like a Board of Education hearing shouldn't cost much. Just you leave it to me—I'll find an attorney for you."

She wanted to object, but there was no time. Her students were waiting for her.

On Saturday she had lunch with Bernard Wallace, the attorney Jim Pargrin recommended. He was a small, elderly man with sharp gray eyes that stabbed at her fleetingly from behind drooping eyelids. He questioned her casually during lunch, and when they had pushed aside their dessert dishes he leaned back and twirled a key ring on one finger and grinned at her.

"Some of the nicest people I ever knew were my teachers," he said. "I thought they didn't make that kind any more. I don't suppose you realize that your breed is almost extinct."

"There are lots of fine teachers on Mars," she said.

"Sure. Colonies look at education differently. They'd be commiting suicide if they just went through the motions. I kind of think maybe we're committing suicide here on Earth. This New Education thing has some results you may not know about. The worst one is that the kids aren't getting educated. Businessmen have to train their new employees from primary-grade level. It's had an impact on government, too. An election campaign is about what you'd expect with a good part of the electorate trained to receive its information in very weak doses with a sickening amount of sugar coating. So I'm kind of glad to be able to work on this case. You're not to worry about the expense. There won't be any."

"That's very kind of you," she murmured. "But helping one worn-out teacher won't improve conditions very much."

"I'm not promising to win this for you," Wallace said soberly. "Wilbings has all the good cards. He can lay them right out on the table, and you have to keep yours hidden because your best defense would be to show them what a mess of arrant nonsense this New Education is, and you can't do that. We don't dare attack the New Education. That's the board's baby, and they've already defended it successfully in court, a lot of times. If we win, we'll have to win on their terms."

"That makes it rather hopeless, doesn't it?"

"Frankly, it'll be tough." He pulled out an antique gold watch, and squinted at it. "Frankly, I don't see how I'm going to bring it off. Like I said, Wilbings has the cards, and anything I lead is likely to be trumped. But I'll give it some thought, and maybe I can come up with a surprise or two. You just concentrate on your teaching, and leave the worrying to me."

After he left she ordered another cup of coffee, and sipped it slowly, and worried.

On Monday morning she received a surprise of her own, in the form of three boys and four girls who presented themselves at her office and asked permission to join her class. They had seen it on TV, they told her, and it looked like fun. She was pleased, but doubtful. Only one of them was officially a student of hers. She took the names of the others and sent them home. The one who was properly her student she permitted to remain.

He was a gangling boy of fifteen, and though he seemed bright enough, there was a certain withdrawn sullenness about him that made her uneasy. His name was Randy Stump—"A dumb name, but I'm stuck with it," he mumbled. She quoted him Shakespeare on the subject of names, and he gaped at her bewilderedly.

Her impulse was to send him home with the others. Such a misfit might disrupt her class. What stopped her was the thought that the suave TV teacher, the brilliant exponent of the New Education, would do just that. Send him home. Have him watch the class on TV in the sanctity of his own natural environment, where he couldn't get into trouble, and just incidentally where he would never learn to get along with people.

She told herself, "I'm a poor excuse for a teacher if I can't handle a little problem in discipline."

He shifted his feet uneasily as she studied him. He was a foot taller than she, and he looked past her and seemed to find a blank wall intensely interesting.

He slouched along at her side as she led him down to the classroom, where he seated himself at the most remote desk and instantly lapsed into a silent immobility that seemed to verge on hypnosis. The others attempted to draw him into their discussions, but he ignored them. Whenever Miss Boltz looked up she found his eyes fixed upon her intently. Eventually she understood: he was attending class, but he was still watching it on TV.

Her hour on television went well. It was a group discussion on *A Tale of Two Cities*, and the youthful sagacity of her class delighted her. The red light faded at eleven-fifteen. Jim Pargrin waved his farewell, and she waved back at him and turned to her unit on history. She was searching her mind for something that would draw Randy Stump from his TV-inflicted shell.

When she looked up her students were staring at the door, which had opened silently. A dry voice said, "What *is* going on here?"

It was Roger Wilbings.

He removed his spectacles, and replaced them. "Well!" he said. His mustache twitched nervously. "May I ask the meaning of this?"

No one spoke. Miss Boltz had carefully rehearsed her explanation in the event that she should be called to account for this unauthorized teaching, but this unexpected confrontation left her momentarily speechless.

"Miss Boltz!" His mouth opened and closed several times as he groped for words. "I have seen many teachers do many idiotic things, but I have never seen anything quite as idiotic as this. I am happy to have this further confirmation of your hopeless incompetence. Not only are you a disgustingly inept teacher, but obviously you suffer from mental derangement. No rational adult would bring these—these—"

He paused. Randy Stump had emerged from his hypnosis with a snap. He leaped forward, planted himself firmly in front of Wilbings, and snarled down at him. "You take that back!"

Wilbings eyed him coldly. "Go home. Immediately." His gaze swept the room. "All of you. Go home. Immediately."

"You can't make us," Randy said.

Wilbings poised himself on the high pinnacle of his authority. "No young criminal—"

Randy seized his shoulders and shook vigorously. Wilbings's spectacles flew in a long arc and shattered. He wrenched himself free and struck out weakly, and Randy's return blow landed with a splattering thud. The Deputy Superintendent reeled backward into the curtain and then slid gently to the floor as glass crashed in the corridor outside.

Miss Boltz bent over him. Randy hovered nearby, frightened and contrite. "I'm sorry, Miss Boltz," he stammered.

"I'm sure you are," she said. "But for now—I think you had better go home."

Eventually Wilbings was assisted away. To Miss Boltz's intense surprise, he said nothing more; but the look he flashed in her direction as he left the room made further conversation unnecessary.

Jim Pargrin brought a man to replace the glass. "Too bad," he observed. "He can't have it in for you any more than he already had, but now he'll try to make something of this class of yours at the hearing tomorrow."

"Should I send them all home?" she asked anxiously.

"Well, now. That would be quitting, wouldn't it? You just carry on—we can fix this without disturbing you."

She returned to her desk and opened her notebook. "Yesterday we were talking about Alexander the Great—"

The fifteen members of the Board of Education occupied one side of a long, narrow table. They were business and professional men, most of them elderly, all solemn, some obviously impatient.

On the opposite side of the table Miss Boltz sat at one end with Bernard Wallace. Roger Wilbings occupied the other end with a bored technician who was preparing to record the proceedings. A fussy little man Wallace identified as the Superintendent of Education fluttered into the room, conferred briefly with Wilbings, and fluttered out.

"Most of 'em are fair," Wallace whispered. "They're honest, and they mean well. That's on our side. Trouble is, they don't know anything about education and it's been a long time since they were kids."

From his position at the center of the table, the president called the meeting to order. He looked narrowly at Bernard Wallace. "This is not a trial," he announced. "This is merely a hearing to secure information essential for the board to reach a proper decision. We do not propose to argue points of law."

"Lawyer himself," Wallace whispered, "and a good one."

"You may begin, Wilbings," the president said.

Wilbings got to his feet. The flesh around one eye was splendidly discolored, and he smiled with difficulty. "The reason for this meeting concerns the fact that Mildred Boltz holds a contract, type 79B, issued to her in the year 2022. You will recall that this school district originally became responsible for these contracts during a shortage of teachers on Mars, when—"

The president rapped on the table. "We understand that, Wilbings. You want Mildred Boltz dismissed because of incompetence. Present your evidence of incompetence, and we'll see what Miss Boltz has to say about it, and wind this up. We don't want to spend the afternoon here."

Wilbings bowed politely. "I now supply to all those present four regular Trendex ratings of Mildred Boltz, as well as one special rating which was recently authorized by the board."

Papers were passed around. Miss Boltz looked only at the

special Trendex, which she had not seen. Her rating was .2—two tenths of one per cent.

"Four of these ratings are zero or so low that for all practical purposes we can call them zero," Wilbings said. "The rating of 27 constitutes a special case."

The president leaned forward. "Isn't it a little unusual for a rating to deviate so sharply from the norm?"

"I have reason to believe that this rating represents one of two things—fraud, or error. I freely admit that this is a personal belief, and that I have no evidence which would be acceptable in court."

The board members whispered noisily among themselves. The president said slowly, "I have been assured at least a thousand times that the Trendex is infallible. Would you kindly give us the basis for this personal belief of yours?"

"I would prefer not to."

"Then we shall disregard this personal belief."

"The matter is really irrelevant. Even if the 27 is included, Miss Boltz has a nine-week average of only 5 and a fraction."

Bernard Wallace was tilted back in his chair, one hand thrust into a pocket, the other twirling his keys. "We don't consider that 27 irrelevant," he said.

The president frowned. "If you will kindly let Wilbings state his case—"

"Gladly. What's he waiting for?"

Wilbings flushed. "It is inconceivable that a teacher of any competence whatsoever could have ratings of zero, or of fractions of a per cent. As further evidence of Miss Boltz's incompetence, I wish to inform the board that without authorization she brought ten of her students to a studio in this building and attempted to teach them in class periods lasting an entire morning and an entire afternoon."

The shifting of feet, the fussing with cigarettes, the casual whispering stopped. Puzzled glances converged upon Miss Boltz. Wilbings made the most of the silence before he continued.

"I shall not review for you the probably deadly effect of this obsolete approach to education. All of you are familiar with it. In case the known facts require any substantiation, I am prepared to offer in evidence a statement of the physical damage resulting from just one of these class periods, as well as my own person, which was assaulted by one of the young hoodlums in her charge. Fortunately I discovered this sinister plot against the youth of our district before the effects of her unauthorized teaching became irreparable. Her immediate dismissal will of course put an end to it. That, gentlemen, constitutes our case."

The president said, "This is hard to believe, Miss Boltz. Would you mind telling the board why—"

Bernard Wallace interrupted. "Is it our turn?"

The president hesitated, looked along the table for suggestions, and got none. "Go ahead," he said.

"A question, gentlemen. How many of you secured your own elementary and/or secondary education under the deadly circumstances Wilbings has just described? Hands, please, and let's be honest. Eight, ten, eleven. Eleven out of fifteen. Thank you. Do you eleven gentlemen attribute your present state of degradation to that sinister style of education?" The board members smiled.

"You, Wilbings," Wallace went on. "You talk as if everyone is or should be familiar with the deadly effects of group teaching. Are you an authority on it?"

"I am certainly familiar with all of the standard studies and research," Wilbings said stiffly.

"Ever experience that kind of education yourself? Or teach under those conditions?"

"I certainly have not!"

"Then you are not personally an authority. All you really know about these so-called deadly effects is what some other windbag has written."

"Mr. Wallace!"

"Let it pass. Is my general statement correct? All you really know—"

"I am quite prepared to accept the statements of an acknowledged authority in the field."

"Any of these acknowledged authorities ever have any experience of group teaching?"

"If they are reputable authorities—"

Wallace banged on the table. "Not the question," he snapped. "Reputable among whom? Question is whether they really know anything about what they write about. Well?"

"I'm sure I can't say just what basis they use for their studies."

"Probably not the only basis that counts—knowing their subject. If I could produce for you an authority with years of actual experience and study of the group-teaching system, would you take that authority's word as to its effects, harmful or otherwise?"

"I am always happy to give proper consideration to the work of any reliable authority," Wilbings said.

"What about you gentlemen?"

"We aren't experts in education," the president said. "We have to rely on authorities."

"Splendid. I now give you Miss Mildred Boltz, whose twenty-five years of group teaching on Mars makes her probably the most competent authority on this subject in the Western Hemisphere. Miss Boltz, is group teaching in any way harmful to the student?"

"Certainly not," Miss Boltz said. "In twenty-five years I can't recall a single case where group teaching was not beneficial to the student. On the other hand, TV teaching—"

She broke off as Wallace's elbow jabbed at her sharply.

"So much for the latter part of Wilbings's argument," Wallace said. "Miss Boltz is an expert in the field of group teaching. No one here is qualified to question her judgment in that field. If she brought together ten of her students, she knew what she was doing. Matter of fact, I personally would think it a pretty good thing for a school district to have one expert in group teaching on its staff. Wilbings doesn't seem to think so, but you gentlemen of the board might want to consider that. Now—about this Trendex nonsense."

Wilbings said coldly, "The Trendex ratings are not nonsense."

"Think maybe I could show you they are, but I don't want to take the time. You claim this rating of 27 is due to fraud or error. How do you know those other ratings aren't due to fraud or error? Take this last one—this special rating. How do you know?"

"Since you make an issue of it," Wilbings said, "I will state that Miss Boltz is the personal friend of a person on the engineering staff who is in a position to influence any rating if he so desires. This friend knew that Miss Boltz was about to be dismissed. Suddenly, for one time only, her rating shot up to a satisfactory level. The circumstances speak for themselves."

"Why are you so certain that this last rating is not due to fraud or error?"

"Because I brought in an outside engineer who could be trusted. He took this last Trendex on Miss Boltz personally."

"There you have it," Wallace said scornfully. "Wilbings

wants Miss Boltz dismissed. He's not very confident that the
regular Trendex, taken by the district's own engineers, will
do the job. So he calls in a personal friend from outside, one
he can trust to give him the kind of rating he wants. Now if
that doesn't open the door to fraud and error—"

The uproar rattled the distant windows. Wilbings was on
his feet screaming. The president was pounding for order.
The board members were arguing heatedly among themselves.

"Gentlemen," Wallace said, when he could make himself
heard, "I'm no Trendex authority, but I can tell you that
these five ratings, and the circumstances surrounding them,
add up to nothing but a mess. I'll take you to court cheerfully,
and get you laughed out of court, if that's what you want, but
there may be an easier way. At this moment I don't think any
of us really know whether Mildred Boltz is competent or not.
Let's find out. Let's have another Trendex, and have it
without fussing around with samples. Let's have a Trendex of
all of Miss Boltz's students. I won't make any promises, but if
the results of such a rating were in line with this Trendex
average, I would be disposed to recommend that Miss Boltz
accept her dismissal without a court test."

"That sounds reasonable," the president said. "And sensible. Get Pargrin in here, Wilbings, and we'll see if it can be
done."

Miss Boltz sank back in her chair and looked glumly at the
polished table top. She felt betrayed. It was perfectly obvious
that her only chance for a reprieve depended upon her refut-
ing the validity of those Trendex ratings. The kind of test
Wallace was suggesting would confirm them so decisively as
to shatter any kind of a defense. Certainly Jim Pargrin would
understand that.

When he came in he studiously avoided looking at her. "It's
possible," he said, when the president described what was
wanted. "It'll upset our schedule, and it might make us late
with the next Trendex, but if it's important we can do it. Will
tomorrow be all right?"

"Is tomorrow all right, Wilbings?" the president asked.

"Where Miss Boltz is concerned, I have no confidence in
any kind of rating taken by our staff."

Pargrin elevated his eyebrows. "I don't know what you're
getting at, but if you've got doubts just send in that engineer
of yours and let him help out. With this extra load the
Trendex men would probably appreciate it."

"Is that satisfactory, Wilbings?" the president asked.

Wilbings nodded. "Perfectly satisfactory."

"Very well. Miss Boltz's class ends at eleven-fifteen. Can we have the results by eleven-thirty? Good. The board will meet tomorrow at eleven-thirty and make final disposition of this case."

The meeting broke up. Bernard Wallace patted Miss Boltz on the arm and whispered into her ear, "Now don't you worry about a thing. You just carry on as usual, and give us the best TV class you can. It's going to be so tough it'll be easy."

She returned to her class, where Lyle Stewart was filling in for her. "How did you make out?" Stewart asked.

"The issue is still in doubt," she said. "But not very much in doubt, I'm afraid. Tomorrow may be our last day, so let's see how much we can accomplish.

Her TV class that Wednesday morning was the best she'd ever had. The students performed brilliantly. As she watched them she thought with an aching heart of her lost thousands of students, who had taken to watching jugglers and magicians and young female teachers in tights.

The red light faded. Lyle Stewart came in. "Very nice," he said.

"You were wonderful!" Miss Boltz told her class.

Sharon, the blind girl, said tearfully, "You'll tell us what happens, won't you? Right away?"

"I'll tell you as soon as I know," Miss Boltz said. She forced a smile and left the studio quickly.

As she hurried along the corridor a lanky figure moved to intercept her—tall, pale of face, frighteningly irrational in appearance. "Randy!" she exclaimed. "What are you doing here?"

"I'm sorry, Miss Boltz. I'm really sorry, and I won't do it again. Can I come back?"

"I'd love to have you back, Randy, but there may not be any class after today."

He seemed stunned. "No class?"

She shook her head. "I'm very much afraid that I'm going to be dismissed. Fired, you might say."

He clenched his fists. Tears streaked his face, and he sobbed brokenly. She tried to comfort him, and some minutes went by before she understood why he was weeping. "Randy!"

she exclaimed. "It isn't your fault that I'm being dismissed. What you did had nothing to do with it."

"We won't let them fire you," he sobbed. "All of us—us kids—we won't let them."

"We have to abide by the laws, Randy."

"But they won't fire you." His face brightened, and he nodded his head excitedly. "You're the best teacher I ever saw. I know they won't fire you. Can I come back to class?"

"If there's a class tomorrow, Randy, you may come back. I have to hurry, now. I'm going to be late."

She was already late when she reached the ground floor. She moved breathlessly along the corridor to the board room and stopped in front of the closed door. Her watch said fifteen minutes to twelve.

She knocked timidly. There was no response.

She knocked louder and finally opened the door a crack.

The room was empty. There were no board members, no technician, no Wilbings, no attorney Wallace. It was over and done with, and they hadn't even bothered to tell her the result.

They knew that she would know. She brushed her eyes with her sleeve. "Courage," she whispered and turned away.

As she started back up the corridor, hurrying footsteps overtook her. It was Bernard Wallace, and he was grinning. "I wondered what kept you,' he said. "I went to check. Have you heard the news?"

She shook her head. "I haven't heard anything."

"Your Trendex was 99.2 Wilbings took one look and nearly went through the ceiling. He wanted to scream 'Fraud!' but he didn't dare, not with his own engineer on the job. The board took one look and dismissed the case. Think maybe they were in a mood to dismiss Wilbings, too, but they were in a hurry."

Miss Boltz caught her breath, and found the friendly support of a wall. "It isn't possible!"

"It's a fact. We kind of planned this. Jim and I pulled the names of all of your students, and we sent letters to them. Special class next Wednesday. Big deal. Don't miss it. Darned few of them missed it. Wilbings played right into our hands, and we clobbered him."

"No," Miss Boltz said. She shook her head, and sighed. "No. There's no use pretending. I'm grateful, of course, but it was a trick, and when the next Trendex comes out Mr. Wilbings will start over again."

"It was a trick," Wallace agreed, "but a kind of a permanent trick. It's like this. The younger generation has never experienced anything like this real live class of yours. On the first day you told them all about school on Mars, and you fascinated them. You held their attention. Jim was telling me about that. We figured that putting this class of yours on TV would fascinate them, too. Wilbings took that special Trendex before you got your class going, but Jim has been sneaking one every day since then, and your rating has been moving up. It was above 10 yesterday, and now that all of your kids know what you're doing it'll jump way up and stay there. So—no more worries. Happy?"

"Very happy. And very grateful."

"One more thing. The president of the board wants to talk to you about this class of yours. I had dinner with him last night, and I filled him in. He's interested. I've got a suspicion that he maybe has a personal doubt or two about this New Education. Of course we won't tear down TV teaching overnight, but we're making a start. I have work to do, now. I'll be seeing you."

He shuffled away, twirling his keys.

She turned again, and saw Jim Pargrin coming toward her. She gripped his hand and said, "I owe it all to you."

"You owe it to nobody but yourself. I was up telling your class. They're having a wild celebration."

"Goodness—I hope they don't break anything!"

"I'm glad for you. I'm a little sorry, too." He was looking at her again in that way that made her feel younger—almost youthful. "I figured that if you lost your job maybe I could talk you into marrying me." He looked away shyly. "You'd have missed your teaching, of course, but maybe we could have had some children of our own—"

She blushed wildly. "Jim Pargrin! At our ages?"

"Adopt some, I mean."

"Really—I've never given a thought to what I might have missed by not having my own children. I've had a family all my life, ever since I started teaching, and even if the children were different every year I've loved them all. And now I have a family waiting for me, and I was so nervous this morning I left my history notes in my office. I'll have to run." She took a few steps, and turned to look back at him. "What made you think I wouldn't marry you if I kept on teaching?"

His startled exclamation was indistinct, but long after she turned a corner she heard him whistling.

On the sixth floor she moved down the corridor toward her office, hurrying because her students were celebrating and she didn't want to miss that. Looking ahead, she saw the door of her office open slowly. A face glanced in her direction, and suddenly a lanky figure flung the door aside and bolted away. It was Randy Stump.

She came to a sudden halt. "Randy!" she whispered.

But what could he want in her office? There was nothing there but her notebooks, and some writing materials, and—her purse! She'd left her purse on her desk.

"Randy!" she whispered again. She opened the office door, and looked in. Suddenly she was laughing—laughing and crying—and she leaned against the door frame to steady herself as she exclaimed, "Now where would he get an idea like that?"

Her purse still lay on her desk, untouched. Beside it, glistening brilliantly in the soft overhead light, was a grotesquely large, polished apple.

Part III: The Consequences of TV

WHILE we don't really have a "dim" view of television, the word does serve as a mnemonic device for the three primary methods by which the consequences of television can occur: *d*irectly, *i*ndirectly, and *m*ediately. Direct effects occur through the message itself, as presented verbally or portrayed pictorally. Indirect effects occur through setting, camera angle, and editing as well as incidental factors. For example, spending five hours a day in front of the tube precludes other activities. Finally, mediated effects occur when members of the audience pass on information to their friends and acquaintances.

As to the specific consequences of television, they are, of course, numerous as well as powerful. However, as several of the following stories illustrate, indirect or mediated factors are usually responsible for the more important effects.

Watching TV may indirectly promote nostalgia, as Jack C. Haldeman points out in "What Time Is It?" What we spent so much time watching as kids, such as "Our Miss Brooks" or "Star Trek," we tend to remember fondly and wish we could see again.

Frank A. Javor's "Interview" considers an even more basic consequence: watching TV may give us ideas about what is true and what isn't (perceptions of social reality). Remember the opinions you formed about each of the Watergate witnesses? Yet even live television is filtered through machines which can sometimes trick us (intentionally or otherwise) into believing something is reality when it is not.

Larry Niven's "Cloak of Anarchy" looks at how being on television affects deviant behavior. Here, as you might suspect, the feeling of being under surveillance, such as by bank cameras, tends to increase fear of punishment, thus reducing the probabilities of deviance. Ironically, however, watching today's TV may have the opposite effect. So much violence is shown that some may see it as a perfectly legitimate form of problem solving.

Theodore Sturgeon's "And Now the News" suggests that watching television might cause information overload and result in disorganization, withdrawal, and despair. Sound ridiculous? Well, according to Alan Toffler (author of *Future Shock*), today's knowledge is less than 3 percent of what will be known fifty years from now. And, according to a psychologist named Ludwig, just exposing people to fairly brief overloads of light and sound may produce feelings of loss of control, perceptual distortions, diminished reality testing, and other worldly feelings.

Television commonly influences values of goodness, rightness, and importance by how, and even whether, it covers certain people or events. In "Very Proper Charlies," for example, science fiction's resident Ph.D. in mass media argues that present coverage of terrorists may indirectly glorify and perpetuate them. So what's the solution? To Dean Ing, it's laughably simple.

Finally, Frank Herbert's "Committee of the Whole" illustrates how television, with the important help of mediators, spreads ideas quickly. Unfortunately, good ideas aren't the only ones that are disseminated. For example, one survey of a maximum-security prison in Michigan found that 90 percent of the inmates had learned new criminal skills from watching TV.

WHAT TIME IS IT?

JACK C. HALDEMAN II

"**I** still say they could have done more." The copilot swiveled around in his well-padded chair. Crumbs fell from his lap.

"What's that, Bob?" The pilot gazed idly at the flashing lights in front of him. All he ever had to do was watch the lights. They told him how well the computers were running the ship.

"I thought at least the vice-president could have been there to see us off. He even shows up at Boy Scout meetings."

"What are you babbling about?" George, the pilot, turned away from the flashing lights to face his copilot. He set his peanut butter and jelly sandwich on the console in front of him.

"Darn it. This *is* the first faster-than-light expedition. They could have done something. Anything. A short speech or a farewell dinner would have been nice. What's wrong with them?" He threw an empty box of candy across the control room.

"Take it easy. Why should they get all excited? This run is going to be a piece of cake."

"What happened to your sense of history? At last the stars are ours. There are no limits to what we can do."

"It'll be years before we get to that. The government just doesn't have the money." George looked back at his lights. Everything was green and normal, as always.

"But there's money to be made out *there*, too. Can't they see that?"

"That's why we're sitting here now. Money." George pulled a comic book from underneath his seat and tried to ignore the ranting of his copilot.

Bob soon caught on to the fact that there was little to be gained by talking to a pilot buried in a comic book. He yearned for the excitement of the old Mars run where you could at least count on a little diversion. With a grin he remembered how the atomic pile had gone bananas every other trip.

He decided that there really wasn't much to do in the control room except sit and watch George read. With the computers taking care of the ship, he, as copilot, was a double redundancy. He stood up and started aft, hoping that he might find something to liven up the trip.

In the narrow passageway he met one of the passengers, an old millionaire from Dallas.

"Howdy, commander. How're we doing?" The old man touched the brim of his stetson with a gnarled finger.

"Just fine. It shouldn't be long now." Bob was a long way from being a commander, but he didn't want to disillusion the old gent.

"We can hardly wait, you know. We've polished up the equipment and everything is ready to go. Would you like to see my Duncan yo-yo? It's a wooden one—very hard to find these days."

"No thank you."

"Monopoly cards? I have a mint condition Marvin Gardens."

"Some other time."

Bob turned back to the control room. Anything would be better than listening to all those old men talk about the past. Besides money, it was all they ever talked about.

As he entered the control room, his years of training told him that something was wrong. His sharp eyes picked out the twenty or thirty flashing red lights on the control panel while his acute hearing noted that the alarm bell was ringing.

George was running around in circles.

"What's happening?" asked Bob, starting to back out the door.

"I don't know. Everything went off at once."

"Did you check the flight manual?"

"Good idea. I'll do that." George started rooting through the stacks of comics and porno that littered the control console. Everything was smeared with peanut butter.

"It's here somewhere. Ah, yes. This is it." He held up a plastic-covered notebook. A blob of jelly slid off the cover.

"Look under lights and bells comma what to do period," Bob suggested hopefully.

"Here it is! It indicates we are coming out of faster-than-light drive."

"Oh my God! What'll that do to us?"

"Nothing. It means we've arrived at our destination. All we have to do is tell the passengers."

"I'll go tell them," said Bob, anxious to get away from the noise and confusion.

He made his way back down the passageway and could hear excited noises from the living quarters. There was no need to notify the old men. They must have heard the alarm. He opened the door.

The twelve richest men in the world were hunched over their equipment. This was the very moment they had paid an inconceivable amount of money for—the ultimate culmination of man's technology. The room was filled with a flickering gray light.

The men were crowded around a large wooden box. It had a three-inch screen with a magnifying glass in front of it. They were watching the fuzzy television images that had left the Earth years and years ago—long before video tape had been around to preserve the signals. Some of the men clutched old television schedules; some wore hats with ears on them. A freckle-faced puppet was dancing on the screen while a clown squirted seltzer water.

All together now.

Hey kids! What time is it?

Interview

FRANK A. JAVOR

LOOKING at the woman, Lester V. Morrison felt deep inside himself the stirring of sympathy, familiar, rising to the sustained, heady rapport that made him know, with the certainty of long experience, that this was going to be another of his great interviews.

He smiled and loosened the fist he'd made unconsciously to emphasize the word "great" when it passed through his mind.

He felt a light touch on his arm and turning, bowed his head so that his lead technician could slip over it the video-audio headband. Its close-fitting temple pieces curved to touch the bone behind his ears and the twin stereo view-finder cameras came down over his eyes.

Lester rather liked to make the subdued bowing movement, the symbolic humbling, it pleased him to think, of his six-and-almost-a-half-foot tallness to receive the crownlike headgear of his craft. A crown heavy, not with the scant two ounces of transmitting metal and optical plastic, but heavy with his responsibility to the billions upon billions of viewers who would see what Lester looked upon, would hear what he turned his ear to; the center of their universe for those moments the spot upon which Lester stood, the signal spreading outward from it like the ripple pattern of a dropped stone.

His technician pressed Lester's arm twice and stepped back. Lester stood erect, his hands and fingers hovering over the twin-arced rows of buttons and rods set in the flat surface of the control console he wore high on his chest like an ancient breastplate. There was no speaking between Lester and his four-man crew, nor any testing of equipment. Lester wore his responsibility with what he considered a suitable humility, but with a firm confidence. Let lesser men fiddle with their equipment, talk, blur the virgin spontaneity of the look that would flash into the woman's eyes with the first impact of Lester's equipment upon her. His men, like Lester, were the absolute best in their field; razor-honed by long close union and good pay until they responded almost symbiotically to Lester and each other.

A clear warning warble from his left earphone, heard only by Lester through the bones of his skull, readied him to begin his task. He stood firmly tall, silent, waiting . . .

A musical bleat. The suddenly glowing red face of the timer in the upper corner of his left viewfinder. He was on the air.

The general view first. Eight seconds to set the scene, to let his viewers see for themselves the sordid slum he was standing in. To see the aged, crumbling buildings, some of them as much as twelve and even fourteen years old, engineered to have been torn down and replaced long ago. Long before a tragedy of this kind could strike. To form their own opinion of a council that could allow such a blight to exist on their planet.

Smoothly Lester pivoted his body, one shoulder leading, a counterbalance for the slightly trailing head, editorializing subtly by what he chose to look at, by what he chose to ignore. Flowingly, easily, compensating automatically for even the rise and fall of his own controlled breathing. A beautifully functioning, rock-steady camera vehicle Lester was. It was the least of his interviewing skills.

A closer shot. His thumb brushed a rod on his breastplate. The view in his finders grew larger. Armor-suited men, resting now, but still strapped in the seats of their half-track diggers. Orange-painted against the greening dust and the bright red glow of the police-erected crowd-control barrier force field like a sheltering dome over them. Through it, visible above and around in all directions, a swirling, shifting mass upon mass of human beings. Some in fliers, others on skimmers. Some strapped in one-man jumpers and even on foot. A boiling, roiling swarm of the morbidly, humanly curious pressing all around, straining toward the little knot of blue-coverall-clad men and their pitifully small, broken burden.

*   *   *

Lester's fingers and palms brushed the rods and buttons of his breastplate-console. Let the rattle and the clank and the sound of the crowd stay as they are. A shade more of the force field's rasping hum to warm his viewer's nerve endings . . . to ready them . . .

The woman's sobbing. His thumb touched a stud. Let it start to come through now. Softly . . . barely hearable . . . subtly swelling.

The little knot of blue-coverall-clad men. A medium shot, then rapidly to a close-up of their burden, the dangling limbs half-hidden by their bodies and the merciful sagging of the blue-green plasti-sheet. A tight shot, but passing . . . the merest flicker. Nothing staring, nothing lingering, nothing in bad taste.

In Lester's right ear was the sound of his own voice, recorded on his way to the scene and before he came upon it so that he would not need to break his silence until his selected moment. His voice giving the boy's age, his group-affiliations, the routine details of his death. All quietly, all monotonously even, the greater to contrast with what was the meat of Lester's program.

Nineteen seconds. The sobbing louder now and growing. The mother, kneeling, body sagged, hands clenched, dark head bowed.

Lester put a hand on her shoulder, letting it show in his finders, knowing that each of his viewers could see it as his own, extended, sympathetic, understanding . . .

The woman did not respond to his touch. Unobtrusively Lester increased the pressure of his thumb, gouging. She stirred under his hand, shrinking, her head lifting.

Lester's hand darted back to his console.

Her eyes. Dark, dulled, beseeching. *Fine*.

And now Lester spoke. He spoke with practiced hesitance, the gentle respecter, for his viewer, of her desire and right to her privacy at a time like this.

"How do you feel to have lost your only child?" His hands hovering, the woman looking at him . . . *now*.

Her eyes widened, flickeringly. Sorrow surging and pain, deep and of the soul, opened to the finder. Raw, fresh.

Great. I'm right never to test, never to speak until this moment.

"Please try to control yourself. I'm your friend, we're all your friends. Tell us." And he repeated his question.

Her head bent sharply back, the eyes half closing now, her mouth open, the lips trembling, the intensity of her emotion visibly choking the sound in her throat, making of her attempt to speak a silent mouthing.

Easy . . . easy does it.

Her hands came up. Fists, pressing against each other and under her chin. "My baby, my baby," and her voice was a moan.

Lester needed only the one hand, his left. The other he stretched toward the woman, touching her hair, his fingertips only, gently, benevolently, seeing it in his finder, looking deep into her upturned face.

In the corner of Lester's finder the sweep second hand began to wipe the red glow from the timer's face. When it came around to the twelve, except for the sponsor break and his verbal sign-off, he would be off the air.

Sobs began to rock the kneeling woman. Lightly at first a mere staccato catching of the breath, but growing. Growing in a crescendo of violence that, peaking, made of her body a heaving, thrashing, straining animal thing.

Great racking, convulsive sounds rasped from her throat. A thread-thin trickle of blood started from one corner of her tortured mouth.

Enough.

Her head dropped, her whole body now bowed and shaking.

Lester watched his hand go out to her, stop in midair. He did not try to hide its trembling. His fingers closed, his hand came back, not having touched her. Leaving her, huddled, tremulous, to herself and her great sorrow.

Slow fade and . . . go to black.

Ninety seconds. Exactly and on the dot and another of his human-interest segments for the intergalactic network was over; another moment in the life story of a lttle person had been made immortal.

Lester eased his headgear off, handed it to the waiting technician, stood rubbing the spots where the temple pieces had pressed. The woman had stopped trembling now and was looking dazed, uncomprehending. *They always do, the subjects.*

Swiftly, but not too roughly, Lester raised up her limp left arm, undid the cuff and stripped off the tiny receptor taped to the wrist. Another he took from her ankle and two more from the back of her skull, from under the concealing black hair. He could have left to one of his technicians this stripping off of the tiny receptors, that, obedient to the commands of his console, sent their impulses impinging upon the nerve streams of his subjects. But Lester felt that doing it himself, this body contact with his subjects, was just one more tiny factor that helped keep fresh his unmistakable feeling of rapport.

His lead technician touched his shoulder from behind, indicating they were about ready for his verbal signature and the one part of his program Lester found distasteful. A compliance with a regulation he felt was onerous and a little demeaning. Someday those who made these artistically point-less rulings would recognize the validity of his technique and perhaps eliminate this abhorrent note. Until then . . .

Lester leaned forward and spoke into the button mike his technician was holding out to him.

And at the end, ". . . The emotional response of the subject was technically augmented."

Cloak of Anarchy

LARRY NIVEN

SQUARE in the middle of what used to be the San Diego Freeway, I leaned back against a huge, twisted oak. The old bark was rough and powdery against my bare back. There was dark green shade shot with tight parallel beams of white gold. Long grass tickled my legs.

Forty yards away across a wide strip of lawn was a clump of elms, and a small grandmotherly woman sitting on a green towel. She looked like she'd grown there. A stalk of grass protruded between her teeth. I felt we were kindred spirits, and once when I caught her eye I wiggled a forefinger at her, and she waved back.

In a minute now I'd have to be getting up. Jill was meeting
me at the Wilshire exits in half an hour. But I'd started
walking at the Sunset Boulevard ramps, and I was tired. A
minute more. . . .

It was a good place to watch the world rotate.

A good day for it, too. No clouds at all. On this hot blue
summer afternoon, King's Free Park was as crowded as it
ever gets.

Someone at police headquarters had expected that. Twice
the usual number of copseyes floated overhead, waiting. Gold
dots against blue, basketball-sized, twelve feet up. Each a
television eye and a sonic stunner, each a hookup to police
headquarters, they were there to enforce the law of the park.

No violence.

No hand to be raised against another—and no other laws
whatever. Life was often entertaining in a Free Park.

North toward Sunset, a man carried a white rectangular
sign, blank on both sides. He was parading back and forth in
front of a square-jawed youth on a plastic box, who was
trying to lecture him on the subject of fusion power and the
heat pollution problem. Even this far away I could hear the
conviction and the dedication in his voice.

South, a handful of yelling marksmen were throwing rocks
at a copseye, directed by a gesticulating man with wild black
hair. The golden basketball was dodging the rocks, but barely. Some cop was baiting them. I wondered where they had
gotten the rocks. Rocks were scarce in King's Free Park.

The black-haired man looked familiar. I watched him and
his horde chasing the copseye . . . then forgot them when a
girl walked out of a clump of elms.

She was lovely. Long, perfect legs, deep red hair worn
longer than shoulder length, the face of an arrogant angel,
and a body so perfect that it seemed unreal, like an adoles-
cent's daydream. Her walk showed training; possibly she was
a model or dancer. Her only garment was a cloak of glowing
blue velvet.

It was fifteen yards long, that cloak. It trailed back from
two big gold discs that were stuck somehow to the skin of her
shoulders. It trailed back and back, floating at a height of
five feet all the way, twisting and turning to trace her path
through the trees. She seemed like the illustration to a book
of fairy tales, bearing in mind that the original fairy tales
were not intended for children.

Neither was she. You could hear neck vertebrae popping all over the park. Even the rock throwers had stopped to watch.

She could sense the attention, or hear it in a whisper of sighs. It was what she was here for. She strolled along with a condescending angel's smile on her angel's face, not overdoing the walk, but letting it flow. She turned regardless of whether there were obstacles to avoid, so that fifteen yards of flowing cloak could follow the curve.

I smiled, watching her go. She was lovely from the back, with dimples.

The man who stepped up to her a little further on was the same who had led the rock throwers. Wild black hair and beard, hollow cheeks and deep-set eyes, a diffident smile and a diffident walk. . . . Ron Cole. Of course.

I didn't hear what he said to the girl in the cloak, but I saw the result. He flinched, then turned abruptly and walked away with his eyes on his feet.

I got up and moved to intercept him. "Don't take it personally," I said.

He looked up, startled. His voice, when it came, was bitter. "How should I take it?"

"She'd have turned any man off the same way. That lady has staples in her navel. She's to look, not to touch."

"You know her?"

"Never saw her before in my life."

"Then—?"

"Her cloak. Now you *must* have noticed her cloak."

The tail end of her cloak was just passing us, its folds rippling an improbably deep, rich blue. Ronald Cole smiled as if it hurt his face. "Yah."

"All right. Now suppose you made a pass, and suppose the lady liked your looks and took you up on it. What would she do next? Bearing in mind that she can't stop walking even for a second."

He thought it over first, then asked, "Why not?"

"If she stops walking she loses the whole effect. Her cloak just hangs there like some kind of tail. It's supposed to wave. If she lies down with you it's even worse. A cloak floating at five feet, then swooping into a clump of bushes and bobbing frantically—" Ron laughed helplessly in falsetto. I said, "See? Her audience would get the giggles. That's not what she's after."

He sobered. "But if she really wanted to, she wouldn't *care* about . . . oh. Right. She must have spent a fortune to get that effect."

"Sure. She wouldn't ruin it for Jacques Casanova himself." I thought unfriendly thoughts toward the girl in the cloak. There are polite ways to turn down a pass. Ronald Cole was easy to hurt.

I asked, "Where did you get the rocks?"

"Rocks? Oh, we found a place where the center divider shows through. We knocked off some chunks of concrete." Ron looked down the length of the park just as a kid bounced a missile off a golden ball. "They got one! Come on!"

The fastest commercial shipping that ever sailed was the clipper ship; yet the world stopped building them after just twenty-five years. Steam had come. Steam was faster, safer, more dependable, cheaper in time and men.

The freeways served America for almost fifty years. Then modern transportation systems cleaned the air and made traffic jams archaic and left the nation with an embarrassing problem. What to do with ten thousand miles of unsightly abandoned freeways?

King's Free Park had been part of the San Diego Freeway, the section between Sunset and the Santa Monica interchange. Decades ago the concrete had been covered with topsoil. The borders had been landscaped from the start. Now the Park was as thoroughly covered with green as the much older Griffith Free Park.

Within King's Free Park was an orderly approximation of anarchy. People were searched at the entrances. There were no weapons inside. The copseyes, floating overhead and out of reach, were the next thing to no law at all.

There was only one law to enforce. All acts of attempted violence carried the same penalty for attacker and victim. Let anyone raise his hand against his neighbor, and one of the golden basketballs would stun them both. They would wake separately, with copseyes. It was usually enough.

Naturally people threw rocks at copseyes. It was a Free Park, wasn't it?

"They got one! Come on!" Ron tugged at my arm. The felled copseye was hidden, surrounded by those who had destroyed it. "I hope they don't kick it apart. I told them I need it intact, but that might not stop them."

"It's a Free Park. And they bagged it."

"With my missiles!"

"Who are they?"

"I don't know. They were playing baseball when I found them. I told them I needed a copseye. They said they'd get me one."

I remembered Ron quite well now. Ronald Cole was an artist and an inventor. It would have been two sources of income for another man, but Ron was different. He invented new art forms. With solder and wire and diffraction gratings and several makes of plastics kits, and an incredible collection of serendipitous junk, Ron Cole made things the like of which had never been seen on Earth.

The market for new art forms had always been low, but now and then he did make a sale. It was enough to keep him in raw materials, especially since many of his raw materials came from basements and attics. There was an occasional *big* sale, and then, briefly, he would be rich.

There was this about him: he knew who I was, but he hadn't remembered my name. Ron Cole had better things to think about than what name belonged with whom. A name was only a tag and a conversational gambit. "Russel! How are you?" A signal. Ron had developed a substitute.

Into a momentary gap in the conversation he would say, "Look at this," and hold out—miracles.

Once it had been a clear plastic sphere, golf-ball-sized, balanced on a polished silver concavity. When the ball rolled around on the curved mirror, the reflections were *fantastic*.

Once it had been a twisting sea serpent engraved on a Michelob beer bottle, the lovely vase-shaped bottle of the early 1960s that was too big for standard refrigerators.

And once it had been two strips of dull silvery metal, unexpectedly heavy. "What's this?"

I'd held them in the palm of my hand. They were heavier than lead. Platinum? But nobody carries that much platinum around. Joking, I'd asked, "U-235?"

"Are they warm?" he'd asked apprehensively. I'd fought off an urge to throw them as far as I could and dive behind a couch.

But they *had* been platinum. I never did learn why Ron was carrying them about. Something that didn't pan out.

Within a semicircle of spectators, the felled copseye lay on the grass. It was intact, possibly because two cheerful, conspicuously large men were standing over it, waving everyone back.

"Good," said Ron. He knelt above the golden sphere, turned it with his long artist's fingers. To me he said, "Help me get it open."

"What for? What are you after?"

"I'll tell you in a minute. Help me get—never mind." The hemispherical cover came off. For the first time ever, I looked into a copseye.

It was impressively simple. I picked out the stunner by its parabolic reflector, the cameras, and a toroidal coil that had to be part of the floater device. No power source. I guessed that the shell itself was a power-beam antenna. With the cover cracked there would be no way for a damn fool to electrocute himself.

Ron knelt and studied the strange guts of the copseye. From his pocket he took something made of glass and metal. He suddenly remembered my existence and held it out to me, saying, "Look at this."

I took it, expecting a surprise, and I got it. It was an old hunting watch, a big wind-up watch on a chain, with a protective case. They were in common use a couple of hundred years ago. I looked at the face, said, "Fifteen minutes slow. You didn't repair the whole works, did you?"

"Oh, no." He clicked the back open for me.

The works looked modern. I guessed, "Battery and tuning fork?"

"That's what the guard thought. Of course that's what I made it from. But the hands don't move; I set them just before they searched me."

"Aha. What does it do?"

"If I work it right, I think it'll knock down every copseye in King's Free Park."

For a minute or so I was laughing too hard to speak. Ron watched me with his head on one side, clearly wondering if I thought he was joking.

I managed to say, "That ought to cause all *kinds* of excitement."

Ron nodded vigorously. "Of course it all depends on whether they use the kind of circuits I think they use. Look for yourself; the copseyes aren't supposed to be foolproof. They're supposed to be cheap. If one gets knocked down, the taxes don't go up much. The other way is to make them expensive and foolproof, and frustrate a lot of people. People aren't supposed to be frustrated in a Free Park."

"So?"

"Well, there's a cheap way to make the circuitry for the power system. If they did it that way, I can blow the whole thing. We'll see." Ron pulled thin copper wire from the cuffs of his shirt.

"How long will this take?"

"Oh, half an hour."

That decided me. "I've got to be going. I'm meeting Jill Hayes at the Wilshire exits. You've met her, a big blond girl, my height—"

But he wasn't listening. "Okay, see you," he muttered. He began placing the copper wire inside the copseye, with tweezers. I left.

Crowds tend to draw crowds. A few minutes after leaving Ron, I joined a semicircle of the curious to see what they were watching.

A balding, lantern-jawed individual was putting something together: an archaic machine, with blades and a small gasoline motor. The T-shaped wooden handle was brand new and unpainted. The metal parts were dull with the look of ancient rust recently removed.

The crowd speculated in half whispers. What was it? Not part of a car; not an outboard motor, though it had blades; too small for a motor scooter; too big for a motor skateboard . . .

"Lawn mower," said the white-haired lady next to me. She was one of those small, birdlike people who shrivel and grow weightless as they age, and live forever. Her words meant nothing to me. I was about to ask, when—

The lantern-jawed man finished his work, and twisted something, and the motor started with a roar. Black smoke puffed out. In triumph he gripped the handles. Outside, it was a prison offense to build a working internal combustion machine. Here—

With the fire of dedication burning in his eyes, he wheeled his infernal machine across the grass. He left a path as flat as a rug. It was a Free Park, wasn't it?

The smell hit everyone at once: a black dirt in the air, a

stink of half-burned hydrocarbons attacking nose and eyes. I gasped and coughed. I'd never smelled anything like it.

The crescent of crowd roared and converged.

He squawked when they picked up his machine. Someone found a switch and stopped it. Two men confiscated the tool kit and went to work with screwdriver and hammer. The owner objected. He picked up a heavy pair of pliers and tried to commit murder.

A copseye zapped him and the man with the hammer, and they both hit the lawn without bouncing. The rest of them pulled the lawn mower apart and bent and broke the pieces.

"I'm half-sorry they did that," said the old woman. "Sometimes I miss the sound of lawn mowers. My dad used to mow the lawn on Sunday mornings."

I said, "It's a Free Park."

"Then why can't he build anything he pleases?"

"He can. He did. Anything he's free to build, we're free to kick apart." And my mind flashed, *Like Ron's rigged copseye.*

Ron was good with tools. It would not surprise me a bit if he knew enough about copseyes to knock out the whole system.

Maybe someone ought to stop him.

But knocking down copseyes wasn't illegal. It happened all the time. It was part of the freedom of the park. If Ron could knock them all down at once, well . . .

Maybe someone ought to stop him.

I passed a flock of high school girls, all chittering like birds, all about sixteen. It might have been their first trip inside a Free Park. I looked back because they were so cute, and caught them staring in awe and wonder at the dragon on my back.

A few years and they'd be too blasé to notice. It had taken Jill almost half an hour to apply it this morning: a glorious red-and-gold dragon breathing flames across my shoulder, flames that seemed to glow by their own light. Lower down were a princess and a knight in golden armor, the princess tied to a stake, the knight fleeing for his life. I smiled back at the girls, and two of them waved.

Short blond hair and golden skin, the tallest girl in sight, wearing not even a nudist's shoulder pouch: Jill Hayes stood squarely in front of the Wilshire entrance, visibly wondering where I was. It was five minutes after three.

There was this about living with a physical culture nut. Jill insisted on getting me into shape. The daily exercises were part of that, and so was this business of walking half the length of King's Free Park.

I'd balked at doing it briskly, though. Who walks briskly in a Free Park? There's too much to see. She'd given me an hour; I'd held out for three. It was a compromise, like the paper slacks I was wearing despite Jill's nudist beliefs.

Sooner or later she'd find someone with muscles, or I'd relapse into laziness, and we'd split. Meanwhile . . . we got along. It seemed only sensible to let her finish my training.

She spotted me, yelled, "Russel! Here!" in a voice that must have reached both ends of the park. In answer I lifted my arm semaphore-style, slowly over my head and back down.

And every copseye in King's Free Park fell out of the sky, dead.

Jill looked about her at all the startled faces and all the golden bubbles resting in bushes and on the grass. She approached me somewhat uncertainly. She asked, "Did you do that?"

I said, "Yah. If I wave my arms again they'll all go back up."

"I think you'd better do it," she said primly. Jill had a fine poker face. I waved my arm grandly over my head and down, but of course the copseyes stayed where they had fallen.

Jill said, "I wonder what happened to them?"

"It was Ron Cole. You remember him. He's the one who engraved some old Michelob beer bottles for Steuben—"

"Oh, yes. But *how?*"

We went off to ask him.

A brawny college man howled and charged past us at a dead run. We saw him kick a copseye like a soccer ball. The golden cover split, but the man howled again and hopped up and down hugging his foot.

We passed dented golden shells and broken resonators and bent parabolic reflectors. One woman looked flushed and proud; she was wearing several of the copper toroids as bracelets. A kid was collecting the cameras. Maybe he thought he could sell them outside.

I never saw an intact copseye after the first minute.

They weren't all busy kicking copseyes apart. Jill stared at the conservatively dressed group carrying POPULATION

BY COPULATION signs, and wanted to know if they were serious. Their grim-faced leader handed us pamphlets that spoke of the evil and the blasphemy of man's attempts to alter himself through gene tampering and extra-uterine growth experiments. If it was a put-on, it was a good one.

We passed seven little men, each three to four feet high, traveling with a single tall, pretty brunette. They wore medieval garb. We both stared; but I was the one who noticed the makeup and the use of UnTan. African pigmies, probably part of a U.N.-sponsored tourist group; and the girl must be their guide.

Ron Cole was not where I had left him.

"He must have decided that discretion is the better part of cowardice. May be right, too," I surmised. "Nobody's ever knocked down *all* the copseyes before."

"It's not illegal, is it?"

"Not illegal, but excessive. They can bar him from the park, at the very least."

Jill stretched in the sun. She was all golden and *big*. Scaled down, she would have made a nice centershot for a men's videozine. She said, "I'm thirsty. Is there a fountain around?"

"Sure, unless someone's plugged it by now. It's a—"

"Free Park. Do you mean to tell me they don't even protect the *fountains?*"

"You make one exception, it's like a wedge. When someone ruins a fountain, they wait and fix it that night. That way if I see someone trying to wreck a fountain, I'll generally throw a punch at him. A lot of us do. After a guy's lost enough of his holiday to the copseye stunners, he'll get the idea, sooner or later."

The fountain was a solid cube of concrete with four spigots and a hand-sized metal button. It was hard to jam, hard to hurt. Ron Cole stood near it, looking lost.

He seemed glad to see me, but still lost. I introduced him. "You remember Jill Hayes." He said, "Certainly. Hello, Jill," and, having put her name to its intended purpose, promptly forgot it.

Jill said, "We thought you'd made a break for it."

"I did."

"Oh?"

"You know how complicated the exits are. They have to be, to keep anyone from getting in through an exit with like a shotgun." Ron ran both hands through his hair, without making it any more or less neat. "Well, all the exits have stopped working. They must be on the same circuits as the copseyes. I wasn't expecting that."

"Then we're locked in," I said. That was irritating. But underneath the irritation was a funny feeling in the pit of my stomach. "How long do you think—?"

"No telling. They'll have to get new copseyes in somehow. And repair the beamed power system, and figure out how I bollixed it, and fix it so it doesn't happen again. I suppose someone must have kicked my rigged copseye to pieces by now, but the police don't know that."

"Oh, they'll just send in some cops," said Jill.

"Look around you."

There were pieces of copseyes in all directions. Not one remained whole. A cop would have to be out of his mind to enter a Free Park.

Not to mention the damage to the spirit of the park.

"I wish I'd brought a bag lunch," said Ron.

I saw the cloak off to my right: a ribbon of glowing blue velvet hovering at five feet, like a carpeted path in the air. I didn't yell or point or anything. For Ron it might be pushing the wrong buttons.

Ron didn't see it. "Actually I'm kind of glad this happened," he said animatedly. "I've always thought that anarchy ought to be a viable form of society."

Jill made polite sounds of encouragement.

"After all, anarchy is only the last word in free enterprise. What can a government do for people that people can't do for themselves? Protection from other countries? If all the other countries are anarchies too, you don't need armies. Police, maybe; but what's wrong with privately owned police?"

"Fire departments used to work that way," Jill remembered. "They were hired by the insurance companies. They only protected houses that belonged to their own clients."

"Right! So you buy theft and murder insurance, and the insurance companies hire a police force. The client carries a credit card—"

"Suppose the robber steals the card too?"

"He can't use it. He doesn't have the right retina prints."

"But if the client doesn't have the credit card, he can't sic the cops on the thief."

"Oh." A noticeable pause. "Well—"

Half-listening, for I had heard it all before, I looked for the end points of the cloak. I found empty space at one end and a lovely red-haired girl at the other. She was talking to two men as outré as herself.

One can get the impression that a Free Park is one gigantic costume party. It isn't. Not one person in ten wears anything but street clothes, but the costumes are what get noticed.

These guys were part bird.

Their eyebrows and eyelashes were tiny feathers, green on one, golden on the other. Larger feathers covered their heads, blue and green and gold, and ran in a crest down their spines. They were bare to the waist, showing physiques Jill would find acceptable.

Ron was lecturing. "What does a government do for *anyone* except the people who run the government? Once there were private post offices, and they were cheaper than what we've got now. Anything the government takes over gets more expensive, *immediately*. There's no reason why private enterprise can't do anything a government—"

Jill gasped. She said, "Ooh! How lovely."

Ron turned to look.

As if, on cue, the girl in the cloak slapped one of the feathered men hard across the mouth. She tried to hit the other one, but he caught her wrist. Then all three froze.

I said, "See? Nobody wins. She doesn't even like standing still. She—" And I realized why they weren't moving.

In a Free Park it's easy for a girl to turn down an offer. If the guy won't take no for an answer, he gets slapped. The stun beam gets him and the girl. When she wakes up, she walks away.

Simple.

The girl recovered first. She gasped and jerked her wrist loose and turned to run. One of the feathered men didn't bother to chase her; he simply took a double handful of the cloak.

This was getting serious.

The cloak jerked her sharply backward. She didn't hesitate. She reached for the big gold discs at her shoulders, ripped them loose and ran on. The feathered men chased her, laughing.

The redhead wasn't laughing. She was running all out. Two drops of blood ran down her shoulders. I thought of trying to stop the feathered men, decided in favor of it—but they were already past.

The cloak hung like a carpeted path in the air, empty at both ends.

Jill hugged herself uneasily. "Ron, just how does one go about hiring your private police force?"

"Well, you can't expect it to form spontaneously—"

"Let's try the entrances. Maybe we can get out."

It was slow to build. Everyone knew what a copseye did. Nobody thought it through. Two feathered men chasing a lovely nude? A pretty sight; and why interfere? If she didn't want to be chased, she need only—what? And nothing else had changed. The costumes, the people with causes, the people looking for causes, the peoplewatchers, the pranksters . . .

Blank Sign had joined the POPULATION BY COPULATION faction. His grass-stained pink street tunic jarred strangely with their conservative suits, but he showed no sign of mockery; his face was as preternaturally solemn as theirs. Nonetheless they did not seem glad of his company.

It was crowded near the Wilshire entrance. I saw enough bewildered and frustrated faces to guess that it was closed. The little vestibule area was so packed that we didn't even try to find out what was wrong with the doors.

"I don't think we ought to stay here," Jill said uneasily.

I noticed the way she was hugging herself. "Are you cold?"

"No." She shivered. "But I wish I were dressed."

"How about a strip of that velvet cloak?"

"Good!"

We were too late. The cloak was gone.

It was a warm September day, near sunset. Clad only in paper slacks, I was not cold in the least. I said, "Take my slacks."

"No, hon, I'm the nudist." But Jill hugged herself with both arms.

"Here," said Ron, and handed her his sweater. She flashed him a grateful look, then, clearly embarrassed, she wrapped the sweater around her waist and knotted the sleeves.

Ron didn't get it at all. I asked him, "Do you know the difference between nude and naked?"

He shook his head.

"Nude is artistic. Naked is defenseless."

Nudity was popular in a Free Park. That night, nakedness was not. There must have been pieces of that cloak all over King's Free Park. I saw at least four that night: one worn as a kilt, two being used as crude sarongs, and one as a bandage.

On a normal day, the entrances to King's Free Park close at six. Those who want to stay, stay as long as they like. Usually they are not many, because there are no lights to be broken in a Free Park; but light does seep in from the city beyond. The copseyes float about, guided by infrared, but most of them are not manned.

Tonight would be different.

It was after sunset, but still light. A small and ancient lady came stumping toward us with a look of murder on her lined face. At first I thought it was meant for us, but that wasn't it. She was so mad she couldn't see straight.

She saw my feet and looked up. "Oh, it's you. The one who helped break the lawn mower," she said; which was unjust. "A Free Park, is it? A Free Park! Two men just took away my dinner!"

I spread my hands. "I'm sorry. I really am. If you still had it, we could try to talk you into sharing it."

She lost some of her mad, which brought her embarrassingly close to tears. "Then we're all hungry together. I brought it in a plastic bag. Next time I'll use something that isn't transparent, by d-damn!" She noticed Jill and her improvised sweater-skirt, and added, "I'm sorry, dear, I gave my towel to a girl who needed it even more."

"Thank you anyway."

"Please, may I stay with you people until the copseyes start working again? I don't feel safe, somehow. I'm Glenda Hawthorne."

We introduced ourselves. Glenda Hawthorne shook our hands. By now it was quite dark. We couldn't see the city beyond the high green hedges, but the change was startling when the lights of Westwood and Santa Monica flashed on.

The police were taking their own good time getting us some copseyes.

We reached the grassy field sometimes used by the Society for Creative Anachronism for their tournaments. They fight on foot with weighted and padded weapons designed to behave like swords, broadaxes, morningstars, etc. The weapons are bugged so that they won't fall into the wrong hands. The field is big and flat and bare of trees, sloping upward at the edges.

On one of the slopes, something moved.

I stopped. It didn't move again, but it showed clearly in light reflected down from the white clouds. I made out something man-shaped and faintly pink, and a pale rectangle nearby.

I spoke low. "Stay here."

Jill said, "Don't be silly. There's nothing for anyone to hide under. Come on."

The blank sign was bent and marked with shoe prints. The man who had been carrying it looked up at us with pain in his eyes. Drying blood ran from his nose. With effort he whispered, "I think they dislocated my shoulder."

"Let me look." Jill bent over him. She probed him a bit, then set herself and pulled hard and steadily on his arm. Blank Sign yelled in pain and despair.

"That'll do it." Jill sounded satisfied. "How does it feel?"

"It doesn't hurt as much." He smiled, almost.

"What happened?"

"They started pushing me and kicking me to make me go away. I was *doing* it, I was walking away. I *was*. Then one of the sons of bitches snatched away my sign—" He stopped for a moment, then went off at a tangent. "I wasn't hurting anyone with my sign. I'm a psych major. I'm writing a thesis on what people read into a blank sign. Like the blank sheets in the Rorschach tests."

"What kind of reactions do you get?"

"Usually hostile. But nothing like *that*." Blank Sign sounded bewildered. "Wouldn't you think a Free Park is the one place you'd find freedom of speech?"

Jill wiped at his face with a tissue from Glenda Hawthorne's purse. She said, "Especially when you're not saying anything. Hey, Ron, tell us more about your government by anarchy."

Ron cleared his throat. "I hope you're not judging it by *this*. King's Free Park hasn't been an anarchy for more than a couple of hours. It needs time to develop."

Glenda Hawthorne and Blank Sign must have wondered what the hell he was talking about. I wished him joy in explaining it to them, and wondered if he would explain who had knocked down the copseyes.

This field would be a good place to spend the night. It was

open, with no cover and no shadows, no way for anyone to sneak up on us.

We lay on wet grass, sometimes dozing, sometimes talking. Two other groups no bigger than ours occupied the jousting field. They kept their distance; we kept ours. Now and then we heard voices, and knew that they were not asleep; not all at once, anyway.

Blank Sign dozed restlessly. His ribs were giving him trouble, though Jull said none of them were broken. Every so often he whimpered and tried to move and woke himself up. Then he had to hold himself still until he fell asleep again.

"Money," said Jill. "It takes a government to print money."

"But you could get I.O.U.'s printed. Standard denominations, printed for a fee and notarized. Backed by your good name."

Jill laughed softly. "Thought of everything, haven't you? You couldn't travel very far that way."

"Credit cards, then."

I had stopped believing in Ron's anarchy. I said, "Ron, remember the girl in the long blue cloak?"

A little gap of silence. "Yah?"

"Pretty, wasn't she? Fun to watch."

"Granted."

"If there weren't any laws to stop you from raping her, she'd be muffled to the ears in a long dress and carrying a tear gas pen. What fun would that be? I *like* the nude look. Look how fast it disappeared after the copseyes fell."

"Mmm," said Ron.

The night was turning cold. Faraway voices, occasional distant shouts, came like thin gray threads in a black tapestry of silence. Mrs. Hawthorne spoke into that silence.

"What was that boy really saying with his blank sign?"

"He wasn't saying anything," said Jill.

"Now, just a minute, dear. I think he was, even if he didn't know it." Mrs. Hawthorne talked slowly, using the words to shape her thoughts. "Once there was an organization to protest the forced contraception bill. I was one of them. We carried signs for hours at a time. We printed leaflets. We stopped people passing so that we could talk to them. We gave up our time, we went to considerable trouble and expense, because we wanted to get our ideas across.

"Now, if a man had joined us with a blank sign, he would have been *saying* something."

"His sign says that he has no opinion. If he joins us he says that we have no opinion either. He's saying our opinions aren't worth anything."

I said, "Tell him when he wakes up. He can put it in his notebook."

"But his notebook is *wrong*. He wouldn't push his blank sign in among people he agreed with, would he?"

"Maybe not."

"I . . . suppose I don't like people with no opinions." Mrs. Hawthorne stood up. She had been sitting tailor-fashion for some hours. "Do you know if there's a pop machine nearby?"

There wasn't, of course. No private company would risk getting their machines smashed once or twice a day. But she had reminded the rest of us that we were thirsty. Eventually we all got up and trooped away in the direction of the fountain.

All but Blank Sign.

I'd *liked* that blank sign gag. How odd, how ominous, that so basic a right as freedom of speech could depend on so slight a thing as a floating copseye.

I was thirsty.

The park was bright by city light, crossed by sharp-edged shadows. In such light it seems that one can see much more than he really can. I could see into every shadow; but, though there were stirrings all around us, I could see nobody until he moved. We four, sitting under an oak with our backs to the tremendous trunk, must be invisible from any distance.

We talked little. The park was quiet except for occasional laughter from the fountain.

I couldn't forget my thirst. I could feel others being thirsty around me. The fountain was right out there in the open, a solid block of concrete with five men around it.

They were dressed alike in paper shorts with big pockets. They looked alike: like first-string athletes. Maybe they belonged to the same order or frat or R.O.T.C. class.

They had taken over the fountain.

When someone came to get a drink, the tall ash-blond one would step forward with his arm held stiffly out, palm forward. He had a wide mouth and a grin that might otherwise have been infectious, and a deep, echoing voice. He would intone, "Go back. None may pass here but the immortal Cthuthu," or something equally silly.

Trouble was, they weren't kidding. Or: they were kidding, but they wouldn't let anyone have a drink.

When we arrived, a girl dressed in a towel had been trying to talk some sense into them. It hadn't worked. It might even have boosted their egos: a lovely half-naked girl begging them for water. Eventually she'd given up and gone away.

In that light her hair might have been red. I hoped it was the girl in the cloak. She'd sounded healthy . . . unhurt.

And a beefy man in a yellow business jumper had made the mistake of demanding his rights. It was not a night for rights. The blond kid had goaded him into screaming insults, a stream of unimaginative profanity, which ended when he tried to hit the blond kid. Then three of them had swarmed over him. The man had left crawling, moaning of police and lawsuits.

Why hadn't somebody done something?

I had watched it all from a sitting position. I could list my own reasons. One: it was hard to face the fact that a copseye would not zap them both, any second now. Two: I didn't like the screaming fat man much. He talked dirty. Three: I'd been waiting for someone else to step in.

As with the girl in the cloak. Damn it.

Mrs. Hawthorne said, "Ronald, what time is it?"

Ron may have been the only man in King's Free Park who knew the time. People generally left their valuables in lockers at the entrances. But years ago, when Ron was flush with money from the sale of the engraved beer bottles, he'd bought an implant-watch. He told time by one red mark and two red lines glowing beneath the skin of his wrist.

We had put the women between us, but I saw the motion as he glanced at his wrist. "Quarter of twelve."

"Don't you think they'll get bored and go away? It's been twenty minutes since anyone tried to get a drink," Mrs. Hawthorne said plaintively.

Jill shifted against me in the dark. "They can't be any more bored than we are. I think they'll get bored and stay anyway. Besides—" She stopped.

I said, "Besides that, we're thirsty *now*."

"Right."

"Ron, have you seen any sign of those rock throwers you collected? Especially the one who knocked down the copseye."

"No."

I wasn't surprised. In this darkness? "Do you remember his—" And I didn't even finish.

"Yes!" Ron said suddenly.

"You're kidding."

"No. His name was Bugeyes. You don't forget a name like that."

"I take it he had big, bulging eyes?"

"I didn't notice."

Well, it was worth a try. I stood and cupped my hands for a megaphone and shouted, *"Bugeyes!"*

One of the Water Monopoly shouted, "Let's keep the noise down out there!"

"Bugeyes!"

A chorus of remarks from the Water Monopoly. "Strange habits these peasants." "Most of them are just thirsty. *This* character—"

From off to the side: "What do you want?"

"We want to talk to you! Stay where you are!" To Ron I said, "Come on." To Jill and Mrs. Hawthorne, "Stay here. Don't get involved."

We moved out into the open space between us and Bugeyes's voice.

Two of the five kids came immediately to intercept us. They must have been bored, all right, and looking for action.

We ran for it. We reached the shadows of the trees before those two reached us. They stopped, laughing like maniacs, and moved back to the fountain.

A fourteen-year-old kid spoke behind us. "Ron?"

Ron and I, we lay on our bellies in the shadows of low bushes. Across too much shadowless grass, four men in paper shorts stood at parade rest at the four corners of the fountain. The fifth man watched for a victim.

A boy walked out between us into the moonlight. His eyes were shining, big, expressive eyes, maybe a bit too prominent. His hands were big, too, with knobby knuckles. One hand was full of acorns.

He pitched them rapidly, one at a time, overhand. First one, then another of the Water Trust twitched and looked in our direction. Bugeyes kept throwing.

Quite suddenly, two of them started toward us at a run. Bugeyes kept throwing until they were almost on him; then he threw his acorns in a handful and dived into the shadows.

The two of them ran between us. We let the first go by: the wide-mouthed blond spokesman, his expression low and murderous now. The other was short and broad-shouldered, an intimidating silhouette seemingly all muscle. A tackle. I stood up in front of him, expecting him to stop in surprise; and he did, and I hit him in the mouth as hard as I could.

He stepped back in shock. Ron wrapped an arm around his throat.

He bucked. Instantly. Ron hung on. I did something I'd seen often enough on television: linked my fingers and brought both hands down on the back of his neck.

The blond spokesman should be back by now; and I turned, and he was. He was on me before I could get my hands up. We rolled on the ground, me with my arms pinned to my sides, him unable to use his hands without letting go. It was lousy planning for both of us. He was squeezing the breath out of me. Ron hovered over us, waiting for a chance to hit him.

Suddenly there were others, a lot of others. Three of them pulled the blond kid off me, and a beefy, bloody man in a yellow business jumper stepped forward and crowned him with a rock.

The blond kid went limp.

I was still trying to get my breath.

The man squared off and threw a straight left hook with the rock in his hand. The blond kid's head snapped back, fell forward.

I yelled, "Hey!" Jumped forward, got hold of the arm that held the rock.

Someone hit me solidly in the side of the neck.

I dropped. It felt like all my strings had been cut. Someone was helping me to my feet—Ron—voices babbling in whispers, one shouting, "Get him—"

I couldn't see the blond kid. The other one, the tackle, was up and staggering away. Shadows came from between the trees to play pileup on him. The woods were alive, and it was just a *little* patch of woods. Full of angry, thirsty people.

Bugeyes reappeared, grinning widely. "Now what? Go somewhere else and try it again?"

"Oh, no. It's getting very vicious out tonight. Ron, we've got to stop them. They'll kill him!"

"It's a Free Park. Can you stand now?"

"Ron, they'll *kill* him!"

The rest of the Water Trust was charging to the rescue.

One of them had a tree branch with the leaves stripped off. Behind them, shadows converged on the fountain.

We fled.

I had to stop after a dozen paces. My head was trying to explode. Ron looked back anxiously, but I waved him on. Behind me the man with the branch broke through the trees and ran toward me to do murder.

Behind him, all the noise suddenly stopped.

I braced myself for the blow.

And fainted.

He was lying across my legs, with the branch still in his hand. Jill and Ron were pulling at my shoulders. A pair of golden moons floated overhead.

I wriggled loose. I felt my head. It seemed intact.

Ron said, "The copseyes zapped him before he got to you."

"What about the others? Did they kill them?"

"I don't know." Ron ran his hands through his hair. "I was wrong. Anarchy isn't stable. It comes apart too easily."

"Well, don't do any more experiments, okay?"

People were beginning to stand up. They streamed toward the exits, gathering momentum, beneath the yellow gaze of the copseyes.

And Now the News

THEODORE STURGEON

THE man's name was MacLyle, which by looking at you can tell wasn't his real name, but let's say this is fiction, shall we? MacLyle had a good job in, well, a soap concern. He worked hard and made good money and got married to a girl called Esther. He bought a house in the suburbs, and after it was paid for he rented it to some people and bought a home a little farther out and a second car and a freezer and a power mower and a book on landscaping and settled down to the worthy task of giving his kids all the things he never had.

He had habits and he had hobbies, like everybody else and (like everybody else) his were a little different from anybody's. The one that annoyed his wife the most, until she got used to it, was the news habit, or maybe hobby. MacLyle read a morning paper on the eight-fourteen and an evening paper on the six-ten, and the local paper his suburb used for its lost dogs and auction sales took up forty after-dinner minutes. And when he read a paper he read it, he didn't mess with it. He read page one first and page two next, and so on all the way through. He didn't care too much for books, but he respected them in a mystical sort of way, and he used to say a newspaper was a kind of book, and so would raise particular hell if a section was missing or in upside down, or if the pages were out of line. He also heard the news on the radio. There were three stations in town with hourly broadcasts, one on the hour, and he was usually able to catch them all. During these five-minute periods he would look you right in the eye while you talked to him and you'd swear he was listening to you, but he wasn't. This was a particular trial to his wife, but only for five years or so. Then she stopped trying to be heard while the radio talked about floods and murders and scandal and suicide. Five more years and she went back to talking right through the broadcasts, but by the time people are married ten years things like that don't matter; they talk in code anyway, and nine tenths of their speech can be picked up anytime like ticker tape. He also caught the seven-thirty news on Channel 2 and the seven-forty-five news on Channel 4 on television.

Now, it might be imagined from all this that MacLyle was a crotchety character with fixed habits and a neurotic neatness, but this was far from the case. MacLyle was basically a reasonable guy who loved his wife and children and liked his work and pretty much enjoyed being alive. He laughed easily and talked well and paid his bills. He justified his preoccupation with the news in a number of ways. He would quote Donne: "... any man's death diminishes me, because I am involved in mankind ...," which is pretty solid stuff and hard to argue down. He would point out that he made his trains and his trains made him punctual, but that because of them he saw the same faces at the same time day after endless day, before, during, and after he rode those trains, so that his immediate world was pretty circumscribed, and only a constant awareness of what was happening all over the earth kept him conscious of the fact that he lived in a bigger place than a thin straight universe with his house at one end, his office at the other, and a railway track in between.

It's hard to say just when MacLyle started to go to pieces, or even why, though it obviously had something to do with all that news he exposed himself to. He began to react, very slightly at first; that is, you could tell he was listening. He'd *shh!* you, and if you tried to finish what you were saying he'd run and stick his head in the speaker grille. His wife and kids learned to shut up when the news came on, five minutes before the hour until five after (with MacLyle switching stations) and every hour on the half hour, and from seven-thirty to eight for the TV, and during the forty minutes it took him to read the local paper. He was not so obvious about it when he read his paper, because all he did was freeze over the pages like a catatonic, gripping the top corners until the sheets shivered, knotting his jaw and breathing from his nostrils with a strangled whistle.

Naturally all this was a weight on his wife Esther, who tried her best to reason with him. At first he answered her, saying mildly that a man has to keep in touch, you know; but very quickly he stopped responding altogether, giving her the treatment a practiced suburbanite gets so expert in, as when someone mentions a lawn mower just too damn early on Sunday morning. You don't say yes and you don't say no, you don't even grunt, and you don't move your head or even your eyebrows. After a while your interlocutor goes away. Pretty soon you don't hear these ill-timed annoyances any more than you appear to.

It needs to be said again here that MacLyle was, outside of his peculiarity, a friendly and easygoing character. He liked people and invited them and visited them, and he was one of those adults who can really listen to a first-grade child's interminable adventures and really care. He never forgot things like the slow leak in the spare tire or antifreeze or anniversaries, and he always got the storm windows up in time, but he didn't rub anyone's nose in his reliability. The first thing in his whole life he didn't take as a matter of course was this news thing that started so small and grew so quickly.

So after a few weeks of it his wife took the bull by the horns and spent the afternoon hamstringing every receiver in the house. There were three radios and two TV sets, and she didn't understand the first thing about them, but she had a good head and she went to work with a will and the can-opening limb of a pocket-knife. From each receiver she removed one tube, and, one at a time, so as not to get them mixed up, she carried them into the kitchen and meticulously banged their bases against the edge of the sink, being careful to crack no glass and bend no pins, until she could see the guts of the tube rolling around loose inside. Then she replaced them and got the back panels on the sets again.

MacLyle came home and put the car away and kissed her and turned on the living-room radio and then went to hang up his hat. When he returned the radio should have been warmed up, but it wasn't. He twisted the knobs a while and bumped it and rocked it back and forth a little, grunting, and then noticed the time. He began to feel a little frantic and raced back to the kitchen and turned on the little ivory radio on the shelf. It warmed up quickly and cheerfully and gave him a clear sixty-cycle hum, but that was all. He behaved badly from then on, roaring out the information that the sets didn't work, either of them, as if that wasn't pretty evident by that time, and flew upstairs to the boys' room, waking them explosively. He turned on their radio and got another sixty-cycle note, this time with a shattering microphonic when he rapped the case, which he did four times, whereupon the set went dead altogether.

Esther had planned the thing up to this point, but no further, which was the way her mind worked. She figured she could handle it, but she figured wrong. MacLyle came down-stairs like a pallbearer, and he was silent and shaken until seven-thirty, time for the news on TV. The living-room set wouldn't peep, so up he went to the boys' room again, waking them just as they were nodding off again, and this time the little guy started to cry. MacLyle didn't care. When he found out there was no picture on the set, he almost started to cry, too, but then he heard the sound come in. A TV set has an awful lot of tubes in it and Esther didn't know audio from video. MacLyle sat down in front of the dark screen and listened to the news. *"Everything seemed to be under control in the riot-ridden border country in India,"* said the TV set. Crowd noises and a background of Beethoven's "Turkish March." *"And then . . ."* Cut music. Crowd noise up: *gabble-wurra* and a scream. Announcer over: *"Six hours later, this was the scene."* Dead silence, going on so long that MacLyle reached out and thumped the TV set with the heel of his hand. Then, slow swell, Ketelby's "In a Monastery Garden." *"On a more cheerful note, here are the six finalists in the Miss Continuum contest."* Background music, "Blue Room," interminably, interrupted only once, when the announcer said through a childish chuckle, *"And she meant it!"* MacLyle pounded himself on the temples. The little guy continued to sob. Esther stood at the foot of the stairs wringing her hands. It went on for thirty minutes like this. All MacLyle said when he came downstairs was that he wanted the paper—that would be the local one. So Esther faced the great unknown and told him frankly she hadn't ordered it and wouldn't again, which of course led to full and righteous confession of her activities of the afternoon.

Only a woman married better than fourteen years can know a man well enough to handle him so badly. She was aware that she was wrong, but that was quite overridden by the fact that she was logical. It would not be logical to continue her patience, so patience was at an end. That which offendeth thee, cast it out, yea, even thine eye and thy right hand. She realized too late that the news was so inextricably part of her husband that in casting it out she cast him out, too. And out he went, while whitely she listened to the rumble of the garage door, the car door speaking its sharp syllables, clear as *"Exit"* in a playscript; the keen of a starter, the mourn of a motor. She said she was glad and went into the kitchen and tipped the useless ivory radio off the shelf and retired, weeping.

And yet, because true life offers few clean cuts, she saw him once more. At seven minutes to three in the morning she became aware of faint music from somewhere; unaccountably it frightened her, and she tiptoed about the house looking for it. It wasn't in the house, so she pulled on MacLyle's trench coat and crept down the steps into the garage. And there, just outside in the driveway, where steel beams couldn't interfere with radio reception, the car stood where it had been all along, and MacLyle was in the driver's seat dozing over the wheel. The music came from the car radio. She drew the coat tighter around her and went to the car and opened the door and spoke his name. At just that moment the radio said *"And now the news . . . ,"* and MacLyle sat bolt upright and *shh'd* furiously. She fell back and stood a moment in a strange transition from unconditional surrender to total defeat. Then he shut the car door and bent forward, his hand on the volume control, and she went back into the house.

After the news report was over and he had recovered himself from the stab wounds of a juvenile delinquent, the grinding agonies of a derailed train, the terrors of the near-crash of a C-119, and the fascination of a Cabinet officer, charter member of the We Don't Trust Nobody Club, saying in exactly these words that there's a little bit of good in the worst of us and a little bit of bad in the best of us, all of which he felt keenly, he started the car (by rolling it down the drive, because the battery was almost dead) and drove as slowly as possible into town.

At an all-night garage he had the car washed and greased while he waited, after which the Automat was open and he sat in it for three hours drinking coffee, holding his jaw set until his back teeth ached, and making occasional, almost inaudible noises in the back of his throat. At nine he pulled himself together. He spent the entire day with his astonished attorney, going through all his assets, selling, converting, establishing, until when he was finished he had a modest packet of cash and his wife would have an adequate income until the children went to college, at which time the house would be sold, the tenants in the older house evicted, and Esther would be free to move to the smaller home with the price of the larger one added to the basic capital. The lawyer might have entertained fears for MacLyle except for the fact that he was jovial and loquacious throughout, behaving like a happy man—a rare form of insanity, but acceptable. It was hard work, but they did it in a day, after which MacLyle wrung the lawyer's hand and thanked him profusely and checked into a hotel.

When he awoke the following morning he sprang out of bed, feeling years younger, opened the door, scooped up the morning paper and glanced at the headlines.

He couldn't read them.

He grunted in surprise, closed the door gently, and sat on the bed with the paper in his lap. His hands moved restlessly on it, smoothing and smoothing until the palms were shadowed and the type hazed. The shouting symbols marched across the page like a parade of strangers in some unrecognized lodge uniform, origins unknown, destination unknown, and the occasion for marching only to be guessed at. He traced the letters with his little finger, he measured the length of a word between his index finger and thumb and lifted them up to hold them before his wondering eyes. Suddenly he got up and crossed to the desk, where signs and placards and printed notes were trapped like a butterfly collection under glass—the breakfast menu, something about valet service, something about checking out. He remembered them all and had an idea of their significance—but he couldn't read them. In the drawer was stationery, with a picture of the building and no other buildings around it, which just wasn't so, and an inscription which might have been in Cyrillic for all he knew. Telegram blanks, a bus schedule, a blotter, all bearing hieroglyphs and runes as far as he was concerned. A phone book full of strangers' names in strange symbols.

He requested of himself that he recite the alphabet. "A," he said clearly, and "Eh?" because It didn't sound right and he couldn't imagine what would. He made a small foolish grin and shook his head slightly and rapidly, but grin or no, he felt frightened. He felt glad, or relieved—most happy, anyway, but still a little frightened.

He called the desk and told them to get his bill ready, and dressed and went downstairs. He gave the doorman his parking check and waited while they brought the car round. He got in and turned the radio on and started to drive west.

He drove for some days, in a state of perpetual, cold, and (for all that) happy fright—roller-coaster fright, horror-movie fright—remembering the significance of a stop sign without being able to read the word STOP across it, taking caution from the shape of a railroad-crossing notice. Restaurants look like restaurants, gas stations like gas stations; if Washington's picture denotes a dollar and Lincoln's five, one doesn't need to read them. MacLyle made out just fine. He drove until he was well into one of those square states with all the mountains and cruised until he recognized the section where, years before he was married, he had spent a hunting vacation. Avoiding the lodge he had used, he took back roads until, sure enough, he came to that deserted cabin in which he had sheltered one night, standing yet, rotting a bit but only around the edges. He wandered in and out of it for a long time, memorizing details because he could not make a list, and then got back into his car and drove to the nearest town, not very near and not very much of a town. At the general store he bought shingles and flour and nails and paint—all sorts of paint, in little cans, as well as big containers of house paint—and canned goods and tools. He ordered a knock-down windmill and a generator, eighty pounds of modeling clay, two loaf pans and a mixing bowl, and a war-surplus jungle hammock. He paid cash and promised to be back in two weeks for the things the store didn't stock, and wired (because it could be done over the phone) his lawyer to arrange for the predetermined eighty dollars a month which was all he cared to take for himself from his assets. Before he left he stood in wonder before a monstrous piece of musical plumbing called an ophicleide which stood, dusty and majestic, in a corner. (While it might be easier on the reader to make this a French horn or a sousaphone—which would answer narrative purposes quite as well—we're done telling lies here. MacLyle's real name is concealed, his home town cloaked, and his occupation disguised, and dammit, it really was a twelve-keyed, 1824, fifty-inch, obsolete brass ophicleide.) The store-keeper explained how his great-grandfather had brought it over from the old country and nobody had played it for two generations except an itinerant tuba player who had turned pale green on the first three notes and put it down as if it was full of percussion caps. MacLyle asked how it sounded and the man told him terrible. Two weeks later MacLyle was back to pick up the rest of his stuff, nodding and smiling and saying not a word. He still couldn't read, and now he couldn't speak. Even more, he had lost the power to understand speech. He had paid for the purchases with a hundred-dollar bill and a wistful expression, and then another hundred-dollar bill, and the storekeeper, thinking he had turned deaf and dumb, cheated him roundly but at the same time felt so sorry for him that he gave him the ophicleide. MacLyle loaded up his car happily and left. And that's the first part of the story about MacLyle's being in a bad way.

MacLyle's wife Esther found herself in a peculiar position. Friends and neighbors offhandedly asked her questions to which she did not know the answers, and the only person who had any information at all, MacLyle's attorney, was under bond not to tell her anything. She had not, in the full and legal sense, been deserted, since she and the children were provided for. She missed MacLyle, but in a specialized way; she missed the old reliable MacLyle, and he had, in effect, left her long before that perplexing night when he had driven away. She wanted the old MacLyle back again, not this untrolleyed stranger with the grim and spastic preoccupation with the news. Of the many unpleasant facets of this stranger's personality, one glowed brightest, and that was that he was the sort of man who would walk out the way he did and stay away as long as he had. Ergo, he was that undesirable person just as long as he stayed away, and tracking him down would, if it returned him against his will, return to her only a person who was not the person she missed.

Yet she was dissatisfied with herself, for all that she was the injured party and had wounds less painful than the pangs of conscience. She had always prided herself on being a good wife and had done many things in the past which were counter to her reason and her desires, purely because they were consistent with being a good wife. So as time went on she gravitated away from the "What shall I do?" area into the "What ought a good wife to do?" spectrum and, after a great deal of careful thought, went to see a psychiatrist.

He was a fairly intelligent psychiatrist, which is to say he caught on to the obvious a little faster than most people. For example, he became aware in only four minutes of conversation that MacLyle's wife Esther had not come to him on her own behalf, and, further, decided to hear her out completely before resolving to treat her. When she had quite finished and he had dug out enough corroborative detail to get the picture, he went into a long silence and cogitated. He matched the broad pattern of MacLyle's case with his reading and his experience, recognized the challenge, the clinical worth of the case, the probable value of the heirloom diamond pendant worn by his visitor. He placed his finger tips together, lowered his fine young head, gazed through his eyebrows at MacLyle's wife Esther, and took up the gauntlet. At the prospects of getting her husband back safe and sane, she thanked him quietly and left the office with mixed emotions. The fairly intelligent psychiatrist drew a deep breath and began making arrangements with another head-shrinker to take over his other patients, both of them, while he was away, because he figured to be away quite a while.

It was appallingly easy for him to trace MacLyle. He did

not go near the lawyer. The solid foundation of all skip
tracers and bureaus of missing persons, in their *modus
operandi,* is the piece of applied psychology which dictates
that a man might change his name and his address, but he
will seldom—can seldom—change the things he does, particularly the things he does to amuse himself. The ski addict
doesn't skip to Florida, though he might make Banff instead
of a habitual Mont Tremblant. A philatelist is not likely to
mount butterflies. Hence when the psychiatrist found among
MacLyle's papers some snapshots and brochures, dating from
college days, of the towering Rockies, of bears feeding by the
roadside, and especially of season after season's souvenirs of
a particular resort to which he had never brought his wife
and which he had not visited since he married her, it was
worth a feeler, which went out in the form of a request to that
state's police for information on a man of such-and-such a
description driving so-and-so with out-of-state plates, plus a
request that the man not be detained or warned, but only
that he, the fairly intelligent psychiatrist, be notified. He
threw out other lines, too, but this is the one that hooked the
fish. It was a matter of weeks before a state patrol car
happened by MacLyle's favorite general store; after that it
was a matter of minutes before the information was in the
hands of the psychiatrist. He said nothing to MacLyle's wife
Esther except goodbye for a while, and this bill is payable
now, and then took off, bearing with him a bag of tricks.

He rented a car at the airport nearest MacLyle's hideout
and drove a long, thirsty, climbing way until he came to the
general store. There he interviewed the proprietor, learning
some eighteen hundred items about how bad business could
get, how hot it was, how much rain hadn't fallen and how
much was needed, the tragedy of being blamed for high
markups when anyone with the brains God gave a goose ought
to know it cost plenty to ship things out here, especially in
the small quantities necessitated by business being so bad
and all; and betwixt and between he learned eight or ten
items about MacLyle—the exact location of his cabin, the fact
that he seemed to have turned into a deaf-mute who was also
unable to read, and that he must be crazy because who but a
crazy man would want eighty-four different half-pint cans of
house paint or, for that matter, live out here when he didn't
have to?

The psychiatrist got loose after a while and drove off, and

the country got higher and dustier and more lost every mile, until he began to pray that nothing would go wrong with the car, and, sure enough, ten minutes later something did. Any car that made a noise like the one he began to hear was strictly a shot-rod, and he pulled over to the side to worry about it. He turned off the motor and the noise went right on, and he began to realize that the sound was not in the car, or even near it, but came from somewhere uphill. There was a mile and a half more of the hill to go, and he drove it in increasing amazement, because that sound got louder and more impossible all the time. It was sort of like music, but like no music currently heard on this or any other planet. It was a solo voice, brass, with muscles. The upper notes, of which there seemed to be about two octaves, were wild and unmusical, the middle was rough, but the low tones were like the speech of these mountains themselves, big up to the sky, hot, and more natural than anything ought to be, basic as a bear's fang. Yet all the notes were perfect, their intervals were perfect—this awful noise was tuned like an electronic organ. The psychiatrist had a good ear, though for a while he wondered how long he'd have any ears at all, and he realized all these things about the sound, as well as the fact that it was rendering one of the more primitive fingering studies from Czerny, Book One, the droning little horror that goes: *do mi fa sol la sol fa mi, re fa sol la ti la sol fa, mi sol la . . .*, inchworming up the scale and then descending hand over hand.

He saw blue sky almost under his front tires and wrenched the wheel hard over, and found himself in the grassy yard of a made-over prospector's cabin; but that he didn't notice right away, because sitting in front of it was what he described to himself, startled as he was out of his professional detachment, as the craziest-looking man he had ever seen.

He was sitting under a parched, wind-warped Engelmann spruce. He was barefoot up to the armpits. He wore the top half of a skivvy shirt and a hat the shape of one of those conical Boy Scout tents when one of the Boy Scouts had left the pole home. And he was playing, or anyway practicing, the ophicleide, and on his shoulders was a little moss of spruce needles, a small shower of which descended from the tree every time he hit on or under the low B flat. Only a mouse trapped inside a tuba during band practice can know precisely what it's like to stand that close to an operating ophicleide.

It was MacLyle, all right, looming well fed and filled out. When he saw the psychiatrist's car he went right on playing, but, catching the psychiatrist's eye, he winked, smiled with the small corner of lip which showed from behind the large cup of the mouthpiece, and twiddled three fingers of his right hand, all he could manage of a wave without stopping. And he didn't stop, either, until he had scaled the particular octave he was working on and let himself down the other side. Then he put the ophicleide down carefully and let it lean against the spruce tree, and got up. The psychiatrist had become aware, as the last stupendous notes rolled away down the mountain, of his extreme isolation with this offbeat patient, of the unconcealed health and vigor of the man, and of the presence of the precipice over which he had almost driven his car a moment before, and had rolled up his window and buttoned the door lock and was feeling grateful for them. But the warm good humor and genuine welcome on MacLyle's sunburned face drove away fright and even caution, and almost before he knew what he was doing the psychiatrist had the door open and was stooping up out of the car, thinking, *Merry* is a disused word, but that's what he is, by God, a merry man. He called him by name, but MacLyle either didn't hear him or didn't care; he just put out a big warm hand and the psychiatrist took it. He could feel hard flat calluses in MacLyle's hand, and the controlled strength an elephant uses to lift a bespangled child in its trunk; he smiled at the image, because after all MacLyle was not a particularly large man, there was just that feeling about him. And once the smile found itself there it wouldn't go away.

He told MacLyle that he was a writer trying to soak up some of the magnificent country and had just been driving wherever the turn of the road led him, and here he was; but before he was half through he became conscious of MacLyle's eyes, which were in some indescribable way very much on him but not at all on anything he said; it was precisely as if he had stood there and hummed a tune. MacLyle seemed to be willing to listen to the sound until it was finished, and even to enjoy it, but that enjoyment was going to be all he got out of it. The psychiatrist finished anyway, and MacLyle waited a moment as if to see if there would be any more, and when there wasn't he gave out more of that luminous smile and cocked his head toward the cabin. MacLyle led the way, with his visitor bringing up the rear with some platitudes about nice place you got here. As they entered, he suddenly barked at that unresponsive back, "Can't you hear me?" and MacLyle, without turning, only waved him on.

They walked into such a clutter and clabber of colors that the psychiatrist stopped dead, blinking. One wall had been removed and replaced with glass panes; it overlooked the precipice and put the little building afloat on haze. All the walls were hung with plain white chenille bedspreads, and the floor was white, and there seemed to be much more light indoors here than outside. Opposite the large window was an oversized easel made of peeled poles, notched and lashed together with baling wire, and on it was a huge canvas, most nonobjective, in the purest and most uncompromising colors. Part of it was unquestionably this room, or at least its air of colored confusion here and all infinity yonder. The ophicleide was in the picture, painstakingly reproduced, looking like the hopper of some giant infernal machine, and in the foreground some flowers; but the central figure repulsed him—more, it repulsed everything which surrounded it. It did not look exactly like anything familiar and, in a disturbed way, he was happy about that.

Stacked on the floor on each side of the easel were other paintings, some daubs, some full of ruled lines and overlapping planes, but all in this achingly pure color. He realized what was being done with the dozens of colors of house paint in little cans which had so intrigued the storekeeper.

In odd places around the room were clay sculptures, most mounted on pedestals made of sections of tree trunks large enough to stand firmly on their sawed ends. Some of the pedestals were peeled, some painted, and in some the bark texture or the bulges or clefts in the wood had been carried right up into the model, and in others clay had been knived or pressed into the bark all the way down to the floor. Some of the clay was painted, some not, some ought to have been. There were free forms and gollywogs, a marsupial woman and a guitar with legs, and some, but not an overweening number, of the symbolisms which preoccupy even fairly intelligent psychiatrists. Nowhere was there any furniture per se. There were shelves at all levels and of varying lengths, bearing nail kegs, bolts of cloth, canned goods, tools and cooking utensils. There was a sort of table, but it was mostly a workbench, with a vise at one end and, at the other, half finished, a crude but exceedingly ingenious foot-powered potter's wheel.

He wondered where MacLyle slept, so he asked him, and again MacLyle reacted as if the words were not words but a series of pleasant sounds, cocking his head and waiting to see if there would be any more. So the psychiatrist resorted to sign language, making a pillow of his two hands, laying his head on it, closing his eyes. He opened them to see MacLyle nodding eagerly, then going to the white-draped wall. From behind the chenille he brought a hammock, one end of which was fastened to the wall. The other end he carried to the big window and hung on a hook screwed to a heavy stud between the panes. To lie in that hammock would be to swing between heaven and earth like Mahomet's tomb, with all that sky and scenery virtually surrounding the sleeper. His admiration for this idea ceased as MacLyle began making urgent indications for him to get into the hammock. He backed off warily, expostulating, trying to convey to MacLyle that he only wondered, he just wanted to know—no, *no*, he wasn't tired, dammit; but MacLyle became so insistent that he picked the psychiatrist up like a child sulking at bedtime and carried him to the hammock. Any impulse to kick or quarrel was quenched by the nature of this and all other hammocks to be intolerant of shifting burdens, and by the proximity of the large window, which he now saw was built leaning outward, enabling one to look out of the hammock straight down a minimum of four hundred and eighty feet. So all right, he concluded, if you say so. I'm sleepy.

So for the next two hours he lay in the hammock watching MacLyle putter about the place, thinking more or less professional thoughts.

He doesn't or can't speak (he diagnosed): aphasia, motor. He doesn't or can't understand speech: aphasia, sensory. He won't or can't read and write: alexia. And what else?

He looked at all that art—if it *was* art, and any that was, was art by accident—and the gadgetry: the chuntering windmill outside, the sashweight door closer. He let his eyes follow a length of clothesline dangling unobtrusively down the leaning center post to which his hammock was fastened, and the pulley and fittings from which it hung, and its extension clear across the ceiling to the back wall, and understood finally that it would, when pulled, open two long, narrow horizontal hatches for through ventilation. A small

door behind the chenille led to what he correctly surmised
was a primitive powder room, built to overhang the precipice,
the most perfect no-plumbing solution for that convenience
he had ever seen.

He watched MacLyle putter. That was the only word for it,
and his actions were the best example of puttering he had
ever seen. MacLyle lifted, shifted, and put things down,
backed off to judge, returned to lay an approving hand on the
thing he had moved. Net effect, nothing tangible—yet one
could not say there was no effect, because of the intense
satisfaction the man radiated. For minutes he would stand,
head cocked, smiling slightly, regarding the half-finished
potter's wheel, then explode into activity, sawing, planing,
drilling. He would add the finished piece to the cranks and
connecting rods already completed, pat it as if it were an
obedient child, and walk away, leaving the rest of the job for
some other time. With a wood rasp he carefully removed the
nose from one of his dried clay figures and meticulously put
on a new one. Always there was this absorption in his own
products and processes, and the air of total reward in everything. And there was time, there seemed to be time enough
for everything, and always would be.

Here is a man, thought the fairly intelligent psychiatrist,
in retreat, but in a retreat the like of which my science has
not yet described. For observe: he has reacted toward the
primitive in terms of supplying himself with his needs with
his own hands and by his own ingenuity, and yet there is
nothing primitive in those needs themselves. He works constantly to achieve the comforts which his history has condi-
tioned him to in the past— electric lights, cross-ventilation,
trouble-free waste disposal. He exhibits a profound humility
in the low rates he pays himself for his labor: he is building a
potter's wheel apparently in order to make his own cooking
vessels, and, since wood is cheap and clay free, his vessel can
cost him less than engine-turned aluminum only by a very
low evaluation of his own effort.

His skills are less than his energy (mused the psychiatrist).
His carpentry, like his painting and sculpture, shows considerable intelligence, but only moderate training; he can construct but not beautify, draw but not draft, and reach the
artistically pleasing only by not erasing the random shake,
the accidental cut; so that real creation in his work is, like
any random effect, rare and unpredictable. Therefore his

reward is in the area of satisfaction—about as wide a generalization as one can make.

What satisfaction? Not in possessions themselves, for this man could have bought better for less. Not in excellence in itself, for he obviously could be satisfied with less than perfection. Freedom, perhaps, from routine, from dominations of work? Hardly, because for all that complexity of this cluttered cottage, it had its order and its system; the presence of an alarm clock conveyed a good deal in this area. He wasn't dominated by regularity—he used it. And his satisfaction? Why, it must lie in this closed circle, himself to himself, and in the very fact of noncommunication!

Retreat . . . retreat. Retreat to savagery and you don't engineer your cross-ventilation or adjust a five-hundred-foot gravity flush for your john. Retreat into infancy and you don't design and build a potter's wheel. Retreat from people and you don't greet a stranger like—

Wait.

Maybe a stranger who had something to communicate, or some way of communication, wouldn't be so welcome. An unsettling thought, that. Running the risk of doing something MacLyle didn't like would be, possibly, a little more unselfish than the challenge warranted.

MacLyle began to cook.

Watching him, the psychiatrist reflected suddenly that this withdrawn and wordless individual was a happy one, in his own matrix; further, he had fulfilled all his obligations and responsibilities and was bothering no one.

It was intolerable.

It was intolerable because it was a violation of the prime directive of psychiatry—at least, of that school of psychiatry which he professed, and he was not going to confuse himself by considerations of other, less-tried theories—*It is the function of psychiatry to adjust the aberrate to society, and to restore or increase his usefulness to it.* To yield, to rationalize this man's behavior as balance, would be to fly in the face of science itself; for this particular psychiatry finds its most successful approaches in the scientific method, and it is unprofitable to debate whether or not it is or is not a science. To its practitioner it is, and that's that; it has to be. Operationally speaking, what has been found true, even statistically, must be Truth, and all other things, even Possible, kept the hell out of the toolbox. No known Truth allowed a social entity to secede this way, and, for one, this fairly intelligent psychiatrist was not going to give this—this *suicide* his blessing.

He must, then, find a way to communicate with MacLyle, and when he had found it he must communicate to him the error of his ways. Without getting thrown over the cliff.

He became aware that MacLyle was looking at him, twinkling. He smiled back before he knew what he was doing, and obeyed MacLyle's beckoning gesture. He eased himself out of the hammock and went to the workbench, where a steaming stew was set out in earthenware bowls. The bowls stood on large plates and were surrounded by a band of carefully sliced tomatoes. He tasted them. They were obviously vine-ripened and had been speckled with a dark-green paste which, after studious attention to its aftertaste, he identified as fresh basil mashed with fresh garlic and salt. The effect was symphonic.

He followed suit when MacLyle picked up his own bowl, and they went outside and squatted under the old Engelmann spruce to eat. It was a quiet and pleasant occasion, and during it the psychiatrist had plenty of opportunity to size up his man and plan his campaign. He was quite sure now how to proceed, and all he needed was opportunity, which presented itself when MacLyle rose, stretched, smiled, and went indoors. The psychiatrist followed him to the door and saw him crawl into the hammock and fall almost instantly sleep.

The psychiatrist went to his car and got out his bag of tricks. And so it was that late in the afternoon, when MacLyle emerged stretching and yawning from his nap, he found his visitor under the spruce tree, hefting the ophicleide and twiddling its keys in a perplexed and investigatory fashion. MacLyle strode over to him and lifted the ophicleide away with a pleasant I'll-show-you smile, got the monstrous contraption into position, and ran his tongue around the inside of the mouthpiece, large as a demitasse. He had barely time to pucker up his lips at the strange taste there before his irises rolled up completely out of sight and he collapsed like a grounded parachute. The psychiatrist was able only to snatch away the ophicleide in time to keep the mouthpiece from knocking out MacLyle's front teeth.

He set the ophicleide carefully against the tree and straightened MacLyle's limbs. He concentrated for a moment on the pulse, and turned the head to one side so saliva would not

drain down the flaccid throat, and then went back to his bag
of tricks. He came back and knelt, and MacLyle did not even
twitch at the bite of the hypodermics: a careful blend of the
nonsoporific tranquilizers Frenquel, chlorpromazine and
Reserpine, and a judicious dose of scopolamine, a hypnotic.

The psychiatrist got water and carefully sponged out the
man's mouth, not caring to wait out another collapse the next
time he swallowed. Then there was nothing to do but wait,
and plan.

Exactly on schedule, according to the psychiatrist's wrist
watch, MacLyle groaned and coughed weakly. The psychiatrist immediately and in a firm quiet voice told him not to
move. Also not to think. He stayed out of the immediate
range of MacLyle's unfocused eyes and explained that MacLyle
must trust him, because he was there to help, and not to
worry about feeling mixed-up or disoriented. "You don't
know where you are or how you got here," he informed
MacLyle. He also told MacLyle, who was past forty, that he
was thirty-seven years old, but he knew what he was doing.

MacLyle just lay there obediently and thought these things
over and waited for more information. He didn't know where
he was or how he had got here. He did know that he must
trust this voice, the owner of which was here to help him;
that he was thirty-seven years old; and his name. In these
things he lay and marinated. The drugs kept him conscious,
docile, submissive and without guile. The psychiatrist observed
and exulted: oh you azacyclonol, he chanted silently to himself, you pretty piperidyl, handsome hydrochloride, subtle
Serpasil . . . Confidently he left MacLyle and went into the
cabin, where, after due search, he found some decent clothes
and some socks and shoes, and brought them out and wrapped
the supine patient in them. He helped MacLyle across the
clearing and into his car, humming as he did so, for there is
none so happy as an expert faced with excellence in his
specialty. MacLyle sank back into the cushions and gave one
wondering glance at the cabin and at the blare of late light
from the bell of the ophicleide; but the psychiatrist told him
firmly that these things had nothing to do with him, nothing
at all, and MacLyle smiled relievedly and fell to watching the
scenery go by, passive as a Pekingese. As they passed the
general store MacLyle stirred, but said nothing about it.
Instead he asked the psychiatrist if the Ardsmere station was
open yet, whereupon the psychiatrist could barely answer

him for the impulse to purr like a cat: the Ardsmere station, two stops before MacLyle's suburban town, had burned down and been rebuilt almost six years ago; so now he knew for sure that MacLyle was living in a time preceding his difficulties—a time during which, of course, MacLyle had been able to talk. He crooned his appreciation for chlorpromazine (which had helped MacLyle be tranquil) and he made up a silent song, "O Doll o' Mine, Scopolamine"—which had made him so very suggestible. But all of this the psychiatrist kept to himself, and he answered gravely that yes, they had the Ardsmere station operating again. And did he have anything else on his mind?

MacLyle considered this carefully, but since all the immediate questions were answered—unswervingly he *knew* he was safe in the hands of this man, whoever he was, he knew (he thought) his correct age and that he was expected to feel disoriented, and he was also under a command not to think—he placidly shook his head and went back to watching the road unroll under their wheels. "Fallen Rock Zone," he murmured as they passed a sign. The psychiatrist drove happily down the mountain and across the flats, back to the city where he had hired the car. He left it at the railroad station ("Rail Crossing Road," murmured MacLyle) and made reservations for a compartment on the train, aircraft being too open and public for his purposes and far too fast for the hourly rate he suddenly decided to apply.

They had time for a silent and companionable dinner before train time, and then at last they were aboard, solid ground beneath, a destination ahead, and the track joints applauding.

The psychiatrist turned off but one reading lamp and leaned forward. MacLyle's eyes dilated readily to the dimmer light, and the psychiatrist leaned back comfortably and asked him how he felt. He felt fine and said so. The psychiatrist asked him how old he was and MacLyle told him thirty-seven, but he sounded doubtful.

Knowing that the scopolamine was wearing off but the other drugs, the tranquilizers, would hang on for a bit, the psychiatrist drew a deep breath and removed the suggestion; he told MacLyle the truth about his age and brought him up to the here and now. MacLyle just looked puzzled for a few minutes and then his features settled into an expression that can only be described as not happy. "Porter," was all he said,

gazing at the push button on the partition with its little
metal sign, and he announced that he could read now.

The psychiatrist nodded sagely and offered no comment,
being quite willing to let a patient stew in his own juice as
long as he produced essence.

MacLyle abruptly demanded to know why he had lost the
powers of speech and reading. The psychiatrist raised his
eyebrows a little and his shoulders a good deal and smiled
one of those you-tell-me smiles, and then got up and suggested
they sleep on it. He got the porter in to fix the beds and as an
afterthought told the man to come back with the evening
papers. Nothing can orient a cultural expatriate better than
the evening papers. The man did. MacLyle paid no attention
to this, one way or the other. He just climbed into the
psychiatrist's spare pajamas thoughtfully and they went to
bed.

The psychiatrist didn't know if MacLyle had awakened
him on purpose or whether the train's slowing down for a
watering stop had done it, or both; anyway, he awoke about
three in the morning to find MacLyle standing beside his
bunk looking at him fixedly. He closed his eyes and screwed
them tight and opened them again, and MacLyle was still
there, and now he noticed that MacLyle's reading lamp was
lit and the papers were scattered all over the floor.

MacLyle said, "You're some kind of a doctor," in a flat voice.

The psychiatrist admitted it.

MacLyle said, "Well, this ought to make some sense to you.
I was skiing out here years ago when I was a college kid.
Accident, fellow I was with broke his leg. Compound. Made
him comfortable as I could and went for help. Came back,
he'd slid down the mountain, thrashing around, I guess.
Crevasse, down in the bottom; took two days to find him,
three days to get him out. Frostbite. Gangrene."

The psychiatrist tried to look as if he were following this.

MacLyle said, "The one thing I always remember, him
pulling back the bandages all the time to look at his leg.
Knew it was gone, couldn't keep himself from watching the
stuff spread around and upward. Didn't like to; *had* to. Tried
to stop him, finally had to help him or he'd hurt himself.
Every ten, fifteen minutes all the way down to the lodge,
fifteen hours, looking under the bandages."

The psychiatrist tried to think of something to say and
couldn't, so he looked wise and waited.

MacLyle said, "That Donne, that John Donne I used to spout, I always believed that."

The psychiatrist began to misquote the thing about send not to ask for whom the bell . . .

"Yeah, that, but especially *'any man's death diminishes me, because I am involved in mankind'*. I believed that," MacLyle repeated. "I believed more than that. Not only death. Damn foolishness diminishes me because I am involved. People all the time pushing people around diminishes me. Everybody hungry for a fast buck diminishes me." He picked up a sheet of newspaper and let it slip away; it flapped off to the corner of the compartment like a huge grave-moth. "I was getting diminished to death and I had to watch it happening to me like that kid with the gangrene, so that's why." The train, crawling now, lurched suddenly and yielded. MacLyle's eyes flicked to the window, where neon beer signs and a traffic light were reluctantly being framed. MacLyle leaned close to the psychiatrist. "I just had to get uninvolved with mankind before I got diminished altogether, everything mankind did was my fault. So I did and now here I am involved again. MacLyle abruptly went to the door. "And for that, thanks."

From a dusty throat the psychiatrist asked him what he was going to do.

"Do?" asked MacLyle cheerfully. "Why, I'm going out there and diminish mankind right back." He was out in the corridor with the door closed before the psychiatrist so much as sat up. He banged it open again and leaned in. He said in the sanest of all possible voices, "Now, mind you, doctor, this is only one man's opinion," and was gone.

He killed four people before they got him.

Very Proper Charlies

DEAN ING

"... I found fear a mean, overrated motive; no deterrent and, though a stimulant, a poisonous stimulant whose every injection served to consume more of the system. ..."
—T.E. Lawrence, *Seven Pillars of Wisdom*

AT the first buzz of the phone, Everett decided to ignore it. He'd planned his selfish Saturday for weeks, determined that official business would positively not deflect him from one last autumn day in the high country. Born a hundred and fifty years too late to be a mountain man, Maurice Everett lived his fantasy whenever he could—briefly by necessity, alone by choice. It wasn't until the third buzz, as he struggled into a turtleneck, that he recognized the buzzer tone of his unlisted number. Only his informants, and probably the FBI, had access to this tenuous link between newsmen and the federal government.

Everett spoke briefly, listened long, and promptly forgot the Rockies that lay in sere majesty on his horizon in Colorado Springs. "You're already en route, then," he said, thrusting the earpiece between head and shoulder as he tugged on heavy socks. "But why the Shoshone-Beardsley intersection? Doesn't the parade go through the center of Pueblo?" A pause. "Sure; handy for you and me, and the tactical squads too. Those mothers must be awfully confident." A final pause. "Maybe fifty minutes if I drive the superskate, but I haven't a CB rig in it. My problem anyhow; and thanks, Leo. Really."

Once before he hit U.S. route eighty-seven and twice after, Everett was noticed by Colorado Highway Patrol cruisers. He kept the tiny Mini-Cooper in racing tune though he rarely had time for his infatuation with the little freeway raptor. The big cruisers invariably saw his honorary highway patrol decals, fell back to check his plates, then let him continue fleeing south at nearly three kilometers a minute. A Federal Communications Commissioner was supposed to be circumspect, and Maurice Everett had been criticized for his maverick ways; but he used special privilege only in the line of duty. Mavericks had settled the West, and they might yet settle the electromagnetic spectrum.

Everett took the second offramp at Pueblo as if the curve were a personal affront, then eased off as he entered boulevard traffic. According to the newsman's tip, he would be at the intersection in time for the terrorist demonstration. Briefly, Everett was reminded of Charlie George, who had sat near him at—what was it, the Associated Press convention? The comedian had opined, in his laconic drawl, "TV will still play whore to any pimp with a machine pistol. We're the tush of terrorism." Everett had laughed at the remedy Charlie had proposed. But then, you were supposed to laugh at Charlie.

Everett spotted vehicles of two different networks as he neared the target area, and forgot about TV comedians. The van, he overtook; the big Honda bike overtook them both, more by maneuverability than speed. *The van gets you status, the bike gets you there first,* he mused. Electronic newsgathering equipment was so compact, newspeople could do ENG with two-wheeled vehicles though the Honda was too small to carry powerful transmission equipment.

Everett kept the van in his rearview and when it stopped, he found a niche for the Mini. From that point on, he was in enemy country.

He hesitated a moment in choosing decoy emblems. His was a camouflage problem: he wanted to avoid a make by newsmen, and a few knew Maury Everett on sight. But he also wanted to avoid getting himself killed. He donned wraparound dark glasses for the first criterion, and an armband over his rough leather jacket to meet the second. Terrorists knew who their friends were; the armband said simply, PRESS.

Following a National Broadcasting Network cameraman on foot, Everett wished he too had a lightweight videotape rig—even a dummy Micam would do. It had been years since a terrorist had deliberately downed a media man, and while Everett's informant could not predict details of the demonstration, it was prudent to suspect gunfire.

The boulevard was lined with spectators enjoying that foolish marvel of autumn anachronism, a homecoming parade.

Everett could not pause to enjoy the brassy polychrome of
assembled high school bands which high-stepped, a bit wearily
by now, between wheeled floats. He focused instead on the
newsmen. One, a bulky Portacam slung over his back, clam-
bered atop a marquee for a better view. Two others from
competing stations took up positions nearer the intersection,
almost a block from Everett. The comforting mass of a stone
pillar drew Maury Everett into its shadow. He could see a
thousand carefree people laughing, pointing, children darting at stray float decorations, cheering the discordances in
the music of these devoted amateurs. Was the tip a false
alarm? If not, Everett thought, this happy ambiance might
be shattered within minutes. And he, one of the famed FCC
Seven Dwarfs, was powerless.

Watching nubile majorettes cavort despite a chill breeze on
naked thighs, Maurice Everett faced his personal dilemma for
the hundredth time since his appointment. Newsmen dubbed
their solution "disinvolvement." You have a job and you
assume its risks. If you are government, you stay in your
bureau and off the toes of other bureaucrats. If you are
business, and most explicitly media newsgathering, you rise
or fall chiefly on informal contacts and you do not interfere
with news. You do not divulge sources for two reasons. The
legal reason is backed by the Supreme Court, and the selfish
reason is that fingering a contact is professional suicide. If
Everett somehow interrupted the impending show after its
careful leakage to TV newsmen by some unknown malcontent, his sources would evaporate instantly, permanently.
And his primary utility lay in knowing the actual nuts and
bolts of ENG, newsgathering by compact electronic gear.
Freedom of reportage, even when irresponsible, was a fun-
damental function of media. Theorists called it surveillance:
Maurice Everett called it hellish.

The Portacam man had shifted position to a second-landing
fire escape next to the synagogue. A thorough pro, he was
taking shots of the parade so that whatever happened, some
sort of story might be salvaged. Everett saw that all the
floats featured the same general theme: athletics. Lumbering
beyond him was a float honoring the 1980 Olympics winners,
a crudely animated statue labeled "Uri" waving three gold
medals. That would be Yossuf Uri, Israel's surprise middle-
distance winner. The hulking mannikin beside it represented
the Soviet weights man, whose heart had later failed under

the demands placed upon it by too many kilos of steroid-induced muscle tissue.

The casual connection of death with the display goaded Everett's mind toward a causal inference, but he froze for too many seconds. A synagogue on the corner, an Israeli hero approaching it, and a vague tipoff by a terrorist. No matter how little the newsmen knew, Maurice Everett clawed his way to a terrible conclusion.

Later, he could regain an uneasy sleep whenever he awoke streaming with the perspiration of guilt; for he *had* vaulted the horns of his dilemma. "Stop," he bawled, and knew his voice was hopelessly lost in the general clamor. Everett sprinted between bystanders, knocked a beldame sprawling, caromed into the side of another float. He was still on his feet, still shouting for attention, when the great torso of Yossuf Uri came abreast of the synagogue and disappeared in a blinding flash.

How Jewish can you get? The stable manager fingered the crisp twenty-dollar bill, smiling down at the signature. "I've saddled up a perty spirited mare, Mr. Rabbinowitz," he said, taking in the wistful smile, the olive skin, the dark hypnotic eyes. "Sure that's what you want?"

"Precisely," the little man pronounced his favorite word, and paced out to the corral. He mounted the mare quickly, gracefully, and cantered her out along the rim of the arroyo. The stableman watched him, puzzled, certain that he had seen Rabbinowitz before. Suddenly, as the figure dipped below his horizon in the afternoon sun, the stableman laughed. Meticulous silken dress and manner made the illusion even better, a youthful cosmetic version of a man more character than actor. "George Raft," he murmured, satisfied.

The mare was no filly, but she had Arabian lines. The rider held her at a gallop, imagining that he was in Iraq and not California. He savored the earthy scents and rhythms of this, a small pleasure he could justify in terms of security. No one, he felt, would bug a bridle trail. Presently he came in view of San Jose rooftops and at that moment—precisely—knew that he was being watched.

He made an elaborate show of patting the mare's neck, leaning first to one side and then the other, scanning—without seeming to—every mass of shrub cover within reasonable pistol-shot. Nothing. His heels pressured the mare. She was already plunging ahead when he heard the girl cry out behind him. He had passed her before sensing her? Most disturbing.

He wheeled the mare and returned, erasing his frownlines for the girl. She was clapping now, a jet-haired comely thing. "Ayyy, *que guapo*," she laughed aloud, showing a pink tongue between dazzling teeth. The gold cross at her throat, the peasant blouse: a latina.

He misjudged her in two ways: "You like the horse?"

"The combination," she answered, growing more serious. Her hands were clearly in sight, fingernails trimmed close, and he did not see how she could hide a significant weapon while showing so much youthful flesh. But still— Now she stroked the mare's nose, looking up at him. He liked that. "Like music," she said, and waited.

The formula should not have surprised him so. "Music by Sedaka?"

"Imsh'Allah," she said. How convenient that a popular composer's name should also, in several related tongues, mean *gift*. Well, this one would give.

He complimented her on the deception, dismounting, walking with her to a tree-shaded declivity. The mare tethered, they sat. "Curious," he began, "how my appetites are whetted by a job well done." They spoke English and then Arabic, softly, warmly, and when he remounted it was not on the mare. Presently they drew apart.

The girl combed her hair with impatient fingers. "You have seen videotapes of the morning's work?"

"Very early morning," he yawned. "I nearly missed my flight to San Jose. But no, I only heard a bulletin. Did we get suitable coverage?"

She nodded gravely. "Hakim will be pleased."

"Of that, I am certain." Their great bituminous eyes locked for a moment before, toying with her, he continued. "But Hakim must have a media center. You are prepared?"

"Prepared? When I hailed you," she riposted, "did you or did you not think I was a local chicana?"

Echoes of repugnance clashed like scimitars behind his quiet words. "You are clever, you are nubile. I speak of greater things than—" and paused after using a grossly sexist Bedouin term for their recent communion. He saw her corneas expand. Pleasure or pain? "I must know whether you have the site, the men, and the equipment I required."

"I cannot say. My instructions are to provide only for the leader himself. He may not arrive. Or he may." She shrugged.

"You *are* clever. But you are prepared for Hakim Arif?"

She said simply, "We are Fat'ah."

"And who am I?" He removed his left small finger at the last joint, replaced the prosthetic tip while she regained her composure. "I signed your instructions, 'Rabbinowitz.' "

"I—sire, you are Hakim Arif," she murmured, seeming to grow smaller.

"So I am. And angry at continued small talk, and impatient for my media. We have another demonstration to plan, depending on the results we see from today's work."

She quickly explained the route to the site she had prepared, naming each landmark three times. He did not remind her of his long familiarity with travel in the United States, but listened with critical approval. It was best to arrive after sunset, she said, which also gave her time to alert the others.

"Two of the three knew you before," she added, and named them. The third had been recruited in Damascus after Hakim Arif's last sojourn there, but Arif had read impressive reports.

"They will serve," he said, rising to collect the somnolent mare some distance away. He flung over his shoulder, "Better perhaps than a woman who deflects my questions." She could not see him smile. He turned the mare and trotted her back to the girl. Again he stared down from a commanding height, stern, refractory: the visage of Fat'ah. "Soon, then," he said, eyeing the sun.

"Sire," she stammered. Her body was controlled; only her voice trembled. "I did not know you. Your face is known to few in Fat'ah."

"Or out of it, as Allah is merciful," he rejoined. "Perhaps I shall be merciful too."

"If God wills," she said in Arabic.

"Or perhaps—" He waited until she met his eyes again. "I shall beat you."

"Perhaps you will," she said, not flinching.

Hakim Arif flogged the mare mercilessly up the trail, enjoying the experience, enjoying the memory of the girl's eyes. They had dilated again at his threat. Under a westering sun he sped back to the stable. He was thinking: *spawn of pain. We Fat'ah are the children of El Aurans after all. . . .*

Two hours later he found the Fat'ah site, temporary as it must be but better situated than he expected. The bungalow commanded a clear view of the San Jose skyline and, on three sides, open pastures beyond carbine range. On the fourth side a swath of scrub oak followed a brook so near the house that he could almost leap from its porch into thick cover. Two men patrolled the greenery, protecting Hakim Arif's escape route. Hakim was pleased. He let his distant smiles and nods say so. Let those idiots in the PLO show all the ersatz egalitarianism they liked: Fat'ah, born of Fat'h, born of Al Fat'h, born of injustice, was effective because he, Hakim Arif, was so.

But despite himself: "Ah," he breathed jubilantly, surveying the media center the girl had assembled. Four small TV sets half-encircled a desk which also faced an expanse of window. Four multiband radios were ranged to one side. All sets had earplugs. Three telephones were within reach. Notepads, blank card files, colored pens, a typewriter, a minivid recorder and two audio cassette machines filled most of the working space. The squat table underfoot was almost hidden by stacks of directories; Bay Area numbers, Los Angeles numbers, Washington numbers precisely as he had specified. Hakim knew the danger of heavy dependence on help supplied by telephone companies. There were ways to trace one from his patterns of inquiry. Unless, of course, one mastered the system.

The girl stood near, gnawing a full underlip, watching him assess the media center. "Rashid and Moh'med," he rapped suddenly. "Are they prepared to spend the night as pickets?"

"Each after his way," she murmured.

"And the husky one, the Panamanian?"

"En route to Santa Cruz. A powered parafoil requires skill. He knows his work; when he secures telephones he will call." She hesitated, then went on, "Yet he does not know how to address you in person." Her inflection said that she shared the man's concern.

The Fat'ah leader had not risen this far by allowing cynicism to show in his voice. "Do we fight for democracy? Is my name Hakim? Then Hakim it is!"

He began to play with his new equipment, not waiting for the latino's call. It was nearly an hour before the news shows, but the girl flicked a finger toward the minivid. He fumbled it into operation and saw that she had edited earlier newscasts into a videotape festival of the Pueblo horror. Hakim Arif settled back into a chair, notepad ready, and watched his favorite show.

*   *   *

Like a dry bearing in his head, a thin pure tone pierced Everett's awareness. "When will I quit hearing that whistle?" he demanded.

The white smock shrugged. "It goes with the injury," the doctor replied. "With luck, another day or so. No, don't try to sit up, you'll disturb the tubes. Follow orders and you'll be up in a few days, Mr. Everett. You're a big healthy animal; give your system a chance."

Everett glanced out the window of the Denver hospital. The fine cloudless day was lost to him, and he to the Rockies. "Hell of a day to be down."

"But a very good day to be alive," the doctor insisted. "Eleven others weren't so lucky, including a whole handful of TV people. You have no idea what an outcry the networks are making over those five particular fatalities."

Thanks to the drugs, Everett did not feel the bruised kidney, hairline fracture, and other modest rearrangements of his middle-aged anatomy. During his thirty-six hours of coma, the Denver people had done very well by him. But there were things they could not do. Curbing impatience he said, "Let's assume I stay put, don't hassle my nurse, and take lunch in approved fashion," glancing at the intravenous feeding apparatus.

The surgeon folded his arms. "If," he prompted.

"If I can trade the nurse for a staff member in here to—"

"Contraindicated. We're trying to excite regrowth around that flap torn in your tympanum, Mr. Everett. At your age, a blown eardrum is tough to repair. The nurse stays, the FCC goes."

"My left ear's okay, though. And even a felon gets *one* phone call."

After a judicious pause: "You've got it." He spoke to the nurse for a moment, stopped with his hand on the door. "We're starting you on solid foods, provided you make that one call and no more. We can haggle too. Agreed?"

"Agreed." Maury Everett watched the door swing shut, thinking of channels. FCC staff to network honchos? A mutual friend? Both too slow, and always loss of fidelity when the message was indirect. The hell with it. "Nurse, I want you to call NBN Hollywood and get one man on the line. I want nobody else, I want him with all possible dispatch, and it might help if you tell him Commissioner Everett is ready to lay the tush of terrorism."

She waited starchily, receiver in hand. "You're to avoid excitement. Is this an obscene call?"

"Everybody's a comedian," he grunted. "But the one I want is Charlie George."

Everett never knew exactly when the whistle died in his cranium. It was gone when he donned street clothes five days later, and that was enough. He was shaky, and wore an earplug on the right side, but he was functioning again. A staff member packed his bag because there was no wife to do it, and brought the taxi because he wasn't going home. The office would simply have to improvise until he had recuperated in Palm Springs—a tender negotiation with militant medics, based on his promise to relax with friends at the California resort city. He did not tell them it would be his first visit, nor that he had met only one of those friends.

Everett did not feel the Boeing clear the runway, so deep was he into a sheaf of clippings collated by his staff. A dozen dissident groups claimed so-called credit for the Pueblo blast, each carefully outlining its reasons, each hopeful that its motive would be touted. As usual, the commissioner noted with a shake of the massive head, our media system accommodated them all.

Only one group was armed with guilty knowledge: Fat'ah, led by the wraithlike Iraqi, Hakim Arif. Shortly after the blast, a United Press International office took a singular call from Pueblo, Colorado. It spoke in softly accented English of a microwave transmitter hidden in a tennis ball on a synagogue roof, and of galvanized nails embedded in the explosive. These details were easily checked by UPI. They were chillingly authentic. The caller went on to demand that Fat'ah, the only true believers in Palestinian justice, be given a base of operations for its glorious fight against Jewish tyranny. Ousted from Jordan, then ostensibly from Syria, Fat'ah was simply too militant even for its friends. It had nowhere to go. It chose, therefore, to go to the American people. Its channel of choice was a hideous explosion which left nearly a dozen dead and three dozen injured, half a world away from its avowed enemy.

When the caller began to repeat his spiel, police were already tracing the call. The message was on its fourth rerun when a breathless assault team stormed a Pueblo motel room. Not quite abandoned, the room contained a modified telephone answering device which, upon receiving a coded incoming call, had made its own prearranged call with an endless tape cartridge. The device was quite cunning: when an officer disgustedly jerked the telephone receiver away, it blew his arm off.

According to the *Newsweek* bio, Fat'ah's leader was a meticulous planner. When Hakim Arif was twelve, U.S. and Israeli agencies had only recently aided Iran in designing its secret police organ, SAVAK. SAVAK was still naive and Hakim already subtle when, during a visit to Iran by the youth and his father, security elements paid a lethal call on the elder Arif. The boy evaporated at the first hint of trouble, taking with him most of the emeralds his father had earmarked for bribes in Iran. SAVAK knew a good joke when it was played on them, and praised the boy's foresight. They would have preferred their praise to be posthumous; in the Middle East, drollery tends to be obscure.

Hakim took his secondary schooling in English-speaking private academies under the benevolent gaze of relatives in Syria, who never did discover where the jewels were. He also came under sporadic crossfires between Arab guerrillas and their Israeli counterparts, and knew where his sympathies lay. The magazine hinted that young Arif may have taken additional coursework in a school of socialist persuasion near Leningrad. How he got into an Ivy League school was anybody's guess, but a thumbnail-sized emerald was one of the better suppositions.

Trained in finance, media, and pragmatism, Hakim Arif again disappeared into the Near East—but not before leaving indelible memories with a few acquaintances. He quoted the Koran and T. E. Lawrence. He was not exactly averse to carrying large amounts of cash on his person. He won a ridiculously small wager by chopping off the end of a finger. And he was preternaturally shy of cameras.

Arif and Fat'ah were mutually magnetized by desire and bitterness, but not even Interpol knew how Arif came to lead a guerrilla band who rarely saw their leader. Thwarted by security forces in Turkey, England, Syria, and Jordan, Fat'ah was evidently fingering the tassels at the end of its tether. Perhaps Arif had sold his last jewel; the fact was clear that the goals of Fat'ah, reachable by sufficient injections of cash into the proper systems, were elusive.

Everett paused in his reading to gaze wistfully at California's mighty Sierra range that stretched away below the Boeing. With the dusting of early snow on sawtooth massifs, it looked as cold and hard down there as the heart of Hakim Arif. What sort of egotist did it take to shorten his pinkie on an absurd wager, yet avoid photographers? A very special one, to say the least. Everett resumed reading.

The conservative *Los Angeles Times* devoted much space to a strained parallel between law enforcement agencies and Keystone Kops. The smash hit of the new TV season was a Saturday night talk show in which a battery of NBN hosts deigned to speak, live, only to callers who were already in the news. Soon after midnight on the Saturday of the Pueblo disaster, a caller identified himself as Hakim Arif. He demanded instant air time. A reigning cinema queen was discussing oral sex at 12:17:25, and found herself staring into a dead phone at 12:17:30. Arif was speaking.

Incredibly, the Iraqi responded to questions; prerecording was out of the question. While Arif launched into the plight of Palestinian Arabs and the need for funding to continue the heroic struggle, network officials feverishly collaborated with police, the FBI, and the telephone company. Arif was obviously watching the show, to judge by his critique of one host's silent mugging.

Arif used no terms objectionable enough to require bleeping; he merely promised to repeat the Pueblo entertainment in larger and larger gatherings until, in its vast wisdom and power, the United States of America found a haven for Fat'ah. And oh, yes, there was one condition: the country of the haven must adjoin Israel.

While voiceprint experts established the identical patterns of the Pueblo and NBN show voices, a co-host asked if Arif realized that he was asking for World War Three. Arif, chuckling, replied that he trusted the superpowers to avoid over-response to Israeli banditry. As Arif chuckled, a Lockheed vehicle lifted vertically from Moffett Field in California for nearby Santa Cruz. Its hushed rotors carried four case-hardened gentlemen over the Coast Range in minutes to a parking lot two hundred yards from the Santa Cruz telephone booth which comprised one end of the telephone connection. Police cordoned the area and awaited the fight.

There was no fight. There was only another clever device in the booth, relaying the conversation by radio. Its sensors noted the approach of the bomb squad to the booth with the "out of order" sign, and suddenly there was no telephone, no device, and no booth; there was only concussion. The *Times* surmised that Arif could have been within thirty miles of the booth. No one, including Arif, knew that the Lockheed assault craft had passed directly over his bungalow in San Jose.

Arif's next call passed through another booth in Capitola, near Santa Cruz, to CBS. He was in good spirits. Government agencies were in overdrive. No one was in a position to corral even one arm of Fat'ah and when Arif was good and ready, he closed down his media center. By the time his bungalow had been discovered, Arif had a two-day start. That is, said the private report compiled for Everett, if it had been Arif. Fingerprint plants were common gambits in disinformation games. The Iraqi's MO varied, but he always knew how to use available channels, including the illegal importation of some of his devices from sources among the Quebecois. There was more, and Everett forced himself to read it. Behind the old-fashioned reading glasses, his eyes ached. Presently he closed them and tried to ignore the faintly resurgent whistle in his head.

Two flights and a limousine later, Maurice Everett declined help with his suitcase and carried its reassuring bulk in Palm Springs heat toward a vacant lot. At least it looked vacant, until he strode through a slot in the sloping grassy berm and realized that this comedian knew how to use money.

The berm surrounded a sunken terrace open to the sun. Around the terrace and below ground level lay the translucent walls of Charlie George's hideaway. It reminded Everett of a buried doughnut, its hole a glass-faced atrium yawning into the sky, slanted solar panels more attraction than excrescence. It was thoroughly unlike the monuments erected nearby: logical, insulated, understated. Already, Everett liked Charlie George better for making sense even when he was not compelled to.

The commissioner was nonplused for an instant by the man who met him at the door like a sodbuster's valet. Denims tucked into beflapped, rundown boots; suspenders over an ancient cotton work shirt; a stubble of beard. Yet there was no mistaking the loosejointed frame or the shock of corntassel hair over bushy brows, familiar to anyone who watched prime time. Beneath the strong nose was a mouth legendary for its mobility, from slackjawed idiocy to prudish scorn. Everett realized with a start that it was speaking.

"You wanted it informal," said Charlie George, and ushered Everett to a guest room.

They talked easily while Everett changed into his scruffies. "I haven't sounded out the rest of the Commission," Everett admitted, wincing as he adjusted his pullover. "McConnell's a reasonable sort, though, and I'll lay it out for him so he'll know you're serious about separating TV from terrorism. These panel talks with the AP and UPI sure haven't excited him—or me. I like your scenario better."

The comedian kept his eyes sociably averted as Everett donned soft leather trousers. "We've been battling out details for an hour."

"Who's we?"

Charlie leaned his head toward the window facing the atrium. "No net veepees, just a couple of pivotal people I told you about." He led Everett through a kitchen saturated with musks of tortilla and taco sauce, into sunlight toward a buzz of voices in a hidden corner of the atrium.

They found two men seated, dividing their attention between sketch pads and bottles of Mexican beer. The smaller one made a point of rising; the taller, a show of not rising. "This is our friend in the feds." Charlie placed a gentle hand on Everett's shoulder. "Maury Everett: Rhone Althouse here, and Dahl D'Este there."

Althouse wore faded jeans and Gucci loafers. Only the footgear and a stunning Hopi necklace belied his undergraduate appearance. He was close-knit and tanned, and his handshake had the solidity of a park statue. It was hard to believe that this pup was a media theorist who had deserted academia for a meteoric rise in gag writing. "I hope you guys move quicker separately than you do together," he said to Everett, with the barest suggestion of a wink.

Everett smiled at this threadbare gibe. FCC decisions never came quickly enough for the industry it regulated. "Don't bet on it," he replied. "I'm still pretty rickety today."

D'Este, doodling furiously on a mammoth sketch pad, stopped to gaze at Everett with real interest. "I forgot," he said in a caramel baritone, "you were the star of the Pueblo thing. Perhaps you'll tell me about it." His tone implied, *some other time, just we two.*

Everett accepted a Moctezuma from Charlie George and eased his broad back onto a lawn chair. "All I know, literally, is what I've read since I woke up. I hope to learn a lot more from you three, in hopes it doesn't happen again."

"Ah," said D'Este, beaming. His elegant slender height was covered by a one-piece burgundy velour jumpsuit which, Everett hazarded, might have been tailored expressly for this event. Dahl D'Este affected tight dark curls, his tan was by Max Factor. He hugged the sketch pad to him and stood to claim his audience. "Well then, the story thus far—" He paused as though for their host's permission and seemed gratified. "Charlie has this—*wild* idea that he can ring in a new era of comedy. Instead of avoiding the issue of terrorism in comedy, and believe me luv, we *do,* he wants to create a fabulous character."

"A whole raft of 'em," the comedian put in. Everett nodded; he knew the general idea but would not rob D'Este of his moment.

"Charlie has seduced the best talents he could find to plan graphics, that's me, and situations, that's Rhone. Of course, that's ironic, because Charlie is NBN, Rhone is an ABC captive, and for the nonce I'm doing CBS sets. I don't know how Charlie beguiled his old *enfant terrible,*" he smirked at Althouse—"to cross traditional lines in this madness." Everett, who knew it had been the other way around, kept silent. "As for me, I couldn't resist the challenge."

"Or the retainer," Althouse drawled in a murmur designed to carry.

The splendid D'Este ignored him. "While Charlie and Rhone brainstormed their little skits, I've been inventing Charlie's logo for the new character. A cartoon of the sort of loser who—how did you put it, Rhone?"

"Rates no respect," the younger man supplied. "If he tried dial-a-prayer he'd get three minutes of raucous laughter."

"Well, my logo will peer out at the world from Charlie's backdrop like a malediction. I really ought to sign it. Behold, a very proper Charlie!" With this fanfare, Dahl D'Este spun the sketch pad around and awaited reactions.

Everett was thankful that he didn't need to surrogate approval. The sketch was, somehow, the face of Charlie George as an enraged Goya might have seen him. Yet the surface similarity was unimportant. Splashed across the paper in hard sunlight was a stylized symbol of repellence.

The head and shoulders of a vicious imbecile faced them as it would glare out at untold millions of viewers. The face was vacuously grinning, and gripped a fused stick of dynamite in its teeth. The fuse was too short, and it was lit. In redundant arrogance, just exactly out of scale as though reaching toward the viewer, was a time-dishonored hand gesture: the stink-finger salute.

Laughter welled up from the group and geysered. Althouse raised his beer in obeisance.

"Ah—about the monodigital scorn," Charlie wavered, darting a look at Everett.

Althouse held his hands open, cradling an invisible medicine ball. "C'mon, Charlie, it's perfect." He too risked a sidelong glance at the FCC man. "And for its public use, our precedent was a recent vice president."

D'Este: "Of which net?"

"Of the United bloody States," cried Althouse in mock exasperation. "Yes it's naughty, and yes it's safe!"

"I'm inclined to agree," said Everett, "if it's done by a questionable character for a crucial effect."

D'Este leaned the sketch against the solar panels. "A proper Charlie," he repeated, then looked up quickly. "Did you know that British slang for a total loser is a veddy propah Chahlie?"

"Poor Dahl," sighed Althouse. "Did you know we picked the name 'Charlie George' in 1975 because semantic differential surveys told me they were the outstanding loser names in the English-speaking world? Bertie is good, Ollie is better; but Charlie George is the people's choice!"

"Thanks for nothing," Everett chortled. "I always wondered why citizens band jargon for the FCC was 'Uncle Charlie.' " Althouse affected surprise, but not chagrin.

Charlie looked out into the middle-distance of his past. "I wasn't too keen to change my name from Byron Krause to Charlie George," he mused, "until I thought about that poem."

Althouse saw curiosity in Everett's face and broke in. "I tacked it up on a soundstage bulletin board, and Charlie saw people react, and bingo: Charlie George." He squinted into the sun, then recited.

"Heroes all have lovely names,
Like Lance, or Mantz, or Vance, or James;

But authors elevate my gorge
By naming losers Charles and George.

There's no suspense on the late, late show;
Big deal: the bad guy's Chas., or Geo.

Goof-offs, goons, schlemiels and schmucks:
Georgies, every one—or Chucks.

Since the days of Big Jim Farley,
Fiction's fiends have been George and Charlie;

No wonder heroes all seem crass
To any guy named Geo., or Chas.

I think I'll change my name, by golly!
My last name's George.
The nickname's Cholly.

Everett grinned, but: "Obviously some of your earliest work," D'Este purred.

"Point is, Dahl, it fitted the image I was after. And it's been good to me," the comedian insisted. "Your logo is great, by the way; it *is* a proper charlie." He paused. "I want you to release it to the public domain."

The ensuing moment held a silence so deep, Everett's ear hurt. D'Este broke it with a strangled, "Just—*give* it away? Like some *amateur*? No"—and there was horror in his husked—"*residuals?*"

"Oh, I'll pay you a great lump. But I want the thing available with no restrictions, for any medium anywhere, anytime. PBS. *Mad* Magazine. The *National Enquirer* maybe."

"Madness. *Mad*ness," D'Este said again, aghast, his normal hyperbole unequal to this task. He reached for a beer.

When Rhone Althouse spoke again it was in almost fatherly tones. "I'm afraid you haven't been listening very closely, Dahl. It's no accident that Charlie and I are planning to spring this idea in different networks. Charlie's the rudder of several committees where the power is in some veepee. I have a little leverage in ABC and with any positive audience response we can slowly escalate the trend. *If* there's no problem in, ah, certain quarters." He raised an eyebrow toward Maurice Everett.

Everett traced a pattern on the label of his beer bottle, thinking aloud. "There shouldn't be any serious objection from us," he began. "It's in the public interest to pit media against terrorism—and if you find yourselves in jeopardy it won't be from the Commission." He could not keep an edge from his voice. "Personally I think you've waited too goddam long."

"They nearly bagged an FCC man, you mean," Charlie prodded.

"No. Yes! That too, I can't deny personal feelings; but I was thinking of ENG men from three networks, casually hashed like ants under a heel. That's why network execs care. That's why your iron is hot. But so far I don't hear evidence of any broad scope in your plans."

The comedian bit off an angry reply and Everett realized, too late, that he teetered on the brink of a lecture that none of them needed. This group represented, not problem, but solution.

Althouse rubbed his jaw to hide a twitch in it. "You came in late," he said softly. "You didn't hear us planning to expand this idea into news and commentary. If you've ever tried to apply a little torque to a network commentator, you know what howls of censorship sound like. Morning news and editorializing are more folksy, a good place to start."

"Start what? Boil it down to essentials."

"It boils down to two points: we turn every act of terrorism into a joke at the terrorist's expense; and we absolutely must refuse, ever again, to do a straight report on their motives."

Everett sat rigidly upright at the last phrase, ignoring the pain in his side. "Good God, Althouse, that really is censorship!"

"De facto, yes; I won't duck that one. But legally it's a case of each network freely choosing to go along with a policy in public interest. Wartime restrictions beyond what the government demands are a precedent, if we need one. And the National Association of Broadcasters could publish guidelines for independent stations. The NAB is an ideal go-between."

The issue lay open between them now like a doubly discovered chess game. Everett saw in Althouse a formidable player who had studied his moves and his opponent. "It's unworkable," Everett said. "What'll you do when some Quebec separatist gang tortures a prime minister? Sit on the news?"

"Maybe not, if it's that big a story. We *can* give coverage to the event, sympathetic to the victim—but we *must* deride the gang as proper charlies, and refuse to advertise their motives."

"While you let newspapers scoop you on those details?"

"Probably—until they get an attack of conscience."

Everett's snort implied the extravagance of that notion. "A couple of Southern Cal people did in-depth surveys that suggest there's no 'probably' to it. Editors print assassination attempts as front-page stuff even if they know it brings out more assassins. They admit it."

"Hey; the Allen-Piland study," Althouse breathed, new respect in his face. "You get around."

"I've been known to read hard research," Everett replied.

"And newsmen have been known to modify their ethics," Charlie George said. "If this becomes censorship, Maury, it'll be entirely self-imposed."

"I'm sure this sounds like an odd stance for me to take" —Everett smiled sadly—"but I tend to balk at social control. Hell, Althouse, you've studied Shramm and his people."

"Right. And I remember something you don't, it seems. Most media philosophers claim that, between simple-minded total liberty to slander and hard-nosed total control over the message, there's something we always move toward when we confront a common enemy. It's called Social Responsibility Theory. We used it to advantage in 1917 and 1942. It's time we used it again."

That the issue would arise in the Commission seemed certain. It was equally certain that Everett must select a principle to override others sooner or later. He had a vivid flash of recollection: a willowy girl with gooseflesh and a baton, bravely smiling after an hour of parading, ten seconds before her obliteration. "I don't like it," he said slowly, measuring the words, "but I don't like wars on children either. You make God-damned sure this social responsibility doesn't go beyond the terrorism thing." His promise, and its limitation, were implicit.

"I don't like it either," D'Este spat. "I seem to be part of a media conspiracy I never asked for. Charlie, you didn't ask me here just for graphics. What, then?"

'Commitment," Charlie said evenly.

"I'm working on CBS specials! How I'm expected to collar newsmen, writers, and producers is beyond me, regular programming is out of my line."

"Nothing in television is out of your line," Rhone Althouse

began, laying stress on each word. As he proceeded, Everett
noted the upswing in tempo, the appeal to D'Este's vanity,
the loaded phrases, and he was glad Althouse did not write
speeches for politicians. "You're independent; you work for
all the nets, you know everybody in key committees all over
the industry, and when you lift an idea you pick a winner.
Charlie can sweet-talk NBN news into using that logo when
there's a place for it—we think—while he develops his satire.

"You know the old dictum in showbiz: if it succeeds, beat it
to death. I'll start working the same shtick in ABC comedy—
Christ, I'm doing three shows!—and I can drop the hint that
this lovely logo is public domain. With any luck, the idea can
sweep NBN and ABC both. News, commentary, comedy.

"And you, Dahl? Will CBS keep out of the fun for some
asinine inscrutable reason? Or will one of its most active—"
he paused, the word *homosexuals* hanging inaudibly in the
air like an echo without an antecedent—"free spirits cham-
pion the idea from the inside? That's really the only question,
Dahl. Not whether you can do it, but whether you *will*."

Intending support, Everett murmured, "It'll take guts, in a
milieu that hasn't shown many," and immediately wished he
hadn't.

"No one corporation owns me, Mr. E." D'Este flung the
words like ice cubes. "I don't have to stroke your armor."

"That's not what I meant. None of you have considered
asking the next question," Everett responded.

Charlie George misunderstood, too. "Ask yourself if it's
worth some trouble to keep this industry from being a flack
for maniacs, Dahl. If we don't start soon, ask yourself if you'd
like to see the FCC license networks themselves when Congress considers tighter government control."

An even longer silence. "Madness," D'Este said at last,
"but in this crazy business—I have misgivings, but I'll go
along." He folded his arms challengingly and stared at Everett. "Licensing? Is that the sword you were brandishing, the
next question you meant?"

Everett swigged his beer, then set it down. His smile was
bleak. "That never crossed my mind; I think Charlie over-
stated. Here's what I meant: if this idea takes hold, the idea
men could be spotlighted, and that means to people like
Hakim Arif. I had a brush with their rhetoric, and they
weren't even after me. See what it brought me." He peeled
his shirt up to reveal the tape that bound the bandage to his

right side. Angry stripes, the paths of debris in human flesh, marked his belly and pectorals beyond the tape.

He hauled the fabric down, regarded the sobered media men. "We have a lot of questions to thrash out, but none of you can afford to ignore the next one: if you take them *all* on—Palestinians, IRA, Chileans, Japanese extremists—what are the chances they'll come after you personally?" For once, he noted with satisfaction, Rhone Althouse sat unprepared, openmouthed.

Hakim's feet were light on the steps as he hurried from the bank. The sheer weight of banknotes in his attaché case tugged at his left arm but failed to slow his stride. Fourteen minutes to rendezvous; plenty of time unless he were followed. His quick pace was perfectly normal in metropolitan New York City. He checked his watch again before entering the cafeteria. No one followed or seemed to loiter outside the place. He bought a chocolate bar to tempt, but not to entertain, his empty stomach. Slipping the candy into a pocket of his silk shirt, away from the extended shoulder holster, he thought of the pleasures of self-denial. He salivated for the chocolate. Later he would watch the girl eat it. He surveyed the cafeteria's glass front through reflective sunglasses. Twelve minutes; time to burn. He left by a different exit, moving unobtrusively down the street.

It was sheerest luck that the antique store was placed just so, and boasted a mirror angled just so. Hakim spotted the glance from a stroller to the unmarked sedan, both moving behind him and in his direction. The stroller drifted into another shop. A tall blond man emerged from the sedan, and in a hurry. Hakim's body braced for action.

He continued his brisk pace. Instead of converging on him they had exchanged tails, which meant he was expected to lead them—whoever they were. Federals, probably, judging from the cut of their suits. He tested the notion of the Jewish Defense League, not so farfetched in Manhattan, and felt perspiration leap at his scalp. But their methods were more direct, and the tail he had picked up must have mooched around the bank for days. And that meant inefficiency, which implied government. He cursed the overcoat that impeded his legs in November cold, then saw the third-rate hotel.

The blond man entered the lobby as Hakim was leaving the stair onto the filthy mezzanine and wasted seconds on two other passages; seconds that saved him. Hakim found the fire exit, burst the door seal, and slithered past the metal grating to drop into the alley. He sprinted for the street, adjusted his breathing again as he slowed to a walk, then turned another corner and risked a peek over his shoulder. The sedan was following with its lone driver.

Hakim had nine minutes and needed seven. He wanted that rendezvous, not relishing the alternative risks of public transportation to Long Island. Nearing the next corner he noted the lack of pedestrians and made his decision. He broke into a run, turned sharply, ran a few steps, then turned back and melted into a doorway. He did not want the driver to pursue him afoot and knew this to be the next option of his pursuer.

A small girl sat on the stair in his doorway at Hakim's eye level, watching silently as he fumbled in his coat. He flashed her a smile and a wink. The sedan squalled around the corner. Hakim gauged his move to coincide with commitment to the turn, made five leaping paces, and fired as many times. The parabellum rounds pierced glass, cloth, flesh, bone, upholstery, and body panels in that order, each silenced round making no more noise than a great book suddenly closed. The sedan's inertia carried it into a forlornly stripped foreign coupe. Hakim held the sidearm in his coat and retraced his steps, winking again at the little girl just before he shot her. Then he reseated the pistol, careful to keep the hot silencer muzzle away from the expensive shirt.

Seven minutes later Hakim hurried up another alley, squirmed into a delivery van, and nodded at the sturdy Panamanian who lazed behind the wheel in coveralls as the engine idled.

The van's engine was mounted between front seats with an upholstered cover. Bernal Guerrero had built an extension just long enough to accommodate a small Iraqi, and the makeshift upholstery would pass casual inspection. Kneeling with the extension cover up, reluctant to relinquish control to the latino, Hakim urged caution. "Drive south first; I was followed." He did not elaborate.

For a time, Guerrero attended strictly to driving. Soon the distant beeps of police vehicles were lost and Hakim directed his driver to the bridge approach. Once over the East River, in heavy traffic, Hakim began to relax but did not stir from his position. Guerrero adjusted the inside rearview. "The funds were on hand, then."

Hakim met his eyes in the mirror. "Was that a question?"

"Deduction, señor. The briefcase seems heavy—and you are smiling."

"A wise man smiles in adversity," Hakim quoted, reloading six rounds into the clip.

"I trust Moh'med was smiling at the last," Guerrero said obliquely. "I liked him."

"Moh'med was a fool. You cannot load down an underpowered aircraft and maneuver it, too."

"A fool, then," Guerrero said. "I agree that a satchel charge would have been simpler."

Hakim's irritation was balanced by the utility of the sinewy Guerrero. The Panamanian's suggestions were good and he did not press them. Yet his conversation always provoked broader answers than Hakim cared to give. "You agree with whom? Have you toured the Statue of Liberty, Guerrero? A satchel charge might disfigure the torch, nothing more. I planned to destroy the thing. Think of the coverage," he breathed, and chuckled.

They were past Queens, halfway to the site in Farmingdale, before Hakim spoke again. "The new funds," he said as if to himself, "will pour into accounts for Fat'ah exactly as long as our coverage is adequate. But our supporters may not enjoy last night's media sport at our expense."

Guerrero nodded, remembering. But to prattle is to reveal, and this time he said nothing. Amateur films had caught Moh'med, his handmade bomb shackles hopelessly jammed, as he veered away from his first pass at the great gray statue, the previous day. The canister weighed nearly three hundred kilos, and as it dangled swaying from the little Piper, Moh'med must have known he could neither land nor long maintain control. To his credit, he had fought the craft into a slow shallow turn and straightened again, kilometers from his target. With any luck he might have completed his run, barely off the surface of the harbor, and crashed directly into the Statue of Liberty. But the new fireboat hovercraft were very quick, faster under these circumstances than the Piper that careened along at all of ninety kilometers an hour.

Hakim sighed. What ignominy, to be downed by a stream of dirty salt water! Still, "The Charlie George show made Moh'med a martyr," he asserted.

"To what? Idiot liberation, they said. And," Guerrero reminded him, "NBN news did not carry the story well. 'A terrorist quenched with a water pistol,' indeed. It is—*la palabra*, ah, the word? Provocative."

"As you are," Hakim said shortly. "Let me worry about media, and let the Americans worry about our next demonstration."

"Our next demonstration," Guerrero echoed. It was not quite a question.

"Soon, Guerrero, soon! Be silent." Again Hakim felt moisture at his temples, forcing him to acknowledge a sensation of pressure. Harassment was the guerrilla's tool; when he himself felt harassed, it was best to cancel the operation. But he dared not. Something in Guerrero's attitude, indeed in Hakim's own response to television's smug mockery, said that Hakim Arif must choke that dark laughter under a pall of smoke.

He shifted his cramped legs to sit atop the attaché case as they skirted Mineola. Soon they would roll into the garage at Farmingdale, soon he would bear the case inside with a show of indifference, reviewing the site again to assure its readiness for—for whatever; he did not know what.

Fat'ah must be ready with only four members now, and he could not easily muster more on short notice. The Damascus site and its people would again be secure for a time, now that Hakim could furnish bribes, but Damascus is not Farmingdale, New York, and Hakim knew he was improvising. Fat'ah could not afford always to improvise. Nor could it afford to delay vengeance for the Moh'med fiasco.

The double-bind was adversity. Hakim forced himself to smile, thinking of smoke. Of black smoke and of media, and of the girl who would be warm against him in the chill Long Island night. He vowed to deny himself the third, which made his smile more genuine, and knew that he could now concentrate on the first two.

Rashid and the girl failed to hide their relief at the sight of the money, stacks of twenties and fifties, which Hakim revealed in due time. During supper their eyes kept wandering to the cash until Hakim wordlessly arose and dumped it all back into the case. "Now we will have sweet coffee," he sighed, the girl rising to obey, "and contemplate sweeter revenges. Even today I struck a small blow; the eleven o'clock news may bear fruit." He was gratified to see curiosity in their silent responses.

Hakim did not expect to occupy the ABC lead story, but grew restive as national, then local news passed. Had his escape gone unnoticed, then? It had not, for, "There was an evident postscript, today, to the blundering attempt on the Statue of Liberty," said the anchorlady. "If anyone can make sense of it, perhaps Richard can."

Her co-anchor gazed out at millions, his backdrop a leering idiot that was becoming familiar. He dropped a piece of typescript as if it were defiled and related little more, factually, than the locale and the killing of Hakim's pursuer. He went on: "What places this below the usual level of crime in the Big Apple, according to one source, is that the gunman's description matches that of a Fat'ah charlie, and his victim was a Daoudist, another terrorist. The current guess is that the victim was trying to make friendly contact, and the gunman mistook him for someone who knew too much." A frosty smile. "Or perhaps that's a charlie's way of hailing a taxi."

Injected by his co-anchor lady: "About the little girl he missed at point-blank range?"

"Maybe he thought she knew too much, too. And compared to these charlies, maybe she does. She's almost five years old."

Hakim used great restraint to continue his televiewing. The girl at his side began with, "But you said—" until Hakim's hand sliced the air for silence.

The weather news endorsed the frigid gusts that scrabbled at the windows, and Hakim's mood was like the wind. He could not have missed the urchin—and his daring coup was against domestic security forces, he was certain. Well, *almost* certain. Was it even remotely possible that the coxcomb Abu Daoudists had intended—? On the other hand, government sources could have deliberately lied to the newsmen with a release designed to confuse Fat'ah.

The girl ghosted to the kitchenette to prepare fresh sweet coffee which Hakim craved, and subsequently ignored, as he lounged before blank television screens. The art of disinformation was but recently borrowed from the Near East, but the Americans were learning. *But if they know I know that Daoud could not know where I am,* his thoughts began, and balked with, *where am I?*

He released a high-pitched giggle and the girl dropped her cup. Hakim angrily erased the rictus from his face and pursued another notion. Daoudists could be behind this, seeking to share the media coverage in their bungling fashion. He, Fat'ah, would need to arrange more talks with his television friends. Not exactly friends, he amended, so much as co-opportunists who could always be relied upon to give accurate and detailed coverage if it were available. *Except in wartime*, whispered a wisp from a forgotten text. It was unthinkable that American television networks could perceive themselves at war with Fat'ah.

Unthinkable, therefore Hakim thought about it.

The same grinning salacious fool was becoming the prominent image behind every news item on terrorism. On competing networks! He thought about it some more. While Fat'ah planned the attack that was to cost Moh'med his life, Ukrainian dissenters had made news by murdering three enemies in the Soviet Secretariat. A scrap of dialogue haunted Hakim from a subsequent skit on the *Charlie George Show*.

INT. SQUALID BASEMENT NIGHT

CHARLIE wears a Rasputin cloak and villainous mustache, leaning over a rickety table lit by a bent candle. He scowls at CRETINOV, who cleans a blunderbuss with a sagging barrel.

TWO-SHOT CHARLIE AND CRETINOV

CHARLIE

Comrade leader, I say we kidnap everyone who calls us fools!

CRETINOV
(bored)

Nyet; where would we keep four billion people?

This established the general tenor of a five-minute lampoon, redolent of impotent fools, on terrorism against the Kremlin. The Ukrainians had enjoyed the sympathy of the United States government. Perhaps they still did, but obviously television moguls thought differently.

When had Hakim last heard a sympathetic rendering of the justice, the demands, the motivations, of a terrorist group? For that matter, he persisted, any factual rendering at all? A harrowing suspicion helped a pattern coalesce in

Hakim's mind as he absently reached for his coffee. Every datum he applied seemed to fit an undeclared war that he should have suspected from this medium. A medium upon which Fat'ah was all too dependent; newspapers brought details, but TV brought showers of cash from Fat'ah well-wishers. Had the Americans at last conspired to rob him of his forum, his voice, his cash?

Hakim Arif retrieved his images of smoke and media, this time imagining a greasy black roil erupting from a picture tube. It should be simple enough to test this suspicion. If it proved to be accurate, Hakim vowed, he would bring war to this monster medium.

He sipped the tepid coffee, then realized that he had forbidden it to himself. Rage flung the cup for him, shattering it against a television set that squatted unharmed. The girl's gasp paced Guerrero's reaction, a sidelong roll from his chair from which the latino emerged, a crouching wolverine, his Browning sidearm drawn. Guerrero was not particularly quick, but his hand was steady. In the silent staring match with the latino, Hakim told himself, he dropped his own eyes first to atone for his rashness.

Hakim stood erect and exhaled deeply from his nose. "We need rest," he said.

"Yes, you do," Guerrero agreed, tucking the automatic away.

Hakim did not pause in his march to the far bedroom. He read the latino's implied criticism, but would absorb it for now. He could not afford to waste Guerrero. Yet.

As long as the National Association of Broadcasters wanted to hold a convention during Thanksgiving holidays, Everett admitted, it was nice to find that Reno was its choice. He wandered among the manufacturers' exhibits in the hotel foyer, grudgingly accepting some responsibility for the presence of so many new security devices. Say what you like about media men, their self-interest is intelligent. Cassette systems shared display space with microwave alarms. One import drew the commissioner's admiration: an outgrowth of an English medical thermovision system, it could display so small a mass of metal as coins in a pocket—unless they were at body heat, no more, no less.

A voice behind him said, "Neat. Any charlie who sneaks

his forty-five past that rig will have to carry it as a suppository," and Everett wheeled to face Rhone Althouse.

Everett's delight was real, though brief. "Thank God for somebody I can ask questions of, instead of just answering 'em," he said.

"I heard your speech on porn," was the reply, "and I can't believe you have any answers. Seriously, I did want to—well, uh, actually Charlie George, um." He cocked his head to one side. "The fact is, our Palm Springs meeting has become the worst-kept secret since the Bay of Pigs. Dahl D'Este couldn't sit on such a juicy tidbit for long. For one thing, his lady-love is a gossip columnist."

"It's a little late, but thanks for the warning. Lady? D'Este makes both scenes?"

A one-beat pause. "Yeah, ob and epi—and thanks for the straight line. Charlie G. and I thought you should know that the word would be leaking. It should have a positive effect in the industry," Althouse added quickly. It had the sound of an excuse.

Everett nodded, hands thrust into pockets of his stylishly discomfiting jacket. "Well, you're answering my questions before I ask. I'll have to deny my part in it for the record; but between us, Rhone, I'm willing to let it live as a rumor. The commission is interested in this ethical epidemic, naturally. I've been asked how long you can keep it up." Raised eyebrows invited an answer.

"Hell, it's popular," the writer grinned. "With CBS taking it up, it's a trendy thing—oh," he amended. "You mean the reprisals?"

This time Everett's nod was quick. "Those Fat'ah pismires cost NBN a bundle when the net refused to air that videotape Arif sent them."

"Fortunes of war," Althouse shrugged. "Don't think our own Charlie isn't hurting, even if he doesn't flinch. He's got a piece of several stations, and those transmission towers Fat'ah destroyed didn't do the dividends any good. Insurance tripled."

"Didn't flush out any friendly envoys from the nets to pay anybody off, I suppose."

Althouse squinted in the subdued light. "I think I would've heard if that were in the mill. If that's the crux of your concern—officially, I mean—I can't answer for the whole industry. Maury, it's become a grass-roots movement, just as I hoped; doesn't have a single spokesman. That's where its strength lies. But it looks to me like a full-scale media war." He hesitated, glanced around them, bit his lip. For the first time, Everett saw something in the writer that was not young, something of the mature hunted animal. "We haven't forgotten those scenarios you laid on us. Do you have—cancel that, I don't want to know. Do you think we should have around-the-clock protection when our names hit the newspapers?"

"Let me put it this way: you and I both know D'Este can put us on the list of endangered species. You think our names are due to hit newsstands?"

"I *know* they are," said Althouse, with a sickly smile that told Everett this was why the writer had flown to Reno: face-to-face admission that Everett could expect the worst. There could be little pleasure in a print-media hero label when it was also a death warrant.

No point in asking how Althouse knew. His pallor said he knew. "Tell Charlie George we are about to learn what it's like to be a popular politico," Everett remarked, fashioning a cross-hair X with his forefingers. As an effort at lightness, the gesture fell flat. "How long before our oh-so-responsible press fingers us?"

"Tomorrow."

Everett drew a long breath. "Goddam the world's D'Estes, we ought to put out a contract on that guy ourselves. Well, can't say I didn't expect this sooner or later. I intended to stay and gamble till Sunday, but somebody just raised the stakes on us and I've decided to find some pressing business elsewhere. Luck, Rhone." He turned and moved away.

Althouse stood and watched the big man, wondering if Everett would hide, wondering if he should disappear himself as D'Este had already done. He took some comfort in Everett's refusal to blame him for the original idea. But the commissioner had known the danger, even while he lent tacit bureaucratic support. D'Este gone to ground, Everett forewarned: better than nothing, yet poor defense against the fury of terrorism which his own scripts had deflected against them all. An unfamiliar itch between his shoulders made Althouse aware that he was standing absolutely still, alone in a hotel, a perfect target. Rhone Althouse walked away quickly. He did not care who noticed that his path was a zigzag.

The news magazines made up in depth what they lacked in immediacy. The article was satisfyingly thorough under its head, "TV: No More Strange Bedfellows?" It began:

For weeks, every pundit in the sprawling television medium had matched his favorite terrorism rumor against the rumors in the next studio. The scathing satire on terrorism, newly unleashed and widespread in TV, was said to originate in an oval office. Or, less likely, that it was a propaganda ploy jointly financed by Israel and England. One pollster claimed that the scripts merely reflect what the American viewer wants to see.

The truth, as it filtered from CBS this week, was both likelier and stranger than whodunits. There had been no tugs at domestic political strings and no foreign influence. But in the persons of four highly regarded media men, there was definitely a plot. The top banana, to no one's great surprise, turned out to be NBN's answer to Jacques Tati, the protean Charlie George. Of considerably more interest was the reputed anchorman, anomalous FCC sachem Maurice D. Everett (see box). . . .

"All bedfellows are strange," murmured Hakim, patting the rump of the girl who slept as he scanned the stack of magazines. He read the four-page article carefully, marking some passages with flow pen, then concentrated on the thumbnail biography of Maurice Everett. The short piece commented on Everett's unpredictability, his sparse personal life, and his penchant for outdoor sport. Hakim did not find these details pleasant; the man could be trouble.

Presently Hakim riffled through other magazines, finding— as he had expected—invaluable information on his enemies. His sullen longing found its focus in names, faces, details which, given time, Hakim could fashion into targets.

Print media made one thing clear: no matter how successful his coup, the terrorist was still to be treated as a proper charlie. Hakim saw this dictum as a simple clash of wills. If the *fait accompli* carried no leverage, one could try the threat. No hollow promise, but one steeped in potency. The sort of threat one could employ when the enemy is isolated, immobilized, and at risk. Hakim wondered which of the four men he would take first and felt a lambent surge of rekindled strength. He turned off the light and nudged the girl. It had not once occurred to the Fat'ah leader that other charlies, less cautious than he, might react with a blinder savagery.

Everett urged his Mini-Cooper up the ice-slick highway out of Golden, Colorado, wishing he had accepted the company of a federal agent. He had refused that and a snub-nosed piece in a shoulder holster on the same grounds: they were both confining and might call attention to the user. The car was repainted and relicensed, though, and during his five days of new celebrity his Denver office had intercepted only a lone ceramic letter-bomb. Perhaps he was exaggerating his importance, but he would feel safer spending his weekend at one of the rental cabins outside the little town of Empire. Even do a little winter stalking, who could say?

The three men who could say kept well to the rear. For a time the driver sweated to keep his BMW in sight of the Mini and settled for occasional glimpses of the tiny vehicle as the terrain permitted. There were few turnouts available after the new snow, and the further Maurice Everett isolated himself, the better they liked it.

Everett chose the roadhouse on impulse, backing the Mini in to assure easy return. He ordered coffee and began shuck-ing the furlined coat before he realized that he was alone with the counterman. He slapped snow from the front of his winter hat, then saw the dark blue BMW ease off the high-way. Everett took his coffee with hands that shook, watching through fogged windows as the sleek sedan began to emulate his parking manners. No, not quite; the BMW blocked his Mini, and only one of the car's three occupants emerged. Three coffees to go, or one commissioner?

Everett saw the raincoated man cradle his long, gaily wrapped package, speak briefly to his driver; Everett noted the Vermont license plate and used his time wisely. He walked to one end of the roadhouse, far from the windows and counterman, and piled his coat high in the last booth, putting his hat atop it. The coffee steamed in the center of the booth table, untasted bait.

Everett stepped directly across the aisle from his end booth into the men's room, hoping that his circumstantial case was

nothing more than that, hoping that the raincoated man
would get his coffee and go to Empire, or Georgetown, or hell.
He did not close the door or try the light switch.

There was nothing he could see in the gloom that would
serve as a weapon, and as he settled on the toilet, fully
clothed and staring at his coffee three meters away, he felt
the toilet seat move. One of its two attachment wingnuts
was gone. Gently, silently, Everett set about removing the
other. Early or late, he reasoned, the audacious bird gets the
worm.

He heard the front door of the roadhouse sigh shut, heard a
mumbled exchange—one voice had an odd lilt to it—at the
counter ten meters from him, heard the counterman open a
refrigerator. So Mr. Raincoat wanted more than coffee?
Cheeseburgers, or diversion?

Under the clank and scrape of short-order cookery, Everett
heard soft footfalls. He stood, breathing quickly and lightly
through his mouth, gripping the toilet lid with no earthly
thought of what he was doing with it. He felt like a fool—*Oh,
hello, I was just leaving, sorry about the lid, didn't fit me
anyhow*—and then Mr. Raincoat stepped to Everett's booth
as if offering his package, one hand thrust into the false end
of the package, and he must have seen that he was confront-
ing an uninhabited hat and coat just as Everett swung the
lid, edge on, against the base of his skull from behind and to
one side.

Everett was appalled at himself for an instant. He had
drygulched a harmless holiday drunk, he thought, as the
man toppled soundlessly onto Everett's coat. The contents of
the package slid backward onto the floor then, and Everett
reflected that harmless drunks do not usually carry sawed-off
automatic shotguns in Christmas packages with false ends.

Everett's snowshoes were in the Mini, and without them he
would be stupid to run out the back way. The counterman,
incredibly, was busy incinerating three steaks and had seen
nothing. Everett wrote the BMW license number on his table
with catsup, though he could have used blood, and wrestled
the raincoat from the unconscious man.

The only way out was past the BMW. He hoped it would
flee at his first warning shot, then realized that the occupants were waiting to hear that shot. How would Mr. Raincoat exit? Backward, no doubt, holding the shotgun on the

counterman. Everett's trousers were the wrong shade of gray but he could not afford to dwell on that.

He slid into the raincoat, which pinched at the armpits, turned its collar up, retrieved the shotgun and checked the safety. Gripped in glacial calm, he reminded himself of Pueblo and quashed his fear with one thought: *My turn!* Everett had time to pity the counterman, but not to question his own sanity, as he moved past windows near the front door and turned his back on it.

The blast tore a fist-sized hole in the floor and sent a lance of pain through Everett's bad ear. The counterman ran without hesitation out the rear door into a snowdrift, screaming, and Everett backed out the front door fast. The BMW engine blipped lustily and a voice called, "In, in, ye fookin' twit," and Everett spun to see a man holding a rear door open with one hand, a machine pistol forgotten in the other. Everett did not forget the weapon and aimed for it. He missed, but blew out the windshield from the inside.

The driver accelerated to the highway, the left rear door of the car flapping open, and Everett fired twice more. The first shot sent pellets caroming off the inside of the sedan and the second was a clean miss. Everett flopped hard into the snow so that he only heard, but could not see, the shiny BMW slide off the highway. It was a long vertical roll to the river but neither of the occupants minded the cold water, being dead at the time.

Everett burst into the roadhouse to find that his first victim was still unconscious, and realized that he had things to set right. The counterman must be tamed, the telephone must be used; but first things first. He needed the toilet lid for a mundane purpose, and *right now*.

The NBN electrician learned from an honest bartender in Burbank that his wallet had turned up minus cash, but with papers intact. He verified that his licenses and the new NBN security pass were accounted for and vowed to forget it.

NBN officials assured Charlie George that the fenced backlot in the San Fernando Valley was secure, far better than a leased location and nearer Hollywood. They did not add that their own security chief disagreed, and avoided mentioning the obvious: backlots are cheap. The new passes, they said, employed dipoles for inexpensive electronic ID. Of course, Fat'ah employed them too.

It was midmorning before Charlie George and his writers were mollified with the script, a tepid takeoff on the attempt at Maurice Everett the previous Friday. The skit had two things going for it: Charlie's Irish accent was uproarious, and he could do pantomimic wonders as an IRA Provisional trying to pull a trigger and chew gum at the same time. They threw out the lines identifying the terrorist driver as French-Canadian. It was faithful to the new connection between separatist gangs, but it was also confusingly unfunny.

They managed a half-dozen takes before noon and, as lunch vans began their setups at unobtrusive distances from the exterior set, Charlie's nose directed his eyes toward the new van which advertised hot Mexican food. Charlie's mania for Mexican food had been duly noted by news magazines.

"Okay, it's a wrap," the unit director called. "Lunch!" Charlie threw off his prop raincoat, ignoring the free spread by NBN. He drifted instead toward the *menudo* and its vendor, Bernal Guerrero.

Only one side panel of the van was raised, for the excellent reason that one side was rigged for lunch, the other for Charlie. The comedian waited his turn. The compact latino appeared to recognize his patron only at second glance, bestowed a grave smile on Charlie and said, "For you, Señor Carlito, something special." Had Charlie not followed Guerrero to the hidden side of the van, Hakim could have fired the veterinarian's tranquilizer gun from inside the van, through his thin silvered mylar panel.

Charlie's smile was quizzical until he felt Guerrero's needle enter his side like a cold lightning bolt. He cried only, "Hey, that hurts," not convincingly, before Guerrero's gristly fingers numbed his diaphragm. Three other patrons on the innocent side of the van turned, then were rediverted as racks of warm lunch items began to spill onto the macadam—one of Hakim's deft touches.

Guerrero grasped Charlie by the thighs and lifted, hurling the limp NBN star against the featureless side panel. The panel swung inward, dumped Charlie at the feet of Hakim Arif, and swung shut again. Guerrero hurried back to see patrons catching the spill of food, made a gesture of hopelessness, said "Keep it," and dropped the open side panel. He found it difficult to avoid furious action before reaching the driver's seat because he could hear, a hundred meters away, screams from the script girl who had seen it all.

As the van howled between two hangarlike sound stages, Guerrero bore far to the right to begin his left turn. He had thirty seconds on his pursuers but Hakim had made it clear that they must expect communication between the exterior sets and the guarded backlot gate. Guerrero smiled, hearing Hakim's curses as he struggled with a dead weight greater than his own, and sped toward the perimeter cyclone fencing. Outside the fence was an access road, deserted except for a small foreign sedan and a larger car towing an old mobile home. These vehicles were motionless.

Guerrero slapped the button in plenty of time but was not pleased. He slapped it again, then pressed it with a rocking motion as he tapped the brakes hard. Fifteen feet of cyclone fencing peeled back as the bangalore torpedo at last accepted his microwave signal, and Guerrero felt the pressure wave cuff the van. He angled through the hole, negotiating the shallow ditch with elan, and exulted in his choice of a vehicle with high ground clearance. As he made a gear change, accelerating toward escape, he could see Rashid in his outside rearview, dutifully towing the decrepit mobile home into position to block immediate pursuit along the access road.

The girl waited for Rashid in her smaller car, the only vehicle of their regular fleet that was not a van. Guerrero waited for nothing, but tossed quick glances to check the possibility of air surveillance. Van Nuys airport was soon sliding past on his right and they would be vulnerable until he reached the state university campus where their other vans waited.

Minutes later, Guerrero eased the van into a campus parking lot. Hakim was ready with the crate and together they wrestled it from their vehicle into the rear of a somewhat smaller van. As Hakim urged the smaller vehicle away, encouraging its cold engine with curses, Guerrero wheeled the kidnap van across the lot and abandoned it along with his vendor's uniform. It might be many hours before the kidnap van was noticed, among the hundreds of recreational vehicles on the campus. Guerrero knew what every student knew: a recreational vehicle was limited only by what one defined as recreation.

He moved then to his last vehicle change, flexing his hands in the thin gloves as he waited for the engine to warm, for the flow of adrenaline to subside, for the next item on his private agenda. He had carefully ascertained that Arif's fingerprints were on the abandoned kidnap vehicle, and that his own were not. On the other hand, Arif had given him only a public rendezvous some kilometers to the west in Moorpark and not the location of the new site, which, Guerrero knew, might be in any direction. The latino grumbled to himself in irritation. Arif's monolithic insistence on sole control was a continuing problem, but Guerrero had to admit the little *palo blanco* was precise. He checked the time and grinned to himself; it wouldn't do to be late picking up Rashid and the girl. Guerrero's masters were precise, too.

By six P.M. Hakim was so far out of patience that he fairly leaped from his seat in the Moorpark bus station at his first sight of Guerrero. The Panamanian bought a newspaper, saw Arif stand, then ambled out onto the street. It was too dark to read the fine print but, waiting for Hakim to catch up, Guerrero saw that they had again made the front page above the fold.

Though Guerrero walked slowly, Hakim sounded breathless. "I told *the girl* to make rendezvous," he said, as they paused for a stop light. "And you are four hours late!"

"The Americans had other ideas," Guerrero growled convincingly. "She and Rashid tried to run a blockade."

"Escape?"

"I was lucky to escape, myself. They were cut down, Hakim."

Hakim's voice was exceedingly soft. "This you saw?"

"I saw. It may be here," he lied again, brandishing the folded newspaper, ready to grapple with the Iraqi if he saw his cover blown. Hakim Arif only looked straight ahead, and fashioned for himself a terrible smile.

They walked another block, forcing themselves to study window displays, checking for surveillance as they went. "The comedian will be conscious soon," Hakim said as if to himself. "He will be noisy, no doubt." Then, as a new possibility struck him: "Was your van compromised?"

Guerrero gave a negative headshake, very much desiring to keep his own vehicle. "It is just ahead there," he indicated. "Do I abandon it now?" Always, he knew, Hakim was perversely biased against an underling's suggestion.

"We have expended twelve thousand dollars in vehicles, and two Fat'ah lives, this day," Hakim snarled. "No more waste. Stay here, wait for my van, then follow."

Guerrero nodded and sauntered to his parked van as Arif hurried away. One cigarette later, the latino saw Arif's vehicle pass. He followed closely in traffic, then dropped back as they turned north onto Highway 23 toward the mountains. Well beyond the town of Fillmore, the lead van slowed abruptly, loitered along the highway until it was devoid of other traffic. Then Hakim swung onto a gravel road; Guerrero sensed that they were very near the new Fat'ah site and philosophically accepted his inability to share that suspicion.

After two kilometers they turned again, and Guerrero saw that the new site was a renovated farmhouse in a small orchard. He hurried to help Hakim unload the crate at the porch, ignoring the awful sounds from inside it. Only when the crate was opened inside did Guerrero learn why Charlie George, gagged and tightly bound, was such a noisy passenger.

The long legs had been taped flexed, so that muscle cramps would almost certainly result. More tape looped from neck to thighs, assuring that a tall man would make a smaller package. Heavy adhesive bands strapped his arms across his chest, the left hand heavily retaped over a crimson-and-rust bandage. Guerrero did a brief double-take, rolling the captive over to see the maimed left hand. Despite the gag, the prisoner moaned at the rough movement. From Guerrero, a sigh: "Will you rid the world of fingers, Hakim?"

The Fat'ah leader knelt to examine the bandage while Charlie tried to speak through the gag. "An ancient and honored custom, my friend," he said, and backhanded Charlie viciously to quell the interruption. "I mailed his small finger special delivery to the National Broadcasting Network people. I added a promise to forward more pieces until my demands are aired," he continued, staring into Charlie's face as he spoke. He wheeled to regard Guerrero. "I might have delivered it there myself while waiting for you!"

"Your demands, not Fat'ah's," Guerrero mused aloud.

"I am Fat'ah," almost inaudible.

"It is reducing itself to that," Guerrero agreed ambiguously, then adroitly blunted the goad. "What may I do now?"

Hakim retained a precarious control. "Familiarize yourself with the house, cook a meal, mend your tongue. I shall arrange for our guest to—entertain us."

*   *   *

The nearest lights, Guerrero found, were over a kilometer off, too far to carry the sounds of the interrogation of Charlie George. The latino took his time, kept away from the "guest" room, and waited for Arif to kill their captive in outlet for his frustration. When the screams subsided, Guerrero began to heat their stew.

The American was stronger than either of them had thought. He managed to walk, a tape-wrapped garrote wire looped as leash about his throat, to the table but fell trying to sit in the folding chair. Hakim's smile was a beatitude, so well did his captive behave. Charlie's nose was a ruin, his right ear torn—"It will come off anyway," Hakim chuckled—but his mouth had been left equipped for conversation. He was not disposed to eat and his hands shook so badly that Hakim laughed; but Hakim needed say only once, "Eat it all," softly. Charlie George ate it all.

Hakim produced a huge chocolate bar for dessert and helped eat it. He felt no desire or need to deny the stuff, while the garrote wire was in his hand. After the chocolate: "You maintain that this satire is too widespread to halt," he prodded the exhausted captive, "and I say you will halt it, piece by piece."

"You underestimate their greed," Charlie replied, scarcely above a whisper. From time to time he squeezed his left wrist hard. "Every nightclub schlepper in the Catskills is inventing stealable material—and the public loves it." He managed something that could have been a smile. "You're a smash, Arif."

Hakim looked at the wall a moment. "And the news series you mentioned? What is the investment?"

"One on ABC, one on CBS," Charlie said. "Buy 'em off if you can. Try ten million apiece. They'll laugh at you." With this unfortunate phrase he trailed off; exhaustion tugged at his eyelids. Hakim reached out with delicate precision and thumped the bloody bandage. "Ahhhhh . . . I don't see what you gain by torture," Charlie grunted. "I have no secrets."

Guerrero, taking notes, gestured at the captive with the butt of his pen. "Perhaps you do not *know* what you know."

"And perhaps you are being punished," Hakim murmured.

"What else is new," Charlie said, and was rewarded by a sudden tug on the wire. "Sorry," he managed to croak.

"Repeat after me: 'I beg forgiveness, Effendi,'" Hakim smiled, and tugged again. Charlie did it. "Now tell us again how your network amassed those extra tapes to be aired in the event one of you was captured." Charlie did that, too. Eventually Hakim saw that the answers were more disjointed, less useful, and led the unprotesting Charlie to the torture room. Guerrero saw the captive trussed flat on a tabletop before Hakim was satisfied, and kept the butt of his ballpoint pen aimed at the doorway, putting away his gear as Hakim returned.

"I will set up the media center," Hakim said mildly. "You will install this lock on our guest's door." It was a heavy push-bolt affair.

Guerrero set about clearing the bowls away as Hakim brought media monitors in. "I saw lights of a village from the porch," Guerrero reported. "With only the two of us left, you might brief me to that extent."

"I might—when you need to know. Information is at a premium now, is it not? We have not even a telephone here. But no matter," he said, setting his small portable TV sets up. "We can do what we must."

Guerrero paused, framed another guarded question, then thought better of it and went after tools for the door lock. From his van, he saw that the windows of Charlie's room were boarded. Returning with the tools, he installed the simple lock, pausing to watch the monitors with Arif. There was no mention of a shootout between Rashid and police—naturally—but there was also absolute silence on the daring daylight abduction of Charlie George. Guerrero saw Arif's subliminal headshakes and was emboldened; the Iraqi might have doubted Guerrero's story if the kidnapping had received major coverage. As it was, Hakim Arif focused only on television as his source of dis-, mis-, and non-information.

When the last newscast was done, Hakim read and made notes on alternative courses of action. At last he replaced the notebook, ascertained that Charlie George was breathing heavily, and sought his own bedroll. Then, for the first time, he missed the girl until he thrust the image of her body from him. "We shall see, tomorrow," he said to the sleeping Guerrero, and fell into a sleep of confidence.

The next morning, there was still no news of the abduction on television. A National Public Radio newscast mentioned

the fact that newspapers carried headlines on a reported
kidnapping while television sources refused comment. Hakim
forced their captive to eat a mighty breakfast and smiled
fondly as Charlie complied. The comedian had bled more
during the night but, Guerrero judged, not nearly enough.
Hakim Arif seemed content to sit in their orchard site until
their food ran out. The noon news was innocent of Fat'ah, but
Hakim was ebullient.

Finally at supper Hakim hinted at his motive for optimisim.
"Your show goes on at eight," he said to Charlie. "If your
people place any value on you, we shall have what we
demand."

"The show was taped in pieces weeks ago, you know,"
Charlie replied, constant pain diluting his voice. "They don't
have to worry about dead air."

"I shouldn't talk so casually about pieces or death, if I were
you," Hakim rejoined. "I shall bet you one ear that we get
coverage."

Charlie made no reply, but tried to read a paperback which
Guerrero had discarded. Shortly after his own show began,
the captive showed signs of distress. Hakim handed the leash
wire to Guerrero, who waited in the bathroom while Charlie
lost his supper. The audio was up, the door nearly closed.
Guerrero took a calculated risk. "You will not leave here
alive, Carlito. If you hope, throw that up, too."

Charlie knelt, face in his hands, rocking fore and aft.
Muffled by his bandaged hand: "Why d'you think I'm so
puking scared? NBN won't cave in; we agreed on that tactic. I
wish I could retract it but I can't. And if I did, *they* wouldn't."
He looked up through streaming silent tears, his hands
bloodily beseeching. "And if they would?"

"You would still die," Guerrero said, wondering if it were
true.

"What can I do?" It was an agonized whisper.

"Die. Slowly, appeasing him, in a week; or quickly, avoiding pain, if you anger him enough." Their eyes met for a long
moment of communion. Charlie retched again briefly and the
moment passed.

The *Charlie George Show* passed as well, without reference
to the kidnapping until the end of the show. Charlie normally
traded jokes with his live audience for a few moments but,
instead of the piece Charlie had taped, his rotund second-

banana comic appeared. Standing before the familiar logo, he mimicked a gossip columnist with barbed one-liners. Finally, he said, there was no rumor in the truth—his tongue pointedly explored his cheek—that Charlie was in a plummet conference with stagestruck terrorists. They wanted a big hand, but Charlie only gave them the finger.

Hakim watched the credits roll, snapped off the set, and treated Charlie George to a malevolent smile. "You win," he said, "and you lose."

"You got coverage," Charlie husked, "and anyhow, you're going to do whatever you want to. NBN got your message, and you got theirs."

"I have other messages," Hakim said, and spat in Charlie's face.

Charlie saw cold rage in the zealot eyes and accepted, at last, that the network would not save him from consequences of events he had shaped. He spoke to Hakim, but looked at Guerrero. "Have it your way, you pile of pigshit. We did a sketch on that: we'll give you coverage in a pig's prat, that's where you rate it—"

The garrote cut off the sudden tirade. Without Hakim's tape over the wire it would have cut more than that, as Hakim used the wire leash to throw Charlie to the floor. Hakim held the leash tight, kicking expertly at elbows and knees until his victim lay silent and gray on the red-smeared floor. He squatted to loosen the wire and nodded with satisfaction as the unconscious man's breathing resumed in ragged spasms, the larynx bruised but not crushed. Guerrero kept his face blank as he helped drag their burden into the torture room, then laid his ballpoint pen on a shelf while Hakim trussed Charlie George to the table.

"Keep him alive awhile," Guerrero urged. To his dismay, he heard Hakim grumble assent.

"He must not cheat me of his awareness," the Fat'ah leader explained, "when I take more souvenirs." He paused, studying the inert hostage, then jerked his gaze to the Panamanian. "What was he really saying, Guerrero? *Damn you*, or *kill me?*"

"Does it matter what the tree says to the axe?"

"If only all your questions were so cogent," Hakim laughed. "That was worthy of El Aurans himself; he who understood pain so well— No, it does not matter. Tomorrow the comedian will be replenished. And wrung empty again."

*   *   *

Charlie was half-dragged to their morning meal; one arm useless, the other barely functional. He moaned softly as Guerrero and Hakim attacked their cereal. Then Hakim, using his own traditionally unclean left hand in private amusement, gravely took Charlie's spoon and began to feed him. Charlie knew better than to refuse, saying only, "You are one strange man."

"You must continue to function, and it is easy to be polite to an inferior. Another thing," he said, watching Charlie's difficulty in swallowing, "your schoolboy taunts will not compel me to kill you. Fat'ah is not compelled. It compels. And punishes."

"The monitors," Guerrero said, indicating his wristwatch.

"You will watch them when we have taken Charlie George to his room." Hakim had tired of his game with the spoon and, with the implacable Guerrero, conveyed Charlie to the room Charlie dreaded.

Hakim trussed Charlie to the table again as Guerrero faced the monitors in the next room, then hauled Charlie's torso to the table's edge. The captive lay face up, hanging half off the table, his head a foot from the spattered floor. He saw Hakim produce the knife, elastic bands, clear plastic tube and gossamer bag, and tried not to guess their uses. Hakim taped him firmly in place as blood gradually pounded louder in the ears of Charlie George.

Hakim brought the knife to Charlie's throat, smiling, and Charlie closed his eyes. Hakim tugged at the torn ear until Charlie opened his eyes again and then, in two quick sweeps, he severed the ear.

Charlie fought his own screams through clenched teeth, sobbing, straining against the bonds. His face a study in dispassionate interest, Hakim stanched the flow of blood and, holding Charlie by his hair, sprinkled a clotting agent over the gory mess before he applied a rough bandage.

It took Charlie George four tries to say, between gasps, "Why?"

"Questions, questions," Hakim sighed. "Your ear will go to the *Los Angeles Times* and its coverage may provoke your television people. This may even start a modest media war. And *this* is because I choose," he continued, quickly pulling the flimsy polyethylene bag over Charlie's head.

Hakim snapped the elastic bands around Charlie's neck and stood back, watching the red stain spread past his bandage inside the bag. Charlie's eyes became huge with horror as his first breath sucked the bag against his nose and mouth. After twenty seconds, Hakim thrust the plastic tube under the elastic and into Charlie's mouth, then tugged the bag in place. The tube was short and not entirely flaccid, and Hakim pulled his chair near to hold the free end of the tube away from loose ends of the bag.

Hakim waited until the breathing steadied. Charlie's eyes were closed. "Open your eyes," Hakim said gently. No response. "Open them," he said, placing a fingertip lightly over the tube's end. Charlie's eyes flew open and Hakim's finger moved back.

"Have you heard of the dry submarine, my friend? You are wearing one. The wet submarine is favored in Chile; it features a variety of nasty liquids in the bag. Yours may soon qualify as wet," he added, seeing the runnel of crimson that painted the bag's interior in Charlie's feeble struggles.

"Why, you ask, and ask, and ask," Hakim continued, crooning near as though speaking to a valued confidante, a beloved. "Because you will perhaps return to your sumptuous life, if it pleases me. You will be my message to your medium, a man who knows he has been totally broken. El Aurans, the Lawrence of Arabia, broke after long torture and found ambition gone. Few were his equal, but—" The dark eyes held a soft luminosity as he quoted, " 'My will had gone and I feared to be alone, lest the winds of circumstance . . . blow my empty soul away.' I do not think you can avoid carrying that message," Hakim added. "This is true Eastern martial art: corner the enemy, and leave him nothing. Your Machiavelli understood."

From the other room came Guerrero's call: "Coverage, Hakim!"

The little man turned in his chair, picked up the severed ear, and released the tube which lay nearly invisible against the bag. In three strides he was through the door, to loom at Guerrero's side.

The item was insignificant, merely an admission that an NBN star was a possible kidnap victim. Television was carrying the news, but obviously was not going to dwell on this event. "So I must contact another medium," Hakim said, and held up his ghastly trophy.

Guerrero blinked. "It has been quiet in there."

"He no longer complains," Hakim answered, deliberately vague.

"You are finished, then," Guerrero persisted.

It was Hakim's pleasure to joke, thinking of the abject terror in the eyes of Charlie George. "Say, rather, *he* is finished," he rejoined, and turned back toward the torture room.

Guerrero followed unbidden, his excitement mounting. He saw their captive hanging inert like some butchered animal, his head half-obscured in glistening red polymer. He could not know that Charlie George had spent the past moments desperately inhaling, exhaling, trying with an animal's simplicity to bathe his lungs in precious oxygen. Charlie's mind was not clear but it held fast to one notion: Guerrero was anxious for his death. Mouth and eyes open wide, Charlie George ceased to breathe as Guerrero came into view.

Guerrero's mistake was his haste to believe what he wanted to believe. He saw the plastic sucked against nostrils, the obscenely gaping mouth and staring eyes. He did not seek the thud of Charlie's heart under his twisted clothing and failed to notice the slender tube emergent from the plastic bag. "The poor *pendejo* is dead, then?" He rapped the question out carelessly.

Hakim's mistake was the indirect lie, his automatic response to questions asked in the tone Guerrero used now. "Truly, as you see," Hakim said, gesturing toward Charlie George, amused at Charlie's ploy.

His merriment was fleeting. From the tail of his eye he saw Guerrero's hand slide toward the Browning and in that instant, Hakim resolved many small inconsistencies. Still, he flung the knife too hastily. Guerrero dodged, rolling as he aimed, but could not avoid the chair that struck him as he fired. The Iraqi sprang past the doorway, slammed the door and flicked the bolt in place as chunks of wallboard peppered his face. He counted five shots from the Browning but knew the damned thing held nine more. Half blinded by debris from Guerrero's slugs, Hakim elected to run rather than retrieve his own automatic which lay at his media display in the path of Guerrero's fire against the door lock.

Hakim reached his van quickly, almost forgetting to snap the hidden toggle beneath the dash, and lurched toward the road with a dead-cold engine racing and spitting. He dropped low over the wheel, unable to see if Guerrero followed. He had cash and an exquisite Israeli submachinegun, Fat'ah's survival kit, behind him in the van.

Hakim considered stopping to make a stand on the gravel road but checked his rearviews in time to reconsider. Guerrero was there, twenty seconds behind. Hakim would need ten to stop, ten more to reach and feed the weapon. He would fare better if he could increase his lead, and guessed that Guerrero would withhold fire as they passed through the village of Piru. It was worth a try.

Slowing at the edge of the little town, Hakim saw his rearview fill with Guerrero's van. Whatever his motive, the Panamanian evidently had a hard contract to fulfill and might take insane chances. Hakim wrenched the wheel hard, whirling through a market parking lot. A grizzled pickup truck avoided him by centimeters and stalled directly in Guerrero's path, and then Hakim was turning north, unable to see how much time he had gained.

The road steepened as Hakim learned from a road sign that Lake Piru and Blue Point lay ahead. He searched his rearviews but the road was too serpentine for clear observation, and Hakim began to scan every meter of roadside for possible cover.

He took the second possible turnoff, a rutted affair with warnings against trespassers, flanked by brush and high grass. The van threw up a momentary flag of dust, a small thing but sufficient for Guerrero, who came thundering behind, alert for just such a possibility.

Hakim topped a low ridge and did not see Guerrero two turns back. Dropping toward a hollow, he tried to spin the van but succeeded only in halting it broadside to the road. He hurtled from his bucket seat, threw open the toolbox, and withdrew the stockless Uzi with flashing precision. Two forty-round clips went into his jacket and then he was scrambling from the cargo door which thunked shut behind him. If Guerrero were near, let him assault the empty van while Hakim, on his flank, would cut him down from cover.

But he had not reached cover when the van of Bernal Guerrero appeared, daylight showing under all four tires as it crested the rise before the mighty *whump* of contact.

Hakim stopped in the open, taking a splayed automatic-weapons stance, and fitted a clip in the Uzi.

Almost.

It may have been dirt from the jouncing ride, or a whisker of tempered steel projecting like a worrisome hangnail; whatever it was, it altered many futures.

Hakim dropped the clip and snatched at its twin, missed his footing, and sprawled in the dust. The van of Guerrero impended, crashing around Hakim's wheeled roadblock into the grassy verge, a great beast rushing upon him. Guerrero set the handbrake and exited running as Hakim, his weapon hoary with dirt, essayed a multiple side roll. He was mystified when Guerrero merely kicked him in the head instead of triggering the automatic.

Hakim waited for death as he gazed into the dark nine-millimeter eye of the Browning. "Daoudist," he surmised bitterly.

"I am Fat'ah," Guerrero mimicked, breathing deeply. His face shone with sweat and elation. "And in Panama, a *Torrijista*, and everywhere, always, KGB." He wiped dust from his mouth, the gun muzzle absolutely unwavering and much too distant for a foot sweep by Hakim. "Rise, turn, hands on your head." Hakim obeyed.

The latino marched him back to his own van and forced him to lie prone in the pungent dust. While Guerrero ransacked the tool box, Hakim listened for distant engines, voices, a siren. In the primeval mountain stillness he could even hear ticks from his cooling engine, but nothing remotely suggested deliverance.

Presently, standing above the little Iraqi, Guerrero ordered his hands crossed behind him. Hakim recognized his garrote wire by its bite and was briefly thankful it was not about his neck. At further orders, Hakim stalked to Guerrero's own vehicle and lay on his face beside it as he tried to identify a succession of odd sounds.

"Had you the wit to take a four-wheel-drive path," Guerrero mused pleasantly as he worked, "you might have escaped. Since the day before yesterday my front differential housing has been full of transceiver gear." Guerrero leaned into his van, arranged the controls, flicked the engine on and stood back. "You wanted coverage, Hakim? Well, turn and stand—and smile, you are live on Soviet television."

The camera in Guerrero's hand looked very like a ballpoint pen but, unlike the unit left in the torture room, it did not store audiovisual data. It merely fed its impressions to the transceiver equipment packed into the van's dummy differential case. Hakim considered the possibility of a hoax until he heard the fierce whine of a multikilowatt alternator over the whirr of the engine, and then saw the great inflated meter-broad balloon, spidery metallic film covering its lower segment, that sat on Guerrero's horizontal rear cargo door. Almost certainly a dish antenna, he marveled, for a Molniya satellite in clarkeian orbit.

Hakim did not show his relief but remained docile as Guerrero shoved him down at the base of a manzanita shrub. Such equipment was fiendishly expensive and tallied well with Guerrero's claim to be a KGB infiltrator, which meant Soviet control. Hakim was limp with gratification; at least his captor represented law and order, not capricious revenge by some gang of charlies.

"There was no American blockade," Hakim accused, and drew a hissing breath as the wire tugged at his wrists.

"What does it matter to whom I turned them? It was neatly done except for the girl, and a bent mount on the differential housing," Guerrero replied, slitting Hakim's sleeves, tearing away the fifty-dollar shirt. "Rashid is entertaining the KGB—as you would be, had we known your idiotic choice of sites in advance. We opted against a motorcade, and then I was unable to transmit our location." Pride forbade him to add that he had not been furnished with sophisticated receiving gear, so that feedback to Guerrero was by relatively primitive tonal signals.

"You are a fool; they could have homed in on your unit, had you only kept it going."

"And so might you, with the noise and microwave interference." Hakim took a stinging slap. "That was for the lecture." Another slap, with an effect that shocked Hakim. "And that was for making it necessary to interrogate you here; I dare not pass that village again before dark."

Hakim swallowed hard. It was not Guerrero's brawn that bred such terror with each small successive violence. Hakim and pain were dearer friends than that. Yet he felt a rising sense of dread, and of something else; a betrayal of faith. And how could this be so, when Hakim's only faith was in Hakim?

Guerrero stepped away and laid the pencil-slim camera on an outcrop of weathered basalt. "You have seen these before," he chided. "A similar device recorded your last tender sessions with the comedian. Later I will retrieve the microcorder and feed those scenes to the Molniya."

As he spoke, he took a slender case from an inside pocket. Hakim feared the hypodermic but, far worse, dreaded the fact that he was bathed in sweat. He prepared to flail his body, hoping to destroy the injector or waste its unknown contents.

Guerrero was much too battle-wise. He chose a nearby stick of the iron-hard manzanita and, with a by-your-leave gesture to the camera, suddenly deluged Hakim with blows. It became a flood, a torrent, a sea of torment, and Hakim realized that the thin shrieking was his own. He, Hakim Arif, mewling like any craven berber? He invoked his paladin's wisdom: ". . . *no longer actor, but spectator, thought not to care how my body jerked and squealed.*" Jerking and squealing, Hakim cared too much to feel the prick of the needle in his hip.

Hakim rallied with great shuddering gasps, rolled onto his back, and fought down a horror he had expected never to meet. His emissary, pain, had turned against him.

Guerrero leaned easily against a boulder, tossing and catching a drycell battery of respectable voltage. "You have long been a subject of KGB study at Lubianka in Moscow," he glowered, "and I am impressed by our psychologists. You built a legend with your vain volunteer anguish, Hakim, and never knew that the operative word was *volunteer.*" His face changed to something still uglier. "You will divulge two items. The first, Fat'ah accounts. The second is your new Damascus site." He raised the stick and Hakim cowered, but the things that touched his naked flesh were merely the drycell terminals.

Merely an onslaught of unbearable suffering. Hakim needed no verbal assurance to learn that the drug made each joint in his body a locus of gruesome response to even the mildest electrical stimulus. When his spasm had passed he had fouled himself, to the syncopation of Guerrero's laughter.

"Your funds," Guerrero said, extending the drycell, and Hakim bleated out a stream of information. Squinting into the overcast as if to confirm the satellite link over thirty-six thousand kilometers away, Guerrero grinned. "Coding, I am told, is automatic, and *gracias a Dios* for small favors. But it may take some minutes to check your figures. Perhaps in Los Angeles, perhaps in Berne or at Lubianka. But if you lie, you must understand that I will quickly know it. Lie to me, Hakim. Please. It justifies me."

Raging at himself, Hakim hurriedly amended crucial figures. The pain in his joints did not linger but its memory overhung him like a cliff. Through it all, degrading, enervating, the sinuous path of Guerrero's amusement followed each of Hakim's capitulations.

When Hakim fell silent, the other pressed his demand. "You are learning, I see. Now: the Damascus site, the new one. The Americans would like to know it, too, but they tend to impose order slowly. We shall be more efficient even without pentothal." Hakim squeezed his eyes tight-shut, breathing quickly, wondering if it were really possible to swallow one's tongue—and then the drycell raked his bicep and jawline.

Hakim was transfixed, skewered on a billion lances that spun in his body, growing to fiery pinwheels that consumed him, drove all else from his being. Hakim was a synonym of appalling agony. Guerrero, who had previously laughed for the necessary effect, punished his lower lip between his teeth and looked away. He wished he were back soldiering under Torrijos, hauling garrison garbage, anything but this filthy duty.

Yet appearances were everything and, "Again? I hope you resist," he lied, and had to caution Hakim to answer more slowly. Under the torture, answers came in a fitful rhythm; a phrase, shallow breathing, another strangled phrase, a sob, and still another phrase. Hakim was finished so soon that Guerrero knew embarrassment. He had hurried, and now he needed only wait. The military, he shrugged to himself, must be the same everywhere.

Waiting for his van's radio speaker to verify or deny, Guerrero viewed his keening captive with glum distaste. "The girl was more man than you," he said in innocent chauvinism. "Rashid accepted capture, but not she. Another agent took her knife. She fought. When he pointed the knife against her belly she embraced him. I never heard the sound of a knife like that before, it . . ."

"Kill me," he heard Hakim plead.

"Before I know how truly you betray Fat'ah? For shame."

"Yes, for shame. Kill me."

"Because you are so quick to surrender? Because you are not your beloved Lawrence, but only a small puppeteer? Absurd, Hakim. Think yourself lucky to know what you are, at last: a primitive little executive, a controller—even of yourself as victim. Is it so much more glorious to be a masochist pure and simple, than what you really are?"

"Enough! End it," Hakim begged.

"As you ended it for the comedian, perhaps. I waited for days to record your disposal of that man. Without those orders, my work would have been simpler." Guerrero spat in irritation.

Hakim stared. The Soviet security organ had waited only to obtain a video record of Fat'ah killing the comedian? He fathomed the KGB logic gradually, concluding that they could use the evidence to justify reprisals if it suited them.

Another thought brought a measure of calm: he still had control over Guerrero's future. Hakim exercised it. "It was not my intent to kill Charlie George," he said distinctly. *"And we left him alive."*

Guerrero said nothing for ten seconds. "The video record will show that he died," he asserted, licking lips that were suddenly dry.

"It will show his breathing tube, and also what we both knew: that he is an actor." Their eyes met in angry silence.

Guerrero insisted, "The record will vindicate me," and Hakim knew that Guerrero too was posturing for the benefit of the camera pickups. His own effectiveness contaminated by haste, Guerrero would be forced to return and kill Charlie George himself.

Guerrero approached again with the drycell and locked his gaze to Hakim's for the last time. Torture would prove nothing more, and Guerrero feared what it might seem to prove. The crowning irony was that under further torture, Hakim might further compromise his torturer. Hakim trembled in tears, but did not drop his gaze. Guerrero laid the drycell on a stone.

Hakim did not recognize the coded sequence from the van but saw Guerrero register relief at a musical signal. In any case, Hakim in his weakness had spoken the truth. Guerrero was lashing Hakim's feet with wire at the time, and resumed the job until his prisoner was positioned feet spread, knees bent, face up. Enraged at Hakim's revelation, Guerrero had chosen a vengeance option. He enjoyed that choice but realized only half of its full expense as he stalked to his van and returned.

Guerrero tore a strip of tape, placed it dangling from a branch before Hakim's eyes, and stuck a capsule to the tape within range of Hakim's mouth. "Before I knew you, Arif, I would not do what I do now. Let us say it is for Moh'med, whom I hated to sacrifice. Did you think the bomb shackles jammed themselves?" He read the surge of anger that raced across Hakim's face. "So: no, I will not end your life—but *you will*. I wonder if you are devout, and if your followers are. In any event, the capsule acts quickly. Exercise your control, Hakim; take one last life on television," he finished, whisking Hakim's van keys away. He brought the drycell near Hakim's side and the Iraqi arched away as well as he might, lashed to bushes by lengths of his garrote wire.

The drycell went beneath Hakim's naked back, centimeters from contact. Guerrero trotted away with one backward look and Hakim strained fitfully to hold his arch. Weeping, laughing, Hakim knew that Guerrero had left his own van to permit transmission of Hakim's option. But Guerrero did not know of the toggle beneath Hakim's dash panel, which reduced the Panamanian's own options to zero.

There was no sound of starter engagement, only the slam of a door before, a moment later, a heavy concussion wave. The ground bucked and Hakim, muscles already past endurance, fell back. He cared nothing for the rain of metal and flesh that showered around him but, deafened and half stunned by the five kilos of explosive he had buried in the van, Hakim could still exult. The drycell had been turned on its side.

Hakim spent nearly ten minutes scrabbling at debris before he managed to grasp a stone that would abrade the garrote wire. He kept enough tension on the wire to satisfy his hunger for torment, all the while glaring at the Soviet camera. He could perhaps make use of the van equipment. He might find most of the money in the wreckage of his own van.

And after that, what? His exploitation of media finally smothered, he had known for weeks that the enemy had found an offense that could destroy him. Even before ransacking by the KGB, his coffers were too empty to maintain Fat'ah. The Soviet videotapes would produce hatred and scorn in the people who had previously financed him as easily as they bought English country estates and ten-meter limousines. Hakim would find respect nowhere—not even within himself. There was no more Fat'ah and Hakim was Fat'ah. Therefore there could be no Hakim.

The wire parted silently and Hakim rolled away. Eventually he freed his feet, then sat squatting before the drycell. He had triumphed over Guerrero, but that triumph was his last. He could not bring himself to touch the drycell.

Hakim took the capsule from the tape with gentle fingers, smashed the camera. "Forgive, *El Aurans*," he whispered, and swallowed. It was minutes before he realized that the capsule was a harmless antihistamine, Guerrero's malignant joke, and an hour before he found that the injection, as Guerrero had known from the first, was the slow killer. But by that time Hakim had stumbled, twitching, into a stream far from the silent smoldering wreckage and was past caring. The body, a source of concern in some shadowy circles, was never found.

Maurice Everett did not attend the private cremation service for Charlie George in Pasadena, on advisement of his Government Issue companion. Rhone Althouse attended, then was driven with two vehicle changes to his rendezvous with Everett. Althouse gained entry to the building by way of a conduit tunnel with its own guarded entrance. The only identification procedure was handprint analysis but its brevity was deceptive. Gas chromatography assured that the whorls were not synthetic while standard optical matching assured that they belonged to Althouse. The writer dismissed his burly aide temporarily and found the waiting room alone.

"Somehow I never thought of you as a redhead," was Everett's first remark as Althouse entered the room.

"Welcome to the puttynose factory," Althouse returned, taking the hand he was offered. "They do very good work in this clinic; you think facelifts will improve our chances?"

"I couldn't afford the tab," Everett pointed out. "For those bent on nudging it, a free society gets awfully expensive. I'll make do with a bodyguard until we've slid off the back pages of the newspapers."

"That shouldn't take long, now that Charlie George is dead." Althouse smiled at the consternation that fled across Everett's face. "Hey, Maury, we must think of it that way. Charlie George is *dead!* Defunct, expired, cashed in his chips, a dear departed. But my old friend Byron Krause," he said, wagging a gleeful forefinger, "is still suckin' wind."

"I keep forgetting. Look, do we really have to wait for visiting hours?" They glanced together at the wall clock. "Let's jump the gun a few minutes."

"Don't say 'gun,' " Althouse grumbled, leading the way to the elevator. Moments later they submitted to another print-check outside the private room of one Barry Shaunessy, alias Byron Krause, no longer Charlie George. The attendant who accompanied them into the room never spoke, but he did a lot of watching. Everett thought it wise to make every gesture slow and cautious.

The face behind the bandages must have tried to smile, judging from the crinkles around the mouth and eyes. "Ow, dammit," said a familiar voice. "Maury, good to see you. Listen, Rhone: the first one-liner out of you, and my silent partner here will cut you down."

"Don't say 'cut,' " Althouse muttered, then slapped his own mouth.

Everett found a chair, Althouse another. They learned from the NBN star that federal agents had found him half alive, six hours after they began to backtrack from the explosion near Lake Piru. They were aided by tire tracks, reports of a high-speed chase, and fingerprints linking the destroyed van with the avowed kidnapper of Charlie George. "They had the good sense to keep me under wraps from the locals and the media too," added the comedian. "I spent a lot of time thinking before I passed out, and decided I'd rather be a live Krause than dead with all the other charlies. Funny thing is, that sadistic little shit Arif messed me up so much, cosmetic surgery would've been necessary anyhow."

"And that finger?"

"They tell me they can make me another real one, even though it may be stiff. The ear, too. You knew they took my goddam ear? Some agent stepped on it. Boy, some of the apologies I get," he finished, shaking the bandaged head ruefully.

Everett leaned back, folding his arms. The emotional sharing of close friendship came rarely to him and he detested what must be said. "You know, Char—Byron, I can't be allowed to know who you'll be, or what you'll look like. Not for a long, long time anyhow. Just in case . . ."

One eye winked in the bandage. "That's what I didn't want to tell *you*, Maury. Like you said: not for a long time. Though I gather from the news that Fat'ah was creamed by some other bunch in Syria—and Arif is feeding flies all over the Los Padres National Forest."

"No he isn't," Everett said, and shrugged into the silence he had created. "This is for your ears only, and God knows it's little enough, but my contact wouldn't tell me more. It seems the Soviets get nervous when outsiders try to panic the American public. They were helpful enough—don't ask me why—to tell us that Arif turned his whole fanatical gang under interrogation. Probably the kind of interrogation we don't like to do; anyway, he got away into the mountains afoot after that explosion. They think he was dying."

"But they don't know," Althouse whispered. "Now I will damned sure get that facelift."

"Nothing's for sure. Disinformation at all levels," Everett replied. "It's inevitable."

"We're part of it," said Byron Krause. "Letting Charlie George die is really like dying, for me. But if my new face works as it should, and if they can alter my larynx to fool a voiceprint, there may be a retreaded top banana cavorting on your set one of these days. And if not—well, I don't have to work. Then in a few years we'll have a reunion. Without D'unspeakable Este."

"I really want that," Everett said.

"Could happen sooner than we think," Althouse put in. "I keep my fingers into surveys at ABC. It'd be easy to include a few items to find out who the public sees as enemies of terrorism. If the names change quickly I could see that the data gets published, for every charlie on earth to see it's the idea, and not the man, they're up against. If I'm wrong and the same few names keep cropping up . . ." He spread his hands in a characteristic gesture.

"You'll falsify the names," Everett suggested.

"I will like hell," said Althouse quickly. "I have *some* ethics. Nope; but I wouldn't publish the data either."

"That's a relief," said Byron Krause. "Your media theories

have cost us enough bits and pieces. Oh, quit looking at me that way, Rhone, I wasn't blaming you. You were right about the solution."

"And Maury was right about the risk," Althouse sighed.

"All the same," gloomed the commissioner, "I'll miss the *Charlie George Show*."

"Just remind yourself it was all a lot of hype," Rhone Althouse said, grinning at the bandaged face for understanding. "When you think of the odds this guy beat, you realize he was never a very proper charlie."

Committee of the Whole

FRANK HERBERT

WITH an increasing sense of unease, Alan Wallace studied his client as they neared the public hearing room on the second floor of the Old Senate Office Building. The guy was too relaxed.

"Bill, I'm worried about this," Wallace said. "You could damn well lose your grazing rights here in this room today."

They were almost into the gantlet of guards, reporters and TV cameramen before Wallace got his answer.

"Who the hell cares?" Custer asked.

Wallace, who prided himself on being the Washington-type lawyer—above contamination by complaints and briefs, immune to all shock—found himself tongue-tied with surprise.

They were into the ruck then and Wallace had to pull on his bold face, smiling at the press, trying to soften the sharpness of that necessary phrase:

"No comment. Sorry."

"See us after the hearing if you have any questions, gentlemen," Custer said.

The man's voice was level and confident.

He has himself over-controlled, Wallace thought. *Maybe he was just joking . . . a graveyard joke.*

The marble-walled hearing room blazed with lights. Camera platforms had been raised above the seats at the rear. Some of the smaller UHF stations had their cameramen standing on the window ledges.

The subdued hubbub of the place eased slightly, Wallace noted, then picked up tempo as William R. Custer—"The Baron of Oregon" they called him—entered with his attorney, passed the press tables and crossed to the seats reserved for them in the witness section.

Ahead and to their right, that one empty chair at the long table stood waiting with its aura of complete exposure.

"Who the hell cares?"

That wasn't a Custer-type joke, Wallace reminded himself. For all his cattle-baron pose, Custer held a doctorate in philosophy, math and electronics. His western neighbors called him "The Brain."

It was no accident that the cattlemen had chosen him to represent them here.

Wallace glanced covertly at the man, studying him. The cowboy boots and string tie added to a neat dark business suit would have been affectation on most men. They merely accented Custer's good looks—the sunburned, windblown outdoorsman. He was a little darker of hair and skin than his father had been, still light enough to be called blond, but not as ruddy and without the late father's drink-tumescent veins.

But then younger Custer wasn't quite thirty.

Custer turned, met the attorney's eyes. He smiled.

"Those were good patent attorneys you recommended, Al," Custer said. He lifted his briefcase to his lap, patted it. "No mincing around or mealy-mouthed excuses. Already got this thing on the way." Again he tapped the briefcase.

He brought that damn light gadget here with him? Wallace wondered. *Why?* He glanced at the briefcase. *Didn't know it was that small . . . but maybe he's just talking about the plans for it.*

"Let's keep our minds on this hearing," Wallace whispered. "This is the only thing that's important."

Into a sudden lull in the room's high noise level, the voice of someone in the press section carried across them: "greatest political show on earth."

"I brought this as an exhibit," Custer said. Again, he tapped the briefcase. It *did* bulge oddly.

Exhibit? Wallace asked himself.

It was the second time in ten minutes that Custer had shocked him. This was to be a hearing of a subcommittee of the Senate Interior and Insular Affairs Committee. The issue was Taylor grazing lands. What the devil could that . . . *gadget* have to do with the battle of words and laws to be fought here?

"You're supposed to talk over all strategy with your attorney," Wallace whispered. "What the devil do you . . ."

He broke off as the room fell suddenly silent.

Wallace looked up to see the subcommittee chairman, Senator Haycourt Tiborough, stride through the wide double doors followed by his coterie of investigators and attorneys. The senator was a tall man who had once been fat. He had dieted with such savage abruptness that his skin had never recovered. His jowls and the flesh on the back of his hands sagged. The top of his head was shiny bald and ringed by a three-quarter tonsure that had purposely been allowed to grow long and straggly so that it fanned back over his ears.

The senator was followed in close lockstep by syndicated columnist Anthony Poxman, who was speaking fiercely into Tiborough's left ear. TV cameras tracked the pair.

If Poxman's covering this one himself instead of sending a flunky, it's going to be bad, Wallace told himself.

Tiborough took his chair at the center of the committee table facing them, glanced left and right to assure himself the other members were present.

Senator Spealance was absent, Wallace noted, but he had party organization difficulties at home, and the Senior Senator from Oregon was, significantly, not present. Illness, it was reported.

A sudden attack of caution, that common Washington malady, no doubt. He knew where his campaign money came from . . . but he also knew where the votes were.

They had a quorum, though.

Tiborough cleared his throat, said: "The committee will please come to order."

The senator's voice and manner gave Wallace a cold chill. *We were nuts trying to fight this one in the open,* he thought. *Why'd I let Custer and his friends talk me into this? You can't butt heads with a United States senator who's out to get you. The only way's to fight him on the inside.*

And now Custer suddenly turning screwball.

Exhibit!

"Gentlemen," said Tiborough, "I think we can . . . that is, today we can dispense with preliminaries . . . unless my colleagues . . . if any of them have objections."

Again, he glanced at the other senators—five of them. Wallace swept his gaze down the line behind that table— Plowers of Nebraska (a horse trader), Johnstone of Ohio (a parliamentarian—devious), Lane of South Carolina (a Republican in Democrat disguise), Emery of Minnesota (new and eager—dangerous because he lacked the old inhibitions) and Meltzer of New York (poker player, fine old family with traditions).

None of them had objections.

They've had a private meeting—both sides of the aisle—and talked over a smooth steamroller procedure, Wallace thought.

It was another ominous sign.

"This is a subcommittee of the United States Senate Committee on Interior and Insular Affairs," Tiborough said, his tone formal. "We are charged with obtaining expert opinion on proposed amendments to the Taylor Grazing Act of 1934. Today's hearing will begin with testimony and . . . ah, questioning of a man whose family has been in the business of raising beef cattle in Oregon for three generations."

Tiborough smiled at the TV cameras.

The son-of-a-bitch is playing to the galleries, Wallace thought. He glanced at Custer. The cattleman sat relaxed against the back of his chair, eyes half lidded, staring at the senator.

"We call as our first witness today Mr. William R. Custer of Bend, Oregon," Tiborough said. "Will the clerk please swear in Mr. Custer."

Custer moved forward to the "hot seat," placed his briefcase on the table. Wallace pulled a chair up beside his client, noted how the cameras turned as the clerk stepped forward, put the Bible on the table and administered the oath.

Tiborough ruffled through some papers in front of him,

waited for full attention to return to him, said: "This subcommittee . . . we have before us a bill, this is a United States Senate Bill entitled SB-1024 of the current session, an act amending the Taylor Grazing Act of 1934, and the intent is, as many have noted, that we would broaden the base of the advisory committees to the Act and include a wider public representation."

Custer was fiddling with the clasp of his briefcase.

How the hell could that light gadget be an exhibit here? Wallace asked himself. He glanced at the set of Custer's jaw, noted the nervous working of a muscle. It was the first sign of unease he'd seen in Custer. The sight failed to settle Wallace's own nerves.

"Ah, Mr. Custer," Tiborough said. "Do you—did you bring a preliminary statement? Your counsel . . ."

"I have a statement," Custer said. His big voice rumbled through the room, requiring instant attention and the shift of cameras that had been holding tardily on Tiborough, expecting an addition to the question.

Tiborough smiled, waited, then: "Your attorney—is your statement the one your counsel supplied to the committee?"

"With some slight additions of my own," Custer said.

Wallace felt a sudden qualm. They were too willing to accept Custer's statement. He leaned close to his client's ear, whispered: "They know what your stand is. Skip the preliminaries."

Custer ignored him, said: "I intend to speak plainly and simply. I oppose the amendment. Broaden the base and wider public representation are phases of political double talk. The intent is to pack the committees, to put control of them into the hands of people who don't know the first thing about the cattle business and whose private intent is to destroy the Taylor Grazing Act itself."

"Plain, simple talk," Tiborough said. "This committee . . . we welcome such directness. Strong words. A majority of this committee . . . we have taken the position that the public range lands have been too long subjected to the tender mercies of the stockmen advisors, that the lands . . . stockmen have exploited them to their own advantage."

The gloves are off, Wallace thought. *I hope Custer knows what he's doing. He's sure as hell not accepting advice.*

Custer pulled a sheaf of papers from his briefcase and

Wallace glimpsed shiny metal in the case before the flap was closed.

Christ! That looked like a gun or something!

Then Wallace recognized the papers—the brief he and his staff had labored over—and the preliminary statement. He noted with alarm the penciled markings and marginal notations. How could Custer have done that much to it in just twenty-four hours?

Again, Wallace whispered in Custer's ear: "Take it easy, Bill. The bastard's out for blood."

Custer nodded to show he had heard, glanced at the papers, looked up directly at Tiborough.

A hush settled on the room, broken only by the scraping of a chair somewhere in the rear, and the whirr of cameras.

"First, the nature of these lands we're talking about," Custer said. "In my state . . ." He cleared his throat, a mannerism that would have indicated anger in the old man, his father. There was no break in Custer's expression, though, and his voice remained level. ". . . in my state, these were mostly Indian lands. This nation took them by brute force, right of conquest. That's about the oldest right in the world, I guess. I don't want to argue with it at this point."

"Mr. Custer."

It was Nebraska's Senator Plowers, his amiable farmer's face set in a tight grin. "Mr. Custer, I hope . . ."

"Is this a point of order?" Tiborough asked.

"Mr. Chairman," Plowers said, "I merely wished to make sure we weren't going to bring up that old suggestion about giving these lands back to the Indians."

Laughter shot across the hearing room. Tiborough chuckled as he pounded his gavel for order.

"You may continue, Mr. Custer," Tiborough said.

Custer looked at Plowers and said: "No, Senator, I don't want to give these lands back to the Indians. When they had these lands, they only got about three hundred pounds of meat a year off eighty acres. We get five hundred pounds of the highest grade proteins—premium beef—from only ten acres."

"No one doubts the efficiency of your factory-like methods," Tiborough said. "You can . . . we know your methods wring the largest amount of meat from a minimum acreage."

Ugh! Wallace thought. *That was a low blow—implying Bill's overgrazing and destroying the land value.*

"My neighbors, the Warm Springs Indians, use the same methods I do," Custer said. "They are happy to adopt our methods because we use the land while maintaining it and increasing its value. We don't permit the land to fall prey to natural disasters such as fire and erosion. We don't . . ."

"No doubt your methods are meticulously correct," Tiborough said. "But I fail to see where . . ."

"Has Mr. Custer finished his preliminary statement yet?" Senator Plowers cut in.

Wallace shot a startled look at the Nebraskan. That was help from an unexpected quarter.

"Thank you, Senator," Custer said. "I'm quite willing to adapt to the Chairman's methods and explain the meticulous correctness of my operation. Our lowliest cowhands are college men, highly paid. We travel ten times as many jeep miles as we do horse miles. Every outlying division of the ranch—every holding pen and grazing supervisor's cabin is linked to the central ranch by radio. We use the . . ."

"I concede that your methods must be the most modern in the world," Tiborough said. "It's not your methods as much as the results of those methods that are at issue here. We . . ."

He broke off at a disturbance by the door. An Army colonel was talking to the guard there. He wore Special Services fouragere—Pentagon.

Wallace noted with an odd feeling of disquiet that the man was armed—a .45 at the hip. The weapon was out of place on him, as though he had added it suddenly on an overpowering need . . . emergency.

More guards were coming up outside the door now—Marine and Army. They carried rifles.

The colonel said something sharp to the guard, turned away from him and entered the committee room. All the cameras were tracking him now. He ignored them, crossed swiftly to Tiborough, and spoke to him.

The senator shot a startled glance at Custer, accepted a sheaf of papers the colonel thrust at him. He forced his attention off Custer, studied the papers, leafing through them. Presently, he looked up, stared at Custer.

A hush fell over the room.

"I find myself at a loss, Mr. Custer," Tiborough said. "I have here a copy of a report . . . it's from the Special Services branch of the Army . . . through the Pentagon, you understand. It was just handed to me by, ah ... the colonel here."

He looked up at the colonel who was standing, one hand resting lightly on the holstered .45. Tiborough looked back at Custer and it was obvious the senator was trying to marshal his thoughts.

"It is," Tiborough said, "that is ... this report supposedly ... and I have every confidence it is what it is represented to be ... here in my hands ... they say that ... uh, within the last, uh, few days they have, uh, investigated a certain device ... weapon they call it, that you are attempting to patent. They report ..." He glanced at the papers, back to Custer, who was staring at him steadily. "... this, uh, weapon, is a thing that ... it is extremely dangerous."

"It is," Custer said.

"I ... ah, see." Tiborough cleared his throat, glanced up at the colonel who was staring fixedly at Custer. The senator brought his attention back to Custer.

"Do you in fact have such a weapon with you, Mr. Custer?" Tiborough asked.

"I have brought it as an exhibit, sir."

"Exhibit?"

"Yes, sir."

Wallace rubbed his lips, found them dry. He wet them with his tongue, wished for the water glass, but it was beyond Custer. *Christ! That stupid cowpuncher!* He wondered if he dared whisper to Custer. Would the senators and that Pentagon lackey interpret such an action as meaning he was part of Custer's crazy antics?

"Are you threatening this committee with your weapon, Mr. Custer?" Tiborough asked. "If you are, I may say special precautions have been taken ... extra guards in this room and we ... that is, we will not allow ourselves to worry too much about any action you may take, but ordinary precautions are in force."

Wallace could no longer sit quietly. He tugged Custer's sleeve, got an abrupt shake of the head. He leaned close, whispered: "We could ask for a recess, Bill. Maybe we ..."

"Don't interrupt me," Custer said. He looked at Tiborough. "Senator, I would not threaten you or any other man. Threats in the way you mean them are a thing we no longer can indulge in."

"You . . . I believe said this device is an exhibit," Tiborough said. He cast a worried frown at the report in his hands. "I fail . . . it does not appear germane."

Senator Plowers cleared his throat. "Mr. Chairman," he said.

"The chair recognizes the senator from Nebraska," Tiborough said, and the relief in his voice was obvious. He wanted time to think.

"Mr. Custer," Plowers said, "I have not seen the report, the report my distinguished colleague alludes to; however, if I may . . . is it your wish to use this committee as some kind of publicity device?"

"By no means, Senator," Custer said. "I don't wish to profit by my presence here . . . not at all."

Tiborough had apparently come to a decision. He leaned back, whispered to the colonel, who nodded and returned to the outer hall.

"You strike me as an eminently reasonable man, Mr. Custer," Tiborough said. "If I may . . ."

"May I," Senator Plowers said. "May I, just permit me to conclude this one point. May we have the Special Services report in the record?"

"Certainly," Tiborough said. "But what I was about to suggest . . ."

"May I," Plowers said. "May I, would you permit me, please, Mr. Chairman, to make this point clear for the record?"

Tiborough scowled, but the heavy dignity of the Senate overcame his irritation. "Please continue, Senator. I had thought you were finished."

"I respect . . . there is no doubt in my mind of Mr. Custer's truthfulness," Plowers said. His face eased into a grin that made him look grandfatherly, a kindly elder statesman. "I would like, therefore, to have him explain how this . . . ah, weapon, can be an exhibit in the matter before our committee."

Wallace glanced at Custer, saw the hard set to the man's jaw, realized the cattleman had gotten to Plower somehow. This was a set piece.

Tiborough was glancing at the other senators, weighing the advisability of high-handed dismissal . . . perhaps a star chamber session. No . . . they were all too curious about Custer's device, his purpose here.

The thoughts were plain on the senator's face.

"Very well," Tiborough said. He nodded to Custer. "You may proceed, Mr. Custer."

"During last winter's slack season," Custer said, "two of my men and I worked on a project we've had in the works for three years—to develop a sustained-emission laser device."

Custer opened his briefcase, slid out a fat aluminum tube mounted on a pistol grip with a conventional-appearing trigger.

"This is quite harmless," he said. "I didn't bring the power pack."

"That is . . . this is your weapon?" Tiborough asked.

"Calling this a weapon is misleading," Custer said. "The term limits and oversimplifies. This is also a brush-cutter, a substitute for a logger's saw and axe, a diamond cutter, a milling machine . . . and a weapon. It is also a turning point in history."

"Come now, isn't that a bit pretentious?" Tiborough asked.

"We tend to think of history as something old and slow," Custer said. "But history is, as a matter of fact, extremely rapid and immediate. A President is assassinated, a bomb explodes over a city, a dam break, a revolutionary device is announced."

"Lasers have been known for quite a few years," Tiborough said. He looked at the papers the colonel had given him. "The principle dates from 1956 or thereabouts."

"I don't wish it to appear that I'm taking credit for inventing this device," Custer said. "Nor am I claiming sole credit for developing the sustained-emission laser. I was merely one of a team. But I do hold the device here in my hand, gentlemen."

"Exhibit, Mr. Custer," Plowers reminded him. "How is this an exhibit?"

"May I explain first how it works?" Custer asked. "That will make the rest of my statement much easier."

Tiborough looked at Plowers, back to Custer. "If you will tie this all together, Mr. Custer," Tiborough said. "I want to . . . the bearing of this device on our—we are hearing a particular bill in this room."

"Certainly, Senator," Custer said. He looked at his device. "A ninety-volt radio battery drives this particular model. We have some that require less voltage, some that use more. We aimed for a construction with simple parts. Our crystals are common quartz. We shattered them by bringing them to a boil in water and then plunging them into ice water ... repeatedly. We chose twenty pieces of very close to the same size—about one gram, slightly more than fifteen grains each."

Custer unscrewed the back of the tube, slid out a round length of plastic trailing lengths of red, green, brown, blue and yellow wire.

Wallace noted how the cameras of the TV men centered on the object in Custer's hands. Even the senators were leaning forward, staring.

We're gadget-crazy people, Wallace thought.

"The crystals were dipped in thinned household cement and then into iron filings," Custer said. "We made a little jig out of a fly-tying device and opened a passage in the filings at opposite ends of the crystals. We then made some common celluloid—nitrocellulose, acetic acid, gelatin and alcohol, all very common products—and formed it into a length of garden hose just long enough to take the crystals end to end. The crystals were inserted in the hose, the celluloid poured over them and the whole thing was seated in a magnetic waveguide, while the celluloid was cooling. This centered and aligned the crystals. The waveguide was constructed from wire salvaged from an old TV set and built following the directions in the *Radio Amateur's Handbook.*"

Custer reinserted the length of plastic into the tube, adjusted the wires. There was an unearthly silence in the room with only the cameras whirring. It was as though everyone were holding his breath.

"A laser requires a resonant cavity, but that's complicated," Custer said. "Instead, we wound two layers of fine copper wire around our tube, immersed it in the celluloid solution to coat it and then filed one end flat. This end took a piece of mirror cut to fit. We then pressed a number eight embroidery needle at right angles into the mirror end of the tube until it touched the side of the number one crystal."

Custer cleared his throat.

Two of the senators leaned back. Plowers coughed. Tiborough glanced at the banks of TV cameras and there was a questioning look in his eyes.

"We then determined the master frequency of our crystal

series," Custer said. "We used a test signal and oscilloscope, but any radio amateur could do it without the oscilloscope. We constructed an oscillator of that master frequency, attached it at the needle and a bare spot scraped in the opposite side of the waveguide."

"And this . . . ah . . . worked?" Tiborough asked.

"No." Custer shook his head. "When we fed power through a voltage multiplier into the system we produced an estimated four hundred joules emission and melted half the tube. So we started all over again."

"You are going to tie this in?" Tiborough asked. He frowned at the papers in his hands, glanced toward the door where the colonel had gone.

"I am, sir, believe me," Custer said.

"Very well, then," Tiborough said.

"So we started all over," Custer said. "But for the second celluloid dip we added bismuth—a saturate solution, actually. It stayed gummy and we had to paint over it with a sealing coat of the straight celluloid. We then coupled this bismuth layer through a pulse circuit so that it was bathed in a counter wave—180 degrees out of phase with the master frequency. We had, in effect, immersed the unit in a thermoelectric cooler that exactly countered the heat production. A thin beam issued from the unmirrored end when we powered it. We have yet to find something that thin beam cannot cut."

"Diamonds?" Tiborough asked.

"Powered by less than two hundred volts, this device could cut our planet in half like a ripe tomato," Custer said. "One man could destroy an aerial armada with it, knock down ICBMs before they touched atmosphere, sink a fleet, pulverize a city. I'm afraid, sir, that I haven't mentally catalogued all the violent implications of this device. The mind tends to boggle at the enormous power focused in . . ."

"Shut down those TV cameras!"

It was Tiborough shouting, leaping to his feet and making a sweeping gesture to include the banks of cameras. The abrupt violence of his voice and gesture fell on the room like an explosion. "Guards!" he called. "You there at the door. Cordon off that door and don't let anyone out who heard this fool!" He whirled back to face Custer. "You irresponsible idiot!"

"I'm afraid, Senator," Custer said, "that you're locking the barn door many weeks too late."

For a long minute of silence Tiborough glared at Custer. Then: "You did this deliberately, eh?"

"Senator, if I'd waited any longer, there might have been no hope for us at all."

Tiborough sat back into his chair, still keeping his attention fastened on Custer. Plowers and Johnstone on his right had their heads close together whispering fiercely. The other senators were dividing their attention between Custer and Tiborough, their eyes wide and with no attempt to conceal their astonishment.

Wallace, growing conscious of the implications in what Custer had said, tried to wet his lips with his tongue. *Christ!* he thought. *This stupid cowpoke has sold us all down the river!*

Tiborough signaled an aide, spoke briefly with him, beckoned the colonel from the door. There was a buzzing of excited conversation in the room. Several of the press and TV crew were huddled near the windows on Custer's left, arguing. One of their number—a florid-faced man with gray hair and horn-rimmed glasses, started across the room toward Tiborough, was stopped by a committee aide. They began a low-voiced argument with violent gestures.

A loud curse sounded from the door. Poxman, the syndicated columnist, was trying to push past the guards there.

"Poxman!" Tiborough called. The columnist turned. "My orders are that no one leaves," Tiborough said. "You are not an exception." He turned back to face Custer.

The room had fallen into a semblance of quiet, although there still were pockets of muttering and there was the sound of running feet and a hurrying about in the hall outside.

"Two channels went out of here live," Tiborough said. "Nothing much we can do about them, although we will trace down as many of their viewers as we can. Every bit of film in this room and every sound tape will be confiscated, however." His voice rose as protests sounded from the press section. "Our national security is at stake. The President has been notified. Such measures as are necessary will be taken."

The colonel came hurrying into the room, crossed to Tiborough, quietly said something.

"You should've warned me!" Tiborough snapped. "I had no idea that . . ."

The colonel interrupted with a whispered comment.

"These papers . . . your damned report is *not* clear!" Tiborough said. He looked around at Custer. "I see you're smiling, Mr. Custer. I don't think you'll find much to smile about before long."

"Senator, this is not a happy smile," Custer said. "But I told myself several days ago you'd fail to see the implications of this thing." He tapped the pistol-shaped device he had rested on the table. "I told myself you'd fall back into the old, useless pattern."

"Is that what you told yourself, really?" Tiborough said.

Wallace, hearing the venom in the senator's voice, moved his chair a few inches farther away from Custer.

Tiborough looked at the laser projector. "Is that thing really disarmed?"

"Yes, sir."

"If I order one of my men to take it from you, you will not resist?"

"Which of your men will you trust with it, Senator?" Custer asked.

In the long silence that followed, someone in the press section emitted a nervous guffaw.

"Virtually every man on my ranch has one of these things," Custer said. "We fell trees with them, cut firewood, make fence posts. Every letter written to me as a result of my patent application has been answered candidly. More than a thousand sets of schematics and instructions on how to build this device have been sent out to varied places in the world."

"You vicious traitor!" Tiborough rasped.

"You're certainly entitled to your opinion, Senator," Custer said. "But I warn you I've had time for considerably more concentrated and considerably more painful thought than you've applied to this problem. In my estimation, I had no choice. Every week I waited to make this thing public, every day, every minute, merely raised the odds that humanity would be destroyed by . . ."

"You said this thing applied to the hearings on the grazing act," Plowers protested, and there was a plaintive note of complaint in his voice.

"Senator, I told you the truth," Custer said. "There's no real reason to change the act, now. We intend to go on operating under it—with the agreement of our neighbors and others concerned. People are still going to need food."

Tiborough glared at him. "You're saying we can't force you to . . ." He broke off at a disturbance in the doorway. A rope barrier had been stretched there and a line of Marines stood with their backs to it, facing the hall. A mob of poeple was trying to press through. Press cards were being waved.

"Colonel, I told you to clear the hall!" Tiborough barked.

The colonel ran to the barrier. "Use your bayonets if you have to!" he shouted.

The disturbance subsided at the sound of his voice. More uniformed men could been seen moving in along the barrier. Presently, the noise receded.

Tiborough turned back to Custer. "You make Benedict Arnold look like the greatest friend the United States ever had," he said.

"Cursing me isn't going to help you," Custer said. "You are going to have to live with this thing; so you'd better try understanding it."

"That appears to be simple," Tiborough said. "All I have to do is send twenty-five cents to the Patent Office for the schematics and then write you a letter."

"The world already was headed toward suicide," Custer said. "Only fools failed to realize . . ."

"So you decided to give us a little push," Tiborough said.

"H. G. Wells warned us," Custer said. "That's how far back it goes, but nobody listened. 'Human history becomes more and more a race between education and catastrophe,' Wells said. But those were just words. Many scientists have remarked the growth curve on the amount of raw energy becoming available to humans—and the diminishing curve on the number of persons required to use that energy. For a long time now, more and more violent power was being made available to fewer and fewer people. It was only a matter of time until total destruction was put into the hands of single individuals."

"And you didn't think you could take your government into your confidence."

"The government already was committed to a political course diametrically opposite the one this device requires,"

Custer said. "Virtually every man in the government has a vested interest in not reversing that course."

"So you set yourself above the government?"

"I'm probably wasting my time," Custer said, "but I'll try to explain it. Virtually every government in the world is dedicated to manipulating something called the 'mass man.' That's how governments have stayed in power. But there is no such man. When you elevate the nonexistent 'mass man' you degrade the individual. And obviously it was only a matter of time until all of us were at the mercy of the individual holding power."

"You talk like a commie!"

"They'll say I'm a goddamn capitalist pawn," Custer said. "Let me ask you, Senator, to visualize a poor radio technician in a South American country. Brazil, for example. He lives a hand-to-mouth existence, ground down by an overbearing, unimaginative, essentially uncouth ruling oligarchy. What is he going to do when this device comes into his hands?"

"Murder, robbery and anarchy."

"You could be right," Custer said. "But we might reach an understanding out of ultimate necessity—that each of us must cooperate in maintaining the dignity of all."

Tiborough stared at him, began to speak musingly: "We'll have to control the essential materials for constructing this thing . . . and there may be trouble for a while, but . . ."

"You're a vicious fool."

In the cold silence that followed, Custer said: "It was too late to try that ten years ago. I'm telling you this thing can be patchworked out of a wide variety of materials that are already scattered over the earth. It can be made in basements and mud huts, in palaces and shacks. The key item is the crystals, but other crystals will work, too. That's obvious. A patient man can grow crystals . . . and this world is full of patient men."

"I'm going to place you under arrest," Tiborough said. "You have outraged every rule—"

"You're living in a dream world," Custer said. "I refuse to threaten you, but I'll defend myself from any attempt to oppress or degrade me. If I cannot defend myself, my friends will defend me. No man who understands what this device means will permit his dignity to be taken from him."

Custer allowed a moment for his words to sink in, then:

"And don't twist those words to imply a threat. Refusal to threaten a fellow human is an absolute requirement in the day that has just dawned on us."

"You haven't changed a thing!" Tiborough raged. "If one man is powerful with that thing, a hundred are . . ."

"All previous insults aside," Custer said, "I think you are a highly intelligent man, Senator. I ask you to think long and hard about this device. Use of power is no longer the deciding factor because one man is as powerful as a million. Restraint—*self*-restraint is now the key to survival. Each of us is at the mercy of his neighbor's goodwill. Each of us, Senator—the man in the palace and the man in the shack. We'd better do all we can to increase that goodwill—not attempting to buy it, but simply recognizing that individual dignity is the one inalienable right of . . ."

"Don't you preach at me, you commie traitor!" Tiborough rasped. "You're a living example of . . ."

"Senator!"

It was one of the TV cameramen in the left rear of the room.

"Let's stop insulting Mr. Custer and hear him out," the cameraman said.

"Get that man's name," Tiborough told an aide. "If he . . ."

"I'm an expert electronic technician, Senator," the man said. "You can't threaten me now."

Custer smiled, turned to face Tiborough.

"The revolution begins," Custer said. He waved a hand as the senator started to whirl away. "Sit down, Senator."

Wallace, watching the senator obey, saw how the balance of control had changed in this room.

"Ideas are in the wind," Custer said. "There comes a time for a thing to develop. It comes into being. The spinning jenny came into being because that was its time. It was based on countless ideas that had preceded it."

"And this is the age of the laser?" Tiborough asked.

"It was bound to come," Custer said. "But the number of people in the world who're filled with hate and frustration and violence has been growing with terrible speed. You add to that the enormous danger that this might fall into the hands of just one group or nation or . . ." Custer shrugged. "This is too much power to be confined to one man or group with the hope they'll administer wisely. I didn't dare delay.

That's why I spread this thing now and announced it as broadly as I could."

Tiborough leaned back in his chair, his hands in his lap. His face was pale and beads of perspiration stood out on his forehead.

"We won't make it."

"I hope you're wrong, Senator," Custer said. "But the only thing I know for sure is that we'd have had less chance of making it tomorrow than we have today."